Of Love and Asthma

We should have awakened to the sun
streaming in from across the valley, but this is
not a story about things as they should be, and
it was a dark blustery morning, blasting the
blossom off the may. Only in the shelter of the
high hedgerows down in the lanes streaked
with red mud was there any escape from the
wind and the rain. The Colonel had shooed us
out. He was already trembling with fear of our
boredom.

Just as we were putting on our boots, I
pinned down the unidentified fear of the night
before. I had slept without my asthma pillow.
It was not the first time. Twice before, I had
forgotten to take it away with me, once on
purpose to avoid the shame of explaining it to
a schoolfriend. Both forgettings had been
punished by long and violent spasms. But this
was the first time I had slept without it and
not properly noticed until the morning after.
This must, I thought, be love. Would it be
punished too?

Of Love & Asthma

FERDINAND MOUNT

OF LOVE

AND ASTHMA

Ferdinand Mount

Mandarin

A Mandarin Paperback
OF LOVE AND ASTHMA

First published in Great Britain 1991
by William Heinemann Ltd
This edition published 1992
by Mandarin Paperbacks
an imprint of Reed Consumer Books Ltd
Michelin House, 81 Fulham Road, London SW3 6RB
and Auckland, Melbourne, Singapore and Toronto

Reprinted 1992

Copyright © Ferdinand Mount 1991

A CIP catalogue record for this title
is available from the British Library
ISBN 0 7493 1064 2

Printed and bound in Great Britain
by Cox & Wyman Ltd, Reading, Berks

All Asthmatics, being angry or sad,
do fall into Fits oftener than when
they are cheerful.

The Nervous Juice is still as much
unknown as formerly; and therefore
its Affections are inexplicable:
And though it still be a Dispute whether
the Motion of the Heart in a Fever
be by an Irritation of the Fermenting
Blood or the disordered Spirits, yet
it will be the same thing as to Practice.

Sir John Floyer
A Treatise of the Asthma
1698

Narrator's foreword

For approximately seven months, Joseph Dudgeon Follows was one of the top dozen young entrepreneurs in England. By then, he had already made love to his uncle's mistress, his aunt, his aunt's daughter and his professor's daughter, to name but a few. Later on, you will be relieved to hear, he was to be bankrupted, humiliated, paralysed, exiled, and even kidnapped, or so he said (not to mention the suicide attempt and one or two unsavoury experiences which are best left to skulk in the body of the text). Through it all, he remained lion-hearted, freckle-faced, rather short in the arms and legs, and incurably asthmatic, unlike the narrator who was told he had grown out of it. Slippery too he remained, as elusive as the bath soap clutched at in the clouding water. Sightings and newsflashes have had to be strung together, and a good deal of hearsay as well. Even then, his women may seem presences more real than he does – not, strictly speaking, that they were to be called his, with one exception. Other subjects touched on in this strange and melancholy tale include Italian patisserie, the Occult, linguistic philosophy and its decline, motherhood, the Irish problem, the ecology of butterflies and, of course, death, sex and money. I am afraid it is not quite the English Gatsby, but it will have to do for now.

Prologue

It was the sports day that started my attacks off again. True, even if I had not gone, I might have had another attack sooner or later. They say it is unlikely that a single incident could revive a condition which had been dormant so long. The patient, it seems, has usually been brewing up for a reprise, perhaps over a considerable period. Like beech-nuts seeded in the clay of some Chiltern ridge waiting for the sun to warm them, the mast cells play a waiting game. They lurk for years, decades even, in the walls of the bronchial tubes, until mobilised by the approach of an eligible allergen. A cloud of pollen wafts past, a cat sidles up to the patient, the seam frays on a feather pillow, and whoosh, the mast cells discharge their malign granules in one vengeful, triumphant burst. The tube-walls swell, the passages narrow and the attack begins.

'Avoid allergens,' Mrs Fretwell would chant. She might as well have said avoid life (but most asthmatics will do that anyway, without having to be told). The Fret claimed, not without a certain perverted zest, that the granules loved their work. We ourselves had seen how quickly they could inflame our tissues, when we took the skin-prick test on our first morning at the clinic. Up swelled the little row of bumps along our forearms, each measuring sensitivity to a different allergen, in my case sizeable tumuli for dust and feathers, a modest kopje or hillock for cats, dogs somewhat smaller again, for horses and parrots the merest pimples. 'Parrots?' the Swiss boy said, 'in Switzerland we have no parrots.' 'Not even as pets?' 'We do not pet parrots.'

Our bodies were bandit country swarmed over by these frantic tiny guerrilla armies, alternately warring against each other and colluding against the regime. In such frightful terrain, almost anything could trigger off hostilities. In my case, it happened to be the sports day, and especially the fathers' race, that did it.

A blowy day – they always seemed to have a blowy day for the sports, the head master told me, told everyone in fact – and the poplars at the end of the field were bending and rustling in the wind. The finishing tape was bouncing, the flags around the course flicked and fluttered. The dressed-up mothers had to hold on to their hats. The deputy head, a whippety character with a small moustache and bristly hair, was shouting through a megaphone. The wind carried away his words, although a certain precision of intonation still made itself felt. Children shepherded into groups by their teachers shoved each other, then lolled and wrestled on the grass. As the heats of the hundred yards went by, they burst into shrill starling cries of encouragement, then looked bored and fractious again. My godson, a square, silent child, finished second last in his heat, stuffed my present into the pocket of his shorts, thanked me for coming (his parents were abroad) and said he had to rejoin his house-group. I stood by myself, a desultory, null figure, wondering without fretting about it how much longer I ought to stay.

She was underdressed for the occasion, in blue jeans and a thin blue shirt windblown against her thin body. Her fair hair was scraped back, her fair face not changed at all, nor the voice, that sullen dead voice that kept men in their place, and women too, for that matter.

'It's you,' she said. 'I thought it was.'

'You'd spotted me earlier, had you? I hadn't spotted you at all. And this is –'

'You remember her as Bubbins. Margaret now.'

'What an unexpected name,' I said.

'After Peggy.'

The girl too was fair, but a much paler, ethereal kind of fair, with wideset unsettling eyes, not pretty like some of the girls already were even in their drizzle-grey aertex shirts and gym shorts, but not to be missed in a crowd.

'What brings you here?' her mother asked.

'Godson.' I found myself falling, not meaning to, into her economical way of talking.

'That *is* dutiful. But then you always were.'

'Was I? I'd never thought of myself as being.'

'Not like Joe anyway,' she said.

'Not at all like Joe,' I said.

'I expect you'll go in for the godfathers' race.'

'There isn't one.'

'Well, visitors' race then.'

'I wouldn't dream of it.'

'Oh go on.'

'Yes please do, Mum never goes in for anything. She always says she's too tired.' The girl had a bubbly, academic sort of voice, not at all like her mother's, more as if she liked talking and would talk a lot if encouraged.

'All right. But I'm a pathetic runner.'

'That's the whole point,' the girl said. 'We don't want to watch parents being brilliant.'

The deputy head marched down the row of parents on their folding chairs, using the megaphone to stir up recruits for the races. Closer up, he sounded theatrical, melodramatic almost. As the afternoon wore on, he became more peremptory.

'You sir, shoes off for the fathers' race.'

'I'm only a godfather. I thought the visitors –'

'Visitors are sisters and grannies. You must run in the fathers'.'

I shambled over to the limbering fathers, a broad-shouldered, heavy-muscled, hairy-forearmed crew in their stockinged feet and striped shirts. One skinnier father, in horn-rimmed spectacles, was practising sprint starts. He was wearing running shoes. Despair gripped me as this masculine herd crouched for the starting gun.

The sound of stockinged feet drumming on summer turf is a frightening thing, close and urgent, yet also deploying a more distant menace, an enemy who is both at your throat and over the next hill. The panting, elbowing, shouldering ferocity of a fathers' race must be the nearest thing to combat that urban man goes through in peacetime.

My feet were not made for such competition. They are pale, broad, limp flounders, all but archless. On sand they print a full outline, leaving nothing to the imagination. When called upon to step on it, they do precisely that, impacting upon the ground with a confident finality, erasing all animate life beneath. Notions of spring and leverage are alien to them. To describe such feet as flat is to underestimate their positive commitment to stationariness.

By eighty yards, I was well back in the ruck of the trailing group. At the tape, I was second last, the last of the finishers in fact, since the man behind me, a porpoise in scarlet braces, pulled up soon after the half-way mark and strolled back to collect his shoes with his hands in his pockets, trying to give the impression that he had never had the slightest intention of competing but had merely been caught up in some inexplicable stampede.

'Result of the fathers' race,' declared the deputy head, now mingling Olivier's biting attack with the sonorous melancholy of Sir Ralph Richardson: 'first Mr Angelides, second, Mr Stieglitz, third Mr Bevan-Jones. Time 13.5 seconds.'

It must therefore have been some seventeen or eighteen seconds after the starting gun that the first clutching came at my throat and I heard the first hollowed rasp within my chest, the one which sounds imported, seems almost to belong to someone else or to come from some source other than a human body. That primitive imagery of disease as an invader, an alien, is apt at this first onrush of symptoms; resentment, defiance, the defender's cunning are mobilised. But then the intrusive gremlin becomes a familiar, a known quantity, still resented but less keenly so. A kind of surly collaboration takes place, a wheezing accommodation, but always with a view to getting rid of him in the end, taking him by surprise perhaps or boring him into going away. Even so, each second has to be endured separately, each inward breath found space for, each breathing-out quality-controlled and not skimped. When Joe and I were at university, a philosopher who is now not much read and is also dead, not Scrannel although he is dead too, used to invite us to consider the problems of induction and probability by imagining that eternity was made up of a succession of quite separate instants, each totally unconnected to the next one. Scrannel made short work of this hypothesis; it was a meaningless act to expect the imagination to undertake since it involved imagining ourselves away, for the sum of our experience was what constituted us as human agents. It was the hypothesis that created the problem, not the problem which demanded such hypotheses to be made sense of. The only puzzle about time, Scrannel would say, is that so many philosophers should wish to make a puzzle of it. Philosophers are not the only ones. Children and asthmatics do too, and perhaps with more reason, since they both live from moment to moment, especially when they are at their most childish or asthmatic. An ordinary person would not write twelve volumes, twelve in the old Chatto & Windus edition anyway, to witness the discovery that people age but works of art do not, or not so fast. For an asthmatic, though, that is interesting information.

At that moment, gasping, bent forward with my hands on my knees under a wind-tossed ash-tree, with Matron bending alongside to ask if I was all right, I found myself pleasantly distracted with thoughts of time and how much of it had gone under this and that bridge since I had first seen the fair woman with the scraped-back hair. I say 'woman', although in my own thoughts I kept time at arm's length by still thinking of her as a girl.

'Are you all right,' the head master said, a statement not a question.

'I'll be all right in a minute,' I answered.

'Splendid, only we lost a father last year. Actually, we even wondered whether to hold the race this time.'

'Lost?'

'Died on the way to hospital, as a matter of fact.'

'I'll pull through.'

'Good man.'

The head master passed on at cruising speed, his serene, ambiguous gaze focused at a level six to nine inches above the heads of oncoming parents. I returned to my crouching position and tried again to beguile my bronchial tubes with a few memories.

I see now that I have given quite the wrong impressions: myself as a solitary enigmatic character; the mother and the daughter linked to me by mysterious romantic ties; our meeting dunked in regretful insinuations of what might have been. It was not like that at all. I am neither solitary nor enigmatic. Onora did not much care for me, nor I for her, come to that. She and I were a part of the story, but it is not essentially our story, for the two of us were among the survivors, not the victims, and victims get a better view.

I My fellow patients –
The Napoleon of Asthma –
First visit to Shorewinds

We came down from the sanatorium by the bus. First the long swing round the side of the hill, through the pine trees, the tyres muffled on the brown carpet of last year's needles, the smell of the trees, warm silence, half light. Then we turned the sharp corner to begin the descent, wheels spurting the gravel into the grass, patches of late spring snow gone from the shady places only a few weeks earlier, and now the sudden sight of the sea, distant, hazy, milky-gleaming blue, that blue we dream of on wet pavements in the first dark mornings of winter. I am sorry to begin this story on such a lyrical note. The disillusion will come later. Catch the breath now. It will not all be like that, the breath not always regained. If a haze of innocence, or not so much a haze as a bloom, hangs over these early pages, this is as it was.

'It's a respray job you know, this bus. Under that tasteful shade of cream, it's an old army bus. See the traces of khaki along the window-frame.'

'Oh,' I said.

'Fair old engine though. Plenty of poke. Nothing but the best for Smithy.'

Joe Follows had only arrived a week earlier, but he had already taken possession. He knew which of the staff owned which car – Dr Maintenon-Smith's long ground-sweeping Citroen, Mrs Fretwell's Morris Oxford, Miss Ascott's perky Riley. He knew the back way down to the kitchens and where the biscuits and condensed milk were kept and how to open the condensed milk tin with a penknife. He imported the Dodger's arts into our timorous community.

His asthma fits were noisy, uninhibited wheezings, not silent chest-heavings as mine were. He had views about the proper way to breathe and disagreed with Mrs Fretwell the physiotherapist, who was not interested in the exchange of ideas. She took his herbal cigarettes away when he was climbing into bed.

'Hey, where have my weeds gone?'

'The Fret took them.'

'I'm not having that,' he jumped out of bed, wheezing like a loose bicycle chain, and stumped after her along the passage toward the Superintendent's office. From the long windows opposite our beds there was a view inland across the valley to the rolling heathland beyond, but the windows were set too high to see much of it except by standing on the bed. The curtain rail ran below the tops of the rounded arches. The dawn came in through the open flaps at the top, cold and blue at first, then with pink and golden streaks flooding down upon us. I would lie in a waking dream, absorbing the annunciation of the day through these high lunettes, listening to the breathing from the other beds, calmer now that the worst of the small hours was over, the lungs responding to the fresh cold air of the morning. For many of us, though, these would be false dawns. The hour of waking was one of the bad times, likelier even than the approach of night to bring on an attack.

'This must have been the reflectory,' Joe said, after we had got into bed his first evening. Scaly feet thrusting into chill sheets, sanatorium smell of disinfectant conquered now and then by the smell of the pine trees and the tang of the bracken curling in through the open flaps of the high-arched windows.

'Refectory,' I could not help saying.

'That's right, the refectory.' He had a knack of getting quite familiar words slightly wrong. He would add or subtract an 's' at the end of a name, transpose a consonant or two, or slide into a surprising vowel shift. If put right, whether out of pedantry or in genuine search of clarity, he took no offence and would merely say 'yes, that's right', repeating the correct version after me, as though this was what he had said in the first place but I had misheard him.

The Victorian part of the building had been a monastery before it had become a sanatorium. According to the Superintendent, Dr Maintenon-Smith, the half-Frenchman who was also the clinic's half-owner, it was the only clinic for respiratory diseases which was also a language school. Was this a boast worth making?

'Such a beautiful view, darling, and he can learn lovely French while his lungs are soaking up the sea air,' said my father's friend Mossy, who always knew where to go. Whoever heard of anyone going to a sanatorium to learn languages? My father liked the ingenuity of it. The hill-top monastery setting appealed to him too, as the likely scene of a dramatic cure for me. He had no patience with slow healing. He thought diseases could be taken by surprise, much as people in the Middle Ages thought demons could be tricked if you were clever enough.

'Just like Colditz, isn't it?' Joe had said as he was unpacking his bags.

'On a small scale, yes,' I said. 'But the security is tighter here.'

Joe smiled, showing his white teeth. He looked unsuitably healthy, broad-chested, stocky-thighed, square-headed with a great mop of chestnut hair which livened up his plain freckled face – yet not plain entirely, because of his half-truculent, half-whimsical expression, like an Irishman who may be about to charm you or hit you but you cannot tell which. His sandy body was puzzling too. It had an unfinished air to it. His arms were not long enough for the breadth of his shoulders and his fingers were so stubby that they might have been short of a joint. Jackets hung uneasy on him: he looked like a man hunching his shoulders against the cold. He wasn't dwarfish but his body made you think, rather sadly, of dwarfishness. Nor was his artfulness a blithe thing. When he brought up bootleg extras from the kitchen – packets of dates, digestive biscuits, once even a carton of chocolate spread – he returned from his mission with a dogged joyless mien, not seeking to take any pleasure in his daring.

We were exact twins, this desolate jackanapes and I, seventeen that summer. I had been born in the small hours. He did not know the hour of his birth. 'Not the sort of thing I'd ask my mother. She doesn't go in for childbirth. We call her Monkey,' he added, by way of explanation.

The first night he slept in the bed next to me, I thought he might be dying. His spasms were so fierce, the intervals between them so unbearably short. I began to gather an inkling of what my parents must have gone through listening to my own groans. But listening to Joe's made me feel calm and well. It was without a tremor that I heard the nurse asking the doctor whether she should give him an injection and the doctor telling her to wait till the morning. Asthmatics have cold but tenacious hearts, sticky to the touch, like ice from a refrigerator set at maximum.

Joe's herbal cigarettes came in a packet the colour of old parchment with a Victorian engraving of a military type smoking in a bazaar while a man in a turban crouched at his feet sucking at a hookah. The cigarettes looked just like ordinary cigarettes except for being a dirty beige colour, so that Joe could imitate all the actions of the smart smoker, tapping the cigarette on the side of the packet, drawing the smoke deep down into his lungs, flicking the ash into the flower bed, lighting one for me from the one in his mouth. The smoke made me cough, but he swore by them and derided the Fret's scolding (I noticed, though, that he put them away when Dr Maintenon-Smith came round, perhaps fearful that he might support her view).

'They really are bad for you, you know.'

'You need a tube to soothe the tubes, Mrs Fretwell. For your throat's sake, smoke Craven A, the cigarette doctors prefer.'

I preferred the puffer. The dark amber glass with its delicate curved nozzle, the orange-red bulb, the sinister little bottle containing the fluid – this was my hookah, my passport to Nirvana. The anticipation of sure relief as I put the cold glass to my lips, the faint sickly smell before the first clean puff of vapour, like inhaling the mist of a winter morning, a mist which had been somewhat doctored, the instantaneous lengthening and taming of the spasms, so that their rapid brutal clutchings faded into harmless undulating sighs, growing louder, melodious almost, as they became less intense, less frequent, finally settling into a low gravelling mouth-organ drone, and within my chest sweet peace.

At the age of eight, I had no difficulty imagining heaven. Eternal bliss, with its absence of fear or conflict or roughness, would be merely a prolonged equivalent of how I felt after an asthma spasm had died down, relieved and easy, but a little bored too. The challenges of watchfulness and patience, the ferocious chest-stabbings and thumpings which could sometimes be parried by changing one's thoughts or the emphasis of one's breathing or one's position in bed – all this was living at its most intense. Non-asthmatic existence seemed a tepid business by comparison, with modest rewards and penalties.

To be accredited as an asthmatic was to become entitled to a life of seclusion and privilege. When I told my parents how soon I hoped to be up and about again, it was a polite hypocrisy, much as a millionaire behind the smoked windows of his limousine may say how he envies the poor and would like to share their simple pleasures. And always in their eyes the fear that I might die on them – the fear that was both the ultimate source of my power, yet was also irritating to me.

Joe's puffer was bigger than mine – more modern, he claimed. Its metal clamps and rings gave it a clinical industrial look, quite unlike the intimate appeal mine had.

'And zis, dottore', he would say in his comic Italian accent, waving the puffer in front of him, 'is our amazing new suction equipment. Eet could draw six points of sperm from ze average eunuch.' As he elaborated more fantastic uses for the equipment, two patches of red seeped into his sandy cheeks, like the hectic flush of consumption patients in the old days. 'They can't find a single patch on my lungs, though. Clean as a bell in the last X-ray,' he said. Joe was very forward with the details of his condition, unlike the average asthma patient who fears that to talk about his spasms might start off that mysterious sequence of nervous impulses which causes them. Besides, it is the mystery which confers a certain power on the sufferer, making him into a more interesting person, burdened or gifted with certain sensitivities which coarser spirits

5

can neither share nor understand. This inwardness, this reticence feeds on itself. The asthmatic begins to claim the privileges of the important man whose brusqueness is described as 'keeping his own counsel'. He gives a surly grunt or only the most clipped response to questions, both to show how ill he is and because anything fuller might hinder the greater project of getting well.

But Joe was not at all like this. He was the blustering cuckoo in our nest. He would return from the bathroom announcing the state of his bowels in fake tabloid headlines – 'the Big Shit, Joe's Monster Turd' or 'Deadlock – the Day the Arse Stood Still.' He drew monstrous cartoons of the staff. He had an unexpected facility for drawing. His square sandy fist moved across the paper with a self-moved fluency hatching in obscene growths of hair, phallic noses, lolloping bosoms. We laughed, obedient to his doggy requests for approval, but did not really think the cartoons funny. We looked away while he stood naked in the middle of the room before starting to dress, flaunting his sturdy genitals which sprouted raw and angry from his flaky sandy skin. Like me, he had the asthmatic's eczema which left minute fragments of skin in our socks each night and made our cheeks into dust-bowls if we forgot to put the eczema cream on them. About all this he had no shame, waving his socks in the air before putting them on in the morning, so that the tiny flakes of discarded skin danced a brilliant shower in the light from the high windows. The rest of us, especially the Swiss boy and I, would shrink and shield our selves behind our beds as we pulled on our grey flannels and heavy crewneck jerseys.

'I'm basically the dynamic type of asthmatic,' Joe himself said. 'Like Lord Beaverbrook.'

'Lord Beaverbrook?'

'He gets asthma like me. We just happen to have these unusually narrow bronchial tubes. It's a purely physical thing. There's no psychological angle at all.'

Yet in social encounters he was not exactly easy. He was loud and cheerful with us and the nurses, but when Dr Maintenon-Smith came round in the evening, Joe put on an odd wheedling respectful voice, so different that he sounded to us as though he was playing a complicated practical joke.

'Why are you so smarmy to Smithy?' I asked.

'Smarmy? Oh well, he's the only guy who can get me out of this place.' But there was a puzzled note in his voice. Clearly he did not think he was being smarmy at all. His way of speaking, too, was transparent, unguarded, not like an asthmatic's. You could always tell what he was thinking. When he was agitated, he would scratch his wrists and the backs of his hands with little feral clawings.

Dr Maintenon-Smith warmed to him. Joe teased him in the way that important people like to be teased, so that they feel real and still important. Maintenon-Smith saw himself as an entrepreneur, more of a hotelier than a physician. 'We have plans for the long term,' he would say when asked any question about the running of the sanatorium, down to the collection of mail or the coffee pots at breakfast being too small. His suits – pinstriped, double-breasted – and his fleshy unmoving profile looked out of place on the ward. He was a dead ringer for Napoleon in the St Helena years. We liked to think that he had in fact no medical qualifications at all, had once been delivering fruit and vegetables to some hospital and found a spare white coat lying around and in no time at all had given a passable diagnosis of emphysema. The money to buy this clinic must have been raised by some Corsican protection racket, his former colleagues now interred in the concrete foundations of the new radiology block. He claimed to be a great sportsman and promised to take us partridge shooting in 'my little property in the Beauce.'

He liked horse-racing too and one night on his rounds chanced upon me reading an old edition of Cope's Racegoers' Encyclopaedia, then my favourite browsing. Its red cover with the gilt motif of linked horseshoes was in those days as sacred as a missal to me. 'So you are a lover of the sport of kings,' he deduced, with that sinister, triumphant way he had of speaking as though certain long-held suspicions had been justified in the teeth of repeated denials from official spokesmen. 'You follow the form? You must give me some tips.' With typical energy, he had the *Sporting Life* ordered for me and, on those mornings when I was too ill to go down to breakfast, would come and sit on the end of my bed with his pen and yellow notepad at the ready. To start with, I was flattered and took trouble with my selections. But after a couple of early successes, I began to weary of the business and started to dread the plumping down of his bulk on top of my feet and his Dettol breath swamping me as he bent forward to look at the runners and riders.

'So, today Sandown Park? And we avoid the big handicaps.'

'Yes, and the two-year-old race, unless we're really sure. I like this thing, My Josephine, in the three-thirty.'

'Ah,' he said, 'that is the horse for me. It is Napoleon's horse. Vive l'Empéreur. You see the resemblance?' He turned his fleshy profile to me and thrust his arm inside the lapel of his navy-blue pinstriped suit. 'It's amazing,' I said, as though the likeness was striking me for the first time. 'I am the Napoleon of Asthma,' he said.

The thought of the Emperor led him on to Stendhal and *La Chartreuse de Parme* which we were ploughing through as the set book for our exams. Maintenon-Smith's reflections on the pursuit of love and the pursuit of power (in his eyes, much the same thing) would echo down the high dormitory, empty except for the Swiss boy Hugo who was also bad in the mornings. I would wriggle in my bed partly to shift the crumbs of breakfast toast from beneath me but also to evade, without being rude, the blasts of Dettol breath from the Superintendent. 'For Stendhal,' he would say, 'Love is a mountain to be climbed. He is a hiker of *l'amour*, he does not stop to admire the view. In love, Stendhal teaches us we must chase always the unexpected. Why should Louis Quartorze, who could have enjoyed every woman in France, choose to live with a widow of a certain age, very sensible, very devout, in a word, my ancestor Madame de Maintenon? Because he was getting old, because he was frightened of dying and wanted someone to intercede with *le bon Dieu?* No, my friend, because she was a new peak to conquer. Change, Sire, is the greatest aphrodisiac of all, that is what the king's doctor told him when his desire failed. Is that not the case, Monsieur Hugo?' He extended an imperial arm to the far end of the dormitory. 'Yes, I think very good,' the Swiss boy wheezed.

'She was so demure, so modest, this penniless widow, and dressed always in perfect taste. She never asked for anything except one thing.' He patted my knee, to congratulate me on the question I had not asked. 'That one thing was marriage, something no royal mistress had ever dreamed of. It was a unique request, so bizarre, so provocative that the king could not resist it. Just as Madame Bovary found in adultery all the platitudes of marriage, so *Le Roi Soleil* found in marriage all the excitement of adultery. And besides, you know' – leaning close now, Dettol breath zooming in over the pages of the *Sporting Life* open at Man On the Spot's selections for the Guineas meeting – 'she wore the most beautiful underclothes, under her widow's weeds, the most exquisite petticoats.'

These daunting instructions on the art of love – 'the other sport of kings', as Maintenon-Smith called it – were the first I ever received on the subject. Even now, those who persist in talking about love in a speculative way evoke in me only the vanished gusts of Dettol breath. I later discovered that he could not have been descended from Madame de Maintenon, since she had had no children and her family name was something different and Maintenon was merely the town she took her title from and only visited a couple of times in her life. And it was another king who was told about change being an aphrodisiac.

He was compelling, all the same, and Madame de Maintenon took her place along with Stendhal and assorted French kings, as well as Dr Maintenon-Smith himself, in my general picture of love in the French style as something infinitely ruthless and mysterious. These implacable power-seekers seemed to inhabit a different universe from our own sweet fumblings in the back stalls. This, I knew, must be because the English were notoriously bad at love, although that was not an accusation Maintenon-Smith himself went in for making. He preferred to think of love as a universal language. If anything, in fact, he wished to dispel the traditional British illusions about French behaviour. 'We Gauls are an austere people, we do not hop in and out of bed just like that.

Our passions run deep, very deep.' He gave me a look designed to express profundity of passion, but as usual he only succeeded in looking threatening. After a pause, he said: 'I think these horses are too little priced, I will back them double.'

'Short,' I said, 'we say short-priced.'

On the night of the Swiss boy's birthday, the Australian burgundy searing our throats, the high chamber echoing with our breathless laughter, Joe said he would walk round the room without touching the floor. But there was nothing to hang on to, we said, and the window ledges were too far apart to swing from one to the other.

'On the cornice. We used to do it at school.'

Ten foot up, level with the bottom of the windows, there ran round the room a narrow cornice, two or three inches wide. Joe took off his shoes and socks, then stripped down to his underpants.

'Give me a leg up, Hugo.' The Swiss boy stood on his bed. Joe stepped lightly from the bedhead to Hugo's shoulder and swung himself up on to the window sill. With his body flat against the wall, he began moving along the cornice, his bare feet edging along the unforgiving ledge. He looked like a figure in an Egyptian wall painting, flat, serene, head and feet sideways on in obedience to art rather than anatomy. There was something Egyptian too about his odd proportions, the wide shoulders and slender waist, a kind of physical serenity. On the side he started, he had the window recesses to hop on to every few yards. There were beds below to break his fall. But after the corner, he had nothing but the cornice, and stone and lino floor beneath. His chest pressed against the flaking plaster, and plaster dust floated down between his sandy legs.

Sitting on our beds, with blankets round our shoulders (Maintenon-Smith did not believe in over-heating asthmatics), the flask of Emu being passed from mouth to mouth, we were conscious of the great monastic double doors opening and a presence, silent and ominous, in the doorway behind us.

'Good evening, gentlemen,' Maintenon-Smith's suave villain's English also sounded laden with stifled panic. If only the smallest thing went wrong, he might zoom off into a dictator's scream. Perhaps it was just the way he attempted to convey sang-froid. 'Good evening, Mr Follows. Did you take the lift to get up there?'

'Oh hello, Superintendent,' Joe said, his head still facing the wall.

'This is one of your English jokes. A wager of audacity.'

'Yes, I suppose so.'

'Well, the clinic accepts no responsibility for any injury. That is our joke.'

'I don't think it's very funny,' Joe said but in a friendly waggish voice which seemed to relax Maintenon-Smith, almost indeed to congratulate him on joining in the prank so elegantly.

'No, you will have to take your broken bones down to the hospital yourself. We will lend you some skis.'

'Oh Superintendent, you are a cruel man.'

'This is not a sanatorium for spiders.' Maintenon-Smith was becoming entranced with this crosstalk.

'I think he's getting tired,' I said.

'No, I'm all right.'

'I will fetch a ladder myself,' Maintenon-Smith said and strutted off down the passage. His footsteps passed from thud to clang as he passed from lino to cold monks' stone. When he came back bearing before him a battered wooden plasterer's ladder, Joe's legs were sagging, his arms limp. He could not even twist a foot round away from the cornice to put it down on the top rung of the ladder. Maintenon-Smith had to go up himself. He climbed with care, making sure that each shiny shoe was properly anchored on the rung before attempting the next. When he reached three steps from the top, he reached out and took hold of Joe's left foot and guided it down on to the top of the ladder. As Joe transferred his full weight to the ladder, the Superintendent had to clasp hold of his waist to prevent one or both of them falling off the ladder. The Napoleon of Asthma and the near-naked boy stayed thus entwined for a second or two, recovering breath and balance, a weird enactment of the

Deposition. Then slowly they came down together, matching step for step.

The Superintendent was delighted with Joe for allowing him to perform this rescue. From then on, Joe could ask for almost anything. He had touched some vulnerable spot, found a way through the shell. Perhaps Maintenon-Smith thought of him as a long-lost son, although he had two real grown-up sons working in Clermont-Ferrand. Even Madame Maintenon-Smith seemed to be in favour of the friendship. Her sad unobtrusive face lit up when Joe wandered into Medical Stores where he helped out in a desperate sort of way.

I wondered what she thought of her husband's theories about love (his practice of it was a still more daunting thought). 'Once you've had a black woman, you'll never want a white one', 'when a woman lets you know she wants you, she'll never forgive you if you fail to make love to her', 'every woman thinks she can convert a homosexual' – I believed that Maintenon-Smith had invented these sayings himself and was amazed when I heard them crop up in later life. With such maxims buzzing round her ears, no wonder his wife was sad.

Despite their intimacy, Joe still managed to irritate the Superintendent, often without trying to. Even when he got on someone's wavelength, he never could quite hold the frequency. The Superintendent liked to warn us that 'I have the fearful temper of my Gallic ancestors', but we saw him seriously enraged only once, and then Joe merely meant to tease.

'Please, Dr Maintenon-Smith, does sex cure asthma? Is that why people grow out of it, because they start having sex?'

'That is the question of an inky schoolboy. I will not answer it.' The Napoleon of Asthma seemed embarrassed.

'But sir, it's a serious medical question.'

'You must not confuse the body and the heart.'

'But sir, if asthma is a nervous disease . . .'

'Don't be insolent, boy.' Dr Maintenon-Smith's face darkened into umbrage.

'But sir, we need to know.'

I was too shy to admit it, certainly too shy to admit it to Joe, but his question did catch my fancy. All my dreams of love, the disordered impossible night-dreams, became dreams of healthy breathing too. Once desire had been satisfied, it would be possible to throw away the whole apparatus of our infirmity – the puffer and the pills and the asthma pillow which otherwise I had to take everywhere with me, a great rubber encumbrance that doubled the size of my luggage. But was this liberation a realistic prospect, or would we be for ever lumbered with our asthma pillows while we attempted to navigate the treacherous waters of love, as Dr Maintenon-Smith would have put it. Five minutes after the climax of the encounter, would I have to ask whether she would mind moving over a little, so that my head could find the reassuring bounce beneath it?

Joe tried to overcome the handicap by christening his asthma pillow George. 'You wouldn't believe what George and I have been through together,' he would say, 'the trouble is, we never agree about women, do we George?' For my part, I could not shake off the glum conviction that no one could carry his own pillow about with him and still cut a dash.

Through the trees now, we could see groomed back gardens, the first roses lolling over flint and pebble walls, seaside hedges of pink and white flowers bosoming out over the unimpeachable lawns. An old man in viyella shirtsleeves and ginger corduroys looked up, the rumble of the bus distracting him from his weeding. His neck and arms were white and withered, his moustache was jaunty. Round the corner the little parade of thirties' shops, flat-roofed with modernist metal windows – Gable and Gritstone Estate Agents, The Monkey Puzzle Milk Bar, Pelmet Paradise – all peeling and forlorn now, instantly done for, demoded. At the crossroads, the place-names on the white signpost were still painted over to deceive the invader. Milky seaside light.

'This whole place could do with a lick of paint.'

'Yes,' I said.

'You don't really think so, do you? You probably like it shabby. English people always like things shabby.'

'Well, if you know what I think, why did you ask then?'

'Just to test your reactions. I knew you'd agree. English people always agree, to avoid having a row.'

'So what country do you come from?'

'I didn't say all English people.'

It was hot in the bus. There was a sour, warm, pepperminty smell. The sun was shining on the jumble of red and grey roofs below us, the sea sparkling smashed glass.

'What about your uncle?'

'What about him?'

'Is he shabby?'

'Uncle Peter? I don't know exactly. It's surprising he's invited us over really. He's a bit of a pairia.'

'A what?'

'A pairia dog. Well, actually, they all are in our family, I suppose, the Dudgeon side anyway. I mean none of them are ever on speaking terms with each other. And they don't speak about each other either, except my mother did say you will find my brother a strange person, but as she's not exactly Mrs Average herself, I didn't think much of it.'

'You mean you've never met him?'

'Of course not. Nor his wife, well ex-wife actually.'

'I thought he was part of the reason you came here, because he lived so close.'

'I suppose so. It could be one of Monkey's schemes.'

'You didn't make her sound scheming before.'

'Her schemes aren't like other people's schemes. I mean, she doesn't think them up to do herself a bit of good. That's what's so stupid. Really stupid.' He beat his fist on the top of the seat in front.

The bus decanted us by a phone box in front of a guesthouse with leaded window panes and dusty ivy holding the porch in its grip. Joe squatted down to consult the little piece of paper his uncle had drawn a map for us on. I am writing in a grey cottage set in a washy green landscape, rain-blown, far away in time and place from that scene, but for some reason it is often that sandy figure which hops into my thoughts, crouching by the road in front of the ivy-clutched porch, studying the map with that strange childish concentration he gives to any document, as though he were unused to paperwork and would much rather be up and off on some caper. He looked up and I half expected him to jump off past me with a frog spring. But instead he said:

'These instructions are hopeless. We'll have to ring, but I haven't got any change.'

'You could reverse the charges.'

'In our family, nobody has ever managed to reverse the charges, never. None of us would dream of accepting the call.' His voice was glum and fierce. 'No, I'll just have to rattle dem bones.'

'What?'

He grinned and disappeared into the telephone box. Through the grimy windows, I could see his stubby fingers dialling a long sequence of numbers in a peculiar jumpy way. His creased brow signalled concentration, then frustration and finally rage. He put his head out.

'I can't understand it. Must be a new system. I used to be able to get New York nine times out of ten.' His broad fist slammed the black box. More dialling, followed by a tapping rhythm on the receiver cradle.

'Bloody country. Even the phone boxes are caput.'

'Should I have a go?'

'No point. You need hours of practice to get the timing right.' He exuded the professional's scorn for the amateur who had no idea of the hard work that went into these things. And he had already extracted a certain respect from us for his criminal diligence. Once, he told us, he had wheezed all night in a broom cupboard – he was allergic to the dust and to the feather duster too – in order to creep into the maths master's study and copy out the calculus paper, which he then sold to his classmates at five shillings a throw. He was not much of a cricketer and not much of a mimic either, he said, but he took up wicket-keeping, because that was where the action was, and practised quite hard to learn how to imitate the sound of a bat-snick and how much time to leave before shouting a confident appeal for a catch. I could not help finding this dedication impressive in a squalid sort of way.

'Well, it must be down there, I suppose,' he said.

He led me along a winding avenue of slanting pine trees, many of them burnt by the wind or broken-branched, with peeling white villas behind them, low pre-war blocks with broken-spoked beach umbrellas limp on their deserted terraces. Joe strode on without sparing a glance for these forlorn pleasure lodges. At the end of the winding avenue, we saw the sea through a white gate in the evergreen hedge.

'Damn, we must have gone wrong. What a pathetic map. We'll have to get there along the shingle.'

We climbed over the gate and stumbled and slithered along the high leg-sapping bank of tawny brown and grey pebbles. The rasping cascading noise of our feet blotted out the dull slap of the slack tide. Along the beach, old tank traps reared up, like rusty lobster cages or giant barnacled toast-racks, relics of a heroic era which to us was still a remembered time of austerities and certainties but was soon to be mellowed by the same unmeaning glow as the rest of the past. Joe scampered towards these strange ferrous skeletons, a small-brained shellfish heading towards its fate.

The sandy-pink crab-figure hopping over breakwaters, scuffling over the shingle, swinging in and out of the rusty, barnacled struts of the tank-traps, began to lose what resemblance to *Homo sapiens* it had started with. The beach was empty except for an elderly couple eating sandwiches in the fetid lee of a breakwater, and it was a welcome solitude. I could ignore his hoarse cries – of what? invitation, delight, I neither knew nor cared. It was like taking a pet for a walk, or rather being taken, for there was a tugging, nagging importunity about his mewing.

On the inland side, behind wire fences and staked hurdles, there were blown thickets of ilex and tamarisk and tumbled quirky lutyensy gables and chimneys. A few yards further on, the shoreline curved in to begin tracing the little muddy reedy estuary. Right on the bend, a concrete gun emplacement reared above the shingle, crumbling and ochreous now, its gunslits blocked by a rusty fuzz of barbed wire. On top of this abandoned souvenir of national defiance was standing a burly man in a sort of beach robe, gauzy with gilded threads which shone in the sun.

As I came closer, he raised one hand in which he was carrying a round wire object the size of a football and began to shake the object up and down with a vigorous pumping. He was square-rigged, hard-weathered, the sunburnt skin of his face inflamed by vesuvian encrustations. He had an air of belligerence which even at a hundred yards' distance suggested kinship to Joe.

The two crustaceans caught sight of each other at the same moment and formed the same impression. Joe climbed up the shingle towards the concrete pillbox in a hunched crab's scuffle. The man on the pillbox extended his hands towards Joe, clasping the wire object between them. The sleeves of his robe billowed in this priestly gesture and made him seem more human, more benign, a cutprice Prospero offering an indulgent welcome to his Caliban.

'You must be the Monkey's boy,' he said, 'we did not expect you to attack from the sea.'

'The directions,' panted Joe. 'You put the second left and it should have been the third.'

'A simple test of your ingenuity.' The twitch of ill-humour suggested that he was unused to criticism. 'And this is your bookish friend.'

I gave a weak gesture of deprecation, hoping to indicate my rounded, unpretentious nature.

'Sorry about this bloody nightie. Only thing I can find that doesn't irritate my skin. Have to wear something in the sun, even when I'm just popping out to dry the lettuce. Soggy lettuce is the curse of the English salad. I favour Major Barnes's receipt for the dressing, no sugar and the cheap olive oil, not that overrated virgin muck. Feed you all right up there, do they? Institutional food is always filthy. I ran away from school to escape the macaroni cheese.'

17

He led us through a little gate in the pebbledash wall, ducking to avoid the blowsy tamarisk branches overhead. The gate made a twanging noise as he opened it and I noticed that an enamelled tin sign was hanging loose from the top bar. The sign said Shorewinds with windswept pothooks on the 'h' and 'd' and serpentine s's fore and aft. Dudgeon held himself like a boxer, with a boxer's strut in his plastic flip-flops. The back of his neck was a moonscape of crumble-edged craters.

There was a queer, foreign emptiness about the garden. The lawn was scrubby and neglected, the bushes wind-burnt, bare-branched. The pitched and hipped roofs came low to the ground with leaded windows squinting out from under them.

'Order you about a lot, do they?' He turned his encrusted visage to me with an abruptness which seemed to demand a brisk answer.

'No, we're mostly left to our own devices.'

'Your own devices. A fine phrase. Devices, that's the stuff, an infernal device, a banner with a strange device. Pity they debauched that noble word "craft", so now people just think you mean weaving bloody corn dollies in some damp hovel in the Cotswolds. You'd better come over to what I expect you call the Pat-Eye-Oh. The girls are already out there kippering. Peggy is anyway. That little piece of Nottingham lace has to stay under cover, because her skin is so awfully delicate.'

In the far corner of the garden, the shrubbery was thicker or seemed so from a distance, looked impenetrable even. Peter Dudgeon slipped through an unsuspected gap to lead us into a bushy enclosure no more than fifteen foot square, sheltered and private, yet with the same forlorn look as the rest of the garden, the grass scrubby and the bushes bare-branched.

'Welcome to cosy nook,' he said, waving the lettuce basket like a censer.

In the middle of the grass, a woman lay on a lilo, dark glasses shutting out the sun. She sat up as we came out, half-turning to look at us, but very slowly, as though on doctor's orders to avoid sudden movement. She made no effort to hide her narrow brown sharp-tipped breasts. Behind her in the corner, there was a strip of white cotton drowsily flapping in the breeze, with three corners tied to the bare branches of the bushes and the fourth to a wooden chair with a wicker seat. Beneath this improvised canopy we caught glimpses of another woman lying quite sheltered from the sun. The canopy was so low that it must now and then have brushed her body; the glimpses were quick and partial: the trailing of a milky thigh, a crooked elbow, a flash of golden down. She seemed asleep, unstirred by the slop-slop of the sheet. In the bright light, these split-second intimations of her nakedness were somehow distanced from us, seemed to have the remoteness in space or time of an underexposed photograph. The older woman, rising now to greet us with a half-smile, was just as unnerving.

'Aunt Peggy?' Joe asked.

'Oh no, not Aunt, I think, not now.' Her voice was slow and caressing, slightly nasal too, not so much musical in the ordinary way as suggestive of some unfamiliar instrument, ethnic perhaps, which sounds monotonous to us only because we are listening for the wrong sort of variation in it. She took off her dark glasses and shaded her forehead with her thin hand. My eye trying not to was caught by her round stomach and impudent navel winking out over her blue bathing pants, so unlike the spare elegance of her upper body and her fine greyhound head. Her hair was scraped back under a red and white kerchief.

'And Onora. Wake up, you lazy girl. This is Onora from Nottingham.'

'I was fast asleep.' Murmur from under the slopping sheet.

'No you weren't,' Dudgeon said to the girl. A hand reached out for a towel and he slapped it. 'You say hullo to my nephew and his shy friend.'

'Why do you always say from Nottingham? I don't say where you're from.' Her voice was slow and dead, a kind of provocation.

'It has a ring to it – Onora from Nottingham.'

The girl sat up and looked at us without interest, refusing to make an identification in this parade of suspects. Her sweet boat-shaped face was vacant, her pale eyes unseeing. When she swept her long straw hair out of her eyes there was no coquetry about it, only the crossness of the midday heat. If it had not been for the spots around her chin, she would have looked like a naughty child in a Victorian illustration.

'Do you like that sulky look? Some men do. They like the threat of trouble. I prefer smiling faces around me. Onora, cheer up. Think of the *pommes dauphinoises*. She started life as plain Nora, you know. But then we all have our way to make.'

'You always talk about food. It makes me sick.'

'Because it's all you understand, my child of nature, that and –'

'I'm not a child of nature. That's a horrible thing to say.'

'Oh it's not so bad, Onora dear,' the older woman said. 'But don't fuss, it's such a nice day.'

The girl got up and stalked off through the gap in the hedge with her towel and a floppy bag slung over her shoulder.

'She used to be a sweet-natured girl when she was looking after the beach umbrellas. But I'm afraid she has no devices of her own.'

'Don't be so priggish, Pietro.'

'I'm not usually accused of *that*, even by you.'

'Well, you are a prig, you know.'

Inside, the house was wooden-panelled, umbrous, neglected. Murky passages led to square rooms which were always smaller than expected. In the cloakroom, I knocked into relics of an abandoned sporting past – mildewed fishing waders, a battered set of hickory-shafted golf clubs, a canvas fishing bag with torn netting. In the gents, a dark framed photograph of some people in alpine costume standing in front of an alpine hotel. Below this, a photograph of two grinning young men holding a fish that was almost as tall as they were. That cold dark texture of pre-war photographs had taken these scenes deep into an unimaginable past. The pair of ebony hairbrushes on the little glass ledge above the basin had the dank smell of clubmen long gone and their discontinued brilliantines.

Peggy Dudgeon – if that was still her name – sat in the dining-room chair, exhaling a delicate surprise. She picked at the rich, vinous, olive-laden stew with a certain amused tolerance. It was hard to tell whether this house had once been her home, or whether this was the first time in her life she had been in it. I was intoxicated by this lack of commitment, also by the wine, the first I had tasted which tasted of all those things that serious wine is supposed to taste of – oak and earth and plums and a faint murmur of drains.

'Have some more of this, the wine crooks call it full-bodied. What they mean is it gets you drunk quicker. Don't whatever you do go out into the sun afterwards. I call it a nice siesta wine. Onora, more bread.' The girl rose from her seat, mute, robotic grace, as she opened the panelled door into the kitchen. Her pale cold skin brushed my arm as she passed.

'She is a well-built girl, though you wouldn't think it when she's dressed.'

'Oh Pietro.'

'You got any girls up there?'

'No, girls don't seem to have breathing trouble so much,' I said. 'There are two women with emphysema, but that's all.'

'Sounds like a morgue. Come down here whenever you like. Onora will look after you if I'm not about. You might like to borrow my study for your book-worming.' He gave me a fierce smile. 'I spend most of my time in there, occasionally I go into town for a natter with what I call the inshore expats because they've all come down here to escape from somewhere else but they're too idle to cross the Channel. Actually, I prefer the more elegant term "inquiline". You've got such an inquiline nose, don't you think, I said once to old Reggie D'Arms, he of the grogblossom hooter. He didn't see the joke at all. They're a dismal crowd, you know. Drink far too much. I wrote a little satire on them once, *à la* Juvenal. Called it The Ancient Mariners, after the pub we frequent. Had them all over here for a reading. Didn't go at all well.'

'Are you surprised, dear?' Peggy sat with her head thrown back, gently unfurling a thin plume of smoke through her nostrils.

'Not surprised, Peggy, merely irritated by their lack of sodality. Though since they know sod all . . . ah the advantages of a classical education. I was an usher once, boys, in the locust years before the war. The Upper Sixth classical set sat at my feet, or rather trembled. I kept order, and I taught gym, and woodwork too.' He glared down the table.

'And very good for you it was too,' said Peggy.

'How could you know, my dear? You had not yet swum into my ken. More of the full-bodied, Onora. It was all in the B.M. era. Before Marriage. Not that I didn't make quite a presentable husband, in my own way.'

'That's for me to say.'

'Wives are no judge of these matters, ex-wives worse still.'

Peggy smiled and leant forward to cut a slice of the runny cheese. I was surprised how much she managed to eat. There seemed no tenseness between them, or so little that I had begun to wonder if Joe had been right about them being divorced. Where I was brought up, divorced couples would not speak to each other except about money and the children and then only at a careful distance to prevent a quarrel.

'Come into my *rifugio*. Joe will take the girls down to the beach, or the shingle to be more exact. Well this is it, the old cave of making, as Wystan used to call it, cave of slaking more often in my case. I am by nature a solitary drinker. One cannot drink and think and talk all at the same time. Have a swig of this for a change. The *bersaglieri* used to cauterise their wounds with it. Bloody good anti-freeze it makes too.' Dusty gourd-shaped bottle. Chunky orange glasses received the mist-coloured liquid with a faint susurration. Dudgeon's strong shoulders, mahogany in the dim light of the shuttered room; his massive head now handsome and imperial, the encrustations obscured; he sat rather upright in his cane-backed chair, giving audience.

Above his head, there was a strange picture in thick clotted oils. A naked woman with large black eyes in a crouching posture with her hands upraised, clawing at the air like a heraldic lion. Behind a palm tree in the middle of the picture, a monster of blackish hue glared back at her. The monster's anatomy was so confused in the tropical vegetation that I could not distinguish between tail, legs and phallus. Along the top of the picture ran a scroll of crude golden symbols, a mixture of geometry and alphabet.

'Evilly bad, isn't it?' Peter Dudgeon said. 'Poor Meriel thrust it into my hands when they were selling up the old magic box of tricks. You'll meet Meriel in town I expect. Not what she was these days, I'm afraid. Whatever else she may have discovered, it certainly wasn't the elixir of eternal youth. But then who has, dear boy, what did you say your name was, no, it doesn't matter. Don't want to deliver yourself into my power. We all took names, you know. I was Gnoph-Hek, the Hairy Thing. Derek was Shub-Niggurath, the Goat with a Thousand Young, Lord knows why. That's Derek, married to Meriel for a hundred years now, no young to speak of, though. Or was Derek the Faceless One? Should have been, of course, although he was thought to be quite the coming thing in the fraternity. Still, we had some fun, or I did rather. I don't know whether they ever quite cottoned on to me not being a hundred per cent believer.

'I am a child of the Enlightenment, a spoiled child but a child all the same. In the dear dead days when we all followed the sun, I used to collect superstitions, *canards*, old wives' tales, mares' nests. That was the coast for them, you know. South of Naples, they'd believe anything if it made a good story. Christianity bored them – child born of a virgin seduced by the Holy Ghost, stale buns. What about the priest who gave birth to twins after treading on an adder, *davvero!* Or the siren who had it off with a lobster. More *anticongelante*, drink up.' The high walls of books leant in towards me. The musty smell began to irritate my throat. My breath came shorter.

'That was when I met them all, you know, the bright-eyed mariners, well not so bright-eyed now, more like a load of bloody albatrosses in fact. But then, well, it was all a different story, but I don't feel like telling it just now. In fact, I think it's time for you to bugger off and have a swim. This is the hour consecrated to my snooze. Would you be a dear chap and send Nora up to me? I find it so difficult to nod off properly these days without a bit of help.'

Dudgeon levered himself up from the rickety cane chair and walked over to a tall cupboard in the corner of the room. He took out his long robe, which glimmered pale and gauzy in the murk and drew it over his head. As its ghostly hem fluttered down to his ankles in the dim afternoon light filtered through the closed shutters, I felt I was attending the robing of a priest in some esoteric and not altogether savoury cult.

'Always wear a nightie for your snooze, my boy. It's the only way to keep off a chill on the stomach.' He waddled round the edge of his desk and the cane chair and lowered his bulk onto a dirty old settee covered with a paisley shawl, then swung his legs under the shawl. An unexpected briskness. With a drowsy murmur which I could not decode, he drifted off.

Out beyond the panelled door, the lawn was hot, silent, empty. The scrubby bushes scented the air. The sea was a hot milky blue. Beyond the pebbledash wall at the end of the garden the sound of voices on the shingle, unreal, near, like the creatures of a delirium which insists that the voices are talking about you, although you cannot make out what they are saying. My head ached, but the impending asthma attack seemed to have gone away or perhaps retreated to regroup.

At first sight, the beach was quite empty. It was only when I was three or four yards from the sea that I caught sight of them hidden by the rearing bank of shingle. Coming upon the little group I had the sensation of doing something I or someone like me had done a hundred times before: the same figure awkwardly edging down over the shingle, sending the odd spurt of pebbles scampering and bouncing, the same absorbed figures below looking up with the slow half-interest of the sun-drugged.

'Come on in. It's lovely.'

'I've got a headache, from all that full-bodied stuff.'

'The water will wash it away, really.'

'Oh yes, do have a swim. It's so . . . fresh.' A caressing hesitation before the word, as though no one had ever used such a word before, or not in such a context, also a faint intimation that I was lucky to be there to hear it. Peggy lay on the same lilo which

I had first seen her on, her basking shell. Onora, straw-hatted now, sat with her back propped against a strut of the tank trap, staring down at her toes dangling in the water. Joe waded out of the sea. His strong thighs were already reddening in the sun. He was naked.

'You seem to be very eager to get a tan,' I said.

'Silly boy, he forgot to bring his bathing-suit.'

'Well, we're all adults here,' Joe said.

'Hmm,' Peggy crooned, faintly reproving not the sentiment but Joe's crass way of putting it. Joe's lack of inhibition clearly pleased her. It was a sign of knowing how to behave, much as her grandmother might have been pleased by a young man removing his hat.

'Mr Dudgeon wants you,' I said to Onora.

'Oh ye-ess.' The lengthening of the yes sounded deliberate, but I could not tell whether it was meant to be ironic, or whether she was imitating someone, or if so, who.

'Run along dear.'

'Or Mr Dudgeon will be crawss . . .' This time Onora's parody of Dudgeon's crusty drawl was exact.

'Well, you know . . . what he's like,' Peggy said.

'I know.'

'Really, couldn't you have one more quick swim first?' Joe beseeched. 'Surely Uncle Peter wouldn't mind waiting and it is so awfully hot.'

'I'm afraid he's rather *punctual*,' Peggy said. 'And it does ruin the day if he gets in a fuss.'

Onora sighed and began to trudge back up the shingle towards the pebbledash wall of Shorewinds.

'Why are we Brits always so worried about being punctual?' Joe said. 'Isn't it meant to be all *dolce far niente* on holiday?'

This was the first time I remember hearing anyone talk of himself as a Brit. Joe would often be the first to use a new word or turn of phrase, sometimes even before you came across it in the newspapers. Yet he did not, I think, consciously try to pick up the latest idiom or even to imitate the jargon of any world he happened to find himself in. He naturally absorbed the new, sometimes not getting it quite right, but never offering any resistance. He was a verbal flypaper.

'Well, there's *niente* and *niente*,' Peggy said.

A hot sandy breeze set up a rustle in the fringe of the reeds which were just visible at the far end of the shingle wafting the smell of the sewer outfall, that insistent smell which still brings back to me the sea-shimmer of that coast.

'My daughter Gillian can't stand the smell,' Peggy said. 'She never comes down to the beach when she's here.'

'I'd like to meet her. Will she be coming here soon?' Joe asked.

'I rather doubt it, dear. She doesn't get on with Pietro at all. I thought perhaps when he became an ex-step-father, but . . .' Her hand traced a despairing circle in the air. 'Anyway, she can't really stand sun-bathing, either. She's too pink-skinned, and she won't take trouble like Onora.'

'Well, I'm pinkish too,' Joe said. 'But I love the sun.'

'Oh you'll go a lovely honey colour. I can see that already, but you must take it gently.'

'I am a bit red,' Joe said, twisting his head to try and see his shoulder blades.

'My daughter goes utterly lobster. And of course being rather overweight doesn't help.' The expiring sigh underlined the mysteries of heredity. 'So she tends to stay with the Colonel in Devon.'

'Your first husband was a colonel? I didn't know that.' Joe spoke gravely. He took facts seriously. Dates, statistics, useless information of all sorts he handled like precious objects. When he was talking facts, he never fluffed a word or muddled a figure.

'Oh not a real colonel, at least he wasn't when I was married to him. Later perhaps . . .' her voice trailed away into a desert of incuriosity. 'No, he just looked like a colonel when nobody else did. Gillian gets on very well with him, I can't really think why. Nobody else does.'

For the past five minutes, I had felt the attack brewing as the sun beat down upon my forehead. Futile search for shade in the lee of the tank trap's rusty struts. Aertex shirt drenched with sweat. Hair damp on throbbing brow, breath shortening and beginning to concertina.

'Oh do have a swim. Nobody will see. You can keep your pants on.'

'I'm afraid . . . a bit wheezy . . . be all right in a minute.' The diapason began to sound. Its gravelly resonance picked up speed. The falling-away groan which ended each breath started to cut short before being strangled into muteness. The diapason climbed half an octave, from its full, almost melodious beginnings to a thinner, shriller note, someone trying to cry a warning in a high wind. Peggy and Joe came up the shingle from the sea and stood looking up at me while I wheezed away under the tank trap, visitors to the Reptile House agape before some panting saurian. It seemed somehow worse, more indecent to be having an attack with these naked or near-naked figures hovering, worse even than the time when I was stricken in the middle of a fancy dress party and was surrounded by anxious people in leopard skins and Mickey Mouse outfits.

'Poor you.'

'It's probably the smell.'

'It could be almost anything. He's got a list of allergies as long as your arm. Literally. When they did the tests on his arm, every one came up a bump – dust, feathers, horses, cats, parrots.'

'Parrots?' Peggy murmured.

'A lot of asthmatics are allergic to parrots.'

'Not parrots,' I gasped.

Out of my pocket I pulled the little blood-red pill box, as elegantly ovoid as an eighteenth-century snuff box. Under the little wad of cotton wool, the precious yellow pills lay, the full rich yellow of golden eggs in a fairy story. I broke one in half down the line of its shallow incision and slipped it under my tongue. Its sickly sweetness filled my mouth. I let it dissolve as slowly as possible to prolong the anticipation of relief, its delight not to be too greedily grasped at. I could see Peggy and

27

Joe dressing and gathering up their belongings below me. They seemed to be moving with a drowsy slowness, as though they too had been drugged. My breathing was coming soft and slow again. The last jerks and catches smoothed out. The stone against my calves felt deliciously cool. The pills are banned these days. Even thirty years ago, I felt there was something illicit about them.

Dudgeon had changed into a cream linen jacket and pale blue cotton trousers. His wavy grey hair had been carefully brushed and slicked down. He was immensely but precariously neat, a choleric consul who had just returned from a hard afternoon in the consulate.

'Did you amuse yourselves?'

'The poor boy was not at all well.'

'Oh.' He looked crossly at me. I had come to know that look. People who hated illness really hated it not out of fear of infection or even of inconvenience but because of its claims upon attention and sympathy. Not holding with illness was a refusal of allegiance to the invalid's feudal rights.

'It's just a little go of asthma. I'm quite OK now.' Post-spasm heroics, the asthmatic's patter.

'The Albanian colonists in the part of Italy where I used to live called it the strangling sickness,' Dudgeon said with a glare dipped in menace. 'They believed all respiratory diseases to be highly infectious and would abandon sufferers to the mercy of the elements, particularly the children. The moment you started wheezing, they frogmarched you up over the pass to a godforsaken dry valley without a house or tree for twenty miles. It's still known as the Valle degli Affanni, the Valley of Wheezes, although of course that might simply be a corruption of degli Albani, the Albanians. Old Norman Douglas took me up there once in the days when we used to do a lot of walking. There was the devil of an echo. Think of the groans' – the glare became more menacing – 'ricocheting to and fro between those silent cliffs. But then the little buggers had a stroke of luck. They took refuge from the pitiless sun in the limestone caves. And it turned out to be the best thing possible for their wheezing. The air was enriched by the oxygen molecules trapped in the limestone. And while they were breathing nice and deep up in the mountains, the Italians down in the plain were being wiped out by malaria. Of course, they all attributed their survival to the cave-gods, and pretty soon everyone for miles around was panting up to cast their coins in the cave-pools and demanding miracle cures for cancer and the pox and broken legs and so on, and then going on to pester the cave-gods with requests for any old desire that came into their heads. So they now call them the Caves of Desire and Asthma. It's a sort of Lourdes for heavy breathers. You ought to go out there and see if the cave-gods can sort you out.'

'Oh Pietro, you don't want to *expose* the poor boys.'

'A little exposure never did anyone any harm.'

Already I saw the two of us crouching in a Cave of Desire and Asthma, gulping down the enriched air, our eyes blinking as we looked back at the sundazzled mouth of the cave.

'You could reproduce that atmosphere by artificial means, I expect,' Joe said.

'What a bloody boring suggestion. What's wrong with a decent old cave?'

'There's no need to be rude,' Peggy said. She threw a shawl round her shoulders with the fine dignity of a Russian countess socially doomed by a wastrel husband. She was, I supposed, in her early forties then, if that; looked by the calculus of droop and wrinkle a good five or ten years younger. Yet this was not how we thought of her that evening. She seemed beyond anything as petty as having an age.

'And how is your dear mother?' she inquired, leaning forward to look more closely at Joe.

'Oh the Monkey, she's all right. Very busy. Just got a couple of new kids, from Gandia.'

'Where?'

'It's in Africa, on the West coast.'

'Oh yes, Gambia.'

'That's right, Gambia. She's got fifteen kids now. I don't know how she finds room for them all.'

'Amazing,' Peggy said.

'It's all a bit much for Dad. I don't think he minds living in the stables so much, but she does drive herself so hard and he sometimes finds it difficult to keep up.'

'My sister,' said Peter Dudgeon looming out of the blackness, 'is what I believe is known as a human dynamo. But should dynamos try to be human, that is the question? Or humans try to be dynamos, come to that. It is a question of *function*.' His broad square fist punched the table, but lightly, testingly.

'My sister disapproves of me,' he added.

'Who wouldn't, dear?'

'And I disapprove of her. A typical English sibling relationship, wouldn't you say? We see each other once every two years. After we have embraced, she immediately reminds me of some discreditable chapter in my past, and I riposte with some subtly disparaging remark, designed to undermine her self-esteem, but without much luck. As for my elder brother John – we are a decayed family, you know, but not nicely decayed.'

'Pietro, just because you and Monkey always fight, you don't have to be rude to poor Joe about his – '

'Josephus, I apologise, I crave absolution, I am an utter bastard, forgive your poor old Uncle Pietro. I am living up to or rather down to everything you have doubtless been told about me.'

'I think Monkey rather admires you actually. After all, that's why she sent me here, to the san, because you recommended it.'

'Did I really? I had quite forgotten. Have I become a sort of Gabbitas and Thring for sickly youths? Bring me your pubescent cripples, your juvenile incurables. Cruise ships and sanatoria across the world will tremble at my frown. Spas which have been visited by my displeasure will become ghost towns. Those that prosper under my wing will take my name in gratitude – *visitez Dudgeon-les-Bains, vaut bien le voyage*.'

'I want to show the boys the old fort before it gets dark.'

'It's black as pitch already.'

'There's still the light from the sea.'

30

'Stumble into the ditch if you want to. Count me out.'

The sandy lane glimmered pale through the darkness. A bare arm thrust itself into mine.

'You can't leave me behind,' Onora said.

'So it seems,' Peggy said.

'Link arms, we must all link arms.' The darkness had untethered something like gaiety in her.

The four of us walked arm in arm down the lane between seaside walls of flint and chalk. My gym shoes slipped on the loose gravel. The women's arms were cool and warm against mine.

'Stop a minute, let me light a cigarette,' Peggy bent over the match Joe held out to her. The flame did not waver in the still evening. I could see by the light of the match that Peggy was smiling with the cigarette in her mouth.

The lane bent into a grove of pine trees. Our footsteps were muffled by the needle carpet. Strong pine scent hovering around us. We came to the end of the trees and there in front of us was the low squatting outline of the fort. From where we stood, it seemed toy-sized, unserious. Beyond it, there was a caravan site and the sound of pop music and laughter.

'We won't go back tonight,' Joe said.

'No, not tonight,' I said.

The lane burrowed down into the shadow of a high grassy bank. The curve of the miniature battlements was just visible above its brow.

'It's sunk, you see, with the passing of time, like the rest of us,' Peggy said. 'You can get in round the back.' We stumbled over rough ground, then in and out of a clump of thorn bushes. Thorns prickled through my thin shirt. After a couple of false starts, Peggy found the gap in the outer dyke and we walked up along a narrow path staring up at the massive masonry, silvered now by the light of the climbing moon.

'I think it was Henry VIII who built it, something to do with his marriage troubles. People do the oddest things when they're in a state, don't they?'

'Was it ever besieged?'

'Oh no. I don't think anyone ever bothered. It's far too out of the way.'

The walls above me seemed to sway in time to the distant music from the caravans. They were playing 'She wears red feathers and a huly-huly skirt'.

'Where have they got to?'

'What? Oh, I hadn't noticed,' I mumbled.

'Onora is not one for ruins, not unless they're human anyway, I expect she's – '

'Shall I call them?'

'I wouldn't bother. She'll bring him home. Is your friend always as quick off the mark as this?'

'No idea. I've only known him for three weeks.'

'Asthma doesn't seem to slow him down much.'

'No. He says he's not a typical asthmatic.'

'And you are?'

'I'm afraid so.'

The caravan radio had got to 'She lives on just coconuts and fish from the sea, with love in her heart . . .'

'We'd better start back. I can feel the chill creeping up.'

The silence we walked in was not companionable. Peggy did not hurry back down the lane, but her languor had gone. As we came through the front door and into the dark hall, she seemed tense.

'Where's Onora?' Dudgeon, a half apprehended shadow at the back of the hall, his voice an animal growl.

'Coming. With Joe.'

'Well, she'd better bloody well hurry up then.'

'She knows the way.'

'Of course she knows the way. That's not the fucking point.'

'Don't make a fuss,' she said wearily. 'You can't expect twenty-four-hour service at your age.'

'What do you mean by that?'

'Oh, *you* know.'

'Do I? What do I know?'

'Do I have to – what is that tiresome phrase – spell it out for you?'

'Like what?' I said.

'Well, if the first time you saw her, you saw her – like that.'

How strange the purity of speech, as though to name the parts were to break the spell.

'I don't see why it should make any difference.'

'Don't you?' He looked surprised. 'Don't you have any feeling about there needing to be mystery? Do you know what Peggy told me about her, after she'd gone up to the house. About how she was conceived?'

'What?'

'I shouldn't really say.'

'Go on.'

'Well Peggy says her father went mad and had to be locked up. And her mother went to see him, in a kind of waiting-room, and either she was sorry for him or because she wanted to have a child – '

'What are you chaps gassing about?' Heini, the consumptive who liked to practise his English, wandered into the day-room, with his hands deep in his dressing-gown pockets and an unnaturally non-chalant gait, like an actor in an old-fashioned musical comedy.

'Go back to Switzerland, Heini. There's enough salatoriums in your own country without you and Hugo taking up space down here.'

'Sanatoriums, I think you mean, my friend. We came down here to make your English correct.'

'I'll bust your cuckoo clock if you don't watch out.'

It was all a far cry from Herr Settembrini and Herr Castorp. I am still surprised that there should have been two Swiss boys there. Could they not have learned their English in the purer air of the Alps? Perhaps Maintenon-Smith had offered their parents cut rates as an advertisement for the reputation of his clinic. What else? The ceaseless clucking of the ping-pong ball, the flipping of the greasy cards on the little wooden table with its peculiar deckled edge, the slithery flap of slippers on the long lino passages. The clearness of these sounds in the long silences.

Mrs Fretwell brought us a blow-football set with little white metal goal-posts and bamboo reeds to blow through and a plastic ball painted leather-brown. 'It's Chinese,' she said, 'it will exercise your lungs.' We looked at the game with some disdain but in the end tedium forced us to try it and, against our inclination and sense of dignity, we became obsessive players, crouched over the table for as long as we could manage before we had to stop to get our breath back, cheeks puffed out like zephyrs, brows sweating. Joe had a strange technique modelled, he said, on the Continental style which involved taking short breaths and bobbling the ball about in his own half of the green plywood pitch. I preferred to gather my strength for a long slow blow which sent the ball scudding down his end to rebound off the back wall right up my end again. It was hard to say whether these gruelling encounters did much good to our crippled lungs, but Dr Maintenon-Smith, passing by on his rounds, would pause to watch with a Napoleonic smile on his lips.

Sometimes, like a commanding officer, he would ask for our views on the food. It was always easy to recall the meals of the previous day. Their sad aromas – the watery Irish stew, the sickly macaroni cheese, the Bisto-laden gravy – would still be with us the morning after. Despite its windy hilltop situation, the sanatorium was a place that odours seemed to cling to. Even in the rose garden, the Superintendent's pride, one could not quite avoid the smell from the lavatories at the end of the truncated cloister. And within our hearts, the growing hatred of being shut up and the longing to get out. All the same, it was a magic mountain still. The chill of the cloister in the morning, the mist stealing up from the woods in the afternoon, the sense of being suspended out of time – the experience of it all is with me yet, and not just because of how it ended.

II

Breathing exercises –
Trull and Rickshaw drop anchor –
The Mariners Rest

The chairs we sat in were thronelike, gothic-backed, finialled. We sat in them like six pale dauphins. Our skimpy shorts slid over the greasy wood, our pimple-cold flesh snagged on the splinters. Maintenon-Smith had saved the chairs from the bonfire of furniture after the monastery had been derequisitioned at the end of the war. 'They have style, don't you think?' The circumstances of this liberation were unclear, best not enquired into. Still, there cannot have been too many claimants for a draughty monastery on top of a hill or for its furniture and fittings.

Faint smell of soup and scalded coffee (or what we called coffee, there was still a lot of chicory in it) swam into our nostrils, as we breathed in, flaring our nostrils as Mrs Fretwell taught us. Our fingers splayed on our cold torsos, just below the ribcage, sternum thrust forward, our sad shrunken chests pretending to greatness. Then out through our mouths, lips protruded into a trumpet shape. Mrs Fretwell was snugly wrapped up in a chunky mauve jersey, handsome in an embarrassing way with proud scarlet lips which trumpeted of their own accord. We wore only our white gym vests and the shorts. The vests were hitched up to make sure our fingers pressed the cold flesh properly. The whole exercise felt so futile. How could all this thrusting and trumpeting and bellows-work ever amount to more than a pathetic imitation of the real thing? The project of growing one's own body seemed a fantasy. Now and then, Mrs Fretwell would cut out items from her trade magazine to show us. *Breathing Space* it was called, an ill-printed newsletter with a blotchy orange cover. She read out encouraging stories of hopeless asthmatics who had gone on to win medals in cycling championships, of former martyrs to eczema who had won beauty contests. Once she read us a letter from an old patient of hers who had just climbed the Matterhorn and claimed he owed it all to her breathing exercises. We did not believe him.

Joe became impatient during the Fret sessions. I found them quite soothing. My mind drifted off. The exercises worked on me like a primitive version of those exercises people now take to aid meditation. The terrace outside the window, the little grove of larch and fir below, and beyond, the hills and heathlands. I fancied myself somewhere in the Himalayas, accompanying a party of men of action in the search of the secret of life, to be tracked down in some remote cave or lamasery where She who must be obeyed had sought final refuge from the modern world.

Past the long window I became aware of a woman's figure, silvery, drifting. She was walking slowly between the rosebeds. Behind her, another shorter, more voluptuous woman swinging her hips in a full skirt. Joe, quicker off the mark, was already up out of his chair and at the window, slapping the glass to attract their attention. The silvery figure turned and waved and disappeared from sight, as a Napoleonic figure came into view directing her towards the door.

'And here you see our friends are learning how to breathe again.' By the time they came into the room, Maintenon-Smith had assumed the character of a head master taking prospective parents round the school, benign, omnipotent.

'They look like ghosts,' Peggy said as she stopped to look at the six of us in our white gym kit, sitting upright on the monastic chairs.

'Oh their flesh is too, too solid,' Maintenon-Smith quipped. He patted Joe on the shoulder, cattle dealer appraising fatstock. He was keen on Shakespeare, or *Hamlet* anyway, which he often quoted. 'To be or not to be' was a favourite, handy for any situation involving multiple choice.

'Oh do let them come now. It's so lovely down at the beach,'

Peggy was imploring the Superintendent while Onora behind her was already smiling at Joe.

'What do you say, Mrs Fretwell? Can you release our two young ghosts?'

'He can go,' the physio said, pointing her muscular finger at Joe, 'but he,' pointing at me, 'has his foot therapy now.'

'Surely we could change his appointment.'

'I've got to get back by lunchtime. He must have his treatment now.'

'We can wait in your lovely garden,' Peggy said. 'Those roses. Did I see Gloire de Dieppe, such a pretty colour?'

'Yes, yes,' Maintenon-Smith said vaguely. 'Please make yourself at home.'

Mrs Fretwell led me next door into the back room where she had her apparatus already set up: black bakelite box with dial and two red rubber tubes with electrodes. The idea was to shock the tendons in my feet into contracting, thus training them to form the high arches which nature had denied me. Maintenon-Smith claimed that his clinic, although specialising in respiratory diseases, offered every medical facility. My father had called his bluff by challenging him to cure my flat feet. Once a week Mrs Fretwell brought her apparatus along and shocked me.

'Shall we try and manage a hundred and ten today?'

'Let's not.'

'Come on, don't be a silly,' she said, slowly moving the brass knob which controlled the current.

'That's enough, please,' I cried, as the tickling thump became unendurable.

'You're enjoying it really, aren't you? I can tell.'

'I'm not. I'm not.'

Three grinning faces at the window. Onora in particular seemed gorged with pleasure. Perhaps, as with many people, the spectacle of pain made up for the lack of a sense of humour.

Their faces were blurred by condensation on the windowpanes. Only the white teeth could be seen with any clarity. Pumpkin masks. Sherlock Holmes and the Yellow Face. That ancient terror of something going on behind the skin, behind the eyes even, of something or someone looking at you without being looked at in return. This terror was compounded by being shut in, trapped, while the wandering consciousness outside prowled from window to window, now pressing its mask against the pane, squashy nose, steamy breath, now moving away to become a pale glimmer.

These disjointed thoughts slid in and out of my efforts to cope with the pain. Mrs Fretwell moved on to my right foot. The left foot still trembled. The twitches in its tendons spread and faded like pond-ripples, as she turned up the juice on the other foot.

The three faces at the window began to amuse themselves by swapping places with each other, then sidling along in line together like a song-and-dance act, first to the right, then to the left. Then Joe led them in some of the primitive physical jerks we did in the mornings, swinging his outstretched arms up and down, forwards and backwards, clapping his hands as they met.

'Your friends are most amusing,' Mrs Fretwell said.

'That's what they think.'

'Right now, see if we can manage a hundred and ten on this foot too.'

'This foot's perfectly all right as it is.'

At last, she let me put my shoes and socks on. She packed her instruments of torture away and opened the door on to the terrace. After the shocks, there was always a sense of exhilaration. The world seemed clear and fresh. The view on the terrace, the long, still, silent view of trees and heathland, seemed to present itself for the first time. And the three of them standing there with arms linked, rosy-cheeked, scarves tumbling about their shoulders in the spring sunshine, looked like healthy strangers, like people you see out in the country. Here in the clinic, where we were used to morbid pallor and sinister flush – a blotchy redness high on the cheekbones – they were unmistakably visitors, if not a visitation. Even the way they touched one another, caressingly yet firmly, suggested a kind of confidence in life that was out of place at the clinic. As though to remind me of this, one of the emphysema patients appeared at the far end of the terrace. He was a horse-faced man in early middle age with lank slicked-down hair and a certain air of nobility as he threw back his head to give his ruined lungs a chance. He wore his long badger-striped woollen dressing-gown with a casual swagger too as he strolled between the rose beds.

'Hi, Mark,' Joe called.

The man stopped and mumbled a greeting, then realising that the words had not come out clearly, he waved, with the graceful wave men of the world give when they see a friend at the other end of a restaurant.

'Poor sod, used to be a sixty-a-day man,' Joe said. 'And a fantastic ladies' man too apparently.'

'Oh he does look sad.'

'Would you like to go and change?' Peggy allowed no hint of hurry into her voice, but we went off to discard our gym kit as promptly as to a sergeant-major's command. She herself did not care to linger on the terrace, nor did she look over towards Mark, who was making in our direction, the dawn of a smile on his pale stretched horseface.

'I hate hospitals,' Peggy said. 'I know one shouldn't but I do.'

'Oh it's not really like a hospital,' Joe said.

'Anywhere with ill people is like a hospital.'

Only when we were almost down in the town and the motionless dark fir trees had given way to shimmery dappled young cherry and weeping willow did she begin to relax.

'We're going to the cove for a picnic. The Sirens' cove.'

'Will we see any, do you think, sirens, I mean?' Onora asked.

'Don't be silly, we're taking the sirens with us.'

'Oh Joe,' Peggy sighed. 'I think I'm past the retiring age for sirens.'

'There's no age limit.'

'Are you sure?'

To me, Joe's chaff sounded awkward, learnt or half-learnt from some manual, but the awkwardness seemed unimportant to the others. Perhaps they did not even notice it. Intimations of desire, if that was the right way to describe them, neutralised the critical faculties.

In fact, although I only came to understand this later, the awkwardness might actually be an advantage. It sharpened and made plain the motive. A subtler, more nuanced approach might leave room for doubt. Ambiguity had its uses, but it could be overdone. Joe as a whole person, if you could call him that, seemed to me as ambiguous as anyone could be. But in any single thing he said or did, there was a hungry clarity. You could not avoid knowing what he was after.

We drove along a sandblown track between clumps of buckthorn. The hiss of tyres on the sand, the climbing sun, a sense of languor stretching down my calves to my abused feet. Halt in the spring-fresh silence. Through a gap in the bushes up a winding path, goat-footed, rejuvenated by the morning, appeared Peter Dudgeon, priestly in his gauzy vestment, through which could be discerned the outline of dark bathing trunks.

'Welcome to these echoing groves.'

That day was my first experience of leisure. Not inert absence of occupation, nor a hectic seeking of pleasure, but a determined, experienced, almost professional living through of time, a savouring of each moment. There was nothing said about the day or the place at all. Nobody exclaimed what a delightful spot it was, or how long it had taken to get there or that they must be thinking about getting back soon. How provincial and harassed all the picnics of my childhood seemed by comparison. Here the food and the wine were simply there, and somehow when we talked about them, it made them more delicious, not less.

'You do like the angels' wings, don't you. *Ale degli angeli*. It comes from those goats up on that hill behind Naples, the one like a dowager's hump.'

And even that fetid tang seemed good and right, although my taste in cheese was for the bland and creamy.

We sat on a little grassy bluff overlooking the cove. Clear waters of the palest green, tongues of pale sand licking the low rocks, in the distance the dots of windbreaks on the unfashionable beach.

Round the corner of the rocks came the chugging of a small outboard engine. Dudgeon lying on his elbow, Silenus recumbent, stiffened at the prospect of invasion, and rose to confront the opposition.

The boat was a grimy cockleshell, single-masted, with a rust-coloured sail furled. Two men in it, the taller, straw-hatted, bare-chested, gazing out to sea. The other, steering the boat, was wearing dark glasses and watching the shallows. This helmsman's pale blue shirt was sweaty and torn. They might have been a couple of outcasts in a South Seas tale, hugging an unfriendly shore in search of a place to settle, perhaps some abandoned trading post they could occupy and scratch a living from. And yet, as they came into shore and began to make the boat fast, these first impressions slipped away. Their forlorn state had a chosen, willed look to it. If they were victims at all, it seemed more probable that they had succumbed to their own fantasy rather than to a pitiless destiny. The way they sauntered up to our grassy bluff did not suggest that they were entirely unhappy with themselves.

'It's Rickshaw and Trull,' Peggy declared.

'I told you they were coming.'

'I know, but Rickshaw's so unreliable.'

Handshakes all round, gentlemen abroad. The taller of the two, Richard Shay, and yet not so much taller as he first seemed, was bleached by the sun, his eyes the palest blue, his body driftwood pale.

'Oh Rickshaw,' Peggy said. 'And darling Trull.' The shorter one, but not so much shorter when they stood side by side, was sallow with dark stubble round his soft jowl. His open mouth, a cupid's bow almost, was encouraging, on the verge of a smile; his eyes impermeable behind dark glasses.

'We had hoped to sail the whole way and surprise you. But the wind died.'

'It took long enough as it was, even with the engine.'

'Trull's a terrible pilot. Never stops fretting about the engine.'

'I don't fret. I whine,' the shorter man said.

Shay squatted on his hunkers and described their journey in a soft, confiding voice which at times was hard to hear, a muted voice. How old was he then? Thirty-five perhaps, but the driftwood bones and pale blue eyes were not easy to date. Like Peggy he bypassed the age question, not by clinging to youth but by a kind of poise. He had a reputation then already, I think, but an elusive sort of reputation. In fact, being elusive was what he was best known for. Since he had to be pinned down to something, he admitted to being a traveller and writer, but the two things were not to be vulgarly confounded.

He did not travel in order to find material for his writing. Still less did he write in order to earn the wherewithal to travel. The two pursuits, both exacting solitude and detachment and cunning too, were different ways of being free. At all costs, his privacy had to be defended, and the continuous, arduous business of defending it gave his conversation a peculiar flavour. Eloquent, witty, fantastic, fact-packed cadenzas would, without warning, trail away into halting, evasive fragments, or into silence. The cumulative effect was as frustrating to the inquisitive listener as listening to a radio beset by failing batteries. But how he could describe things! When I ran into him in London a year or so later, how electrifying it was. He hailed me on a zebra crossing near the British Museum and described taking tea with some Grand Mufti in Asia Minor somewhere, and evoked all the charm and malice and halitosis of that evil old character so brilliantly that I felt no desire ever to leave the traffic island on which we had been standing for twenty minutes or more. Then unthinkingly I asked where he was staying and he said in a manner both abrupt and vague, 'with my mother in Battersea', and he disappeared in the gap between two passing cars with only a glimmer of a wave.

He would begin to talk hesitantly, sketchily, before working up to a full tableau. The story he told, of a hunch-backed alchemist who claimed to have been made a cardinal by Pope Alexander III and who sailed the Mediterranean selling fools' gold to credulous dukes and princes, took strange turnings. After years of success as a conman of the high seas, the alchemist genuinely got religion and, by now excommunicated from the true Church, founded his own monastic order of false friars. These esoteric brethren, a mixture of defrocked priests, reformed pirates and common or

46

garden layabouts, continued to roam the seas, demanding alms at each port of call when the proceeds from the gold ran out. Yet there were those among them who sickened of the protection racket and stayed on shore and wandered inland to become hermits in the mountains. These Brothers of the Sea became notable for the austerity of their lives and the fervour of their devotions. The alchemist-cardinal-abbot disappeared from view for years, only to appear at the head of an armed column in the Third Crusade and died gallantly at the siege of Acre, although some said this was another Brother John, perhaps the younger brother or nephew of the first one.

'You're a romancer, Rickshaw.'

'No, he's a romantic, Pietro.'

'Comes to the same thing. You make the whole thing too bloody amusing. The past is a serious business, you know. It wasn't all wizard fun. Most of those vessels furrowing the wine-dark sea were carrying Jewish bankers and Norman military engineers. There might be a few raving friars and Circassian maidens in the hold, but they were merely business expenses.'

'Ah, *professore*.' Shay bowed his head, unwilling to contest the point. He was not an arguing man, nor one to entrench himself.

How else could he have managed to go on talking as he did, with that generous curiosity, that sunny uppishness? How he made the people of those forgotten highlands and sequestered valleys live, set our ears ringing with the chatter of Ladino shepherds – the Swiss, not the Sephardic ones, he threw away as though it were hardly worth saying – the guttural keening of Bosnian monks – his mimicry was a kingfisher's flash – how quick his eye for the telling incongruity, the tailfins of the old Chevvy bouncing down to Trebizond with the belly-dancer with the machine gun peeking out of the back window. I began to notice something curious about these anecdotes, namely the lack of any malice in them. This discovery did not make me feel cheated, as if I had spotted that the drinks we were drinking were non-alcoholic. On the contrary, it induced a cheerful clean feeling.

Yet I felt uneasy too. Whether they were listening or not, the

Dudgeons were so relaxed. Peggy reclined on the rough grass, pale brown arm trailing through a clutter of little pink flowers; her ex-husband motionless on a rock, toad-emperor. Now and then Joe asked a question, which Rick Shay answered always with accommodating friendliness but without losing his stride.

'Oh I believe rather less than a third actually worship in those rocky perches, but at Easter and Advent they still take those flat sugary cakes and the entire village, some of us rather the worse for wear from that terrifying plum spirit, climb up Saint Pantaleimon's path to that very peculiar chapel of ease.'

'Come for a swim,' Joe said. He pulled Onora to her feet and led her round the corner of the rocks.

'What a handsome couple they make,' Keith Trull said.

'Fuck off, Trull,' Peter Dudgeon said.

Trull gave a goblin chuckle. His cupid's mouth bloomed into the shape of a split fruit when he smiled.

'Wouldn't it be great if they never came back and when we went to look for them we only saw goats' footprints leading into the sea? Or tyre marks. Goats are a bit old-fashioned, E.M. Forstery.'

'Oh Trull.'

'Or perhaps just two little heaps of smouldering embers and a faint smell of burnt pork.'

'You're a creep, Trull.'

Trull grinned wider, acknowledging this accolade by pushing his shades up onto his forehead, and gazing at us. His eyes, blank and blinking, gave him a docile, biddable look. Without his shades on, old ladies might have asked him to carry their groceries.

'Why do you like younger girls, Pietro?' he asked.

'Because they're attractive and because I'm getting on. Use your loaf, Trull.'

'But not all middle-aged men do. Often they prefer women in their thirties, don't they? There must be some psychological reason for it.'

'There's a bloody good physical reason for it, but I'm not going to give you the satisfaction of spelling it out.'

'What is it, Pietro? I'm a writer, I have to know these things.'

48

'No, you don't. And anyway who gave you permission to call yourself a writer? All you've written is those creepy stories.'

'Oh did you like them? I didn't know you'd read them.'

'No, I did not like them.'

'But he absolutely devoured them, Trull, like chocolates,' Peggy said.

'Shilling shockers, that's all they are, horror comics. I felt unclean after reading them, like watching an old woman undress when she doesn't know you're there.'

Trull emitted the crooning gurgle of a baby approving a lullaby.

'I suppose you'll want to quote that on the back of the dust jacket,' Dudgeon added.

'Can I really? It would be such a help.'

'Bugger off, Trull. Take that young fellow there for a walk. I'm going to have my snooze.'

We strolled, Trull and I, along that empty shore in the calm white heat of afternoon. The sand was white as wheat. Above us, little thickets of scrub, shimmering at a stray skim of the breeze. In one of them, the sound of voices, love chuckles dying away to low murmurs. Trull turned, took his shades off and looked up at the feathery bushes with the attentive stillness of a nature watcher.

'Young love, young love. Have you had much sexual experience?'

'No.'

'I thought not. You can always tell, you know, by the way people walk. At least you can with men. With girls, it's more the way they talk.'

'What do you mean?' I said, despite myself.

'There's a kind of freedom in the language. After they've had it.'

Trull put his dark glasses back on and went on walking. He had seemed fleshy and sluglike beside Shay's spare figure, an indoor person. But now as we walked along in the heat, I saw that he was square-rigged like Peter Dudgeon, robust, built to last. He pursued his indecent interrogation with calm persistence, and I blushed and became flustered. I resented this line of questioning and could not cope with it at all. Yet I had to confess that, for some reason I could not pin down, I did not dislike him.

'And when did you have your first real erection? People can often remember because it's such a surprising thing to happen.'

'Do you ask everybody you meet questions like that?'

'Everybody.'

'Why?'

'They're the questions we all want to know the answers to, deep down. And of course, lots of people like answering them.'

'I'm sure lots of people don't.'

'You'd be surprised how few. I think I'm performing a sort of public service.' He gave his luscious split-plum smile to the sky. I noticed that his head rarely turned in my direction. It was not that he seemed reluctant to meet my face or anyone else's, more that he cultivated the impersonality of the priest in the confessional.

Ridges of rock, black and tarry, in front of us now, high rearing in comparison with the low perambulable shore line but scarcely casting a shadow on the afternoon. On the other side of the rocks, the sand was dirty grey, almost black. Inland, the ground was steeper, sweeping straight up to the hills behind.

'I do like black sand,' Trull said. 'It upsets people so.'

'Are you travelling with Rick Shay?'

'In a manner of speaking. I mean we sail together, but when we reach port, our ways usually part.' He gave a snorting sort of giggle.

'How do you mean?'

'Well, our tastes differ. He can spend hours talking over a glass of water to the local greybeards. I feel the need of something a little more stimulating.'

'Really, just a glass of water?'

'Yes, he doesn't take stimulants at all for choice. He'll have a glass of wine to be sociable with Pietro, but that's all.'

'Why do you travel together if you're so different?'

'Well, my main use is to sail the boat. We're just trying it out here first.'

'You're the skipper.' This somehow took me aback more than anything else he had said.

'Rickshaw can't sail for toffee. He can't do anything like that, can't drive, or cook. He can ride a bicycle because he did through the German lines in Greece during the war, but that's about all he can manage in the technical line. He says you cannot hope to see the world, really see it, if you're fiddling with machines the whole time.'

'And you can do all those things.'

'Yes. I was Junior Firefly champion at Burnham-on-Crouch, and I'm a qualified mechanic, and I've done a Cordon Bleu course and so on.'

'How did . . .'

'Well, if you'd been brought up by a couple of elderly school-teachers in Ipswich, you'd acquire a skill or two, partly to keep your parents quiet and partly to get the hell out of the place. And they love Rickshaw's books, you see, so they're delighted to think of me sailing the old wine-dark with him. At present they are under the impression that we are doing a sort of miniature Kon-Tiki. Could the Egyptians have sailed far enough up the Aegean in order to have seemed like the mysterious tribe from the north who founded Greek civilisation? They think we're going to potter about the Mediterranean in a replica of a 3000 BC rowing boat. But what do I care, as long as the money is there when I want it.'

As he sketched out his background, that shy serenity began to fracture into a kind of agitation which wavered between the impish and the irritable. I was conscious of being shown round a part of his personality which had not yet been arranged, a glimpse through a half-open door of a rumpled bedroom.

'You probably think Rickshaw's queer. Most people do when they first meet him.'

'I hadn't thought about it one way or another.'

'I expect you had really, but you're too polite to say so.'

'No, I hadn't thought about it.'

'But he isn't, he's just nothing. If you saw his mother, you'd

51

think he was. She's a tough cookie and collects Staffordshire china. But that doesn't always make people turn out queer.'

'I'm sure it doesn't.' We turned round, and began to retrace our steps. Our footprints in the sand looked fragile and doomed.

Trull's attention wandered off along the beach, though I could see nothing to disturb the hot silence or the pale sand.

A hundred yards ahead, a young couple stepped out of the willow scrub. Honey-brown, broad-shouldered, they walked away from us, languid-stepped. The man with surprisingly short arms.

'Sometimes I think that envy is stronger than desire, in sex anyway,' Trull said. 'But then who is to be envied? Here we are, throbbing with jealousy, tremendously alive. And they are, well, depleted, a little sad, wondering what happens next. They have, as the saying goes, had it.'

'I don't think it's quite like that.'

'Just trying to keep our peckers up, am I? Well, nothing wrong with that.' Trull began to hum, not tunelessly, just not trying for a tune, the noise of a telephone after the receiver has been replaced, not the honey tone of contentment, anything but.

We had almost caught up with the bliss-weary couple by the time we reached the little bluff where we had picnicked. As we came down the little winding path between the bushes, they turned to us and spread their hands wide in a gesture of emptiness. No one there. Then a pointing hand.

We looked out to sea. About a quarter of a mile offshore, in the thickening light of late afternoon, the grimy cockleshell could be seen moving in a slow curve. The sea was no longer milky now that the best of the day was gone, and the boat's wake drew a white arc in the water, and then a white semi-circle, before cutting back round over its own track. A single figure sat still and slight on the stern.

'Oh, he's jammed the rudder again.' Trull's groan.

'But where are the others?'

'Gone home, I expect. Oh the silly bugger.' Trull waved, a fierce commanding wave, then made a jerking, lifting movement with his hands together to show Shay how to free the rudder. The figure in the boat acknowledged this pantomime with a slow wingbeat of his raised arm, but made no move to follow the instructions.

'He'd be quite happy to stay there all night, you know,' Trull said, his irritation fading now, and a certain admiration almost creeping in. 'The one thing, the only thing he says a traveller needs to learn is how to wait. If you get heartburn every time you find the visa office closed or you have to wait four days in some godforsaken place for the spare part to arrive, then you really ought not to travel. He's just giving a demo.'

'Couldn't he turn off the engine?'

'No, because he won't be able to start it again. I'll have to sort it out for him.'

Trull stripped off. He was wearing sensible black bathing trunks. He made a neat pile of his clothes with his dark glasses on top and then strode into the waves and swam a slow comfortable crawl out to the boat. He freed the rudder with a single confident wrench and steered the boat back to land. The whole process took no more than five minutes.

As we dragged the boat up the beach, the scalding smell of a hot diesel engine came to my nostrils, intoxicating elixir of my childhood, the great lung-calmer. My asthma was not choosy. Any oil derivative – petrol, diesel, mower lubricant – had power to tame the spasms. Even now, as I pass some ramshackle body repair shop under the railway arches (although the Cyprus Re-spray and Valeting Centre has other associations too), the old fumes, heightened to almost unbearable balminess by the solvents in the paint spray, move me with powerful memories of suddenly being well again, the sweat growing cool on the forehead, the pyjamas no longer a straitjacket, the viyella soft and pleasant to the touch now, the anxious face of my mother all at once losing its stretched, twisted aspect. For milder spasms, my father would prescribe a ride in the old Morris which might have been designed by some imaginative therapist for the purpose, since not only the air inside it, but the wrinkled brown upholstery and even the old black *AA Book of the Road* all seemed impregnated with the petrol smell. The rough, frank springing was also a kind of companion, quite unlike the smooth alien roll of modern suspensions. Bouncing through the lanes with their diverting glimpses of cottages and copses and the creamy satisfying whiteness of the long white-washed and thatched walls, now almost gone from hi-tech farmyards, all these sensations are conjured up for me by that simple phrase 'after the war'.

'I think,' Rickshaw said, 'that I should have preferred a longer radius. The views were lovely, but my eyes had no time to dwell on them and they came round too often.'

'I told you how to free the rudder. This sort always gets stuck.'

'I didn't want to deprive you of your Byronic swim.' Shay was humoured by the diversion, might almost be suspected of having set it up if Trull had not said that he was hopeless with machines. Anyway, I was already beginning to see that subterfuge of this sort was beyond him, and would have destroyed the point of the incident, like removing an inconvenient card to make a patience come out. The adventurer had to shun calculation, if he was not to tarnish the purity of the adventure. Happenings must be allowed to flow through him, while he himself remained as colourless as a glass prism. Rickshaw's helplessness and the pleasure he had taken in contemplating the scene had nothing affected about them. He hopped over the edge of the boat and greeted us with the affability of one who has been for the trip round the bay, just as advertised.

'The others? Oh, they pushed off. Pietro seemed a little . . . impatient.' Here perhaps there was a hint of weakness, a wish to avoid trouble which could not be quite hidden.

'So who cares? He is always so impatient,' Onora said, with a forgiving smile, the sort that comes most naturally when one is forgiving oneself. I could not have expected her to serve Peter Dudgeon's needs for ever, but her standing by the boat so bright-eyed and wide-awake offended my feelings of propriety, which were formidable then. She began stowing our belongings under the seat in a brisk manner and then put her strong shoulders to the gunwale as we manhandled the boat back into the water. All her sullenness had gone. She even gave me an amiable shove in the back when she thought I was not pushing hard enough. She seemed to have more of a life of her own now, an individual destiny in which she had her own say and a character of her own which made itself felt. Perhaps Joe, with or without meaning to, had brought off a kind of rescue.

'Will the boat take all of us?'

'Easily. Hop in. I am not steering. You may bind me to the mast and stop my ears, or my mouth if you prefer. Can we sail, do you think, Trull?'

'Not till we get over the bar.'

'Did someone say bar? Mine's a gin and tonic.'

Joe's Colonel Chinstrap imitation died on the breeze.

Trull put on his dark glasses, piled the rest of his clothes under the helmsman's seat and pushed the boat back into the sea. Cautiously, he piloted it through the translucent shallows, the outboard motor raised almost out of the water, so that its screw could be seen burbling behind us. We came out of the rocky nook where we had picnicked towards the more open water into which the little river flowed out of the reedy marsh. Trull opened the throttle. We felt the bump, the prolonged friendly nudge of the sandbar, and then we were in open water.

Crouching in the bows, I watched Joe and Onora sitting with their backs against the mast and its rust-coloured sail still furled. There was not enough wind, and we wouldn't get back before dark if we tried to sail, Trull said. Rickshaw began to tell his stories. With unhurried ease, shy trafficker all the same, he undid his corded bales. He had an unrivalled stock of encounters with the displaced: bogus Bessarabian counts, drunken Dutch drug smugglers, smelly mystics from the dusty hills of Anatolia, Maltese sword-dancers (or part-Maltese – he said his mother was a Fraser from Inverness), a Croatian taxidermist who had been a ferocious partisan until his sex-change, a dwarf prostitute in Sumatra who was a keen admirer of the pony stories of the Pullein-Thompson sisters, a rubber of bridge with a party of alligator-hunters in a hut in the Florida swamps (they refused to play his strong no trump), a Central American ambassador who sang Masefield shanties to him in the Ritz hotel in Madrid (for Rickshaw had no inverted snobbery about such haunts), a game of football under the starry Odessa night in mid-winter with some Russian sailors (Rickshaw played in goal and got frostbite in both feet).

He was describing a sight he had seen in the square of a little town, somewhere in Apulia, I think, or was it Macedonia (my head began to whirl): a melancholy old man in an army greatcoat who carried on his back a beautiful contraption made of old pieces of wood and bits of harness, brass and leather polished to a high sheen, with a peculiar roof, a spire almost, fashioned out of corrugated iron, and through the bars at the back shone the great green eyes of a wildcat and every time the wildcat snarled the old man's face lit up into the most seraphic smile and the women crossed themselves against the evil eye and the men clattered an amazing quantity of coins into the brass cup the old man held out to them, and as the old man limped off out of the square Rickshaw had followed him down the hill to the garage by the main road where the old man put the cage into a smart little Fiat and drove off.

'They must be very poor, the people in those villages,' Joe said.

We all fell silent. Even Joe could see that he had said the wrong thing – no, wrong is too pallid a word. He had smashed up the whole conversation, reduced its delicate assumptions to smithereens.

'Oh yes, desperately, desperately poor,' Rickshaw said, rallying as best he could, 'they live on black bread and olive oil and a little goat's cheese when they can get it' – but even this sounded too enviable.

'Are you interested in poverty?' Peggy enquired, letting her long fingers trail in the foam.

'Well, no more than anybody else really,' Joe said. He began to scratch his wrists, then his forearms, raking up sandy cloudlets of skin-dust.

'My daughter Gillian is interested in poverty. That's why she doesn't like going to poor places. Do you remember, Rickshaw, those funny little villages with little round houses made of flaky stone where the people were so poor and Gillian felt sick. Like beehives, you must remember.'

And he did remember. But as he began, gingerly now, to lead us off again, I was conscious of a certain depletion in him. The delights which he generously scattered over his audience were fragile and he knew it, for the poverty which preserved them was all too visibly doomed. They were precious shards of old Europe lying at the sea-bottom, barnacled, half-covered with sand, glimpsed by the divers while shoals of silver fish darted in and out (Rickshaw loved diving with the local boys, without all that lumbering equipment, and coming up with a single fragment to toss on the professor's table under the flapping awning of the tent). Soon they would lie too deep under the layers of affluence to be recovered, and even the memories of those who had seen them would be silted over by the incuriosity of succeeding generations. The hoarse whisper of the foam, the engine's off-beat thud, the smell of the diesel and the suntan oil, Onora's arm, or was it Peggy's, felt cool through the thin cotton shirt on my back, Rickshaw's voice light, chuckling at itself, inexhaustible through the warm late afternoon.

In Dudgeon's refuge too, there were scattered other remnants of old Europe, most of it as mildewed now as the fishing waders in his lobby; I had taken to browsing there in the afternoons while Joe and Onora went off. In his grumpy way, Dudgeon was glad of company and would lie on his bed in his robe talking now and then as I peered along the disordered shelves: the *Badminton History of Squash Rackets* next to *The Great Illusion, The Book of the Dead* and *Heidi*. Joe said the house gave him the creeps, but its musty tranquillity soothed me. The smell of damp books was another thing that seeemed to calm my bronchial tubes, whatever the doctors might say, or perhaps it was simply the smell of failure that was so congenial to me, and so hateful to Joe, but then he hated being cooped up anyway.

To be his fellow patient was like being shut up with a hunting dog – the scratchings at the door and prowling up and down, the low heaving growl. He jumped at the prospect of excursions with his uncle. When Peter Dudgeon let him out of the back seat of the little car, he bounded puppyish out on to the desolate, down-at-heel quayside, dragging Onora with him. The two of them disappeared into the little town to cash a cheque. Reggie D'Arms and Dudgeon and I ambled up from the harbour with its few neglected dinghies rotting on the stonestrewn greenslimed foreshore. The street which led to their weekly rendezvous was a steep twisting lane with a few dismal junk shops strung along it. D'Arms pressed his strawberry nose to the grimy windows and stared with mildewed eyes at the Coronation mugs, horse brasses and battered barometers and fire-irons, he himself no mean model for a Toby jug with his red-and-white spotted neckerchief and his choleric mien.

'What a load of old rubbish. No wonder the place is so god-forsaken. I sometimes wish I had my little flat in South Ken back again. Well, here we are, journey's end. Not much sign of lovers meeting, though. The Mariners Rest.' A grubby white canvas lifebelt festooned with tarry ropes hung above the door. Bottle-glass windows refracted warming-pans and Windsor chairs. Little wooden 'Licensed' signs in gothic script hanging from the ceiling reassured the fretful toper. Dark Sicilian waiters leaning against the coffee machine on the bar. Dusty dim lit noonday calm.

'Oh rest ye brother mariners, we will not wander more.'

'He says that every time, you know, every bloody time.'

'Look, there's Derek.'

A plump elderly man in spectacles raised his glass to us, and returned to his *Daily Telegraph*.

'I have tried to like Derek, you know, over the years.'

'Not very hard you haven't.'

'We ought to introduce this young man to Derek.'

'I don't see why anybody *ought* to be introduced to Derek.'

'Derek,' D'Arms persisted, 'was one of Aleister Crowley's last young men. When the Beast took refuge in these parts, Derek was, well, whatever you call it, his ADC or acolyte. Quite brilliant at laying on black masses and that kind of thing.'

The plump man greeted me with a firm handshake, clutching his newspaper with a certain desperation as though we might be going to snatch it from him.

'The market seems to be very weak again, I see,' he said.

'What?'

'It's this trouble in the Middle East.'

'Did you use to be in the City?'

'In the City?' He seemed aghast at the question. 'No, no, I've no head for business.'

'Our young friend wants to hear about the beastly goings-on, in the old days.'

'Does he really?' The plump man looked up at me with a mixture of panic and disbelief. 'It was all very tame, really. One has to be careful. People are so inclined to get the wrong idea. It was mostly white magic, you know, healing and so on. People just don't understand how technical it all is. You have to arrange everything just so and you can't always lay your hands on the materials you need. Menstrual blood, for example. Awfully hard to get hold of just when you need it. And then one's collaborators tend to be so unreliable. Often the worse for drink, you know. I had to speak to Crowley himself about that more than once.'

'Come off it, Derek, no one ever conjured up Old Nick on *acqua minerale*.' Peter Dudgeon raised a glass of some glowing brown potion, which had been brought to him unasked by a silent waiter, then held it out to us in a parody of consecration, before swallowing it at a gulp.

The plump man looked at him with displeasure.

'No, no. It is absolutely vital to fast first, cleanse the body before – oh cripes, there's Meriel.' He rose and waved his newspaper to a short woman in a flowery dress and straw hat, the hat-string tied in a big bow under her round chin. The thongs of her sandals were cross-tied round her ankles. With her floppy straw shopping bags, she might have been bringing bread and cheese and cider to sunburnt sicklemen.

'Meriel my dear,' Dudgeon rose to salute her with a courtly

bow. 'We were just reminiscing about the old days and you know what.'

'Peter, I am just not having it, you know. You take advantage of Derek's good nature. We simply do not talk about all that any more, not ever. At the time, it may seem all very amusing, but it upsets him for days afterwards.'

'We weren't really, I mean . . .'

'Well, you certainly aren't going to now I'm here. Let's talk about something sensible for a change. I'm sure this young gentleman doesn't want to hear about all that nonsense.' She turned to me to be introduced. Her dark round eyes seemed to have been stolen from their rightful owner and transplanted into her pink pug-face, or the real she might have been standing behind the face and peering through the sockets in a funfair. Her bossy bustling words sounded off-key, not true to what she was like or had once been like. Once she was sat down and a little calmer, and the silent waiter brought her a capuccino, her voice softened. She undid the strings of her hat, threw her head back.

'Well now,' she said, 'what on earth are you doing with these old buffers?'

'I'm at the sanatorium, for my asthma.'

'Oh, you're his nephew. The son of that peculiar sister. Well, she *is* peculiar, Peter. You must admit it.'

'I wouldn't dream of denying it, Meriel, but this is not my nephew.'

'Well, you *have* had a lucky escape, my dear,' she gave a throaty chuckle, flirtatious now as a barmaid in an Edwardian novel. 'I don't mind telling you she's a real pain, even worse than this old sod here. But she is very *good*, though. I mean she does a lot of good, doesn't she, Peter?'

'I fear so. I tried to stop her, but I couldn't even slow her down. Perhaps Derek could have put one of his spells on her, put a little eye of newt or toe of frog in her herbal tea.'

'Peter, I said stop it and I meant it.' But she seemed less perturbed now and pursed her lips to suck in the coffee through the white foam with an almost languorous pleasure, then wiped the foam from her lips with a plump finger. 'Oh that is lovely. There's something about Giuliano's coffee.'

'It just comes out of a machine. It's always the same wherever you have it,' her husband said.

'No Derek dear it isn't. And in any case, you couldn't possibly know because you never have coffee – because of his heart tremor, you see. Whenever we come to that bit in Good King Wenceslas . . . fails my heart, I know not how – I always think of Derek.'

'I should think that last time you sang Good King Wenceslas must have been about twenty-five years ago.'

'As a matter of fact, it was last Christmas Eve when we all stood round the Todhunters' piano and sang like angels for simply hours. When I say we, I do not include my poor dear husband who was laid low with, well, I won't say what. Let's just say he was indisposed.' She brought out the word with a purr, lengthening the final syllable. 'Oh, macaroons, my favourites. Giuliano, you spoil me rotten. Don't you love that bit in *The Leopard* when he goes to the convent to taste those delicious little pink and green *amaretti* that the nuns make? You haven't read *The Leopard* yet? Such a lovely book.'

'They were not *amaretti*, Meriel,' Peter Dudgeon said. 'They were *mandorlati*, little almond cakes.'

'Exactly. Macaroons.'

'Not macaroons, Meriel dear.'

'Since when were you a pastrycook, Pietro?'

'It's simply a question of using the right word. They were not macaroons.'

'If you'd ever made macaroons, you'd know.'

'If you had read the book in Italian, *you'd* know . . .'

'Perhaps they were *tortiglioni*.'

'No, Reg, *tortiglioni* are a different sort of cakes, the twisty ones with coffee beans for eyes. In any case, what matters is what it says in the book, which is *mandorlati*. And *mandorlati* are *not macaroons*.'

The purple encrustations throbbed, the grogblossom nose quivered with passion, yellow rheumy eyes blazed, gnarled fists hammered on the rickety table.

'That's not how you make bloody macaroons. You have to grind the almonds first and *then* you add the sugar and then you work in the egg-whites.'

'Sheer bliss. Like ski-ing in virgin snow.'

'Rubbish,' said Dudgeon, 'like every third-rate cook, you're making a ludicrous fuss about the whole thing. All you have to do is mix the whole lot in together, and then add the arrowroot.'

'*Arrowroot?* You're not making a blancmange, you know.'

'Of course I'm not trying to make a bloody blancmange. I simply happen to be giving you the proper ingredients for a *perfectly straightforward macaroon.*'

All four of them were leaning forward across the table now, shouting, stirring and beating the air with their hands. The silent waiter slipped another glass of brown liquid into Dudgeon's out-stretched paw. He sank it in one great swallow, leant forward as if about to speak, then fell back convulsed by a thumping blow, like a man shot in a gangster film. With terrible slowness, he toppled sideways off the chair onto the dusty carpet, shattering the glass in his fall and lay slab-still, his face a dreadful swollen purple.

This seizure filled me with awe. I had never seen a heart attack before, or anything of the sort. But Dudgeon's companions reacted with a promptness which startled me. They gave the impression of being in training for such things. Reggie D'Arms assembled four of the Mariners' dayglo-orange cushions. Meriel took the stem of the glass out of Dudgeon's hand and laid him out on the cushions as firmly and surely as a nurse. Derek had rushed off through the bead curtain to summon an ambulance. We crouched on our knees round the motionless effigy. His fist was still clenched in rigid defiance.

'Come on, old boy. Gee up. Don't peg out on us now. He's still breathing. Silly sod. All that brandy.'

In the back of the ambulance, I sat next to Meriel, our bottoms jammed together on the narrow bench. As we jolted along, she began to cry. I felt grateful for her tears.

'Funny chap, Pietro,' D'Arms said. 'Wanted to be a priest. Then lost his whatsit and became a schoolmaster. Next best thing, I suppose. That was before he went south. Then he couldn't make up his mind whether it was boys or girls he preferred. Tried both, didn't really get on with either. Prefers his own company really. I've seen him sitting all by himself there down at the Mariners reading some old adventure story – John Buchan, Dornford Yates, that kind of thing – laughing to himself, happy as a sandboy. Not an intellectual at all. Ah, here's the bloody doctor, and about time too.'

The doctor, a lugubrious young man in a dirty white coat, briefly examined the motionless body on the trolley, then wrenched his stethoscope from his ears with an irritable twist of his wrist.

'This man is dead. He ought not to be here. Take him away.'

'He's not . . . he was breathing . . . five minutes ago.'

'Can't you give him artificial respiration?'

'He is dead. The porters will take him down to the mortuary.'

But Joe had already brushed past the doctor and was flattening his square sandy hands on his uncle's chest and pumping it with fierce thrusts. His own shoulders rose and fell in a seeming supplication. Their humping motion stirred other thoughts too, of other risings and fallings, in Dudgeon's case so fruitlessly undertaken, at least if we were to believe Reggie D'Arms. Perhaps he had reasons of his own to embellish the unhappiness of Peter Dudgeon's sexual career. Just because life ended in the quest for a perfectly straightforward macaroon, there was no call to assume that earlier quests had not had their satisfactions. My father too was interested in such questions. There was, for example, his famous obsession with the origins of mayonnaise which I will not go into here, except to recall that it occupied several days, perhaps weeks, in the public library. But he was certainly not a man to admit dissatisfaction in love. Quite the opposite. It was the irrepressible fertility of his affections that overwhelmed him.

I have not mentioned the entry of Joe and Onora into the hospital ward. An entry is what they made. The two of them stood hand in hand under the globe-light above the double doors, both so sandy in the sickly light. They looked round the ward, not at first seeing Dudgeon's trolley in the far corner of the room and the rest of us sitting on folding plywood chairs along the wall beside him.

But their gaze, indeed their whole bearing, was commanding, almost imperial, suggesting a visit of qualified medical personnel to some primitive establishment where even the staff might go about barefoot.

'I didn't know you knew about first aid,' I said afterwards.

'I did a course, as part of my cadet training, and I've also picked up a few tips from watching ambulance teams handling road accident victims. I wish I'd got there ten minutes earlier.'

'Do you think you could have saved him then?'

'No, but he might still have been breathing and it would have been good experience. With his lifestyle, he was probably a goner in any case. Poor old Uncle Pete.'

Did Joe really say lifestyle, or is it only my remembered irritation that makes me attribute the term to him years before anyone else used it?

'He was an extraordinary man,' I said, surprised by a spurt of sympathy for the deceased.

'I'm in charge of the funeral, you know,' Joe said. 'Next of kin.'

'Oh I suppose you are.'

'Peggy's gone home, to her cottage in the West Country. She doesn't go to funerals.'

'Why not?'

'She just doesn't. Anyway, she's an ex-relative now, I suppose. I only wish Uncle Pete had thought about that and pulled his finger out as far as the lawyers were concerned.'

'Changed his will, you mean?'

'Yes, she still gets everything. I mean, everything's not a lot, really, only the house and a few thousand, mostly in gilts which are practically worthless now, but it's the principle.' He looked seriously bereft, a bedraggled leprechaun caught in a downpour. Then he assumed a mysterious solemn look.

'Would it be all right if Onora came to the funeral?'

'She must come.'

'It wouldn't be out of order, in view of, well, the former relationship?'

'Don't be silly.'

And so we sat in the back of an old Humber saloon with Derek the magician in front and Meriel at the wheel, the magician being a non-driver, following Reggie D'Arms's taxi down the bosky laburnum lane that led to the cemetery.

'Very good of you to come,' Derek said to me. 'Pietro would really have appreciated it. He loved young people, got him into one or two scrapes, of course, but he was awfully good with the parents. People just cannot understand how one can be fond of the young even if one is getting on a bit.'

'Shut up, Derek.'

'I was talking purely of friendship, my dear.'

'Shut up.'

'I wasn't thinking in any way of – '

'You just weren't thinking.'

'There's the chap. Ask him.'

'We're looking for Mr Peter Dudgeon's funeral.'

'Would that be Dudgeon with a D in the middle?'

'Yes.'

'He's my uncle,' Joe said. 'I booked this funeral.'

'Funny name, isn't it? I thought at the time it was a funny name. Here we are then, ten-thirty, I'm sorry to say you've missed it, sir.'

'But I booked it for eleven o'clock, definitely eleven o'clock,' Joe said.

'That's right, sir. But we had a cancellation, and they moved it forward half an hour, because we were double-booked at eleven. You'd be surprised how many cancellations we get here, cancellations *and* double bookings. People not letting the left hand know what the right hand is doing, that's what it is.'

'What shall we do? We can't not say goodbye to old Pietro.'

'We've got to say goodbye.'

'We could go and look at the grave. Then we could drink his health.'

'Health doesn't sound quite right, not at the graveside.'

'Memory then, we could go back to the Mariners and drink to his memory.'

'We could sing a hymn.'

'Not at the Mariners. Giuliano wouldn't like it.'

'No, not at the Mariners. We could sing a hymn here.'

'I don't think you sing in cemeteries, not if the parson's gone home.'

'Well, we could sing in the car.'

'Look at the grave first and *then* sing in the car.'

So we went to look at the little green oblong. The gravediggers had just finished putting back the squares of turf and were barrowing away the earth that Peter Dudgeon had displaced. Then we got back in the car and Reggie D'Arms led off 'There is a Green Hill Far Away' in a high tenor, and now I cannot help thinking of the green hill as being Dudgeon's grave, although in fact the grave raised scarcely more of a hillock than my allergy tests for horses and parrots had. The car windows steamed up with the singing.

It was only a few days later that, on the strength of a single telephone call to Dr Maintenon-Smith, my father decided that I was cured, and without consulting me sent me the money for my fare home. He had faith in the Napoleon of Asthma and felt bound to respond with alacrity to this all-clear. Myself, I was not so sure about the cure.

Joe, my crass, lovable, word-fluffing twin, stayed on.

III

Himself and the Monkey –
The Guns of Navalone –
Tea at the Gryphon Hotel

'That's Dad's den over there, that converted loose-box arrangement.'

Low red-brick stables, half-moon windows either side of the stable arch, the upper row curtained, the lower dust-frocked and grimy. Above the arch, '1892' in curly cream lettering. Grass grew between the square cobbles in the yard. Straw blowing. Coal dust. Old farm machinery rusting in the corner. To the right, the opening above the wooden partition wall had been glassed in and the passage blocked off by a front door painted a grubby green. The signs of dwelling only added to the desolation. Under the shadow of the arch, cardboard boxes neatly stacked implied organised activity but of a transient furtive sort, otherwise derelict premises commandeered for storage by a band of train-robbers.

Brisk tippety footsteps at the back somewhere. A thin whistling, the tune fugitive, not perky, more to keep up the whistler's courage. And a short, square cobbly-faced man opened the grubby green door. He came out into the archway, paused to blink at the light, then gave a gesture of despair, the sweep of his hand too extravagant for an audience of two.

'The trailer was meant to be here at eleven. If all this kit doesn't reach the showground by lunchtime, I'm done for. And the clutch is slipping. Why do clutches always slip? I used to know how to change a clutch-plate. In the Army. I was a sapper, funny thing being a sapper, you know. Other regiments look down on you and yet in a way they respect you. For your technical know-how, though

I'm not really very technically minded but the road surfaces were so bad. In France, you know.'

'Couldn't Monkey take you in the van?'

'No, she left at dawn. With the Koreans. At least I think they were Koreans. They had high cheekbones. Charming children but they make the toughest infantry in the world. Not of course that I've seen them in action, but – '

'What was she doing with the Koreans?'

'Oh some religious festival or other. National cultures. You know what she's like.' Joe's father came up very close to the person he was addressing. His head bobbed at Joe's chest like a bird pecking at berries. He ended each sentence with a chucklish uh-huh sort of noise except that it was not an ending so much as a brief slowing and muting before picking up volume again.

'Pony club day,' he said, bobbing at me now. 'Total chaos. I'm the Hon. Sec. *For my sins*, people always say that, don't they? For my sins. A strange phrase, but then people use a lot of phrases they don't quite understand. My wife never uses a word that isn't exactly what she means. Extraordinary precision, like a microscope. Very valuable gift when you're in admin like me. Quite mad to take it on. But then we're all mad here. When Monkey started with the kids at the Big House, I had to have my own show to run. Gosh, there she is now.'

A battered Ford van came round the corner of the buildings and blistered to a halt, chassis rocking. A weathered woman's face, not especially monkey-like, poked out of the driver's window.

'What's all that stuff still doing there, Him?'

'The dratted trailer hasn't turned up, Monk.'

'Oh all right, load me up then, but I haven't got all day. I've got to pick them up again at two.' She jumped down from the van and flung open its rear doors. We started humping the cardboard boxes across from under the arch.

She stood to one side issuing instructions, her dark fringe bouncing, blue jeans and bush jacket quivering with impatience as she saw us putting them in the wrong place. I had scarcely deposited the last cardboard box in the back before she slammed down the overhead door and jumped back into the driving seat.

'Hullo,' she said through the window. 'There's cauliflower cheese in the fridge. Tell Himself to heat it up properly this time.'

She let off the hand-brake and the van shot away round the corner again.

'Damn, I should have gone with her. She won't know where to put the rosettes or the stuff for the collecting ring. They're bound to end up in the Young Farmers' tent again. That is, if there is a Young Farmers' tent this year. They were threatening to amalgamate it with the NFU marquee, over my dead body, I might say, but then perhaps they are right, depends on the size of the marquee and the weather, of course. We usually have rather good weather, not always, of course, three years ago we had that extraordinary hurricane which drowned all those people in that yachting race on the Solent, was it? I was never much of a sailor although we were brought up within sight of Southampton Water.'

'I'm sorry Monkey was so rude,' Joe said. 'She's very bad at greeting people. When I came back from the san after nine months, she just said, oh Joe, there's a pipe burst in your room.'

'What?' Joe's father seemed even more distracted than before his wife had come and gone. 'She's been hellish busy, has the Monkey. Thrives on it of course, can't bear to be idle. The thing about being idle is . . .'

Behind us, across the yard from the stables, stood a big square brick farmhouse, with yellow tiles surrounding its doors and windows, late Victorian also. There were white bars on the windows. At an open window on the first floor, two little girls were looking out through the bars. One of them waved. Their faces were olive-brown. Even from this distance I could see how white their teeth were. They looked happy enough, but their situation could not help reminding me of children in a story, prisoners perhaps or at any rate in an ambiguous position which was not at all what it seemed.

'That's the Big House,' said Joe's father, 'and there's Kim

69

and Anna,' and then waving back to them, 'Hullo, Kim and Anna. Come upstairs and see if there's any Nescafe left, if you like Nescafe, that is. I could try you with my elderflower wine which is not the same thing as elderberry wine, of course, not at all the same. Popular fallacy. Lot of nonsense talked about wine. We don't drink a great deal, I'm afraid.'

At the top of the wooden stairs beyond the grubby green door, there was another green door, leading to a long low room. A couple of tribal rugs on the floor, another one on the long wall. A series of paper lanterns, perhaps made by the children, hung from the rafters swinging in the through draught from the open casements. Old Penguins in the bookcase, tattered green and orange jackets. Low armchairs covered in some dusty brown material, not welcoming. The kitchen next door deterred foraging.

'I'm afraid you'll have to go to the pub if you want any lunch. It seems Monkey has in fact left the cauliflower cheese over at the Big House and I haven't got the key any more.'

'Oh Him. We're going into town anyway, to the pictures.'

'Have you always called your father Him?' I asked as we got in the car.

'Or Himself. It was a joke, something to do with an Irish batman he had when he was in the army.'

'I didn't know we were going to the pictures. What's on?'

'The Guns of Navalone. It's on at the Gaumont.'

'You must have seen it.'

'I have.'

'Well then, why . . .'

'Would you do me a real favour?' It was a strange pleading look he gave me, or perhaps not so much pleading as encouraging, as though he was offering me a chance to do myself a good turn if only I had the wit to know it.

'What?'

'Would you mind going to the cinema on your own? I'll drop you off there.'

'All right, but . . .'

'I've got other fish to fry. It's well, an affair of the heart. I'll

70

explain later. But I don't want to tempt fate by talking about it first.'

'I don't mind at all. In fact,' I added, to preserve a shred of self-respect, 'I missed the first twenty minutes last time, so I'd quite like to go, really.'

'I do feel one of us should. You never know with alibis. The cinema could burn down or something.'

'Yes.'

'Your reward will be in heaven.' These old-fashioned phrases – affair of the heart, tempting fate, reward in heaven – belonging to a much older kind of person, made the arrangement more humiliating. Yet behind my irritation I was dimly aware of rather different feelings about Joe's behaviour. My mood became detached, trance-like. Joe's urge to get on with things made me not so much envious as sad, in a large, vague way, sad for myself perhaps but for him too, though I could not quite say why.

The Gaumont was in the style of a mediaeval guild-hall in the Welsh marches, all black-and-white timbering and shields and bosses. The cavernous vault of the auditorium was lined with painted reliefs of scenes from English history: Raleigh and Queen Elizabeth, the archers at Agincourt, King John at Runnymede, with scrolled captions winging in and out of the feet of the characters. When the lights went down, these figures loomed out of the walls, bulky and monstrous, far more immediate and alarming than the flickering images on the screen. The bangs and cries from the soundtrack seemed to come from the other end of the world. I emerged blinking into the teatime sunlight like a man who has been on a great journey.

Joe was waiting for me on the pavement, puppy-eager, slobbering gratitude all over me.

'How did you like it the second time?'

'I'm not sure I didn't prefer it the first time, without the opening twenty minutes. How did you like it?'

Joe gave me a reproving look but said only, 'I really am incredibly grateful. Would you like a cream tea at the Gryphon?'

'Is this my pay-off?'

'Sort of. There's someone there who is longing to see you again.'

'Who?'

'Someone you'll remember from Shorewinds.'

'Don't be so coy.'

'I'm not being coy. It's just that she doesn't want to bump into my mother, well who would, so she's staying at the hotel.'

Onora had not seemed so sensitive. Still, she had reason to be wary of Joe's relatives and Mrs Follows's welcomes were scarcely overbrimming, but then nor were Onora's own, and it was in dim spirits that I trod the deep dust-laden carpets of the Gryphon Hotel, passing through untenanted lounges and empty writing-rooms with virgin blotters eternally waiting to be deflowered. Here and there, the hotel had tried to modernise itself, to attract a different class of customer, to give the impression of having a future: brocade wallapers, neon signs to reception rooms – the Norfolk, the Trafalgar – in jazzier lettering, a snooker table glimpsed through a glass door, all soon stifled by the stillness and the dust. In the television room, the set skulked in the shadow of a gigantic richly carved oak sideboard with a dog-eared cardboard notice propped against it, saying 'This sideboard is carved with the legend of Hobhoe and the Hoedown Chase. It weights $4^1/_2$ tons. DO NOT TOUCH OR LEAVE GLASSES ON IT.'

In a little side room, shielded from the afternoon sun, indeed from almost everything, sitting at a low glass-topped table already laden with the tea-cakes and scones and clotted cream and strawberry jam, was Peggy.

'Oh,' I said. 'Hullo.'

'You *are* surprised,' she said. 'How exciting. Joe really didn't tell you. Men are so discreet. What *do* you talk about? Isn't this a scrumptious feast?'

Her grey dress made her eyes seem bright and her cheeks and arms, brown in memory, now seemed pale. She held out her hands to me in a foreign, enchanting way. As I took them, her scent, fresh and vernal, all flowers and laundry baskets, quite unlike the heavy musk I was used to in older women, enveloped, invaded me. Her smile invited comradeship, an alliance of everything that was light and simple against the forces of heaviness.

'I didn't fancy running into my dear ex-sister-in-law. Too difficult to explain, don't you think? And if not explained, the complications and misunderstandings. I am too *old* for French farce.' The gentle stress on that word, barely noticeable unless listened for, was a further binding tight of the conspiracy, a declaration at the outset that there was going to be nothing but candour about that side of the affair, that in fact the candour was itself part of the romance, not an obstacle to it. Without the thrilling disparity there would, she seemed to hint, be so much less to the whole thing. If she had been the same age as Joe, would she have looked at him? But that was a thought I could not claim to have thought at the time, that bewildering time of August sunlight coming through the tall, heavy-sashed window, sunlight thick with particles of Gryphon-dust.

'Tea-cakes?' she inquired in a voice bright with parody. 'Or scones?'

'Scones.'

'Quite right. Who knows what might happen if you had a tea-cake? You might get asthma.'

'Food doesn't give me asthma.'

'I thought you were allergic to everything.'

'Not to food, not to any food at all.'

'What about oysters?'

'I haven't tried oysters.'

'Oh I wouldn't. They're awfully risky.'

'What about scallops?' Joe asked. He put the stress on the second syllable, as in 'shallots'. He may even have said 'scallots'.

'Scollups, dear,' Peggy said with a wondering smile at Joe sitting opposite her with a cup of tea clasped like a mug in his square sandy fist. Far from being irritated, she seemed to find his error endearing.

'That's right,' Joe said, adding for the first time since I had met him, 'I often mispronounce things. You've probably noticed that. He always puts me right.'

73

'Do you? How kind of you,' she said, turning her Nefertiti head towards me, still smiling but not with that same wondering indulgence. This was a smile for humouring pedants.

'He's got to learn,' I said.

'I suppose so,' she said.

'I went on a schools rugger tour once,' Joe said, 'to South-West France, round Biarritz and Bayonne, and they gave us all this shellfish. Well, sometimes we didn't know whether it was off or out of season or whatever, so we made whoever were the reserves for the next match taste it first. And as I had this groin strain, I was always reserve. So I had to taste the most gruesome things, squid and so on, but actually I quite enjoyed them.'

'How awful, to have a groin strain the whole time,' Peggy said, after a pause.

'It wasn't so bad. It only hurt when I ran.'

'It always hurts if I *run*.'

'I don't know how you keep so fit then,' Joe said.

'I'm not *fit*. Not ever. Did you enjoy the film?'

'I'd seen it before,' I said with a hint of dourness.

'Oh, had you? I am sorry. You're so kind. You won't tell, will you?'

'No, of course not.'

How gently she drew me to one side, as negligently as if she was tying the cord of a dressing-gown while thinking of something else. With each light tug, she offered the most infinitely modest of appeals. There must be a hundred better things to do, a hundred more important or alluring people to be with, it would be the most ridiculous waste of time if one were to take her part, nothing of the slightest use would come of it. And yet inescapably one was left with the most powerful impression that to stray from her would be a terrible mistake, that some unique experience would have been missed, that one would be storing up a lasting cause of regret. The talk in that sunlit dusty back room was rambling, broken by long pauses. She liked pauses. The tea had grown cold. All the same, when we rose to go, it was a spell that was being broken. She kissed Joe on the lips.

And then me. A kind of promotion. She smelled of the fresh flowering scent.

'You'll ring tomorrow?' she said to him, grasping his forearm, but lightly.

'Yes.'

'First thing?'

'Very first thing.'

As she waved goodbye down the long passage, she was brisk and animated. A spell had been broken for her too and the languor dispelled. At the end of the passage where it took a right angle past the TV lounge, we turned and waved again, but she had gone.

'How will she spend the rest of the evening, do you think?' I asked.

'Oh, reading and writing in her room. She says she writes a lot of letters. She often stays in hotels by herself. It's the only place you can think properly, she says. And it's quite a decent room. Tell me, do you ever get asthma when you're on the job?'

'What?'

'Making love, when you're making love.'

'I've never heard of that happening,' I said.

'Because, at the crucial moment, this afternoon, well, it was all right in the end, but I was dead scared for a minute or two. You don't think that's a common thing to happen.'

'Well, to be honest, I don't really have enough experience to say. But mostly people get asthma attacks after the stress is over, as a reaction, don't they? I do anyway.'

'Perhaps it's because I'm not a typical asthmatic,' Joe said, half to himself, trying to quell inner doubts.

'It may be just a passing phase,' I said. 'Still, it does seem to answer the question you asked Smithy. Sex doesn't cure asthma.'

'It may be a gradual process,' Joe said. But he went on brooding as he drove us back down the dusty rutted track between fields of high corn. Red poppies shivered in the pale dry mud as we bumped along. Wisps of straw in the restless late afternoon.

'If your lungs are affected, is there a risk, do you think, I mean when you're breathing so fast anyway? Could the heart be affected?'

'For Christ's sake, you're not some prima donna dying of consumption. It's just a spasm.'

'I'm not so sure. She's wonderful, you know that?'

'Yes.'

'You've got to understand this, because – hang on, this is the big one.'

The most cavernous pothole yet dealt a shuddering blow. The old car yelped and leapt like a wounded animal, sweating petrol in its panic. The smell of petrol brought back to mind the fumes of Rickshaw's boat and its soothing effect on my tubes.

'Him really ought to do up the road. Says they can't afford it. Doesn't stop them travelling all over the world whenever they please,' Joe said. 'I suppose you like tumbledown farmhouses like you like shabby old towns.'

'I suppose I do.'

'I *hate* them. I hate things falling apart. I hate this old car.' He thrust his foot at the accelerator. The car roared back at him but went no faster.

The jumble of old brick buildings in the failing August sun offered a vespertine welcome. His father had rented the place during the war, Joe told me, then decided to buy it the moment he came pedalling over the ridge, back from the war. I could see how the sight of it, rising up over the low bank of cow parsley and tall grass, unfenced, open to the sky, might stir such feelings of homecoming. Bought for a song and allowed to go gently downhill ever since. Maintenance, let alone improvement, would have broken the spell.

In the yard, the sun had gone behind the stables and the air was almost chilly. Joe's father clattered down the stairs to shoo us up them again.

'The Monk wants us to have supper immediately. It's one of her at-the-double days.'

Upstairs, the earthenware stewpot was already on the table.

A pile of raw vegetables – carrots, celery and bunches of some unidentifiable coarse green leaves – lay adjacent in a wooden bowl.

'It also seems to be whittle-it-yourself time,' Joe said to me, setting to scraping the carrots after he had ladled stew on to my plate. 'Or you could have some soup.' He gestured to the far end of the room where I suddenly noticed his mother standing in front of the fireplace sipping from a small wooden bowl. I got up awkwardly, uncertain where to collect the soup from.

'Oh please don't get up,' Joe's mother said. 'I hate that sort of thing. I'm afraid I always eat like this, can't bear sitting down, but don't mind me. I'll be gone in a jiff.'

'Nobody entered for the Best Kept Pony class, nobody at all,' Joe's father said, slicing the carrots into his plate of stew. 'It's completely gone out of fashion. Nobody seems to care about tack any more.'

'You should find ponies for the Korean children. They'd look after them beautifully. They have a self-respect which we in the West have sadly lost. Don't you think so?' She began washing up her soup bowl rather noisily, then lit a cigarette and, leaning against the sink, looked at me in a hard examining way.

'We have got rather scruffy,' I said.

'*Scruffy*. We're in a terrible mess, physically *and* spiritually. All of us.'

'Why aren't the Koreans?' Joe asked.

'Because they have not lost touch with the Whole.'

'The whole of what?'

'If you need to ask the question, you will not understand the answer.'

'Where would the ponies come from anyway?' Joe's father inquired.

'That's your department, Anthony.' It was a shock to hear his name. He too seemed to flinch at the sound of it. 'Am I expected to find ponies as well as everything else?'

'Of course not, Monkey. You do far too much as it is.'

'I do not. None of us does. We could all do a very great deal

77

more with our lives. I assume from what you say that you have not read Krishnamurti.'

'I'm afraid not,' I said.

'You could start with this.' The book, plucked from the paperback shelf next to the sink, was plumped down next to my plate like a salad deposited by a disgruntled waiter. 'You will not understand a word of it to start with. You have first to learn how to pay attention, how to be aware.'

'Yes,' I said.

'It's so difficult, that. To know that you are half asleep, you have to be fully awake.'

'Do you?'

'It is vital.'

'Surely sometimes you're half asleep and know you are, like you sometimes know it's all a dream,' I said.

'I wouldn't argue with mother,' Joe said, 'It isn't worth it.'

'What the West calls consciousness is a great deceiver.' She smiled through cigarette smoke, not at what either of us said but at having found someone to debate with.

'Well, I don't see what else we have to go by.'

'A trained consciousness is something quite different.'

'Brainwashing you mean?'

'Exactly the opposite. I mean the consciousness that can see through all the brainwashing of the trash and trivia of so-called civilisation – newspapers, television, politics, advertising.'

'I'm afraid we're a bit out of the world here,' Joe's father said.

'On the contrary. We are living in the real world, or doing our best to.'

'That's what I meant, Monkey. It's just that we aren't very worldly . . . in the conventional sense,' he added.

'I do not accept the conventional sense. We are real-worldly. We don't let words get between us and reality.' She dried two more soup bowls with brisk, thorough rubs of the drying-up cloth, then put them on a wooden rack above her head.

The way she spoke – severe, emphatic, downright – did not

sound easy on her. It was not simply that her striving for clarity, her longing to clean up our lazy ways of talking and thinking was such a vast undertaking – tiny bacilli and invisible viruses floating back again and again to re-infect the environment that had been so painstakingly sterilised. It was also that her credentials for the task had always been in doubt, and she was agonisingly aware of this. She told me how and where she had studied, what a struggle it had been to fill the gaps and recover from the wrong turnings in her education. This was glancingly but only glancingly a complaint about the unequal treatment of women and the lack of interest her father and, worse still, her brothers, had taken in what she said. She sometimes worried whether she had ever quite recovered from her brothers' belittling comments. She spoke of her brother Peter without any of the deference I then thought due to the dead. In fact, she spoke of him as if he were not dead at all and had only recently stopped patronising her. But what she really wanted to express was a higher, nobler complaint about the impurity and bluntness of the instruments we had been given to communicate with one another.

'Sometimes I do not talk for days, not a syllable, except to settle practical things. It is very restful. I do not care for organised religion, in fact – ' she interrupted herself, half ashamed to catch herself using such mild words 'I hate churches, all of them. But they used to know something about the importance of silence. There is a language which goes beyond words, is deeper than words. I sense it with my children over at the Big House. There is a depth in my relationships with them which we do not always find in the usual social contacts. The language barrier is sometimes not a barrier at all but a way of communicating. It is our own language that is so often the barrier, isn't it?'

I was thinking how to reply without heaping up further barriers of the sort she complained of when we both caught sight of Joe at the end of the table. His head had drooped, and his body had gently curled itself into the curve of the high-backed chair; sandy lid on flaky sandy cheek, truculence all gone, out for the count.

Joe's mother looked at him and then at me.

'Has he been drinking? I expect you spent the afternoon drinking.' She spoke, not aggressively like a woman fed up with living amongst alcoholics, but rather with a certain pride as though she had made a brilliant guess.

'No, we went to the cinema, the Guns of Navarone,' I said.

'I don't expect you could drink much in the middle of the afternoon, not here,' Joe's father said.

'The pubs would be closed, I suppose,' Mrs Follows said with the air of an anthropologist hazarding a surmise about some technical point in tribal ritual.

'We did have a cup of tea,' Joe mumbled, roused from sleep, unfazed, rather beguiling.

'In that case, there is no reason for you to be tired,' his mother said. 'I must be off on my sandman rounds. The legend of the sandman occurs in many cultures, you know. A lot of children like to think of me as the sandman, which suits me. I'm not much good at playing mother. Joe, will you come too? The Gambian kids wanted to ask you something about football.'

'Monk, I really am too tired.'

'You have been drinking.'

'Just a cup of tea, Monk, honest.' He parodied the quavering voice of a respectful beggar cringing before a lady and indeed there was the ring of a music-hall number about the exchange, half comic, half sentimental, a ballad which would start by mocking the excuses of the old drunk and then turn in the last verse, with a brutal, satisfying twist, to indict the callousness of the rich, the same swinging chorus which had first been sung in a sad, amused tone now repeated with a swelling indignation. Mrs Follows appeared not to be listening to him, though, her mind already on her goodnight rounds at the Big House.

IV Pigotts Hill –
Scrannel's lecture –
First brushes with commerce

From the high window of the flat we could see the mist rolling
lazy along the valley. The willows and poplars which marked
the windings of the river were lost to us. Only a few roofs and
fir trees lower down the lane were outlined in the great misty
wash of the view. We too floated in a haze above the ungrasped
grind of academic life, disoriented by the absence of landmarks,
too unsure of ourselves to delight in the lack of enforcement.
We had been warned that the opening days of the first term
were always like this. All the same, we were surprised by our
own listlessness.

'How did you swing it? I thought everyone had to live in college
their first year.'

'Medical advice. My doctor says the town's too damp and I
need mountain air.'

'But Pigotts Hill can only be about a hundred feet above sea
level.'

'Makes all the difference. You're above it all up here.'

'But I'm much worse than you. You said yourself you weren't
a typical asthmatic.'

'Not typical doesn't mean not bad. The point is, I've got a
better doctor.'

'I wouldn't particularly want to live in Pigotts Hill.'

'That's not the point. Peggy's arriving on Tuesday. I had to
find digs out of town.'

'Won't she find it a bit small?'

'Oh she'll come and go.' Joe was airy now. For him, for me too, this little bedsitter with its utility furniture – the beige octagonal table, the easy chair with wooden arms, the basin in the corner, the sash window which did not close properly – was already a haunt of romance. 'She's promised to come Tuesdays to Thursdays during the term.'

'Where will she be Fridays to Mondays then?'

'She's got this cottage not far from her first husband. He bought it for her in the divorce settlement, so she could be near her daughter, Gillian. I still haven't met her, although I suppose she's almost a cousin.'

'More like a step-daughter, I should say.'

'Please don't try to be funny. It's all very difficult. We have to take things one step at a time.'

The thought of his responsibilities agitated him as he sat hunched in the easy chair surrounded by textbooks. He began the old feral scratching at the backs of his hands and wrists, raking up little puffs of skin-dust to float down onto the pale green cover of Strawson's *Introduction to Logical Theory*. The corrugation of his sandy brow implied perplexity of almost spiritual depth.

'It's a pity Uncle Pete had to die like that,' he said, after prolonged musing.

'How do you mean?'

'Well, he was cut up about me and Onora, really cut up. I could see that.'

'Could you now?'

'I mean I was getting really fond of him and it was such a pity this thing had to come between us, and now it isn't there any more – '

'And nor is he,' I said.

'You're not suggesting, are you, that what he felt about Onora had any connection with him going like that?'

'No, I'm not, but I don't think he'd be all that much happier if he was still here now.'

'You mean, because of Peggy? But that was over years ago, long before they were even divorced. She's told me all about it.'

'Well, all the same, it might look like rubbing it in rather.'

'Really, do you suppose he'd take it that way?' Joe was stricken by the thought of his uncle's inner life being so ramified. 'You really think he'd mind even now?'

'He might.'

'I hadn't thought of that.'

'And how is Onora?'

'Well, she's got this very good temporary job with BOAC. Her new boyfriend is the regional manager, but they only got to know each other properly in the last month when I was there. He's a nice chap, a great skier and very musical, can sing anything you ask him to. And he encourages her textiles too. I didn't tell her about me and Peggy. Of course, she may have found out since we broke up. But I didn't think it was right to tell her myself. I know a lot of people say you should always be completely frank about everything, and I do think honesty is absolutely essential in personal relationships but I don't think it means one has to say everything out loud all the time. But she's a great girl, Onora. Some of her designs are first-class.'

'What will your parents say when they come here? Do they mind about you and Peggy?'

'My *parents?* They wouldn't dream of coming here. I mean, they never visited me at school, or at the sanatorium. Even when I was in hospital in England, they would just drop me and pick me up. They're much too busy for anything like that. I asked my mother once, when I was about nine, if she could come and see me at boarding school, because all the other boys had visitors, it wasn't so much that I especially wanted to see her. And she said, why, is there something wrong with the school? And I said, no, nothing in particular, in fact, it was a pretty decent sort of place. So she said, in that case, Joe, do you really think it's important for me to come because of course I will if you really want me to, I can always get somebody to deputise for me at the aid centre if I give enough warning, but I think both of us should be aware that this would be a serious decision about time allocation and we should make sure we're happy about it before we go ahead.

So of course I said, don't bother. And she said, if you're quite sure.'

Damp air rising from the valley condensed on the window panes. The cold little room seemed very high up, an eyrie. Joe prowled round the furniture in his green jersey like a trainer circling boxers in a ring too small for the three of them. He began to talk of love again.

'How are you doing in that line?'

'What line?' I said, my thoughts elsewhere. 'Oh, I see. Well, I'm a slow starter.'

'I haven't had a woman for three weeks now.'

'Oh dear.'

'I don't feel well without, really. I get headaches.'

'What about your old trouble, those inconvenient asthma attacks?'

'What do you mean?' The truculent look.

'That afternoon when I went to the cinema . . .'

'Yes, well that turned out to be a one-off, touch wood.'

The good-fellow smile he gave me did not quite hide an affronted dignity. This was not a side of life to be pried into, not any more anyway. All the same, Joe dropped the subject and began to talk philosophy, a subject for which he was not well suited, at least philosophy as we were taught it.

'It seems so destructive, the way they simply tear into little pieces the whole of Plato and Locke and Berkeley. I mean, if the great philosophers really are great, then who cares about Walter Scrannel's niggling little criticisms?'

'Surely we have to analyse what the great philosophers actually say,' I said, parroting our teachers.

'But in the end it's the total vision that matters, it's whether their work as a whole actually makes us wiser. Whether they split the odd infinitive or make an occasional *non sequitur* is pretty secondary.'

My dry reproof did not convey, was I suppose dishonest in shying away from the furtive delight I took in the lectures of W. R. Scrannel (it was typical of Joe to have discovered his

Christian name). The lecture room was crowded always. Late-comers had to sidle along the aisle and crouch on the floor, as though doing homage to the great gaunt figure of Scrannel in his rusty gown, billowing in behind us as the clock struck the hour, frizzy wings of ginger hair sticking up above his bony ears, his face a network of ironies, a pattern of dry watercourses with a bright sun of good humour beaming down upon them. To say he looked older than his years – he was only forty-seven then – would be accurate enough if you had seen a photograph of that face in repose, but it was not in repose, never. That fine, strong, wry mouth moved with a high moral pleasure, nothing mean or donnish about it. His gestures were handsome and confident – he had once played football with a rough and reckless vigour. He threw about him the air of great enterprise. And the part he was to play in our story was cut so cruelly short that it is hard to convey the feeling of silence, emptiness, lack of direction that he left behind.

Suppose I was to set down here a few sentences from his published papers, it would only confirm people's contempt, my own included, for the petty quibbles of academic philosophy. Yet it is not the case – how quickly one drops into the false precision of the trade – that it was only his own physical presence that set ancient controversies alight. His famous astringency was not simply like some lotion which refreshes your cheeks by stinging them. He brought alive the singleness, the reality of language, or 'speech acts', to use the sort of jargon he had no time for, made each nerve tingle with an understanding of the rare precision, variety, suppleness and clarity of speech – never to be described in his hearing as 'ordinary speech' – and instilled at the same time a corresponding grasp of the slapdash poverty and bogus pretensions of the terms philosophers invented to lift themselves above the herd, made you feel the full insidious drift of the dichotomies they claimed were so rigorous. How we were taught to watch out for those supposedly blameless either-ors patrolling the street, with what relish Scrannel would unmask them as master criminals who had terrorised the neighbourhood ever since Aristotle's day.

Joe could not see the point of Scrannel's lectures, after only a couple of weeks gave up going to them and patronised instead a pedestrian performer called Cotgrove, who, according to Joe, covered the entire syllabus in a term, while Scrannel had not got beyond destroying Plato's theory of essences. Yet it was Joe who, by dint of living a hundred yards up Pigotts Hill from Scrannel, first was asked to tea there.

'I bumped into Felicia Scammel, the daughter, when I was out for a run down the lane.'

'Scrannel,' I said. 'I suppose you'd talk about their Scammel pipes of wretched straw.'

'Scrannel, that's right. It's the same word, like Follows is the same as Fellowes, means partners.'

'I didn't know you were a philologist.'

'Felicia, Fisha, told me. She's into philology. It's her special subject. You must come too.'

The tea-table was opulently laden, bakery-smelling. The china tea had that thin tremulous fragrance which triumphs over coarser brews and brings back to the memory, years later, the pattern on the china and the expression on the face of the woman pouring it. For me it was thus indissolubly linked with the plump, contentedly frowning face of Mrs Scrannel in her untidy, cushion-scattered sitting-room with Fisha wandering in front of the long window chanting Icelandic word-roots. Scrannel, intensely active, would crouch below sofa level on a stool or even on the floor, as though mimicking in some kind of penance the discomfort we had suffered at his lectures. There was a son too, a tall, shadowy figure, who passed through the tea-party only occasionally, on his way to his own pursuits. The vibrant cheerfulness was too much for him, I fancied. He needed to breathe a less charged air.

'I'm afraid the lardy cake is too gooey again,' Mrs Scrannel crooned into the tea-pot as she homed into my cup. She held the pot very close to her myopic lovely forget-me-not eyes. Stray wisps of her hair brushed against the china.

'You must curb your perfectionism,' Scrannel said. 'It is a

weakness. Many a good sceptic has been undone by it. Always leave room for improvement.'

'No, but it is too gooey.'

'How can you improve unless you aim for perfection?' Fisha said, raising her own forget-me-not eyes from the Icelandic grammar. She had the same round face as her mother. Something about her mouth, perhaps the way her pearly teeth dented her lower lip as she smiled, gave her an old-fashioned charm – she said she was fed up with being told she looked like the young Queen Victoria.

'Ah, aiming for is a different kettle of fish. You aren't really aiming for perfection when you try to improve your forehand drive. If you bother to think about it at all, you are perfectly well aware that the quest for an utterly perfect stroke, one which is unimprovable by so much as a millimetre or a fraction of a second, would be a ludicrous over-investment of time and effort. What one is after is a reliable method of repeating a shot which is merely good. That is the beauty of most practical skills. That's what most things in life are like. The trouble comes when philosophers try and make life follow the rules of mathematics. The pursuit of the incorrigible by the unspeakable. The lardy cake is not gooey, or tilde-gooey as some of my appalling colleagues would say. Why ever they insisted on stealing that inoffensive squiggle from the Spanish I cannot understand. It was perfectly happy sitting where it was on top of the n's in *señor* and *mañana*.'

This manner of speaking – as of a normally dry and prosy man who had just received amazingly good news – was pleasant to me. I had expected to find him offstage, if not a crotchety and clay-footed person, at least diminished by being in his family circle. On the contrary, if anything, he seemed more electric still.

'You may be repelled by my guzzling. A sweet tooth is often the sign of a philosopher, I mean by philosopher of course not a lover of wisdom, but a chap who earns his living at the trade. In my defence, I will plead that I do insist on the cakes being good, home-baked, fresh cream and all that. Dunbabin, for example, that distinguished Hegelian, if such a phenomenon can be said to exist, only likes shop cakes, the more ersatz the better. We do, however, share an enthusiasm for the turf. You will find, boys, and I hope it does not come as a shock to you, that philosophers, far from being immune to the grosser vices, are flagrantly vulnerable to them. The majority of my colleagues are the most embarrassing lechers, the sort who cannot see a bottom without pinching it. Others, of course, drink too much. On the whole, the lechers lecture better than the soaks. Dunbabin and I, who merely lose on the horses slightly more than we can afford, fall somewhere in the middle.'

Mrs Scrannel gazed at him fondly, dreamily, indifferent to the electricity he was giving off, or earthing it and at the same time insulating him from outside interference. The whole ambience of Furze Bank was a gigantic cladding of porcelain and rubber to protect Scrannel from the world. She kept her end up, gently chiding him about some view of Hume he had once held but now thought silly – I did philosophy when I was here, she said in a tone of quiet wonder, that's how I met Walter – but she lacked any combative instincts. Her gentleness was not a second best or a strategy for exercising control in a subtler way but came naturally to her. She was restful without being devitalising. And when she said do come again next Sunday, as I stumbled out into the dark November lane, I was enchanted. Scrannel himself had left earlier, to go to a college meeting, and we had stayed on to finish the lardy cake.

Joe did not share my enchantment. The tea party had left him strangely fractious.

'Scrannel does bang on a bit, doesn't he? I enjoyed it more after he left, though the mother's too placid for my liking.'

Mrs Scrannel was not so critical of Joe. In fact, when I went on my own the following Sunday, they were disappointed. I do not mean Scrannel himself. Like most great men, he was not much concerned about the make-up of his audience, but mother and daughter seemed over-interested in Joe's whereabouts.

'I expect he's very good at rowing. He looks the right shape.'

'As far as I know, he just does it for the exercise,' I said tartly.

'I like his square shape,' Fisha said reflectively. She was doing a tapestry. Head bent over the little floppy beige square, she looked becoming and gentlewomanly until I got a sight of the pattern which was a violent modern design in black and orange.

'You like brick-shaped men, don't you, darling?' her mother said. 'I used to encourage willowy youths to call, but Fisha thought there was nothing to them. She used to be very keen on rugger, you know.'

Fisha smiled her charming, lip-denting smile. I began to feel uneasy. She did not seem to be hearty in the healthy kind of way which would explain these tastes. Scrannel began to talk about theories of probability and whether they had any practical application to gambling. At least this, I think, was the burden of his discourse, but that evening even his brilliance began to wear on me, and I could not stop looking at his daughter. Her hair glowed under the soft light of the converted oil lamps, her warm cheek resting against the faded brocade of the old-fashioned wing chair, the homely burry sheen of her stockings – all this should have been infinitely comforting, but the longer the lip-denting smile lingered, the more I was overcome by an impression of trouble looming.

'You're not too tired, darling, are you?' Mrs Scrannel said.

'I have no reason to be tired,' Fisha said.

'One doesn't always know the reason.'

'There's nothing to make me tired.'

The day after, Joe heard something fall to the ground as he opened the front door. It was a posy of autumn flowers – Michaelmas daisies, loose-petalled roses. They must have been hung on the door knocker. 'Fisha, I expect,' Joe said calmly and put them in water.

The day after, another bunch of flowers. This time they were more securely anchored to the door knocker, by a piece of ribbon which was also threaded through a greetings card featuring a colour photo of two lovers standing by a lily pond. On the back there was written in a bold hand: 'Shall I drown myself in your eyes or in your thoughts?'

'This is getting beyond a joke,' Joe said.

The next day, there was a jar of honey left on the door-mat, with a card which said 'Sweets for the sweet'.

'I'll have to take her out,' Joe said.

For some reason, the arrangement was that she should call round to his flat, although the Scrannels lived only down the road. I was there when she called. She wore a great mauve wool coat and chunky gold bracelets and her hair was up, dramatically up, gathered into a great top-knot.

'I'm trying to look like a fashion buyer,' she said. 'Do you think Joe will like it?'

'He'll love it,' I said. 'He's tremendously unobservant normally, but this will knock him out.'

'I thought it had to be eye-catching.'

'And the scent – I feel weak at the knees.'

'The woman in the shop said it would make me unforget-table.'

'She was quite right.'

Joe came into the room. He had a bath towel round his waist and he was buttoning up the front of a clean blue shirt.

'Fisha, you look terrific.'

'Not terrifying? I think I look terrifying.'

'No, terrific, very good. I like the bracelets.'

'Do you really?'

'I really do,' he said.

'Oh good,' she said and sat down with a sigh of relief, as if approval of the bracelets was all she needed to make her happiness complete. There I left them. The next day he was ruminative, edgy, almost a little scared-seeming but bursting to tell.

'You haven't asked me about my evening with Fisha. She's an extraordinary girl.'

'What sort of extraordinary?'

'I don't think I've ever met anyone like her. She's very strong.'

'What do you mean?'

'Well, she . . . took the initiative. I mean, we'd scarcely sat down, but it was over incredibly quickly and then, well, she just left, just like that, refused to stay or anything. I thought I must have offended her, but she said no, no, it was wonderful, thank you very much for a wonderful evening were the exact words, as if, you know, we'd just been to the movies and had a steak afterwards, and then she was off down the lane. Refused to let me see her home, or anything.'

'She is basically very shy, I suppose.'

'*Shy*, you don't realise . . .'

'Not in that way perhaps, but in expressing her feelings.'

'She's lovely, I thought she was really lovely and kept on telling her, you know, the way one does, because I genuinely did, but she kept on saying no, you don't, you don't really and so on. The trouble is, she's got a very poor opinion of herself, I think, and it's very hard to get over that.'

Joe really did seem at a loss and the days that followed only added to his perplexity. 'Everything seems to be back to front,' he complained. 'I mean, normally the man has to make all the running until she says yes and then perhaps if he's lucky – you know, if she really likes it – then she'll be quite keen to see him, she'll write to him, she might even give him a present – '

'Give him a present?'

'I don't mean a big present, nothing expensive, just a trinket to show her gratitude. I don't mean she ought to be grateful, I'm just describing what often happens.'

'And Fisha isn't showering you with these little tokens of appreciation?'

'That was only an example. I mean I wasn't expecting a daily delivery from the florist, but in view of all the stuff she sent before, and now I have to beg her to go out with me, and she doesn't make any effort at all. She keeps on saying "you don't really want to see me" and the way she looks now the awful thing is I'm beginning to agree with her.'

'Well, she's probably right to stop trying so hard if that's how you feel.'

'No, no. It would be quite different if she really tried.'

His square sandy face was anxious-truculent. Things were going wrong, the position he was in was somehow false through no fault of his own, but he could not wriggle out of the blame for it. He was not simply puzzled by the maze but offended by the injury done to what could only be called his sense of the proprieties – not that he would have dreamed of using such a phrase and would have got it wrong if he had tried. He himself had behaved as men did, as women expected men to behave, or as he thought they expected him to anyway, and Fisha had revealed herself as hopelessly ignorant in such matters. Worse still, she seemed to be quite unable to pick up the language of love.

'I wouldn't mind so much,' Joe said, 'if she complained I was treating her badly or something like that, but she seems to want me to be unkind to her.'

'Perhaps she only wants you for your body.'

'It isn't funny, it really isn't funny. And it's not a physical thing at all.'

Joe's face lightened when Peggy drove down that week. Life became simple again for him and when she came up the stairs and slowly untwined the scarf round her neck and flounced her hair free, he welcomed her with a boyish hug.

'Don't, I'm out of breath as it is. Those stairs – my old legs.'

'Your old legs look all right to me.'

'Oh dear. I would love a cup of tea.'

Between her thin hands, the strong Indian brew in the blue-and-white striped mug was an unsettling libation. We sat opposite her, the two of us, me perched on the table, Joe on the windowsill, staring at her, awed curators of some rare, unlikely creature, a lemur or marmoset perhaps.

'What a room. You really must . . .'

I cannot now remember exactly what it was she did – moved the army-surplus table away from the window, found (but from where?) a lilac-coloured paisley counterpane for the bed, set out Joe's books along some dusty ledge – caressing the chocolate-brown spine of Samuelson's *Economics*. When she had finished her rearranging, the room was light and gay, its air of neglect quite gone.

I saw them the next day, turning into Andrews and Liversedge

92

where he bought her an Italian scarf. The colours went with the things she was wearing, Joe explained to me later, patiently, as one lecturing the tone-blind. In fact, the scarf was hideous, slashed scarlet and sludge stripes. She would never have dreamed of buying it for herself. Arms linked, cheeks flushed, they looked like a dozen other happy couples.

'What are we to do with Joe?' she said just as he was coming into the room, perhaps an instant before she could have heard the door open, threading a kind of sinuous complicity between the three of us as she turned to him and said: 'I was just saying what were we to do with you.' Most of the time, in fact, we had been talking about Scrannel's lectures.

'Why weren't you discussing what to do with *him*?'

'Oh, he doesn't need doing with.'

'And I do?'

'Well, dear, you have your sights set on things, don't you?'

'So do most people. The difference is I don't mind saying it,' Joe said.

'Do most people?'

'Not most people I know,' I said.

'Well, that's what's wrong . . .'

'With this country.'

'Well, it is.'

'You want to be a tycoon, don't you, dear? He wants to be a tycoon,' she interpreted to me.

'There's nothing wrong with businessmen. And you know I don't like being teased.'

'Don't you, Joe? I expect in business they wouldn't tease you. I don't think I know any *businessmen*, except Brod, of course.' It is impossible by any mere emphasis, any pause and dwelling, or even by the most languorous drawl to convey exactly the way she spoke of businessmen, not with dislike or even contempt so much as with wonder and disbelief at the mention of such persons in her presence.

'Who's Brod?'

'Who's Brod? Oh you *are* young. How extraordinary to think of anyone asking that. Well, perhaps he has been a bit out of things up there.'

'Who is Brod?'

'Oh a dear little toad of a man we all used to know a million years ago. He makes cardigans and things – masses of cardigans, not like a clothes shop. And his uncle was Kafka's best friend, or was it his cousin? And he used to be such fun. No, perhaps it wasn't his cousin at all. Perhaps he just said it when we wouldn't take him seriously. He didn't like being teased either. We'll send you to Brod and he'll teach you how to be a tycoon. At least I hope that's all he'll teach you. He used to be awfully wicked. Well, he wasn't really but he liked pretending, and we just liked listening to his English. Which reminds me, Joe, you ought to go to these marvellous lectures of Professor Scrannel's I've just been hearing about.'

'*He* goes to lectures. I don't waste my time.'

'Actually, he's not a professor,' I said.

'Oh,' she said. I wished I had not embarked on the subject, had never tried to convey the magical vitality of the way Scrannel seized on the smallest conjunctions and prepositions.

'It is these inconspicuous little words that often turn out to be the most subtle, elusive and treacherous in the language, the richest in the number of potential meanings and the most misleading'; Scrannel's lecture on 'being sure' was already celebrated. He began, as always, urgently but with a brilliant, alluring simplicity. The examples he took were the way people really talked, the meanings he unpacked from them were so plain, and the mounting excitement came from that plainness, from the sense that extraordinary revelations could be drawn out so simply from the ordinary. And when he stopped, our hearts stopped too, partly because of the electric abruptness of his stopping. As the hour struck ten o'clock – Scrannel refused to lecture after nine in the morning – and the laggard December sun began to come through the high dusty windows of the crowded Small Lecture Room (he refused the six larger halls in the building), he would suddenly stalk out of the room. Having no books or papers, let alone a

94

briefcase to gather up, he created an instantaneous stunning effect. We rose, those of us who had been crouching at his feet, stretched out cramp-struck legs. A feeling of light-headedness brought with it an exhilarating sense of power. We understood all, had mastered the trick of it, the days was ours. The smell of coffee and eggs and bacon came to us from the cafe next door as part of the same experience, as though that too had been laid on by Scrannel to ground us in reality.

How deep and firm he planted us in the earth, and how scornful he was of those philosophers who had attempted to soar or hover above it, dismissing them as short-sighted raptors who always missed their kill.

'They miss because they are hunting for something which is not there, and this is a frustrating pastime, and one that may lead to the kind of delusions to which prospectors of all kinds are notoriously prone. What they are after is certainty. In this pursuit of certainty, they have, with the blind persistence of truffle hounds, sought to identify a class of statements which could be defended as incorrigibly true in all circumstances. Sometimes these statements are said to have been discovered in mysterious caves inaccessible to human senses; sometimes they are tracked down in humble everyday circumstances – a man looking at a stick in the water, for example. What most of the great philosophers will seldom, if ever, admit is that there are no truffles in the wood. There may be truffles to be found elsewhere – in mathematics no doubt, and perhaps in one or two more of the remoter groves of academe. But not here. Not in this wood, not in this world.'

I cannot now recall the exact order of the gestures by which he illustrated what he meant by 'this world'. Did he first rap the lectern with his big knuckles – and then raise his hand to the light coming through the high misted windows of the lecture room? And was it after these gestures that he smiled, bending forward slightly, at those of us sitting at the front like the smallest boys in a school photograph? It is hard to describe these actions without conjuring up something mannered and actor-ish, even without tagging on the sniff with which, nostrils flared, head thrown back, he ended the demonstration. But he did it all with such good humour, such a wry consciousness of how he might appear that we did not think of it as stagey at all. And when I think of it now, as I do much in the way our ancestors must have thought of Dr Johnson kicking the stone and harumphing 'thus I refute Berkeley', I think of it all as flowing naturally out of what he was saying and not as requiring any kind of rehearsal.

'That is not the sort of wood we are in. But this does not mean that we are lost in the wood, or that the wood is dark or menacing. When the trees come into leaf, it may be a beautiful place; when the wind blows, an exhilarating one; when the leaves begin to fall, a melancholy spot. But we have no cause to complain merely because there are no truffles in it.'

With this brief swoop of fancy – rare, perhaps unique, among the philosophers of his school and certainly not to be found anywhere else in his own lectures – Scrannel ended and was, in his typical way, gone.

At tea, the next Sunday, I tried to say how much I had . . . was 'enjoyed' quite the word? 'appreciated' sounded too patronising, I ended up lamely with 'got from' his lecture. Scrannel seemed scarcely to hear what I had said. He was abstracted, but electrically so, plugged into some other circuit, even began to hum like an electrical appliance which was giving trouble. His wife was just as welcoming to me, but her warmth had an anxious tinge to it. Reluctantly, I admitted to myself that it would have been better if Joe had been there as well and I resolved not to come again without him and perhaps in any case not to come for a week or two. Fisha was not there either. In theory, it would not make much difference since she tended to take no direct part in the conversation, preferring to roam round the edge of the room reciting in a disjointed way whatever it was she was learning. Yet it was perhaps by this habit that she defined the family circle, so that the three or four of us sitting close round the crackling and spitting log fire seemed more intimate than in fact we were. And Scrannel too would emphasise this intimacy by looking up from his tea and with a gesture of impatience asking her to prompt his memory, of which she seemed to be the willing keeper.

'Fisha, that place in Cumberland with the scatological carving in the piscina?'

'Dillington Ambo, Pa,' she would reply, something about the exchange – perhaps just her calling him Pa – bringing to mind pert, long-nosed girls in a Dickens illustration by Leech or Cruikshank, although Fisha with her soft round features looked more like one of the orphan heroines who never answered back.

'We are having trouble with the – oh the what, Fisha?'

'The alternator, Pa.'

'Just so. Fisha's a qualified motor mechanic, you know. She is also a compendium of information – one of those popular encyclopaedias no Victorian household could afford to be without.' I thought this deferring to her was less inspired by a practical need than a way of expressing his love without appearing mawkish. And certainly now that she was not there, I was conscious of a certain directionless, bewildered quality in him.

'Where is Fisha?' he asked.

'Oh, she's out, dear.'

'That I can see for myself, but where?'

'If I knew, I'd tell you.'

'She ought to be here to entertain' – he waved at me, not so much forgetting my name as regarding its naming as a waste of breath.

When I closed the heavy, nail-studded door with the bottle-glass peephole and walked up the gravel drive to the lane, I could not help noticing how my spirits rose and how this made me ashamed, for I had been proud of having tea with the Scrannels, had mentioned it to the friends I went to his lectures with, and now already I could feel my admiration beginning to fray at the edges, and a dank melancholy took hold of me, as dank and deep as the fog coming up from the valley and roosting in the fir trees above Furze Bank.

In the darkness by the laurels, Joe was bent over the open bonnet of Peggy's little runabout.

'What a day. I've been trying since lunchtime to find a garage that would come out on a Sunday. The starter's jammed. I think it's been tampered with.'

'What do you mean?'

He gestured down the lane.

'Oh Fisha,' I said, surprising myself by my lack of hesitation, 'but why should she – '

'She's got the motive and the opportunity. And she's been very odd these past few days.'

'Has she? She may not even know about Peggy.'

'She does because I told her.'

'You . . . but . . .'

'They always want to know about previous girlfriends.'

Joe was quick and irritable, an expert pestered by a layman to explain elementary technicalities.

'But she's not previous.'

Joe swept this aside and went on to explain why he suspected sabotage and Fisha. But I was not really listening. The thought was so cruel or, if true, the fact. I had no heart for the practical aspects of it.

'Of course,' Joe pursued his own line of argument, 'it's not exactly logical to jam the car which would be taking Peggy *away* from here, but then I suppose people aren't always very logical in this sort of situation. As it is, I'll have to give her a push start and go with her in case she stalls somewhere between here and Devon. Could you stay here and keep an eye on things? The man's coming to fix the cooker in the morning but the toaster's still OK. Peggy's left some whisky.'

He was almost shouting these last words as he jumped into the car. He wound down the window and passed on further instructions, detaching the housekeys from the key ring and thrusting them into my hand. As he shouted to me to start pushing (the lane was so steep I only needed to set the car in motion and jog along behind it) I became aware of a dark figure curled up in a rug on the back seat. The figure stayed in its cramped concealment, but out of the darkness a slender hand rose and waved gently in my direction.

The car gathered speed, the engine caught, the hand disappeared from sight and Joe drove off with an expressive spurt of gravel. Memories of the hand rising from the lake to seize Excalibur, clothed in white, samite, mystic, wonderful, floated through my unsettled mind. I could imagine all too well the chiding smile on Peggy's face under the rug.

The attic flat was cold and silent, abandoned to the embrace of the night fog. Indignation, followed by melancholy. Nothing much to eat. A jar of gherkins, and the pot of honey. I toasted some sliced bread and drank some of the whisky. As I was slicing a gherkin to put on the toast, I heard a scrabbling noise outside the window, not the soughing of a branch, too purposeful for that, more on the scale of a sizeable animal digging its burrow. I went on slicing and drinking. The scrabbling continued, and – but here I must make something of a confession. Narrators are, on the whole, chosen for their sober and reliable character. Occasionally, they may be overcome by external forces, a blow on the head, a drugged posset. That is quite acceptable. But they do not usually drink themselves steadily but quite slowly into oblivion at a significant part in the story. There may be a hiatus, a row or two of asterisks, but the events in the intervening period will usually be reported later, if they have a part to play. But for the remainder of that night, I am not a reliable witness. I cannot disentangle reality from dream. Even what those philosophers whom Scrannel had torn to shreds would call 'my sense data' or 'my sense impressions' are unfixed, unfocused, hopelessly variable according to my mood. Sometimes I remember one thing, sometimes another, sometimes nothing much at all. One or two of my impressions have over the years become entangled with memories of another night soon after.

At all events – a phrase never more literally intended than now – the scrabbling did continue, and in the end I went down the stairs and out into the cold hall, but all was quiet. Then I went upstairs again, and the scrabbling began again, then stopped and was replaced by the sound of a voice singing, rather low and insinuating. I was not sure whether it was a man's or a woman's. She – it began to sound more like a woman – was singing in a crooning lilting manner, like a night-club singer, but the song, or what I could catch of it, sounded older, a folk-song, a madrigal perhaps with some kind of erotic undertow. My memory sometimes supplies words to the song, hey-nonnies and lovers in the haytime, but I cannot really pretend that they are what was actually sung. I looked out of the window, and there below moving in the bushes was a pale figure, all in some colour that seemed like white, so indistinct that it might equally well have been wearing a night-dress or a raincoat. Then the figure disappeared into the trees and reappeared at a gap further along the low fence where there was a path leading down through a fir plantation into the valley. I ran down the stairs, out into the hall, round the corner of the house. Coming round the corner, I tripped over something taut and fell onto the wet gravel. I remember the sharp wet impact on the palms of my hands (but there were no scratches there in the morning). I could see no one in the small, unkempt garden at the back. The garden had gone completely wild. Anyone could have hidden there without being seen from the windows. When I went back round the house, the wires I had tripped on were slack, I felt them brush against my wet trousers. Upstairs, I drank enough of the whisky to send me off to sleep, three or four more glasses, I should say.

I lay down on the sofa with a rug over me. I remember the weight of it, and the damp trousers ridden up tight as a tourniquet round my legs. Slumber fitful – again never more literally – for I cannot be sure whether it was in or out of a fit that I heard the scrabbling again and went down once more to answer the door, or whether it was then that the door of the flat seemed to blow open, or perhaps I had never closed it, and Fisha merely had to push it open and walk in with her hair wet as a mermaid's. But how odd that I cannot remember what she was wearing when she came closer to me.

'Don't worry,' she said. 'I know they've gone. I saw you in the garden.'

'And I saw you too, I think.'

'You don't have to worry. It's all right. You're quite safe. I've taken out the detonator.' She produced a flat square object the size of a Christmas card (that is what I thought to myself: 'it's the size of a Christmas card', although that is not much of a help as a description).

'Good,' I said, 'that's good.'

'You don't know what I'm talking about.'

'No, probably not. It's very late, and I'm looking after the flat.'

'Yes, I know. I was in the laurels when he was telling you. I'm everywhere.'

'You do seem to be,' I said, or something to that effect.

'Do you always do what he tells you?'

'Not always.'

'I bet you do. I'm going now.'

And I said good-night to her, or in another version she first opens the window, I remember the fog coming in quite distinctly, and then throws the flat square package out of the window and there is a small bang, somewhere outside. But in the morning there is no sign of the package and no marks of burning on the little patch of grass outside or in the bushes round about. She could, I suppose, have picked it up when she got downstairs and taken it away with her.

What I have just written above is bad enough and I can only say that I too would find it distasteful if written by someone else and perhaps even more distasteful since it is written by myself and I do not go in for fantasies and nightmares and hallucinations. I really genuinely am the sort of person who is cut out to be a narrator, cut out like a silhouette in the best cardboard.

But there is more of it to come, unfortunately. Sometimes what follows is interwoven in my memory with the conversation already described, sometimes it forms part of a second visit from Fisha (and that is how I shall tell it here), sometimes there is no sequence or chronology in the recollections at all, they are merely a jumbled jolting mass of incidents, like a herd of cattle frightened by oncoming headlights. I shall, however, attempt to put them in some kind of order for form's sake.

Later on that night, much later, the door blew open again and Fisha came into the room. This time she was definitely wearing a raincoat, white or a light fawn colour.

'It's me again. Hullo.'

'Hullo.'

'I thought you might be lonely.' She took off the raincoat. Underneath, she was wearing a thin white nightdress. I could see her heavy breasts and the dark – no, perhaps I could not really.

'I'm too drunk to be lonely.' That sounds too sharp for me to have said it in the condition I was in, at least not in those words.

'You probably are really, though, all on your ownsome-moansome.'

'I don't like baby talk.'

'That's not baby talk. That's lover's talk. Have you got a lover?'

'Oh, Fisha it's too late to talk.'

'It's never too late. Would you like to come to the bathroom with me?'

'What – '

'Men often like that, don't they? Except I mustn't say bathroom. It's American. Would you like to come to the lavatory with me?'

'Fisha, go to bed, go home, please.'

'Would you like to watch me go to the lavatory? I don't mind at all, I really don't. Come on, do come on.'

I issued a warning as early as I possibly could, that this story would go downhill after the first few pages of sweetness and innocence and, while I do not much care for narrators who intrude upon the reader with their personal and literary problems, it seems necessary to, I think the phrase is, distance myself a little from the above events by reminding you of the warning.

What happened then is even more of a blur. She kissed me on the lips, but a good-night kiss (although I mistook it at first), and the embrace she wanted was only one of consolation. But I cannot exactly say how or how long we held each other or what we did after that. All I do remember for sure is her putting on her white raincoat again, and how strong and muscular her calves and feet were and how useless strength of that sort was. On second thoughts, this last reflection has the serenity of hindsight. All I really minded about was getting her out of the flat.

The next morning was biting clear and cold. Out of the window, I could see the pale golden sheen on the willows along the river bank. The cars snorting up Pigotts Hill came cheerful to my ears, as I lay in bed wheezing, the old aftermath of stress. Joe telephoned from a call box somewhere in Somerset to say that the car had broken down. Something to do with the alternator, a classic method of delayed sabotage, he claimed. He sounded a long way off. I turned over in bed and slept the whole day through. Nobody came to fix the cooker.

Fisha was admitted to the psychiatric hospital two or three days later. Her mother dropped a card through the letter box to explain that there would be no tea party the following Sunday.

In Joe's absence, I began to think about him in a more objective way. I do not repent of the rather sentimental words with which I ended my account of our first experiences together – 'crass, word-fluffing, lovable twin'. Those words, embarrassing as they might sound now, did reflect my feelings at the time. It was simply that while he was away it was possible to consider him more calmly. I was surprised to find that the Fisha affair did not make me think worse of him. He might have pushed her over the edge, but then one could not help thinking that she was waiting, asking even, to be pushed and she would have jumped of her own accord, sooner or later. Would she really have been grateful if Joe had been one of those people who can see madness looming and know how to run away from it?

The first time Walter Scrannel called was early on Sunday evening. The church bells were chiming, the same mellow jangle that usually accompanied the second slice of lardy cake and the other domestic intimacies of tea at Furze Bank. But now the bells sounded harsh as I opened the door.

He was tieless, an old mac thrown on over his shirt. The wedges of frizzy hair above his ears blew wild in the draught.

'Where's Follows?' The use of the surname, so much an antique quirk of academic life, did not sound as menacing as it would have from someone else.

'Still in Devon,' I said.

'*Devon*. Doesn't he know about Fisha?'

'Yes he does. I told him when he telephoned.'

'Well, why hasn't he come back then?'

'I don't know.'

'Not that I'm going to let him near her. He's never going to see her again. You young men don't realise how cruel you are. You don't know how much damage you can do. I'm going to teach that . . . it took two years for Mary to get her right . . . two years, it nearly killed her . . . and now it's all destroyed.'

His distraction was terrifying. He still trembled with physical energy, so clear-headed and bright-eyed. If only he had been drunk, or sad in some other way. I put out a hand in a muddled gesture of sympathy and he swatted it away with a great sweep of his bony arms, jarring the ends of my fingers. Gradually, I wore down the edge of his anger by making him offers – a chair, a cup of tea – which he rejected with intense ferocity.

'I shall come again, you know. He can't hide away for ever. I shall come again and then I shall tell him. And he will never forget, never.'

Yet even at that moment, as he uttered these and other threats of indelible vengeance, I was aware of their clanging emptiness. The wonderful thrilling power of his lectures was entirely absent. Indeed, the vague hovering memory of that power only stressed how defeated he was. I could imagine all too well Joe listening to him with an expression of attention and concern while inwardly rehearsing the grovelling phrases of contrition with which he would turn away Scrannel's wrath in an almost animal act of repentance so that there would seem to be nothing left of the former person who had committed the fault: shoulders in the humility hunch, hands thrust forward in pleading, head tilted and ducked into the plane of sympathy, spine rounded and pliable, eyes as steady, melting, obedient as a gun dog's.

But when Scrannel called again, Joe was not there either. He had gone out to restock the flat, having just returned from Devon with Peggy. Since taking up with her he had developed a housewifely taste for high standards about the house. There were fresh towels in the little bathroom and fresh bread in the even smaller kitchenette, exotic packages from the delicatessen in the fridge.

'He's not here, I'm afraid.'

'But I heard you talking to someone.'

'He'll be back soon. Come in and see for yourself.'

Peggy was sitting on the sofa with her legs tucked under her, greyhound quivering poised. She was reading somebody's memoirs, the brightly coloured book held in the air in a desultory grip as though she was about to flip it on to the table beside her.

'This,' I said, intercepting Scrannel's glare, 'is Mrs Dudgeon. She's . . . Joe's aunt.'

'He's just been staying with me,' she said.

'In Devon?'

'In Devon. I gave him a lift back here.'

'Quite a long way.'

'A very long way. We kept on breaking down.'

'Ah.'

'I've come to see about getting my daughter into a secretarial college here.'

'That should not be too difficult.'

'It may be. She's not very bright.'

'Well, I hope she enjoys it.'

'She's not . . . fussy.'

Although I had thought it a masterstroke when it came to me, I now wondered whether it had been quite so sensible to introduce Peggy as an aunt. At best, after all, she was a retired aunt, and the atmosphere of farcical deception – the unmistakable echoes of *Charley's Aunt* – only added to the strain. I was thinking of some way of softening the atmosphere but was forestalled.

'It's your daughter, isn't it, who's ill. The boys told me about it. I'm so sorry. We've had so much of it in our family. It is an awful thing.'

Scrannel sat down and began to sob. His grief was so free and noble that I felt no embarrassment, only a kind of relief. The tears coursed down the scaly runnels of his cheeks. All the dryness in his life which he strove so hard to counteract seemed to come back to mock him. The tears' long trails appeared to claim, quite falsely, that they were at last moistening a desiccated husk of a person, that he was lucky to have them.

'One cannot run their lives for them, however hard one tries. One's own life . . . difficult enough, don't you think?'

'Oh yes, hellishly difficult,' he said, 'but it seems impossible to refrain . . .'

'. . . from interfering. Or that is what it seems like to them.'

There somehow was a tea-tray and Peggy pouring, quite as soft and unobtrusive and concerned as Mrs Scrannel.

'She is an . . . unguarded character, in every sense of the term. I fear that comes from me, and my poor brother too, I am afraid.'

The melancholy family history unwound itself, as Scrannel slowly recovered his normal eloquence. Peggy appeared to have no other concern in the world than to measure out exactly the right quantity of milk and hot water.

'Should we, is it our duty, to warn every boy who comes round, about the manic-depressive strain? Or is that condemning her to a lifetime as an invalid, making it inevitable that she will be befriended only out of pity? But then is pity such a terrible motive? Perhaps with Fisha it might be a safer basis. I certainly wish I'd told young Follows a thing or two.'

Peggy gently patted his arm to draw his attention to the cup of tea she had poured for him.

'Oh, Joe is, well, he's young,' she said.

'Not too young to behave like a human being. The way he went off without a word . . . for weeks, to Devon – to stay with you, of course. I don't mean . . .'

'No, no. I'm sure he should have been more considerate.'

Walter Scrannel wiped his eyes and looked at Peggy with a brave smile. Another cup of tea was offered and taken. Joe never appeared. It was near the end of term and he had a lot of loose ends to tie up, he said later.

'I'm getting away, as far away from women as possible. I'm heading North, to this chap Brod, to learn about business.'

'On your own?'

'On my own. I need space.'

He asked me to come too, but his fretful, untethered look put me off and I followed my own quiet devices through the early weeks of that summer holiday, reading very slowly books I had read before, listening to the repeats of radio comedy programmes on Sunday afternoons, living off tinned peaches and tinned goulash, passing my father in the hall from time to time and exchanging a friendly low-key word, like colleagues meeting in an office corridor. By the time Joe rang me, I was ready for an excursion.

'You must come. It's fantastic here. Brod's teaching me so much. He'd love to have you to stay. He loves the young.'

'Are you sure? What's he like, would he really want me?'

'Oh he's fantastic. He wants everybody.'

Aspens bent back by the blustering westerlies strained towards the dark Lancashire earth as the branch line took the train away into the hills. I sat on the edge of my seat, still bemused by the speed with which the plan had been carried out. Little church towers of blackened stone beckoned through the blowsy green woods of the foothills, carrying us to a northern strangeness. Out on the bare, peat-black moorland, the heather had hardly grown yet. The station was a starveling halt perched on the side of a hill, with the silence of old country stations set apart from the places they served. Joe greeted me on the platform and pushed me into the back of a shooting brake of antique design and a non-standard chocolate colour. The back was entirely covered, floor, benches and walls alike, by old Turkish rugs, the crimsons and blues faded a little but still rich enough.

'This is Burscough. He's been with Brod how long?'

'Fifteen years, Mr Joe.'

'Brod insists on everyone on the estate being strictly Lancashire, isn't that right, Burscough?'

'Yes, Mr Joe, except Mr Svoboda, of course.'

'Except Mr Svoboda.'

The house, of the same blackened stone, squatted toadish in a grove of Scots pines. Its gothic frills swelled and frowned across the moorland. In the middle of the lawn in front of the porch was a modern sculpture, eight or nine foot high, bulbous, vaguely figurative, aspiring with a coppery gleam towards a leaden sky.

'You like the piece? Dear Henry didn't want it there but Freddy insisted. I tossed a coin and Henry lost. So charming.' This not, I think, of the sculpture but of me whose hands he had clasped in his with a melting gaze straight from Viennese operetta. Short, and indeed toadish like his manor, he had a harsh chuckling voice crowded with every kind of mockery. He was all in black – trousers of some rough, hairy but expensive stuff, silky black polo-neck, black eyes flecked with the yellow of a cat's eye. Between his lips, a cigarette-holder of the same black and cat's-eye yellow, tortoiseshell or amber perhaps.

'Scarisbrick will take your fucking cases.' He gave a jaybird's chuckle at the withered little woman in old-fashioned maid's uniform who limped out through the glass doors, puffing as she tried to pin her white mob-cap on properly. 'Tea in Haynes room, Scarisbrick.'

At the end of the passage visible through the open door, a pale thin man carrying a ledger hovered, then vanished, though not before Brod had shouted at him.

'Tomorrow, Freddy, tomorrow. My partner, F. Svoboda. Like all Czechs, he is a cowardy-custard. You like pictures? You want to see some bloody pictures. I'll show you.'

We came into a room with dark green and plum wallpaper, a floral design: heavy trusses of grapes and gourds grappling with one another and trumpeting arum lilies spurting out of their midst. From the ponderous cornice were suspended massy gold picture frames. Brod switched on the lights above them and all at once we were in the midst of Arthurian revels: sturdy-calved maidens strolled through fields of cuckoo-pint with earnest, lantern-jawed swains, some in armour, others in doublet and hose richly slashed in gold, vermilion and azure. Above, decidedly Pennine woods stretched up to lakeland crags and down to rush-girt meres. In the alcoves at the corners of the room, smaller gothic-arched frames enclosed scenes of mediaeval indoor life – girls on window-seats spinning and weaving and holding goblets to the light.

'W. F. Haynes, the Lancashire Giotto. There is no collection like it anywhere in the world, not even in Manchester. The poor bugger died in Dieppe, of syphilis, but he was solid workman.' His accent thickened, his jay-screech sharpened at the sight of the collection. 'I have loved Haynes' work since I vos small boy. Our factory in Prague did tablecloths from Haynes' pictures. The Vife of Bath vos smash hit.' He stood rapt in admiration, as though seeing the picture for the first time.

'Your friend,' he gestured at Joe, 'is artist too.'

'Well,' I said.

'He has talent. But not enough talent. That is why he must become businessman. I had talent. I was the greatest pianist of my year at Prague Conservatoire, but then, biff, they start this fucking atonal nonsense and nobody wish to hear Beethoven, Mozart again. My career is finished. I am back number, aged eighteen.'

'But surely – '

'I am back number. Beethoven, Mozart, Brod all on shitheap together. So I enrage and become millionaire in my father's business. Then Nazis play sillybuggers. I come to England with cowardy-custard Svoboda, who is not even Jewish, and we start again. We are fucking paupers, but we make grade, we make Lancashire great too. You know Broderia Mill? It is greatest mill in Lancashire. Should be Broderie, like my father's shop, but English love Italian words, so Broderia.'

He seized my arm. His breath smelled of violets.

'My wife is away. I am the spare man. All Lancashire is hungry for me. But tonight we are all three spare men. We shall get fucking drunk together. We shall just have little picnic but big wines.'

The odour of violets quivered in the umbrous air. The faint bubbly hiss of the gas-lamps wafted us back into the nineties. At any moment, a faint knock at the door might herald the beginning of an adventure in the encircling fog outside, the scent of violets heralding a woman in distress shaking the raindrops from her pelisse. Instead Scarisbrick came in with the vegetables. Her strange hustling gait suggested that someone had a gun poked in her ribs. She was a period figure too, despite rather than because of her costume, a kitchen maid outwardly gruff but with a melting heart who would have saved the choice titbits for the young master or uncomplainingly repaired a jacket torn in some escapade, rewarded only by belated thanks flung down the corridor beyond the green baize door – 'Oh Scarry, you are a trump.' No such sentiments were practised here. Brod believed in treating his servants with a continental rigour.

'Scarisbrick, hot-pot is not hot-pot if it is tepid.'

'Oh, it's quite hot,' Joe said.

'You like cold hotpot and drowning cabbage?' Brod's eyes glared with sportive menace.

'It's delicious, really. Do you cook on gas? It must be awfully difficult getting the supply up here.'

'Calor,' Brod said with a certain disappointment. Joe seemed to be falling short of his expectations.

'Wouldn't electricity be cheaper?' Joe persisted.

'Pictures must be seen by gaslight.'

'I see.'

'If you have not made love by gaslight, you do not know life. A woman's skin is different by gaslight, is like moonlight, you know? When you are older, you will like the softer light. It is more gentle. It maintains the mystery. You have to think to yourself, what is that curve, what is that dark place? You must imagine. There was a room in this restaurant in the woods above Moldau, a little outside the city, a *salon privé*. Two candles on the table, then one candle, and then the light of the moon from a little window high up and this old sofa, very rattletrap sofa. You begin to see?'

'Perhaps a gasfire would do instead,' I said.

'Your friend has no fucking soul, Joe,' Brod said. 'You like this Nuits-St-Georges? It envelopes you, I think.'

They resumed their communion beneath the gaze of the sturdy maidens standing waist-high amid the ox-eye daisies.

The daisies grew not quite so thick in the little valley behind the house. The stream from the moors was almost dry. We traced its course in bare feet, holding our shoes, looking for a view or a clump of flowers for Joe to draw. The sketchbook he carried legitimised our childish sploshing in the peaty beck and dodging under the overhanging rowan branches. Joe was beginning to be ashamed of his drawing, though, and spoke of it, a little furtively, as 'a hobby I still have a lot of fun with.' We were both conscious of having passed over the boundary; he eagerly, longing to get on with life, I reluctantly, with dragging steps. Even as we sat on the heather bank, we were dimly aware that the days of our most intense friendship were over and that, however much we kept in touch, our natural differences were likely to grow and harden.

'Like old times at Smithy's,' he said, recognising that he too knew it wasn't.

Later in the morning, we put on jackets and ties and Burscough drove us down to the mill, down the winding side-valley past the rows of neat mill-workers' cottages and the allotments sprawling over the brow of the hill, the first scarlet runner beans beginning to twine up their sticks, then over a little limestone bridge with another chuckling beck flowing under it and into the mill yard. I had not expected the great square italianate tower, with its round-headed Venetian arches and ironwork balconies. The Broderia sign was elegantly scrawled in italic between the first and second-floor windows. Beneath it could be seen the old black capitals of the previous owners, now scarcely legible.

The panelling of the boardroom was pale, the carpets pale and deep. At a long mahogany table, Brod was flipping through swatches of cloth with a scornful hand. In this pale hall of commerce he looked alarmingly foreign.

'English no-good shit, filthy muck,' he shouted to the man standing at his side holding more swatches. 'Joe, you must design some materials for me. All they send me is dogshit. Go in the pantry and find some champagne.'

He waved at a door by the sideboard and I opened it and almost fell over a silver-haired man in a black jacket who was crouching in this airless cubby-hole loading a tray with glasses. He was so pale he might have been kept there for years, only emerging when shouted for to serve drinks.

'Ramsbottom, have a glass of champagne and take these horrible things away.' The man with the books of swatches gathered them up and held them precariously with one arm while swallowing his drink with the other and at the same time nodding hullo to us and walking backwards in the direction of the door.

'Ramsbottom, my managing director,' Brod waved at the retreating underling. 'Brilliant man, absolutely brilliant. He has no taste. But that does not matter, I have taste for ten. Now come and see the weaving sheds.'

He opened a little door the other side of the room from the door where the butler had been crouching with the drink tray. My heart trembled at the prospect of what might be revealed. But there was only a shabby narrow passage with lino on the floor and grubby marks along the walls, a buffer zone between the boardroom and what lay beyond the flimsy swing doors at the end of the passage. As we shouldered our way through these doors into the sharp insistent clacking noise of the sheds, we seemed to be reaching through to the underside of our lives. In that bright high singing clatter, with the girls in their perky white hats and the men in white coats walking between the machines with the unhurried gait of cricket umpires, a guilty excitement touched me, a sense of having burrowed through to the ultimate ground of reality, but only as a visitor on a guided tour, no more able to stay and breathe that air than a tourist anywhere else.

We stood on a narrow ledge with a bright blue guard rail

keeping us from the workshop floor four or five feet below. Brod treated this eminence with the bravura of a dictator on a balcony, throwing out his chest, then leaning forward to smile and wave at the upturned faces of the mill-girls, their fair curls escaping from their perky hats, their cheeks rosy with amusement at the exotic spectacle of their employer. In some subtle fashion of his own, Brod licensed this amusement, seemed to tease it out of them, in fact.

'Lovely girls, best girls in Lancashire. Their mothers bring them to me the moment they leave school.' He spoke with seigneurial relish, so that the women below us seemed translated into an opera chorus of village maidens. Brod, the lustful count, would behave badly in the first act, worse in act two, and then would be redeemed by love in the finale.

Bemused by the bobbins' racket and the long swaying shimmering skeins rising and falling, I was lost in sensory overload. Only now and then could I hear fragments of the questions Joe was asking about the machines. These questions themselves seemed part of the industrial process, like the commentaries of the educational shorts which preceded the main features at school film evenings, so that it was impossible to recall the images of the raw clay rattling down the chute on its way to becoming china, the hurtling whirr of the great rollers in the print works, the ore ship nosing its way into some grimy dock without also hearing the clipped ceremonious voice of the commentator weaving these processes into the fabric of our island story.

Afterwards, Burscough drove the three of us in the chocolate-coloured brake up on to the moors. We spread the red and blue rugs from the back floor out on the springy heather.

'This is the real shooting picnic,' Brod said. 'Game pie, Cornish pasties, your hard English cheese and your hard English eggs.'

'Why did you order it then, Brod?' Joe asked.

'For you ugly boys. I do not eat out of doors.' He lay on the heather a few yards away, smoking, taking an occasional sip of *vin rosé*. He did not appear to eat or drink much; his paunch seemed to grow of itself.

'There's a girl I know who could do designs for you, Onora, she's awfully good.'

'Women cannot design fabrics. Their line is too weak.'

'I promise you, she really is good.'

'Bring her to stay. We need women.' He was scarcely visible in the fold of the heather where he lay, only the outline of his stomach rising and falling like a giant bumblebee browsing on the bellflowers.

'Oh I don't know whether that would be such a good idea. You see, she and I used to have a thing.'

'She is your ex? All the better. When you are older, you will know that the company of your exes is the best. All passion spent but not forgotten. And so much to talk about, now that the game is over.'

'Well, you see, it wasn't all that long ago.'

'She must come.'

But Onora refused to come. Joe sent her what he described as an old pals letter, promising that they would just be friends on holiday together and it would be a brilliant opportunity for her designs which might not come again. Onora replied saying that she was much too busy but she would send her designs to Mr Brod if he really wanted to see them.

This answer infuriated Brod when Joe told him on our next moorland picnic.

'She is stupid girl.'

'I can't understand it. It's such a brilliant opportunity for her. I suppose she could send the designs.'

'If she sends fucking designs, I tear them up. She has no manners, your friend.'

'Perhaps she really is too busy,' I said.

'If she wanted to come, she would come. Women always do what they want to do.'

'Do they?'

'Always. That is why they cannot draw good designs because they are always thinking what do I do next, what shall I say to him when he comes. They cannot concentrate.'

'Are all women like that?'

'All. I know all women. I study them all through to heart.' The guttering bark of 'heart' was carried away on the moorland breeze like the cry of some marauding animal. When he got up, I was always surprised to see how red in the face and out of breath he was.

By the calendar, these moorland picnics were taken at the height of summer. But to me they already had a faint breath of autumn about them.

V

The Assay –
The Pipes of Straw –
Love at last

The meadows had been frozen for a week. The iron-grey sky
was still, the yellowish light beneath the thin branches of the
pollarded willows stayed the same all day. Nothing moved. This
midwinter stillness was calming, lowering. Quiet footsteps in the
quadrangle. From our corner window we watched the passers-by.
In the mist of late afternoon, the way they walked was all there
was to tell them apart: the high-stepping German tutor gathering
his gown about him as though preparing to fly, the mournful plod
of the little bottle-shouldered chaplain, so at odds with his merry
greeting to one and all coming down the steps towards him, the
confident rolling amble of the football players. It was one of these,
the mountainous McIlwain, who had caught our fancy. His great
thighs were so beautifully exhibited in his walk, like two prize
fatlings being shown professionally. His chest and shoulders, let
alone his face (a sturdy blob), seemed merely part of the supporting
cast. The trousers looked pitifully thin, strained beyond endurance
by the effort to contain these magnificent limbs. Sitting in the
window seat, dunking *petit beurre* biscuits in china tea, we enjoyed
a reversion to childhood, or perhaps to mediaeval fantasy, in our
speculation on McIlwain's thighs. They were insured, naturally,
for thousands by the same firm that insured Rubinstein's hands
for a lesser sum. A whole new rock-face was to be blasted at
Mount Rushmore to enable a team of sculptors to carve some
puny likeness of them. They had been left to the nation, and a
specially reinforced floor was already being built at the British
Museum, no, the Natural History Museum, to prepare for them.

'McIlwain's entered for the Assay.' It was as usual Joe who brought hard news from the fact-world. He listened to our fantasies with benign puzzlement, or only half-listened; it was a foreign language he instinctively knew was not worth his learning.

'I imagine everyone else has scratched, out of respect.'

'It would be *lèse-majesté*, to challenge the Thighs.'

'*Lèse*, oh what's the French for . . . *lèse-cuisses*.'

'I thought it was agreed that we were not to mention them by name, even in a foreign language.'

'I'm so sorry, of course I mean the Pair.'

'But it's just a question of weight, the Assay,' Joe said. 'I can think of several chaps who must be heavier.'

'Heaviness is not everything. It is not mere weight that sets McIlwain apart from ordinary mortals.'

'Isn't it demeaning for him to go in for a college competition? After all, if he wins, all he gets is a silver tankard and the privilege of being pushed across the ice in a dirty old wheelbarrow.'

'No, no, you've got it the wrong way round. McIlwain will dignify the Assay by condescending to go in for it. For centuries afterwards, the Assay will be famous because he took part in it. It may well become known as the McIlwain.'

'But suppose he loses.'

'That is always the risk of Incarnation.'

There was indeed something not wholly of this earth about McIlwain as he stood in his grey woollen dressing-gown beside the great scales in the college kitchen. This giant contraption of brass, discoloured by age, its upper portion covered with dust and cobwebs, had been pulled out from the corner where it normally stood into the centre of the kitchen directly under the lights. Its long arms cast gibbet shadows along the high walls. The other competitors, who had already been weighed, stood beneath the shadows. They sported gaudy dressing-gowns embroidered with dragons or with silken lapels and colourful piping. Only McIlwain stood in honest homespun. As he threw it aside to reveal bathing trunks, we exhaled a gasp of wonder.

'We have seen. We are no longer as other men.'

The Dean, in cap and gown, adjusted the weights. McIlwain sat on the scales. There was a clang and a judder. He was massive.

'Another half stone, Mr Edwards.' Fast Eddie, the porter, produced a weight from the pile on the kitchen table.

'Look at Them. How firm, how *huge*.'

'I do not think it is right that we should attempt to describe Them in mere words. We should simply contemplate and be thankful.'

'Another *stone*, Mr Edwards.' Fast Eddie, so called because he was an amazingly nimble saxophonist, brought up another weight from the diminishing pile. By some trick of acoustics, one could hear Eddie playing in the pantry all over the college, so that, although he did not play at all loudly, even in the furthest corner of the annexe phrases of 'Honeysuckle Rose' would float through a window or up a staircase. In early days (he had been there for twenty years or so now) there had, he said, been complaints from jazz-haters, but the laborious compromise which had been reached by the authorities had allowed time for Eddie's playing to become enshrined in college tradition. Small, bespectacled, nut-brown, strangely prim-mannered, he had become a kind of legend and as a result unpopular among his colleagues who suspected he used his status to avoid his share of the work.

'Mr B.J. McIlwain, 17 stone 13 lbs,' the Dean declared. 'I declare Mr McIlwain to be Assayman. Let the Chariot be brought. Light the torches. Let the ice be tested.'

As the feather-brained tipsy throng shuffled up the steps into the yard which gave access to the gate into the meadows, I noticed Joe talking to Fast Eddie. He had a way of talking to college servants, intimate yet commanding, which seemed alien to the rest of us. The servants seemed to like him better than they did us. He took an interest in their work. Another time, I saw the two of them together when Fast Eddie, goblin in slate-grey apron, black waistcoat and winged collar, was polishing the college silver for some festival. The silver was all laid out on strips of green baize at the bottom of high table, and Joe was inspecting it and asking questions. It might have been Joe's silver and Eddie his man servant. But they had just been joking together, as they were now.

The wheelbarrow, an old green wooden one, high-sided, like the wheelbarrows in children's stories, was brought forward by the losing contestants and McIlwain, now back in his dressing-gown, levered himself into it. He had to put his knees up to his chin to squeeze in.

'Might we get one more tantalising glimpse of Them, do you think?'

'The gown might fall open . . .'

'Ah, rapture . . .'

The torches crackled in the cold night air. The hiss of fog, the swirling draught as the high arched doors swung open. As the advance party of half-a-dozen dons came out into the ghostly white shining meadow, the procession began to seem sinister rather than ludicrous. In the vast expanse of meadow, even the great bulk of McIlwain hunched in the barrow began to look small and vulnerable. The dons stood aside to allow the barrow party to go out onto the ice. The robed attendants edged forward. The wheel made a grumbling, ominous noise. The peasant revels had turned into some unpleasant allegory, some warped fable of punishment which was all the nastier because it was being acted out in homely terrain. Behind the lighted windows above, people might be playing cards or drinking. Other natural functions were doubtless going on around us. And there was poor McIlwain condemned to eternal wrath for sins we knew not of. We began to stamp our feet to keep the cold out. The barrow party had a long distance to cover.

'Bit of a rigmarole, isn't it?' Joe said.

'That's the whole point.'

'It's the sort of thing that's suffocating this country, you know.'

The little group shuffling across the ice was scarcely visible now. I moved a few yards away from the crowd in the hope of being able to get some idea of how far they still had to go. I felt a fierce grip on my forearm, an icy clutch which took my breath away.

'Isn't it wonderful?'

'Oh. Fisha. How nice.'

'It really is a mediaeval ritual, you know, although it was only revived in the Victorian era. But of course it wasn't originally for anything so boring as testing the ice for skating. It was one of the midwinter rebirth rituals. In its original form, it was incredibly erotic. It wasn't just weight that was assayed.'

'At least poor McIlwain doesn't have to worry about that.'

'How are you? How's Joe?'

'He's over there somewhere.'

'Oh I couldn't possibly speak to him. I can't ever speak to him again.'

'Well,' I said, 'he's fine. And how are you then?'

'Much better. Ever so much better. Don't you think I look better?'

She spread open her overcoat like a model showing it off. Underneath, she was wearing what looked like a night-dress.

'Is that a good idea, on a night like this?'

'Don't be so stuffy. I had to. I'm home this weekend. Ma and Pa think I'm still in bed. But I couldn't miss the Assay.' She clutched my arm tighter. I thought she was going to fall and I put my other arm round her. She wriggled out of this hold and said, not indignantly, 'I'm quite all right, you know.' Her round forget-me-not eyes and bitten lip looked devout, appealing in the flickering lights of the torches – a baroque picture of some brimming-eyed passionist, except that Fisha looked more amiable, in fact, almost homely, after the fashion of McIlwain and his woollen dressing-gown. A great fondness for her came over me, even a fondness for her craziness which surprised me, since crazy people are usually so trying to the patience.

'I was pretty mad, but I am much better. Isn't it odd how, before you are mad, you imagine that the one thing mad people won't admit is how mad they are, and when you are, you know quite well you are, most of the time anyway, and in fact you spend hours talking about it.'

'Depends on what sort of mad you are, I suppose.'

'I'm a very ordinary sort, I think. Oh look, they're coming back.'

The trundling creak of the barrow came sharper to our ears,

and then went soft, as they came off the ice on to the grass. The barrow-pushers raised the shafts high and tipped McIlwain out in front of the dons in their gowns and mortar-boards. As he rolled over in a melodramatic tumble, there was a flash of thigh below the dressing-gown. McIlwain rose to his feet and bowed three times to the dignatories.

'Assayman, how do you say? Does the ice hold?'

'Until 1947, they did it all in Latin. Much better,' Fisha murmured.

'The Ice Holds, Master,' McIlwain replied. We had never heard him speak before. He had an unusual voice which was both guttural and squeaky. We tried to imitate it later, without success.

The president of the revels gave the signal for the opening of the ice, and most of the crowd began to slide or waddle on to it. The torch-holders marked out the limits of a pitch for ice hockey which their torches were to illuminate. The players stumbled past us, unused to walking on their skates, among them Joe.

'Oh hullo Fisha,' he said. 'I'm so glad to hear you're better.'

'You didn't come to see me.'

'I didn't think you'd want me to.'

'You were quite right. But you couldn't *know* I didn't want you to.'

'Well, that's too complicated for me. Shall I come and see you now you're home?'

'I'm only home for the weekend. And I don't want you to come to the hospital.'

'All right then. The next time you're home.'

'Don't call me, I'll call you, is it?'

'I *will* call. But if you'd rather it was the other way round.'

'You know I wouldn't dare to call on you.'

'I don't know at all. And anyway I think I'll come and see you at the hospital whatever you say.'

'You didn't before.'

'Well, I should have,' Joe said with a rueful smile, shouldering his hockey stick. 'I know I should have.'

'You go and play your silly game. I think it vulgarises the whole thing, playing a stupid Canadian game afterwards.'

'Aren't you being a bit snobbish, Fisha?'

'I just like things done properly, the way they used to be done.'

He stumbled across on his skates to kiss her goodbye. The stumbling seemed somehow controlled, managed even so that he was balanced enough to pause for an instant first and look at her moon-pale face turned up towards him. He skated off with long slashing strides, overtaking others hobbling across the ice.

His leaving made her garrulous in a happy-mad way. Where Ophelia talked of flowers, she talked of rituals and anthropologists – stupid foreigners mostly, she said they were, not fit to brush the boots of a decent English antiquary who knew his county history. Sometimes she used old-fashioned don's language – the argot of club and common-room – and I could hear her father talking in her, and this made me fonder of her still. And yet looking back, I cannot help feeling that his influence made the world a more difficult place for her, not in the sense of keeping her too unworldly as other doting professor-fathers kept their daughters, but rather by encouraging that nervous aliveness which she had inherited from him and which was somehow too much.

More than that, there was a kind of perfectionism in her which stored up impatience and discontent. She had scarcely a drop of her mother's capability to absorb things. I heard her snort as one of the skaters walked past in full American football rig, his padded shoulders black and monstrous against the moonlit ice.

I tried to explain what I meant above the clash of makeshift hockey sticks and the shrieks and oaths of the players and the mournful howling of their supporters and the crackle of the tarry torches beginning to burn low. A silvery moonlight now washed the horizon and only the hockey-pitch still glowed a hectic black and red and orange. Beside us, the dons took sherry from a silver tray. Gravely in their midst McIlwain quaffed his silver tankard. All this, I said, was probably just like the Middle Ages; it was certainly like a Flemish picture, gowned and reverend signors making polite conversation in one corner, boors and yobs carousing in another, ordinary life carrying on around both, a traditional festival of church and community being used as an excuse for a party.

'No, you don't understand,' Fisha said. 'It's all phoney now. Everything's phoney now.'

'Perhaps it always was.'

'You mustn't always sit back and try and make the best of things. You mustn't be so passive.'

'I wasn't being passive.'

'You have to insist. Everything must be done properly. Properly, do you see? You must see what I mean.'

'Don't clutch my arm so hard.'

'I shall, I shall, to make you see. There, that's how hard my hand can squeeze. And there, that's how hard my nails can scratch. I can draw blood – if I want to. There, now, you're frightened. That's better. I'll go now. Good-night.' That butter-soft kiss on my mouth and she was off into the crowd. For a moment, I thought that a responsible adult would follow her to stop her from doing something stupid. Then I wondered whether I really wanted to be a responsible adult.

All night, I thought of forget-me-not eyes and fierce clutching hands and in the morning and at intervals thereafter I wondered how she was and whether some bad news would come, probably as in a film at the moment when least expected, some moment of carefree enjoyment. The hospital said she was a lot better (than what, they did not say), but patients were not allowed to take calls, except from immediate family, and she had said she did not want visitors just yet.

To start with, Scrannel too seemed quite recovered when I saw him next, brisk and scraped-looking in evening clothes at the Pipes of Straw.

'It's a discussion club, started by Scrannel's admirers. You know, those scrannel pipes of straw – Milton,' Joe told me when issuing the invitation.

'I do know,' I said. 'We've been through that before.'

'Have we?' he said. 'It's quite high-powered, I understand. McIlwain asked if I could get him an invitation as he knew I knew the Scrannels.'

'*McIlwain?*' I was aghast at the thought that the Thighs might have developed intellectual leanings.

'Yes, why not? He's doing Eng. Lit. and it's a literary subject this month.'

And there indeed was the Assayman in the middle of the front row in the college reading-room, a mighty stanchion unperturbed by the high-pitched chatter around him. When Scrannel rose, McIlwain's hands sounded in a positively homeric round of applause.

'The stage I am thinking of is almost empty when the curtain rises, if there is a curtain,' Scrannel began. 'Sometimes the bare stage is already fully visible when the audience comes in. Then the play starts when the stage lights come on, or perhaps when one or more of the characters enters.

'Who are these characters? Sometimes they are described as tramps. One of them may wear a bowler hat, or a battered old tail-coat. Or he may have a flower in his buttonhole. Then the audience or the critics may think of him as a clown.

'But he is not an ordinary clown. So far as we can see, he is not attached to any circus. The tricks and jokes he runs through now and then do not form part of any coherent routine. They seem at best to be scraps of old skills, vestigial memories of some former employment, but no such employment is ever mentioned . . .'

I cannot remember exactly how Scrannel went on. All that comes back to me is the light, skipping gait with which he took us through the steps of his argument. By the time he was finished with them, the tramps and their pranks and their pauses seemed as stale and stagey as an old-fashioned West End comedy. Again and again, the playwright was caught in the act of flattering his audience, of sucking up to their self-pity, of indulging their unearned pretensions to possess a tragic sense.

'Nothing that we can create enables us to cheat death. True. Nothing we can do can remedy our mortality. Agreed. For that reason, we are told, it will all be the same in a hundred years, and therefore it is all the same now. That whole compendious apparatus which we have elaborated to describe the differences between things – the apparatus we call language – is now of use only to tell us that in reality no such differences exist, or none of any permanent significance.'

Scrannel paused, gulped a glass of water. His throat sounded rasping dry, but the pause seemed not entirely medicinal.

'I see no logical connection between the steps in this argument. It would first be necessary to prove that significance is logically dependent upon immortality, that in order to possess meaning a thing must also be eternal. But nobody seems to have bothered to mix that particular cement. Indeed, rather inconveniently, human beings have often attributed a most profound significance to the readiness to sacrifice one's own life. If this sacrifice were in reality not a sacrifice at all but a gateway to a fuller life or at least a prelude to a return in the next series, then it would be a trivial thing. It is the finality as well as the pain of it that makes it count.

'The tragic sense rests on a different if not opposite assumption: that both life and death are real and serious, indeed, that the only futility lies in denying the seriousness of one or other of them, thus turning existence into either a meaningless fraud or a fatuous comedy. Our grounds for a denial of either sort seem to me to be thin.

'If I choose to assert that life is worth living, and, what's more, worth living in some ways and not in others, then only that unnameable personage for whom we are not to be caught waiting would have the authority to contradict me. If I choose to consider as equally precious each layer of the onion, from the papery brown casing to the fleshy crinkle in the middle, who else could force me to simulate disillusion or disgust as I peel it? We could know for sure that life was futile only if the unnameable existed, which would apparently be the precondition for life not being futile.

'But there I must draw these ramblings to a close. To have suggested that despair is not necessarily a philosophically sound position is subversion enough for one evening.'

The applause was tepid, despite the measured beat set by McIlwain's massy slabs. And there was a querulous, almost cheated note to the discussion which followed.

'But surely, if people go on unpeeling the onion in the vain hope of finding something marvellous in the middle, surely we are still entitled to speak of their lives as tragic or at any rate wasted?'

'So we might be if the playwright were not himself aiding and abetting the pursuit, at every turn egging them on to discover further emptiness in things which they had previously thought substantial and significant. The tears he weeps for their despair are crocodile tears, since it is he who has guided them into that slough of despond and on the strength of spurious claims to know the way.'

'Isn't he just pointing out to them the realities which they haven't hitherto bothered to think about?'

'I notice,' said Scrannel, not without satisfaction, 'that we are most of us happy to speak of *They* rather than *We*. We appear to be in the position of observers following the manoeuvres of lost sheep through binoculars.'

'Are you opposed to despair?' Joe's voice sounded verging on impatient. He lacked the sportive tone.

'Well,' Scrannel paused again, put off his stroke. 'I'm not sure that it's something you can appropriately be opposed to, like vivisection or nuclear weapons. But I do think that if philosophers and playwrights are to spend much time buttressing despair, the philosophers will need to deploy better arguments, and playwrights will need to write better plays.'

'Thank you,' Joe said in a fulfilled sort of way. This cast a pall over the *conversazione*. It was so out of keeping with the impudent style of academic argument.

Yet even before Joe had intervened, I had noticed a different element in the air, one which I can only describe as a hectic, unsettled impatience. My first impression, that Scrannel himself had recovered, began to be shaken. His electric vibrancy seemed increasingly out of control as the evening wore on. His shoulders trembled when he coughed his dry, interrogative cough. His high cheeks were flushed. The dinner jacket had that greenish bloom you see in institutions where elderly men dine out in damp halls, but he seemed ill at ease with it, as if he had borrowed it for the evening. The fuzz-wings at his ears which had first reminded me of someone in Dickens – one of those jolly, restless characters who cannot stop jerking about – now made him look more grotesque, the victim of some terrible fright, Struwwelpeterish.

At the end of the discussion, I was standing by myself waiting for a glass of wine, irresolute, confused, yet also elated, when Scrannel rushed up to me with the violence of a football defender and came to a halt only inches from me.

'What are you doing here? You haven't been here before,' he said. 'You're not a philosopher, are you?'

'No,' I said. 'Joe said it would be all right if I came along.'

'When I invited Follows, I did not expect him to ask half the college along with him.'

'Oh, I'm very sorry. I should have asked. I thought it was a wonderful paper.'

'I am delighted that you should think so. However, your encomium does not affect the issue. This was intended as a private club.'

'Well, I'll go now.'

'Of course not. You are now my guest. You must take a glass of wine. Would you condescend to the Sancerre? Or had you larger expectations of our hospitality?'

This prickly ferocity was so unlike that blithe, open manner which had first drawn me to him that I was both puzzled and miserable. It was hard to see what I had done wrong or what Joe had done right. Nor did this antipathy appear to wear off as the evening wandered to its close.

'Dr Pritchard-Evans, you have not perhaps yet encountered the stowaway on board our frail bark, unless the excellence of his essays has already commended him to you.'

'Mr Cotton and I are already acquainted, although I wish that we were more so, for I fear that so far he is more conspicuous by his absence than by his excellence.'

'P-E is celebrated for his dry wit,' Scrannel explained to me, with a momentary softening. Then turning to a pop-eyed little man – 'Mudge, you may care to note in the minutes that the fame of our little gatherings is spreading. Here is Mr Cotton who has accorded us the unexpected honour of his presence.'

'I am supposed to have notice in writing of guests. May I make a note of your name and college? And be so good as to remind your host that Gleanings must also be paid in advance.'

The pop-eyed little man I already recognised as G.H. Mudge, whose skinny frame was perched in the professorial chair everyone agreed Scrannel should have had. Mudge, someone had said, was living proof that it is not only the defeated who bear a grudge. The darting pop-eyes swept the room in a perpetual quest for people saying or thinking that he was unworthy. Scrannel did not trouble to hide his own resentment. Pupils were given elaborate and pressing directions to Mudge's lectures, which were known to be of unendurable tedium and poorly attended: 'You will find Professor Mudge in characteristically bracing form on Descartes. If I were you, I should get there a minute or two early in order to secure a place' – or 'May I commend Professor Mudge's little squib on dualism in *Mind*, although you may think it somewhat raffish.'

'I sometimes wonder,' Mudge said, throbbing-veined, scratchy-voiced, 'whether these little gatherings have not strayed from their original purpose. They seem to be turning into a social bunfight.'

'I fear,' Scrannel came back, 'that my effort this evening cannot be exempt from your strictures. However, I am confident that your paper next month – "Are there two Kants?" I believe you said it was to be called – I am sure that will set us back on the right road.'

'I cannot promise any fireworks,' Mudge said.

A few minutes later, I saw Scrannel in conversation with Joe, laughing, throwing his high, gaunt face to the ceiling, coughing, then laughing again with a triumphant, defiant mien, as though someone on the floor above had ordered him to stop.

Since Peggy had come to stay, I had kept away from Pigotts

Hill. Even elegantly rearranged, Joe's flat was small, and its high, embowered situation made one feel both isolated and a little carried away when sitting on the window-seat looking out over the valley and the mist. The intimacy was daunting.

Already, rumours had begun to float down into the city, at first vague, tentative, constrained by the awesomeness of the idea, then gaining confidence and even accuracy, before toppling over into fantasy. Joe Follows had a woman up on Pigotts Hill, a married woman, or if not married then older, much older, old enough to be his mother, or, the rumours then retreating a little to gain credence, not as old as she looked, in any case she was brilliant-looking, but experienced, a woman with a sad history, probably brutal, certainly romantic. Those who had seen them together on Peggy's rare excursions into town could not mistake their relationship, and she was so smart, so high-stepping, both fashionable and old-fashioned, the skirts longer but the legs all the more elegant for it, and the cool greys and blues and the wisp of scarf so quiet, irresistibly condemning other women as puppyish or dowdy.

None of this came from me. I could lay no claim to discretion or loyalty. I was simply dumbstruck. I had supposed, although the whole affair seemed too awe-inspiring for much in the way of precise supposing, that she would come for the weekend or a day or two after and then return to her own unknowable grown-up life. Not that I had any preconception of how she might otherwise be filling the day. But to live with Joe, literally live, that seemed unimaginable.

Besides, beyond the awe there was also the thrilling presentiment of doom. They would be found out, humiliated, sent packing from their attic Eden. Peggy could not simply stay on like that. The world did not permit such pursuit of fancy. They would have to go away somewhere, under a false name. These were the melodramatic musings with which we disguised our fear of disorder, our lack of nerve.

'I need advice, I'm in trouble, in fact, I'm in it up to here.' Joe woebegone on a raw late February afternoon, oarsman's muffler round his neck, cold sores on his truculent lip, healthy-miserable, brimming with self-pity. Something self-satisfied about him, though, not one of his more endearing guises.

'Everyone in college seems to think you're having a whale of a time.'

'How many people know? I don't want anyone to know. You must keep your mouth shut.'

'I do. But if you – '

'We can't live like caged animals. Does the Dean know?'

'I haven't the faintest idea.'

'Don't care if he does. Anyway, that's all sorted out. Walter says he'll drop the Dean a note to say that my aunt is staying on a few weeks to look for a house and he trusts that there will be no objection.'

'Walter Scrannel?'

'Yes, we've become great mates. He seems to have got over the Fisha thing, says it wasn't my fault at all, forgives me or says there's nothing to forgive. He's going to suggest to Fisha that we should come and visit her together, although I think that might be a bit difficult.'

'Scrannel. I can't believe it.'

'Peggy's been wonderful. In fact, that's just the trouble.'

'What do you mean?'

'You see, he's fallen for her. He's crazy about her, can't take his eyes off her, follows her round the room with his eyes, all that.'

'But then how – '

'Oh he doesn't know about us. Or pretends he doesn't. Perhaps he really doesn't, because if he did – '

'He'd shoot you, or himself.'

'Look, Gus, this is a hellish situation, anything could happen. He's talking of leaving his wife.'

'Don't be silly. He can hardly know her.'

'All last summer when we were up at Brod's. She used to come up here.'

'Up here?'

'To Pigotts Hill. To my digs.'

'How on earth do you know?'

'She left that scarf behind, the one I bought her at Andrews and Liversedge.'

'Perhaps she just didn't like it. I didn't care for it much myself.'

'It was a beautiful scarf. The point is, she hadn't been here at all since June, not officially.'

'Perhaps you'd forgotten about her leaving it behind before you went away.'

'Of course I hadn't forgotten. She left it there on purpose for me to see.'

'That's crazy. Why would she do that?'

'Oh come on. To make me wake up. To tell me what she was doing. I should never have let her have the key.'

'But you've seen him with his wife. They're, well, devoted,' I said.

'You haven't seen him with Peggy. Anyway, she wouldn't dream of denying it. She just said straight out as soon as I found the scarf and phoned her. She's absolutely honest about that sort of thing.'

'But why?'

'Well, I'll tell you if you promise not to tell anyone else.'

'All right,' I said.

'Scrannel hasn't got much time left.'

'Time left for what?' I said, the obtuseness relieving my irritation.

'You know that cough he has. In the morning, there's blood in it. He doesn't want to go to the doctor, because he thinks it undignified to put up one of those gallant fights for life that so signally fail to alleviate the obituary columns.'

Recognising a Scrannel turn of phrase softened my peevishness. Even so, I could not help saying that I had never heard anything so crazy in my life.

'Well, you're a sensible person, Gus. Basically Scammell's a romantic, you see.' This return to the old word-fluffing drew me back to Joe's side more than anything else he had said. His position was so odd and precarious that I temporarily forgot how he had reached it. He was wearing a jersey of nordic knit, too small for him. He had recovered that vulnerable ragamuffin look which was, you could say, the making of him.

'What does Peggy think about it all?'

'I suppose she just wants to make his last months happy. She says it's basically only companionship. But it's so hard to know what she's thinking. I don't mean that she keeps her cards close to her chest, she confides in me a lot, but even when she does you can't really tell her plans, you know, what she's going to do next or anything.'

'Can she tell yours?'

'What do you mean? And if you're talking about Fisha, I don't want to discuss it. I don't think it's fair, I don't mean on me but on her, because if you do talk about it, you have to say about how it started.'

His rumpled brow, betokening hurt chivalry, left me cold. That soft, steamy collusion which he exacted was so suffocating. I did not fancy being made silage of.

'But anyway,' he said. 'She respects his brain.'

'What's left of it,' I said.

'Why do you talk like that? Walter's been through hell these past weeks.'

'I'm sure he has and I think it's unhinged him.'

'Well, I only know he's been very decent to me.'

'That is not the only test of sanity,' I said.

'I thought you'd be more supportive.'

Can he really have said 'supportive'? The word had surely only become fashionable in the last few years. Perhaps I am fathering it on him out of malice. Yet it sounds right in memory's ear. He did have this kind of sixth sense for apprehending clichés of the future. Perhaps the magical properties of his reddish-golden colouring had suffered some kind of cruel debasement, so that, whereas previous generations of coppernobs could foresee great calamities or cure arthritis by letting their rufous hands hover near the affected part, Joe had only the power to reproduce the language of some half-baked sociologist ten years hence. Ah no, that will not do. Other inexplicable happenings were to be observed within his magnetic field. Like it or not, one could not deny that he was something of a poltergeist of the affections.

There was nothing supernatural, though, about the leaden March morning when I saw on the noticeboard the two-line notice: Dr Scrannel's lectures for the remainder of this term are cancelled, because of ill-health.

'So,' I said, 'he really is ill.'

'Of course he's ill, I told you he was.'

'He must have gone to see the doctor, I suppose.'

'No, perhaps. I don't know. I shouldn't think so. That is not it.'

'What is it then?'

'You are slow.' He looked up, thrusting his misery at me.

'Oh.'

'She's gone off with him. To try and help him over the worst time. Because he wanted it so much. All that kind of thing. He probably isn't ill at all. Just knew how to make her sorry for him.'

'He must be – no, I suppose not all that much older.'

'Only five years. I worked it out. Nothing like the gap between us, but who cares?'

'Where are they?'

'Don't know. She didn't say in the letter, to stop me going after them, she said. Not that I would, that's not my bag.'

'What about Mrs Scrannel?'

'No idea how she feels, and I'm not going to find out either. I've suddenly had enough of the Scrannels.'

'It is a shock. Well, it's extraordinary.'

'I told you she respected his brain. She's a raging intellectual snob. Well, I tell you what I'm going to do. I'm going straight down to McIlwain's rooms and sign up for the college eight. And then I'm going to train like a fucking maniac until my arms are as thick as McIlwain's thighs. If she thinks she's been living with a bone-headed hearty, I might as well be the real thing. She can sit up all night talking about the tragic sense of life if she likes,

I'm going to get on with my life, my bloody ordinary, beta minus, crude thicko life.'

This intention was carried out to the letter, with a cromwellian thoroughness. Glimpses of this grim self came now and then through that cold, wet, late spring: a string of oarsmen pounding heavy-footed along the mist-strangled towpath, led by a neat high-stepping little cox yapping instructions through the thick air, his chin jutting above the swathing mufflers, and gasping behind them right at the back Joe, mud-spattered, puffing horribly in the damp air, stumbling, scarcely able to keep up; or in Butts Yard, scrumming down with his comrades into a peculiar tortoise-shell formation, then stamping their feet in unison, and chanting some indecipherable cry; or in the dining hall, sitting together at the end of a table, subjecting one of the crew to some humiliation ritual long abandoned by other members of the college, its name now escaping me or rather being obliterated by the ritual of 'budgering' we had elaborated as a sophisticated parody of such rude customs. Joe's immersion in this exclusive brethren, this unremitting monastico-muscular discipline, made us shake our heads in disbelief. It was a defection which, it seemed to us, even the most terrible disappointment in love could not justify. We tried to keep our spirits up.

'He must by now have seen the Thighs, naked and unashamed.'

'The splendours of the Groin have been unveiled to him.'

'Blessed are they that have not seen and yet have believed.'

In truth, Joe's therapy seemed fitting, and I did not think much about him. It was more after Scrannel and Peggy that my thoughts limped and strayed. The stillness of a country-house hotel; he caged, impatient, pacing; she poised yet anxious – take some more of that cough linctus, you must keep the throat wrapped, that confiding allure which she lent to the simplest phrases, her sheer economy of speech calming Scrannel as he looked out over the dripping rhododendrons and the desolate hard tennis court. She would beguile him through the slow meals in the hushed dining-room and, with some imperceptible inflection, send up the waitress – coffee *in* the lounge, or in the *lounge*? Scrannel would be vulnerable to her style, or rather to her saturating everything with style, so that even the way she undressed at night and then approached him would seem so natural that he would not be able to help himself and yet at the same time would be quite unlike anything else in his experience. And his fears that he might bore her, be too dry, too academic, or, for he would not be crippled by false modesty, too clever for her, well, she would know how to deal with those fears too. She would – these fancies began to build upon each other, so that I began to fret on their behalf like an oversensitive courier – she would slow him down, place that cool, confiding hand on his arm and ask him – no, not to say it all again in words of one syllable – that would remind him too much of the differences between them. Somehow he would never feel inclined to talk beyond her. He would adapt himself to her pace, feel rested, be surprised, even, how little he minded not smoking. And when the darker broodings came, the terror and the guilt, for he must feel appalling guilt (I was convinced of this), she would convey, in the most thoughtful way without going on about herself, how well she knew those dark hours. There was no comfort to be offered, except that the hours would pass and that was no comfort at the time.

But my thoughts were not as clear as I have made them sound, for my horror was really too great for me to think straight. And there was a vindictive spark in my musings, that had to be admitted, a willingness to inflict punishment. There would be hours of boredom too, unfilled afternoons, drizzle on the rhododendrons, drizzle on the hard court. The silent passages, the muffling carpets would begin to strangle their happiness. And so there would be humiliations, sexual failure, veiled recriminations afterwards, comparisons made – and comparisons were invidious whatever Scrannel might say.

His house was a house of doom. The cheerful red tiles, fake timbers and pink roughcast walls came to seem like a gothic horror-villa. When *Psycho* came on at the Regal, I was instantly reminded of Furze Bank, although there was no real likeness. I avoided the house on the rare occasions I came up to Pigotts Hill, took the long way round from the bus-stop. The house could only be guessed at in its enveloping muff of dark pines and spruces.

'Oh hullo. Haven't seen you for ages. But then I hardly see anyone with Walter away.'

I was alarmed to see Mrs Scrannel, could scarcely bear to look at her, terrified of seeing her misfortune in her face. But the forget-me-not eyes looked at me undimmed. In her belted camel-hair coat and Jaeger scarf, she was a comfortable body, might have been untroubled by anything.

'With my two invalids away, I can really get on with tidying the house. But they're both much better, you know. Walter sent an ecstatic postcard from the seaside.'

'From the seaside?'

'Oh didn't you hear, Joe's aunt has so kindly taken him down to stay with them, down on the South Coast. I was a bit nervous about whether her husband would want a strange invalid on his hands. But of course you must know him, because it's near where you were in the sanatorium, isn't it? Anyway, they all seem to be getting on like a house on fire. When I first met her, well, I have only met her about twice, I thought she wasn't going to be my sort at all. But she's an extremely warm character, I don't mean gushing but friendly. After ten minutes, you feel you've known her for ages, you know?'

'I do know.'

'Walter was getting so fidgety, with having to give up smoking and lecturing and so on, and the house is so damp. Well, everywhere's damp just now, isn't it? Anyway, you must come on Sundays again, because Fisha comes out regularly now, and she's really awfully chirpy, or chirpy-severe anyway. She's right back to her old form, putting me right and correcting me and so on. But it's wonderful about Walter too. They asked me to go down as well, of course, but I couldn't leave Fisha, and in any case I didn't want to cramp Walter's style. He really needed to get away, and having your nearest and dearest with you is never quite getting away, is it, not properly.'

There is nothing quite like the first time you hear a serious adult lie. Artists do not usually deploy their full imaginative power to describe the encounter, for artists are liars by trade. They are chauffeurs of desire, not truth-accountants. They may, I suspect, find it hard to imagine how much we pedestrians take truth for granted, how upset we are to come across it being desecrated. The plainer sort of evil – malice, rage, cruelty – is not quite so shocking. Even the greater treachery of which the lie may be only a minor instrument is more expected, less undermining. When Mrs Scrannel said 'husband' in her gentle, trotting way, I trembled. The evidence of the con's success, the innocence with which it was relayed was acutely distressing.

To have resurrected an ex-husband was so audacious, so brazen. The ingenuity, the neatness of it teased the moral sense. You would not have thought of it because you would not have dared to think of it and, for that reason, you were a little disabled, if not disarmed by it. And Mrs Scrannel there outside the library, in her Windsmoor and Jaeger armour of innocence, she too was drawn in, rabbit-dazzled by the weasel's gaze. She did not know what to think of it at all, probably could not be certain in her mind what it was she was keeping up her usual kindly face for – her husband's health or her own self-respect. Was she also lying now, if only to herself, caught up in the terrible lazy reach of the lie?

Mrs Scrannel's smile seemed – though this was probably an illusion – to accept some doubt implied on my side, some unspoken accusation that she was making the best of a situation which was not to be made the best of. She looked tired, but the solitude of the past few weeks had already shed a luminous calm upon her face. She was sad, yet not done for. Our talk dribbled to a halt. We were standing in the back entrance to the University's library. Down the narrow service alley skulked a smell of damp and drains. Boiler-steam threading the high black iron gates; fumes of singed cabbage from the canteen; delivery van reversing towards us, so that we had to jump apart; a little old man wheeling tall grey dustbins back towards the loading bay.

Joe was impatient and matter-of-fact when I told him. He was track-suited and running on the spot as I talked.

'Peggy did say that they would try to make it as easy as possible for the family,' he said.

'But did they need to pretend about Peter? Do stop jogging up and down.'

'You think of a better way. I mean, she's quite entitled. If Uncle Pete was too lazy to change his will when they got divorced – '

'But when Mrs Scrannel finds out – '

'Perhaps she won't. Perhaps Scrannel will see through Peggy quicker than I did. Perhaps she'll realise what a boring old fart he really is. Then we can all go back to square one and live happily ever after.'

He began his stationary jog again, stamping his feet into the cobblestones of the yard. As his knees rose and fell, he began to gasp for breath and his eyes began to fill with tears. The self-pity which suffused him was no less alarming than his breathing spasms. He was as prickly-fierce as Mrs Scrannel was gentle and resigned. Even as I tried to calm him, I could not help noticing how little talent he had for the sardonic. When he tried to be world-weary, he sounded merely puzzled. The words came awkwardly to him, as if this was not his first language and these phrases – back to square one, live happily ever after – were being given a try-out after having been picked up from some passing contacts with the natives. Even the words of derision were tentatively launched, suggesting that he was uncertain whether they might be too violent or alternatively were hopelessly out of date and now used only by people who themselves were ludicrous. The lie or lies were of no more interest to him than if I had told him which train Peggy and Scrannel had left on.

'The real problem is Gillian,' Joe said, stopping to catch his breath.

'Gillian? Why? She can't be surprised by her mother's – I'm sorry, Joe, what I mean is that she doesn't even know the Scrannels or anything.'

'No, no, she's coming here tomorrow and she's expecting her mother to be here to settle her in, and I shall have to explain, or make up some sort of story about why she isn't.'

The echoes of *Charley's Aunt* started up again in my mind. The approach of these farcical crises – the bodies to be hidden under the sofa or pushed into the cupboard, the explanations which had to be thought up on the run – merely paralysed me. But Joe rose to them briskly. He was wonderfully consequential, a man for contingencies, no repiner.

We did not know what to expect. 'You must have seen a picture of her, in a family album,' I pressed Joe, incredulous when he said he had no idea what she looked like.

'Can you imagine the Monkey keeping a family album? Well, in fact she does keep an album, but it's entirely group photos of the children at the Big House.'

But Gillian knew Joe instantly. He was still peering along the platform when she came up behind him and tapped him on the shoulder.

'Joe, isn't it? Hi.'

He turned eagerly, anxiously towards her. He had said to me that he wanted to do his best for her, that she must have had a rough childhood, and so on. But he must also have hoped to find something of her mother in her, to capture here and there reminiscences of her cool enchantments. Even if Peggy had been maliciously accurate in making us think of her daughter as plump and awkward, there would surely be elements of her charm to be traced, made perhaps more charming still by being spied in a fresh sort of person, a younger Peggy-and-not-Peggy, thus bringing up again in a thrilling way the question of age and the erotic vibrations which trembled in its vicinity.

'Hi, I'm Gilly. It's super to meet you at last after all these years.'

She wore a coat and skirt of thick pink wool, very pink, very thick. Afterwards, we argued about whether there had been a hint of inverted commas about the 'super'. But about the sturdy legs and the icing-pink lipstick and the bright brave smile there was no argument. We took turns to carry her heavy suitcase down the platform, each of us numb with embarrassment and fear of being seen. Gillian seemed unwounded by these ignoble sentiments. I thought she scarcely even noticed us. She rattled on about the school she had just left, about the secretarial college she was going to, and eventually, to our terror, about her mother.

'Actually, the most amazing thing, Mum's suddenly taken to doing good. She's whisked this frightfully ill old professor off down to Uncle Peter's house, well, her house now, I suppose. Not that it's exactly the healthiest place I can think of and I expect she'll just lounge about and fry as per usual when she gets there. All the same, she will have to look after this poor old prof and wipe his bottom for him. Honestly, *Mum*, can you imagine?'

As we reached the end of the platform, an elderly man limped up carrying a tea-chest, wheezing as he went.

'Oh you are a goodster – gosh it sounds as if you've got asthma, I am sorry, I should never have asked you – Joe has asthma too, don't you, Joe? It must be absolutely frightful. Well, I really am awfully sorry and it was incredibly kind. Cripes, that was awful, wasn't it, making that poor old chap carry the chest, but otherwise it might have got carried on to lord knows where.'

She put her hand to her mouth to stifle her giggles. She did not really seem much flustered. As she shook back her hair, she did have a look of her mother. Her cheerful babble and her wide laughing mouth seemed like a kind of revenge.

'I was absolutely scared rigid about coming here because of everyone being such terrifying brain boxes, but then I started counting up all the people I knew and it didn't sound quite so scary. I mean there's you two, although I didn't actually know you, but I'd heard such loads about you and then there's Diggory Paish, and Gervase who's a sort of cousin and not a bad bloke for a rock-chopper, and Richenda Vincent who used to be a real mucker of mine and the two Bogrollers, except that one of them's just left, and Catriona who's at the tech doing textiles and who's a real ace. Anyway, I got the body count up to fifteen, so I thought I wouldn't actually die of loneliness. Oh and Topsy of course, Toppers is doing the same course as me.'

Our harassment turned to desolation. We crept through the streets, carrying the tea-chest, with furtive funereal gait. All our resolutions to be kind to this luckless waif had shamefully fled. But our nerve had gone too, and our embarrassment was no match for her invitations to tea.

The initial count had been an underestimate. Crammed into Gillian's little room over the hardware shop were closer on thirty. We knew none of them. They were quite unlike any of the people we knew. They were so exuberant, so loud.

'I expect your rowing friends are like this,' I said as we stood jammed face to face in a corner with a hispid pot-plant nuzzling our ears.

'Not at all,' Joe said indignantly. 'Even when they're drunk, they're soberer than this lot.'

They were all so defined and expressive, as though they had never known the blobbiness of youth. Gervase, tall, crow-like, his face velvet-moled, announced without provocation that he was a Ninian Comper groupie and was going to saturate himself utterly in church furnishings for three or four years before going into the City to make pots of money so he could build a Comperesque chantry on to his parents' dreary little Georgian box. Diggory was going to tour Canada with his pack of bassett hounds and then sell them because of the quarantine regulations and meet up with the elder Bogroller who hadn't left after all because he'd made an utter horlicks of his geography finals. And Richenda Vincent, stately plump Richenda, was certain to fail her exams because she had to spend her whole time fighting off her Mediaeval French tutor who was a hunchback with bad breath but so devastatingly quick.

Some of this information came from Gillian herself, some from the tea guests. None of them seemed at all reluctant to talk about themselves.

'Isn't it fantastic, the way Gilly plunges in? She's only been here a week and already it's total bedlam.'

'Yes.'

'I don't know how you got on before she came. Down in Devon she *is* social life, always has been since the age of nought, making up for her mother, I suppose.'

'How do you mean?'

'Well, she's awfully stand-offish, isn't she, Mrs – well, I can't really keep up, Dudgeon is it still?'

'I wouldn't have thought stand-offish exactly.'

'In Devon she is, I can tell you. Wouldn't catch her coming to any local do. She is attractive, though, you have to admit it.'

'Who is? Mum, I bet. It's so frightful, whenever I hear anybody saying some woman is attractive, I know they're talking about Mum.'

'Well, she is, Gilly.'

'Of course I know she is. It's just so frightful everyone saying so the whole time. Can't you see that?'

'I can indeed,' I said.

'Do you say indeed often? I don't think I know any man who says indeed.'

'It sounds fantastically grown-up,' her friend Richenda said.

'No, I just like it,' Gillian said.

'I can say it again if you like.'

'No, it has to come out naturally. It's awfully hot in here. Come out on the landing, and say indeed again.'

The landing was cold and narrow. Greenish veined marble lino. A Chinese-style lampshade rocking in the breeze from the half-open window. Fire escape, black, long unused. Slipping slated roofs. She turned and kissed me. Gin-scented, smoky, immemorial kiss.

That eager, simple kiss scattered my ignoble instincts. Walking home with Joe, I joined in the mockery of the proceedings, but my heart had gone over to the other side. Diggory, Richenda, the Bogrollers and the rest would have to be swallowed. All this can with hindsight be written off as desire taking control. Yet even now, when so much has happened to harden the hearts of all concerned, I still think gently of my going over to Gillian's side.

She took me up and led me about. I trotted along beside her, proud and content, with her arm in mine. Her clothes – always a little too tidy, too formal – her tendency to wear jewellery that might even have been genuine, her high heels – none of this I minded at all, still less the pronounced arch of her eyebrows, and the scarlet of her lips. Amid the jeans and sloppy jerseys, she was exotic. Even Richenda, in other respects her twin, had surrendered to jeans, but Gillian refused to follow her.

I went along with her to hunt for clothes. Her hand ran along the rail, plucking out something which might do, flattening the dress against her body, smiling at me with her head on one side, but not really asking for my opinion, more talking to herself, or almost talking to the dress or the skirt, regretfully deciding that it was too short or too straight or much too expensive, but now and then congratulating the garment in tones of delighted surprise – oh I *like* the collar – as though she had been warned against it. She did not in fact have more money to spend on clothes than any of her friends, but every now and then some old chum in the shop – they were soon all old chums – would let her have a skirt or a belt which ought to have been in the sale but had been missed out for some reason. And while these little rituals were being played out – you'll get the sack, no, you really ought to have it and so on – I would rock on a chair or crouch on a cushion scattered on the steps at the back of the shop and look on with the weary nonchalance of an old dandy gnawing his cane. Now and then the curtain protecting the dressing cubicle would be not quite fully drawn and I would be slipped a glimpse of some warm sliver of flesh, dusky peach behind the thick curtain. Or Gillian or a friend of hers would come out in stockinged feet to ask if the waist was not a little too low.

I noticed how comforted she was if she knew the name of the material or the technical word for the cut. The knowledge made up for not being sure how she wanted to look. The shadow of her mother hovered in the cubicle, cool, slender, no doubt smiling that quizzical smile.

'Oh my arms, they're like a coal-heaver's or a navvy's' – and these words also, so old-fashioned and borrowed from an earlier generation, added to her endearingness.

Her directness of speech was magical to me too, like the direct-ness of a fairy story. Coming from a family where everything was expressed obliquely, in guarded or euphemistic terms, I found her exclamations as seductive as musky scent. 'This bath is simply crawling with pubes,' she would say, and my heart would leap. And her unexpurgated thoughts were all the more entrancing as I came to see how stoic she was, how she had put up with being dragged about or neglected as a child and how uncomplainingly she would carry out some dreary task if she thought it had to be done.

There was a girl she knew who had been stricken with rheumatoid arthritis and although still mobile, for the disease was in its earliest stages, was clumsy with her hands and began to feel pain after quite mild exertion. Having got permission to paint her college room, she could not face the task and so Gillian did it for her. The girl and I sat drinking tea with the scent of the lavender in the college garden coming in through the high mullioned window, while Gillian in ragged Bermuda shorts moved her step-ladder round us. 'Oh I simply must shave my legs tonight,' she said, sitting on the step-ladder cradling a cup of tea. 'Wouldn't it be lovely to have slim hairless thighs, and not ever have the curse? Oh shit, I'll have to go over that bit again.'

She was the opposite of her mother who made being a woman such a mysterious thing. Perhaps she had set out to be the opposite, so that every time she said 'take cover, there's a monster fart coming' or 'my crutch is itching – do you think I've got crabs?' this was one more leap away from her mother's silken shadow. But for me Gillian's way carried an even greater erotic charge. In fact, when I thought of my first encounters with Peggy – on the beach and in the Gryphon Hotel – that elusive drawing-on now seemed staged and empty.

Gillian was elusive too, all the more so because she seemed so open. All that spring, she held out a kind of promise. 'When you come to Devon . . .' she would start. 'All will be revealed?' 'Don't be silly. No, you'll just see how different everything is.' 'Different from what?' 'You'll see when you come.' 'Is it all tremendously idyllic?' 'No, not idyllic, though I do love it. But it's more . . . interesting, really.' Even that delphic beckoning was enough to draw me on, since most of us did not think of where we came from as interesting, and it was a cool, low-key word for her to have used, an adjective which would have come more appropriately from Peggy.

She did not discourage the idea that there was some sort of secret to be uncovered, but what sort I could not make out. It seemed to have something to do with what she thought of me, with how far she wanted us to go in any sense, but then it seemed to have other connections.

'It's odd, isn't it, how none of your family had ever met Joe before.'

'Not really. If you'd been to Devon, you'd see. It's non-speaks all round. And then there's politics too.'

'Politics? What kind of politics?'

'All kinds – family politics, political politics. You'll see. You really are coming after the end of term, aren't you? Promise. It is rather bliss.'

She half-closed her eyes. A kind of prayer that I should come or an intimation of the rather-bliss? This slow dropping of the lids softened the way she talked, lent her a languor which her language denied. Devon, this drowsy red-earthed county, grew in my mind into a lotusland. The posters on the railway platform – the high-hedged red-earthed lanes, the whitewashed long houses and the swooping purple moorland – were invitations to romance. Their flat shadowless colours and simplified outlines were by then already dated, but they were also timeless, unchanging icons, shunning banal likeness to the actual lanes and villages. Ever since, when someone says he is going to Devon, I have a twitch of envy for my younger self and the all-consuming anticipation of those weeks.

Her father's house was a plain roughcast box, large-windowed with a bay window glaring out over the washy green valley. Ferns were growing out of the cracks in the plaster of the porch and out of the stone gutters draining the gravel drive which rose from the lane below and curved up and round the back of the house to end in a dripping yard. Under the lean-to shed, round the yard, old cars rusting, a few straw bales, wet logs piled in a corner. Dogs barking. At the back door was a large red-faced man drawing fiercely at a cigarette. He rushed forward to welcome me out of the station's taxi and tugged my luggage out of the boot with nervous haste.

'Sorry about condemning you to the fly. I'm afraid the fleet's all in dry dock here. Here, I'd better open that door for you. If you pull it too hard, the glass shatters. Now watch out for the hole in the carpet.'

He moved with light and brisk tread ahead of me, warning me of the approaching pitfalls or removing them from my path. These instructions multiplied as we went up the broad stairs – 'like an ice-rink, Mrs Yeo's pride and joy – if the water's a peaty colour, don't worry, that's according to regulations, but if it's actually rusty, please report to the management, or of course if it's freezing cold. We've got the boiler at full steam ahead in your honour, but it's an in-and-out runner at the best of times.' He put himself out for me with an almost frantic energy, allowing no gap in the conversation, as though I was sure to use even a fractional pause to make demands on him which he could not hope to satisfy. 'We've asked John Dudgeon over for dinner to entertain you,' he said, opening the door into the sitting-room. This news seemed intended as compensation for my inevitable disappointment, offered in the vain hope of warding off the tedium that must by now be suffocating me after at least five minutes in his company. 'Ah, Mrs Yeo has lit the fire,' he said, conveying both relief and amazement, perhaps even a hint of pride too at this extravagant display of hospitality.

His size – he must have been six foot four and sixteen stone – and restless loquacity made it difficult to know where to put myself or what to say if given a chance. I moved to the left of the high-backed sofa intending to admire the view from the bay window. He intercepted this harmless project from the other side of the sofa and waved his hand at the bookcase – no, waved is too airy and languid a word, he agitated his whole arm up and down fiercely like a railway signal gone wrong: 'Books, this house is full of books, plenty to read when it rains, has been known to rain in the West Country, you know, now and then.' I smiled encouragingly, but not enough to stop his face sagging as he repented of this sortie into irony. 'We get forty-five inches a year. Up on the moor they get sixty, more some years. My wife couldn't stand it, don't blame her. Couldn't stand me either but there you are. You have to be born in gum boots to survive here. Where on earth has Gillian got to – ah.'

The sigh of relief as his daughter came into the room was succeeded by wild panic at the sight of the towel turbanned round her hair and the dressing-gown she was wearing.

'My God, G, this isn't a Turkish bath.'

'I have been washing my hair, Colonel, in honour of ex-uncle John.'

'Ex-uncle John wouldn't notice if you came into dinner entirely bald.'

'Hullo,' she said to me, 'what bliss.' The word repeated now here, after sibilating in my head ever since she had made me promise to come, was itself a fulfilment. It was only two days since I had seen her, but the sight of her standing by the door in her jade-green turban was of someone long lost, long hoped for.

Her father snatched up a paisley shawl which had been draped over the back of the sofa and tied it round his head. 'Will this do?' he said.

'Oh Colonel, don't be stupid. Do you want Low to see the hole in the loose cover?'

'Who's Low?' I asked.

'Same as ex-uncle John. Elder brother of Joe's mum. Also known as Low to distinguish him from his father, High Dudgeon.'

'Why was he called High?'

'Every reason you can think of.' Gillian and her father broke into eager cross-talk – 'foul temper, really horrible temper, and bells and smells,' 'fantastically High Church,' 'crypto left-footer if you ask me, huge great fellow,' 'bigger than me, drank like a fish,' 'absolutely stupendously pissed, very popular in the county, don't ask me why,' 'fell down dead at the sheepdog trials,' 'no the horse show,' 'I promise you it was the sheepdog trials,' 'Low's quite a different kettle of fish, very different.' This recital filled them with gusto, flushed their cheeks. When they finished, they

147

had the satisfaction of a couple who have danced themselves to a standstill. There seemed to me some ancient and improper quality about this enthusiasm.

John Dudgeon was a skinny little man with a soft handshake and green teeth which he flashed in a snake's-tongue flicker of a smile. How nice it was, I said, to meet him after having recently met both his brother and sister, his brother just before his death.

'We are not at all alike. Do you think we are alike?'

'No, not at all.'

'I had not seen either of them for some time. We used to meet in court.'

'In court?'

'When we quarrelled about money. We were constantly engaged in litigation, after my father died. They were bitter, I think.'

'Ah.'

'We never shared the same interests. Down here I do not go in for social life. The organisation takes up my energies such as they are.'

'The organisation?'

'We shall not speak of it. The Colonel does not care for the subject. He thinks I am a bad influence, don't you, Alec?' He turned to our host, separating his words with the deference due to the slow-witted.

'Now, now, dear boy,' Gillian's father said.

'The English shy away from such things. They prefer to blur the issue. Muddling through, I believe it is called.' Snake's glitter in his eyes, hen's cackle on his spittle-traced lips. 'In my organisation . . .'

'John, the children don't want to hear about your toy soldiers.' Gillian's father, now incandescent with port, chuckled out the rebuke with hostly ease, his earlier frantic mien all swallowed up in *bonhomie*. His smoking jacket, deep rose like his face, had a slept-in comfort. Opposite him, John Dudgeon was as neat and dark-suited as an undertaker.

'Not in front of the children, no sex and politics. Mustn't bandy a woman's name in the mess.' The clichés were rattled out with mirthless scorn. 'What can you expect of a country where the ruling class are educated by pederasts? Ha. What percentage of your ushers were pederasts, would you say?'

'Oh I don't know,' I said. 'Sort of half and half, I should think.'

'Perhaps you yourself were – what is the conventional phrase for it? – interfered with.'

'No.'

'Unless of course you were doing the interfering.'

'I was not.'

'John, John,' Gillian's father said.

'Whenever I hear people saying John, John, I know I have gone too far. I have revealed that I am not an English gentleman. Have I gone too far?' He appealed to me.

'Yes.'

'You must forgive me. I am not a gentleman. Do you wish to know the hideous truth?' He leant across the table towards me cupping his thin hand to his thin lips. A faint aroma of wine and peppermint. 'My mother was Italian. I am a half-breed. I do not suffer from your conventional inhibitions in these matters. *In partibus infidelium* this is a distinct handicap. My dear friends in the organisation tend to be puritanical to a man. They recoil from the erotic arts. I despair of the county – with the exception of your mother, of course. You have met Gillian's mother?'

'Yes indeed.'

'Now there is a woman. One might almost say, with Sherlock Holmes, *the* woman. When I pass that little bolthole on the hill, Alec, I always think what a fool you were to let her go.'

'It was a long time ago,' the Colonel mumbled. 'Lot of water under the bridge. Gallons and gallons.'

'I remember it like yesterday. How bright and flushed with love she was. You remember that, dear boy?'

'I don't want to hear this, Uncle John,' Gillian said.

'Ah, but you must hear it,' John Dudgeon said. 'One must understand that one's parents are capable of love.'

'I was glad to let her have the cottage, very glad. Close enough to keep an eye on Gillian.'

'My brother Peter was not worthy of her. Behind that great bullfrog façade, he was a sexual faintheart. He did not deserve her, he was not up to her weight. I told him so. Ha, ha!' Something approaching a laugh shook his body. 'We never spoke a word since, not a single word.'

'I was cut up about the whole business. Of course I was, wouldn't deny it for a moment. But then it was all over, these things do blow over in the end, you know, and we haven't had a cross word since.'

'Shut up, shut up, shut up,' Gillian was out of the room, the slam of the door and the final scream almost coinciding.

'We have gone too far. Candid to a fault – that will be my epitaph. We must not talk of ex-wives, even if we can see their lights from the window. That cottage must be valuable, Alec.'

'I suppose it is worth quite a bit.'

'Thirty thousand, forty thousand, what would you say? Now that Peggy's got Shorewinds too she must be a woman of substance.'

'The cottage is on the mains now, you know.'

'Quite so, let us talk of drains and electric light. Anything to keep off sex and money and death.'

'Oh stow it, John.'

'You're not a Catholic?'

'No,' I said.

'You don't look like a Catholic. I can always tell. Two things I can always tell – the size of a chap's member and whether he's a Catholic. I'm never wrong. The other two lapsed, you know. Peter, poor little Pete, went in for that noble pagan rot, utter twaddle, you know, you could always see the altar boy's surplice peeping out from under that silly kaftan. And my dear sister sublimates her dry urges with those naked fakirs. Well, they aren't even naked nowadays, probably better if they were.'

The milk-white glass lampshade above the dining table began to swing drowsily to and fro, stirred by some uncovenanted draught. Pale mothlight fluttered across our heads. Dusky, religious light. The thought of a censer swinging, laden with peppermint fragrance. John Dudgeon at the altar, neat, quick-gesturing to the altar boys.

150

'Father Royle does not care for me. He thinks I am up to no good. He may be right. Do you think he is right? He would not let me advertise my little rally in his tin hut. Only authorised material is to be posted on the notice board in the vestibule' – hideous parody of keening Irish voice – 'Just a tin hut, I told him, that's all it is. *Vestibule.*'

'I think I'm – would it be all right, if I went upstairs,' I said.

The polish of the stairs shone even in the half-light. The shallow treads sloped downhill. A curious feeling of resistance, gentle yet firm, to my climbing them. Even the polishing, so unlikely in that dusty, murky ambience, was a kind of warning. My lurching brains set me adrift on the landing. I opened a door which looked like mine.

She stood in the middle of the high-ceilinged bedroom still but not startled. She might have been smiling before I opened the door and smiled more now only because I had confirmed her expectations.

'Sorry about being starkers,' she said.

'There's no need to apologise,' I said. Yet it did not seem odd that she had, or was it only the word she used that, in some obscure corner of my fuddled head, appeared to need explaining away? The white feet on the bare boards – but this is not my story, and I mention the incident only because it cannot be left out. Any touch of bitterness that may creep in later on needs to have its cause identified. This moment, so unrepeatable, so unarranged yet so ached for – well, such things are not the same in the retelling.

'Lovely navvy's arms,' I said.

'Do you often sleep with navvies?' she said.

'I don't often get the chance.'

'This is a chance.'

At a later stage, some dolphin apprehension surged and plummeted in and out of my sweet lassitude, too quick and slippery for me to catch. My brain seemed too embarrassed to name it to me, let alone to Gillian. Now and then the fear came close enough for me to touch the edge of it, then it dived down into the drowsy deeps and was lost again. Listening to Gillian's magnificent easy breathing, I became convinced that there was nothing to be frightened of, nothing that could not wait till morning anyway.

We should have awakened to the sun streaming in from across the valley, but this is not a story about things as they should be, and it was a dark blustery morning, blasting the blossom off the may. Only in the shelter of the high hedgerows down in the lanes streaked with red mud was there any escape from the wind and the rain. The Colonel had shooed us out. He was already trembling with fear of our boredom.

Just as we were putting on our boots, I pinned down the unidentified fear of the night before. I had slept without my asthma pillow. It was not the first time. Twice before, I had forgotten to take it away with me, once on purpose to avoid the shame of explaining it to a schoolfriend. Both forgettings had been punished by long and violent spasms. But this was the first time I had slept without it and not properly noticed until the morning after. This must, I thought, be love. Would it be punished too?

'I'll show you the Bolthole, Mum's cottage. There's nobody there now. They're still at Shorewinds. I wonder how she's getting on. She loves the beach, of course. But she doesn't like invalids.'

'Poor old Joe.'

'Do you think so? Or lucky old Prof? Come on, we'll do the loop.'

When I think of England, it is of that valley that I think. Not enchanted so much as embalmed, or perhaps merely playing possum, changing all the time while pretending to represent an unchanging dream. Stuttering steps down the steep curve into the village. Gates off their hinges, tied to the gatepost with orange string. Bracken and brambles in the corner of the fields. The gravel of the country road pricked my thin soles. The complicitous cow parsley fronds and the new shoots on the slashed hawthorn branches were in full fig now. On the bend beyond the hummocked bridge we stopped to look back at the little stream. Bright green cress-strands caught in the barbed wire which dipped into the water along the cow-hooved banks. The cluster of council houses curved along their lay-by. Two youths sprawled under their old Morrises, radio crackling out Slim Whitman's sad, twanging tremolo over the revving engines. Mothers leaning over the privet as the sun came out cast severe sidelong looks at the near-gentry crossing the road to church, clicking their white garden gates behind them. China figures on the window ledge, heavy pale-blue trusses of wistaria under the well-groomed thatch, Sunday papers left folded on the firestool. Vicar hurrying past, with his vestment case, a tardy conjuror. Salutations, mild, distant, awkward. The smell of sour beer outside the pub, then disinfectant as a woman slopped out a bucket with a cheerful fling of her bare arms. And Gillian passing through all this with a brisk manorial mien.

The road steep and overgrown again beyond the boarded-up Ebenezer chapel and the ramshackle sheds of a farmyard disused since amalgamation with a larger holding. I dreaded that she would ask me to enthuse about the village, but she said only: 'Not much of a place, is it? The Colonel only bought the farm ten years ago. It's the Dudgeons who are the squires and even that's only hobby farming, the Colonel says.'

'What's the secret about the place? You said there was a kind of secret.'

'Did I? Well, if there is, let's keep it a secret. You *are* unfit.'

I had tried not to notice the undertone to my breathing, the gravelly muttering as of some malign old man keeping time or an unfriendly gremlin jeering at me. Now what is he playing at – I imagined this wizened familiar wheezing as he tightened his grip on my bronchial tubes. Yet these early stages of an attack were not entirely unpleasant. They had a playful sparring side to them, even though the odds were stacked against winning. There was satisfaction to be taken in the wry fortitude with which one noticed the enemy forces massing: the damp house, the dust in the upholstery, the forgotten pillow, the dear, delicious stress – and its aftermath.

'Oh you're going to have an attack, aren't you? Let's go in and sit down in Mum's kitchen.' The look of panic in her eyes, the old tribute exacted by the asthmatic, was the more wonderful being bedewed with love, or so it seemed to me. There are delights which only spasmodic tubes can procure. Arm in arm, brushing away the overarching brambles with our free hands, we climbed the narrow track to the keeper's cottage. My lungs were now achieving the clank and rumble of a ship's boiler. We stopped by the back door and looked back across the valley to the Colonel's house while I caught my breath or tried to catch my breath catching itself.

'Last night . . . it was the first time . . .' I panted.

'Oh. I didn't realise . . .'

'No, no, the first time I slept without my asthma pillow.'

'Oh you shouldn't have.'

'Well, I couldn't exactly – '

'Of course you couldn't. You poor dear.'

She hugged my gasping body. The revelation seemed to make her love me more. I could not believe it. It was probably the happiest moment of my life, and I could scarcely breathe during it. At any rate, there on the little patch of lawn at the back of the cottage, the dew still on the grass, my peculiar ecstasy reached its high point. What followed was downhill a good deal of the way.

The noise from inside the cottage came to our ears as vague, confused: human voices certainly, but muddled up and uncertain. Then perhaps because they had come downstairs or into a nearer room, a man and a woman, the pitch raised, quarrelling or joking or calling to each other through a door. Although the voices were louder than normal, there was intimacy about their interchange or perhaps it was the loudness that showed how intimate they were, the lazy loudness of Sunday morning bickering. Peggy, yes, but it was Joe, not Scrannel.

We stood stock still. Gillian began brushing her thick black hair out of her eyes with a slow, awaking movement.

'We'd better not go in,' she said sadly.

'No,' I said, and we turned away.

We had not the heart to talk about it. I thought about saying 'poor old Joe' in an ironic way, but even that seemed likely to deepen her misery. It was the sheer unexpectedness of her mother's movements that kept on knocking her sideways. Peggy always managed to avoid the net and the chloroform jar. Never caught, never pinned down, she fluttered on past her daughter's head.

Walter Scrannel, we later learned, had been removed to a nursing home a week earlier. He had been too weak on his return from Shorewinds for his wife to look after him properly. But, she said, he was frighteningly alert and in high spirits. Every day she visited him, he gave her a sheaf of notes to be typed up.

Look, she said, holding out half-a-dozen pages of neat tiny handwriting. When I said how exciting, I'd love to read them, she put them into my hands with a kind of relief. 'Why don't you borrow them if you promise to drop them in on Phyllis tomorrow. You know where she lives.'

They were jottings, fragments, uncollected to this day. In my room, I made copies of them before handing them to Scrannel's secretary. I am not quite sure why, some fumbling act of communion, perhaps. It was these copies that I came across the other day at the bottom of a drawer. In fact, it was the discovery of them that provoked these recollections. The sight of my own handwriting, larger and wilder than it is now, moved me. My emotion was not, I think, just self-pity. If there was nostalgia in it, it was not for my youth but for those few glimpses of what I then thought greatness and still do.

Our foolish ancestors, one of Scrannel's jottings went, *used the same hurrah word for everything: the right answer, the right of free speech, right conduct, honesty and honour, legal and loyal all innocently confused. They thought accuracy could be moral as well as mathematical. But how terrible if goodness turned out to be a science, after all.*

The beauty of an impoverished vocabulary.

Other jottings were briefer. Sometimes I was proud of catching the reference and could see what he was driving at: *of that which we cannot speak, thereof we must never stop trying to speak. Silence is the great temptation.*

The ego and the id – what ready-made excuses. Oh that damned id again, I'm afraid the super-ego's on holiday till Monday and the place is in a shambles.

Sometimes, the musings arose from his situation. *How easily we forget our betrayals. How oddly arranged Dante's circles of hell seem to us now. But those we have betrayed have wonderful memories. The sense of guilt dies out, the desire for revenge is as strong as ever, what a lopsided world.*

Or: *I have never felt so weak, or so noble.*

If I had been a permanent invalid, how much more I would have loved my body. Now each cough and fart seems precious to me.

I do not regret the cigarettes. I only wish I could have smoked more of them in the time available.

Some of the other reflections, particularly in the bundles which Mrs Scrannel gave me later on (she was pleased that I enjoyed them so much and used to drop them in on me on her way back from the nursing home), seemed to me more peculiar or more pointless.

Sister is a stupid cow. Must smuggle these notes out if I go on writing such things. But would she bother to read them if she found them? No, patients are not agents.

Patch of sunlight on the wall. Bees buzzing. Childhood and death.

If only art did not have to be fresh, like fish. The vision of the new makes us unhappy.

Professor = confessor. Own up. But I am not a professor.

Posterity fades like a face the nearer you get to it.

For a few weeks that summer, I had the illusion that time had been made to stand still, that pleasure would be endless. Mrs Scrannel's visits – the hope in the forget-me-not eyes, the bundles of her husband's notes and cheerful anecdotes of life in the ward – hinted that even lung cancer could be made to wait. The honey-coloured stone glowed in the sun, the chill of the alleys and quadrangles was delicious, and bacon and eggs sizzled in the cafe and Gillian strode down the high street in her candy-pink summer frock waving her floppy bag as she saw me. It is not always true that we do not know when we are happy, and it was not true then.

Towards the end of term, Mrs Scrannel no longer called on me and I walked up to Furze Bank one afternoon. I could see her from the lane sitting on a bench in the garden with her head bowed in desolation. She told me her news quickly, without thinking twice whether I was the right person to receive it. Scrannel had told her about Peggy. Of course, the thought had crossed her mind, she was not half-witted. But Mrs Dudgeon had seemed such a kind woman and with her nursing experience it had all seemed so ideal. She had always wondered whether, if such a thing happened, she would prefer to know about it or not, and now she knew the answer was not. This was the end of everything. It was even worse than Fisha, different certainly but worse. In a way, she was almost relieved about having to leave the house. Professor Mudge had just written to inform her that since it was now medically confirmed that Dr Scrannel would be unable to resume his duties, the college was reluctantly obliged to ask her to leave Furze Bank by the autumn. The visiting Pinfold Lecturer – Professor Sharpstone from St Louis – had a wife and four children to accommodate. The college would be glad to offer her a sunny flat nearer the shops. All gone, she said, all gone.

The asthma attack I had started outside Peggy's cottage was the last I was to suffer in England for twenty years. For me at any rate the answer to the question that Joe had so annoyed Dr Maintenon-Smith with seemed to be ultimately, triumphantly yes. A month later, after a few more experimental nights without it and no ill effects, I gave my asthma pillow to a Humanist Association jumble sale.

VI The flight to Footprint

The postcard has now been lost. At any rate I cannot lay my hands on it. For years I kept it as a bookmark in Black's Medical Dictionary. The message on it comes to mind, though, with some exactitude: Here we are where it all began, come and stay, love Joe and Peggy. And then the address, also in Peggy's neat, clerkly hand: The Palisades, Lake Drive, Footprint City. On the other side, a view of low, reddish hills against a cloudless sky. In the foreground, the imprint of a giant claw in the dry mud, about a yard across, and a couple looking at it, the man in shirtsleeves, the woman in an old-fashioned flowery summer dress. Even when impatiently thumbing through the dictionary to interpret some new ache or rash, I could not help pausing when I came upon the bookmark and recalling the magic of that empty landscape and my strange days in that bright air.

Their running off together shocked us all, except for Low Dudgeon, who cackled, 'Have you heard about the flight of the Unholy Family?' It seemed such a final disappearing act. The word irresponsible was used, more than once. Yet it was not quite clear who was being irresponsible. Gillian, who had the most cause for anguish, thought Joe was being unfair to her mother, who was beginning to be too old to live at such a pace. Her father, she said, blamed Peggy for destroying Joe's prospects. Everyone agreed that Joe should not have dropped out of university. We who had not dropped out said so too, but we said it mostly out of irritation at being made to feel so small and retarded. Our timid hopes of adventure had been outbid before we had even sorted our cards.

The stars came out in the desert sky as I crossed the state line. The state troopers in their broad-brimmed hats searched my car for liquor and colorado beetles. Before me, the road dipped and bobbed in the gentle dusk for miles and miles until it was lost in the black hills. The huge hired car sighed and swallowed the bumps and rolled with a lazy slurp as the camber changed. The sleepy-voiced preacher on the radio blessed us all, and the sad twang of country guitar welcomed us to the Slim Whitman Hour. How broad and easy and empty it all was compared to that narrow cluttered valley we had left behind. How right the dinosaurs had been to make for the open spaces.

Yet, sad too. So empty, so accidental the whole thing. As a principle, survival of the fittest had its own grim consolations. In that way, Darwin was the last hope of finding a purpose in life. But random selection, the casual mutation of a limited gene pool, where was the point in that? All those great Victorian purpose-hounds, with their prodigious industry, their great sweeping vistas, their ferocity in argument – not much of them left now. Marx and Freud gathering dust, *The Golden Bough* covered with lichen.

Lonesome. Only Slim Whitman could mew the word. Not a word for Europeans to use, but here at the beginning of the desert and the beginning of the night, what feeling other than self-pity, what other word was there? Here, as the shadows stole down the low red hills, there was no consoling angelus, no beckoning towers and classical arcades. The apparatus of settlement and civilisation was too thinly spread. Each town I had come to that long afternoon had filled me with relief but also with a fresh stab of melancholy at the thought of the miles of emptiness around it.

At the roadside, giant black and yellow signs, a little faded, showed dinosaur prints and the distance – fifty miles, forty miles, thirty. I imagined a dusty little place with a bar and a couple of gas stations, like the last one I had passed through in the flatter country beyond the state line. But Footprint was bigger. A sprawling town, huge black shapes roaring out of the western night: billboards, building sites, factory chimneys dwarfing the two old tourists' hotels with their balconies and wicker seats glowing under the veranda lights.

'The Palisades? You want old George Lake's trailer park just the other side of town. Drive straight on through. Can't miss it.'

'Are you sure that's the place?'

'That's the only Palisades I ever heard of in this town.'

I had imagined a rambling ranch house, with a white picket fence and in the distance the shining waters almost too bright to gaze on.

A mile out of town, I turned off at a sign to the Palisades lit by a single neon tube. The ruts jarred my tired limbs. The red dust stung my throat. The track took a sharp uphill bend. Even the soft American springing could not tolerate the pot-holes. Amid a glade of tall trees, the pale blobs of caravans nestled in the dark. As I turned the final corner, there was a view of the lights of Footprint City below, then the streaks of car lights on the road I had come. Then nothing, except the shimmer of the night sky beyond the low hills.

A family was sitting out on the steps of the first caravan, chuckling and jostling each other as I walked down the neat path past them.

'Hey, you looking for the English couple? It's the last one on the left. The big yellow one by the picket fence.' A lanky man in a sweatshirt directed me with a wave. As I thanked him, he made a peculiar nasal noise, a donkey's bray.

The trees ended at a sandy cliff. The caravans at the end of the line looked out over a wide canyon towards the western horizon. Peggy was sitting out on the step of their caravan with a cigarette glowing in her hand. She greeted me with the enthusiasm of the long marooned.

'Joe's not here, I'm afraid. He's working. At the Footprint Inn. You must have passed it. He's a kind of head waiter, except he's dressed in hunting pink, with a hard hat.'

'Why isn't he dressed as a dinosaur?'

'It's a classy joint – it's called the Huntsman Restaurant – although they do serve Bronto steaks. He loves it.'

'I don't see him as Nature's head waiter.'

'Don't you? He's awfully good at it. He's got no pride, you see. You wouldn't like the job at all.'

'Oh,' I said, 'you think I'm proud?' I could feel my cheeks flushing in the cool night air.

'Not like Pip in *Great Expectations*. But you do have – expectations.' This caressing, thoughtful way of talking was intoxicating after driving through three thousand miles of polite impersonalities.

'I didn't think you'd come,' she said. 'All this way.'

'Well, it is supposed to be a travelling fellowship. I'm meant to drive miles and miles. That's all I have to do, in fact.'

'A *travelling* fellowship,' she murmured. 'They pay you to be a gypsy. How nice.'

All at once, the broad philanthropic aims of the Foundation seemed to crumble into nothing. The understanding between peoples, the deepening of cultural links, the cementing of personal friendships – all those things in which the founder placed such hopes sounded quite implausible.

We sat on the step and she drew a shawl round her shoulders, and she told me how they had fetched up there. They had nearly died of thirst when their car broke down in New Mexico, then they had been arrested and had to spend a night in jail for a traffic violation because they had not got the money for the fine, the jailor had been sweet to her but Joe's cellmate had attempted to assault him when he was asleep – 'how odd the Americans are, they are either being unnervingly polite or trying to pull one's trousers down.' She herself had had trouble with Ed, the man with the donkey bray, who had tried to push her into the bushes every time she walked up the path, until Peggy had threatened to tell his wife. It was a long way from the terrible dinner party in Washington they had been to with this Senator whose hand reached up her skirt the moment they sat down. In a way, she and Joe did feel like pioneers, the further west they came, the rougher the going seemed and the poorer they were.

'Come inside and see our very own covered wagon. Let me fix you something to eat.'

Inside, there were bright curtains, red and gold and silver, glass vases holding artificial flowers hanging from the walls and a low table with a gilt frieze round the edge. The upholstery was draped with garish paisley shawls.

'You see, we're all gypsies here. I found the place in Footprint, where the cowboys buy their caravan stuff. So cosy. One must be cosy at the end of the world, don't you think? I love being at the end of the world. It's so definite. You don't have that awful feeling that there's something a bit further on which might be better. Would hamburgers and salad do you?'

I watched her cooking in the kitchenette, behind the drawn-back curtains, the steam rising in the little alcove, cool arms smeared with tomato sauce. Through the window, I could see the stars coming out over the hills.

'Do you like onions in the tomato sauce? You simply must have onions.'

'If I must.'

'That can't be Joe, it's too early.'

The tall man in the sweatshirt stumbled over the threshold and fell into the squashy paisley-covered armchair the other side of the table.

'Hi, I'm Ed. Sorry to intrude. You found it OK.'

'Yes. Hi.'

He was older than I had thought in the half-light outside his caravan. Long lines hatched at the corners of his mouth, wrinkles round his stary eyes, hollow-cheeked, grey bristle hair – the look of a cowboy who had spent too long away from people.

'Ed, you should knock, you know,' Peggy said, unlike her, some oblique role being played.

'Not with friends. With friends you don't knock, you come right in, unless it's a bathroom. Then you knock. In a bathroom, you sure as hell knock.' Glazed smile, not securely focused.

'In England, we lock the door.'

'She's a lovely lady, you know that? The loveliest lady in this park. You in love with her, what you say your name was?'

'Gus.'

'You in love with her, Gus? Because I'm in love with her I don't mind telling you.'

'Ed, you know what I said about telling Arlene.'

'You know what I said about telling Arlene.' The high, finicky imitation was startlingly like Peggy and effortlessly produced as if he was in possession of a small internal device that could mimic such affected English voices. 'Arlene knows I have an eye for a woman. She knows I fool around. You ain't telling her nothing she don't know already.' The white sweatshirt was grubby round the armpits. His long white arms hung over the sides of the chair. He exuded fatigue, but you could see he could go on talking all night. 'I had plenty of girls to choose from, back in Parkersburg, West Virginia. Plenty. I passed up dozens of opportunities.'

'Why did you pass them up?'

'Well, I was the bookish type. That may surprise you, Gus, but that was what brought us together, Peggy and me. I saw her carrying all those books down to the trailer and I offered to help out. And that was the bond between us. Books. I'd have had twice as many women if it wasn't for the books.'

'What kind of books did you . . .'

'All kinds,' he replied fiercely. 'Except religious. I am not a religious man. I went to a Baptist college and I bear the scars and stripes of it. I can't abide bigotry, that's the way I am. If I see a preacher coming my way, I'm off quicker than a jack rabbit down a hole.'

'But why did the books stop you from making all these conquests, Ed?'

'They contaminated my libido, Peggy. That's what they did.' He laughed, and she laughed back, caught up in this lazy-lidded skirmish. 'Contaminated it till it weren't no bigger than a cactus prickle.'

'Oh Ed, how sad.'

'So I came out West to harden my body. That's what I've been doing out here, reviving my organic energies. Hey, you ever read the works of Anthony Trollope?'

'One or two.'

'I've read all his books. What that guy didn't know about the clergy – their conspiring and finagling, their creeping and crawling. He really blew the whistle on these gentlemen. He ought to come out here and make an exposay of these creeping jesuses, these phoney radio reverends, really show them up.'

'I'm afraid it's a bit late for that, Ed.'

'You think I don't know he's dead? You think I'm just an ignorant cowpoke?'

'I thought you were a seed salesman.'

'You think I know fuck all about anything. Well, for your information, Miss Fancypants, Anthony Trollope died in December 1882 of a paralysing stroke, leaving no less than three novels unpublished or partly published, including *Mr Scarborough's Family*. You ever read *Mr Scarborough's Family*? It's one of my favourites.'

'Don't be so touchy.'

'I ain't touchy, but I ain't ignorant either.' His great donkey bray made the caravan tremble. He snuggled up to Peggy and put his long white arm round her. 'You know Gus, I just love conversation, all kinds of conversation, literary conversation, and carnal conversation, or intercourse, as you may prefer to call it. You can't beat good old intercourse American-style.'

'Oh, Ed, it's bedtime.'

'At last we understand each other.'

'No, Ed, time to go.'

'I'll say. Let's really go, baby.'

She wriggled out of his embrace, but he caught her again before she could get the other side of the table. They lost their tempers at the same moment. She tried to knee him in the groin, but only kneed the corner of the table. He was trapped in the narrow space between the table and the sofa and could not bring her closer to him. Fuming at arm's length, locked in his grip, Peggy was angry, a sight that was new to me.

This sight was so odd that I scarcely noticed the door open and Joe come in immaculate in red coat, cream breeches and shining riding boots. At the sight of him Ed let her go and dropped his arms to his side.

'What the hell do you think you're doing?'

I couldn't catch Ed's mumbled reply. In a trice, this magnificent apparition had reduced him to an idiot hulk.

'Just get out of here and don't come here again until I invite you back. Is that clear?'

Ed shambled out. Joe slammed the door behind him and threw his velvet hard hat on the table. Flushed with victory, hair tousled, he might have been an Irish huntsman after a day with some rough pack.

'The end of a perfect day. I've already had to chuck out three drunks from the restaurant, and two of them insisted on shouting tally-ho as they hit the sidewalk.'

I must have looked too sympathetic, for he added quickly: 'It's terrific fun, you know, I love every minute. They're a great bunch. You should see me dish up the Tyranno Salad – it's a kind of Waldorf Salad with crawfish, or crab claws if we can't get the crawfish. And of course the hours are ideal to fit in with my business. Peggy didn't tell you? I'm into property. I've got a prime site in Footprint. As soon as the new zoning law is through the State Senate, its value will multiply by ten. That's why I'm working my butt off now, to pay the interest on the bank loan till I cash in. My credit's Triple-A at the moment, because they think I'm a rich English rancher, but the moment they find I'm waiting table at the Footprint, they may call the loan. So the timing's all a bit hairy.'

'Isn't living here a bit . . .'

'Oh, I have a business address in Footprint, more of an accommodation address really. That's all right because my bank account's down in Madison, so I'm OK until someone from the bank fancies coming up here for a Bronto steak or something, which I don't think they will. It's wonderful here, you'll find you breathe brilliantly. You'll feel your lungs blowing as big as watermelons. I haven't had a wheeze in six months. The whole atmosphere is pure oxygen, and so clean. Wyoming champagne they call it. You'd probably like some wine. I really drink only Coke now because most people I deal

165

with are dry and it's best to go along with them. But Peggy likes a drop.'

'You make me sound like an old soak.'

'I'm afraid it's awfully boring for her sometimes up here.'

'Not at all,' Peggy said, 'there's never a dull moment. Sometimes she sits and thinks, sometimes she sits, and sometimes she listens to Ed talking about Trollope.'

'I'm sorry about Ed,' Joe said. 'When he's sober, I'm really going to have a talk with him.'

'Oh, I don't mind. I prefer him outdoors, though. He makes me feel like a girl on a dirty postcard. Was she chaste? Chased all over the caravan site.'

The cigarette smoke once more exhaled through those delicate nostrils, her eyes bright-mocking, self-mocking, head at a Modigliani angle – the whole tableau re-established. She watched Joe expand on his plans. This great mud-palace of projects piled one on top of another amused her. She watched him like an adult watching a child on the beach, wincing only now and then at the mention of money. As his explanation branched and turned and doubled back on itself, the suspicion stole upon me that all this must have needed some cornerstone of cash to start with, and for that I could think of only one source. But with Joe nothing was allowed to stay in the dark for long. He could not abide twilight in practical matters, or so it seemed then. 'Of course,' he said, 'I could not have started the whole thing without the ten thousand dollars Peggy lent me.' He threw her a coltish glance of love. She shrugged and pursed her lips to dismiss the subject as trivial.

'That was the key,' Joe went on. 'Once I could show the bank a bit of collateral, they were quite happy to up the gearing and ease the repayment schedule.'

'Tally ho,' Peggy said.

'Oh.' He looked down at his cream breeches and gleaming boots. 'I'll change.'

'No, don't. You look sweet. Don't *change*.'

That soft, half-emphasised word came and went in my dreams. Tossing on the old mattress in the empty caravan next door, I had a black night peopled with words rather than images. Change lingered into changeling, belled into clang, then faded into clay. I do not hear of other people having these bleak, pictureless, verbal dreams. The words come up in flickering white letters on a black scratchy screen, captions on a silent film. Perhaps such dreams are too dull even for the most self-entranced dreamers to recount them.

The morning light woke me through the uncurtained window of the caravan. Outside, the air was clear and cold, the sun bright. Path through the trees behind the caravans. The sound of a shotgun once. Twice. In a clearing half a mile above the trailer park, I came upon Ed propping himself up on a fallen tree at the side of the loggers' track winding up the hill. Crack. Down came the squirrel from the high pine tree.

'You a hunting man, Gus?' He turned to me with a lazy grin.

'Not really.'

'I thought all Englishmen were. Trollope was a hunting man.'

'Well, he worked for the Post Office, but we aren't all postmen.'

'Hey that's neat. Arlene left last night, you know.'

'How do you mean left?'

'Walked out on me, with the kids.' He picked up the dead squirrel and stroked its fur.

'Oh dear.'

'Happened before. She's jealous of Peggy, of course.'

'She looked quite cheerful last night, sitting out on the steps.'

'Well, I had a load on, and that she cannot tolerate. To tell the truth, I think she minds the drinking more than the women. Lord, keep me sober and keep me chaste, but not yet amen.'

He lay on top of the tree trunk with his arms folded over his pump-action shotgun, the effigy of a fallen frontiersman, his baseball cap jammed down over his eyes, so the peak almost rimmed his grin. From under the cap, his sidelong glance homed in on me looking out over the glittering icing-pink hills and the white and grey-gold mountains beyond.

'Best goddam dinosaur country in the world, you know that?'

He said. 'Finest bronto prints any place, so wide and deep you could bathe a three-year-old kid in them.'

'Not very bright, were they, the brontos?'

'That's your mammal prejudice showing through. Don't you go badmouthing the big lizards. Those Triassic predators were one hell of a lot smarter than they got given credit for. How else would they have lasted so long, millions of years longer than *homo sap*. Only difference between them and us is they carried half their brains in their butts, well, maybe not so different from some ladies I could mention.'

'What are you going to do about Arlene?'

'Oh she'll go back home to Helena, Montana. We only come this far south in the sowing season.'

'So you have a permanent home up there?'

'What's permanent? That's marriage like it should be, you know – together, apart, together. Who needs routine? Arlene understands. She's frontier people. She's got the dirt of Montana between her toes. Peggy's the same. With dames I can always tell.'

He flicked the leather braces which held up his jeans and nimbly swung himself off the tree-trunk like one of the dancers in *Seven Brides for Seven Brothers*. He had shed about twenty years. In his red lumberjack shirt and his baseball cap, he looked wholesome. Even his stary eyes were sparkling.

'Come on up to the top of the mountain.'

The air was warming up as we scrambled up over the shale and pine needles with the sun full on us, turning the patches of sawdust to a dazzling white.

'You out of breath?'

'No, I'm fine. I'll just sit down for a bit,' I gasped. Far from expanding to the size of watermelons, my lungs felt as though they were being squeezed like old toothpaste tubes.

'Sounds like asthma to me.'

'Can't think why I've got it. I thought I was growing out of it. Joe said this place was brilliant for breathing.'

'Not this high up. The bronchi seize up at this altitude. Just sit down and breathe long and easy, not deep, just long.'

'You seem to know a lot about it.'

'I was an orderly on a respiratory ward once. Let me try something on you.'

He sat me down on a flat rock in the sun and pulled up my shirt. His long fingers interlocked across my diaphragm. They felt warm and supple, not cold and rigid like the fingers of Mrs Fretwell and the other therapists who had tried to teach me how to breathe. Ed seemed to draw the spasms out of me. My chest grew light and free, a bird-cage when the night-blanket is removed.

'That's terrific.'

'It's just a trick. You just sit here a while.'

I sat on the rock, panting gently, listening to the spasms weaken. He looked at me with his appraising look.

'You will grow out of it,' he said. 'I could always tell the ones who would grow out of it. When I was in the Navy – '

'You've been around quite a bit, Ed.'

'Oh I've done it all – cabin boy, piano-player in a cat-house, insurance salesman. Never could settle to anything. It'll look good on the back of my best-seller when I get around to writing it. This afternoon, I'll take you over to Long Pond and teach you how to catch fish.'

He seemed to have taken me on or over. I felt like a small boy in a Hemingway story. Any moment now, he would start telling me how to handle a woman or make a good fire. Yet my chest still fluttered its gratitude, and his company gave me a sense of freedom. There was an indifference to the passage of time about him which reminded me of my father, an indifference all the more seductive to the asthmatic whose panics were so unappeasably time-driven. I did not think of such people as necessarily being happy – my father was not and Ed's situation had its drawbacks – they simply possessed something which was beyond my reach.

Long Pond lay over the back of the mountain, at the bottom of a narrow valley surrounded by thick forest. Ed's beat-up orange station-wagon drew up alongside a little cabin made of green planks at the water's edge. The open sides of the cabin were covered in mosquito netting. Inside, the smell of creosote and the heat of the

afternoon made us drowsy. We seemed like insects in a homely
wooden trap, moving around the confined space in a heavy, listless
fashion.

Peggy sat down at a warped wooden table and began to play
patience with a pack of miniature Viennese cards. Her slender
fingers tickled the cards into place. Now and then, she paused to
look out over the heat-hazed lake. Ed and I stood on the rickety
jetty, casting out into the still water. Joe was crouched in the corner
of the hut with a beer. He was reading some best-seller about how
to succeed in business. The afternoon went slowly. The feeling of
isolation from the rest of the human race was oppressive.

Peggy rose and tapped Joe on the shoulder.

'We're going for a swim. Round the corner, we don't want to
shock Gus again.'

'What on earth do you mean?'

'You remember, at Uncle Pietro's.'

'I wasn't in the least – ' but they were off along the sandy path
into the bushes. Only the occasional fragmented cry skimmed
across the water to us, perhaps now and then a far-off splash.

No fish bit. Not a ripple on the lake. Ed became irritable when
I snagged the line in the rocks. All at once, fishing crossed the
dividing line, so narrow, so unsuspected, between play and work.
Its delicate rituals – tying and re-tying the flies, untangling the
cast – became unendurable tasks. Insect bites began to raise red
bumps on my arms, but not in the neat line of the allergy tests. Our
lines straightening on the pond, the fly sinking into the placid water,
all seemed to have no purpose in life except to keep us occupied.

The sound of a car bumping along the sandy track distracted
us from our boredom. It was some kind of official car, green
with a revolving light on the top. A grinning man in a brown
Stetson and brown uniform got out of the driver's seat and held
the rear door open. Peggy and Joe clambered out, looking dishev-
elled.

'Darlings, have you got any money to keep us out of jail?'

'Sorry about this, ma'am. Normally we just warn minor vio-
lators. But we've been told to crack down on indecency-related

offences in the National Park. And we've already had complaints about you and your . . . brother.'

Peggy laughed and shook her wet hair off her shoulders. She had not bothered to button up her shirt to the top. Joe was cross and tousled, his T-shirt sodden against his chest, water dripping down his sawn-off jeans.

'Come on, show me the article in the State lawbook which says – '

'Don't get sassy with me, friend.'

'I've got your number.'

'You're welcome to it.'

'Ease off, Joe.' Ed ambled forward, failing to grasp how much Joe relished such brushes with authority.

'Stay out of this, Ed.'

'I'm afraid they don't cotton to skinnydippers in this country.'

'Look, I'm talking to the officer.'

'Ain't nothing to talk about, friend. You just pay the fine and I'll go.'

'Pay the man, Joe.'

'You my lawyer or something?'

I looked out up the valley to where the dense trees began to thin out and only a few scrubby bushes clung to the steep grey-green slopes gashed by the earth-red slashes of landslides. The further peaks were a soft pinkish blue now, the haunts of bear and coyote, Ed had told me earlier when we had been happy fishing. Paradise corralled if not lost, even the lonesomeness a kind of cheat, an ambiguous comfort for the lack of something less easy to pin down, compensation for a basic disenchantment which might explain why Ed could take things so easy and be so desperate at the same time. Joe's capacity to get cross – whether he was in the right or not was neither here nor there – was ludicrously European. He kicked up a fuss because he was the sort of person who kicked up fusses. He did not really expect to be taken seriously. His protest was merely a sign of life. But to the park warden or patrolman, his behaviour was threatening.

Joe must be up to something, even if only to make the warden look stupid.

'Well, I'll leave you folks to harmonise your relationships,' the warden said as he smoothed the dollar bills into his folder. The dust settled as he drove away.

Peggy smiled, shrugged her shoulders, buttoned up her shirt. Joe patted Ed on the arm. Ed rubbed Joe's back in a reconciling frottage. The moment of ill-humour was to be exorcised, not dwelled on.

I did not leave until the next day, but it was that moment that I thought of as our last together. The amiable cook-out beside the caravans that night seemed like something in a brochure, not a real experience. The view of the lights of Footprint City below was so obviously a picture postcard. It was the four of us standing there in the reddish dust of the warden's car, Peggy and Joe still wet from their bathe, that I remembered a couple of months later as I drove across the Rockies and back down towards Footprint again.

The road twining back through the mountains came down into thick woods. On the left, the end of a long, curving lake. Sandy shore and pebbles. LONG POND the green National Park sign said, and underneath, a couplet from some poem, presumably by a local poet, something about my green native shore being dearer to me, by George Foster Brown, or some such name. I was driving too fast to take it in properly. Although it was so recently that we had been fishing and bathing at the other end of the lake, my earlier visit seemed to have happened years ago.

'I chose here because I still feel a bit embarrassed to go into the old Footprint Inn,' Joe said, as we sat down in the lobby of the other hotel.

'I'm sure you needn't. In this country, they like people who make good.'

'Yes, but to see Sancho wearing my old red coat gives me a jolt all the same.'

At present, Joe was wearing a cream linen suit.

'You really do look like a million dollars.'

'Well, not quite as much as that. A coupla hundred thousand at most when we've cleared the legal expenses. They re-zoned the district two weeks ago and we sold a week later. It makes a start. We're going straight into mobile catering. Hi.' He waved at another man in a cream suit, crossing the hotel lobby. The man stopped, surprise and pleasure breaking over his rugged features. He came over and enmeshed Joe in a complex embrace.

'Gus, this is Marty, my partner. Marty, this is Gus, my old friend from college.'

Together they spread out their dream of high-quality fast food. 'Joe's Limeyburgers' would soon be a familiar sight at every rodeo, air display, cattle show, stock-car race meet, convention, Independence Day picnic, even commencement and graduation ceremonies. Quality would tell. The subtle blending of pickles and relishes would transform the basic materials. Later, these too would be varied – Cumberland sausages and fancy German breeds would offer a whole new range of options.

We lolled on the squashy cushions of the Dino Diner under the heads of the plaster diplodocuses which reared out of the walls and the skinny wings of the pterodactyls suspended from the ceiling. Marty's strong, hairy-backed hands expanded on a future to me no less fantastic than the past here commemorated. The pterodactyls swayed gently in the breeze of the electric fans. Their bronze-green heads seemed to nod a keen assent to Marty's plans. Their diving beaks, open and outstretched, looked eager for a slice of the action.

'I still worry whether Joe's Limeyburgers is really right. Shouldn't we try for a brand-of-distinction approach – the Oxford, the Shakespeare and so on.'

'No, no, they want it fancy, but not that fancy. Joe's Limeyburgers is swell. Let's get back to the tax-break strategy.'

Joe's hesitancy, his near-stutter had all gone. Not a figure nor a contract sub-clause eluded him as they plotted the financial details with a conspiratorial rapture. As we walked back in the summer dusk to the new home he was renting, Joe was skimming along.

The house had steps leading up to it, a white wooden porch and a spreading tree rustling in the night breeze. The house was dark, and the lower half of the big window next to the front door was smashed.

Joe switched the light on in the sitting-room. It had a bright, tasselled shade, part of the gypsy decor from the caravan. The chair had the gypsy shawls thrown over them, and I recognised the diamond-shaped cut-glass mirror over the fireplace too. Spread out in this large high room all these things looked tawdry, not warm and gay as they had in the caravan. Peggy was lying half-on, half-off the sofa. Her face was swollen and she was bleeding from the corner of her lip. That pleading, bruised victim's look, familiar from many films, was in real life so much more accusing, melting. The eyes so open, so helpless. Her first words I cannot recall exactly but were something like: 'Ed. He's gone, I threw a shoe, out there.'

Joe took her in his arms, laid her on the sofa and closed the window, gentle and quick as he was in response to calls for action. He went to the telephone and looked at her, and she told him not to telephone the police.

The sight of her hurt and weak covered me with a kind of shame. It was something that I ought not to have seen. This feeling of indecency was because of Peggy more than because of what had happened to her. With most people, I thought, it would have been different. In their humiliation, they would still have been recognisably themselves, but she was so reduced and changed. The relief of seeing something of her old self return when she was wrapped up in a dressing-gown and drinking a cup of tea had more than simple charity in it; it was a comfort to think that personality could not be so easily destroyed. She was badly knocked about, she would go to a doctor tomorrow, she would not go to the police. She did not know why she had annoyed Ed so particularly. He had made a pass, but that was not for the first time.

'Go and see him, Joe, just go and see him. Ask him why. No, don't say you'll kill him. Don't be silly. No, it's best if you don't go. Gus can go. You stay here.'

'Whatever you say, darling. Gus, would you?'

'Of course,' I said, thinking why on earth should I and wondering why we couldn't send for the police, but not daring to say so because I knew that would be crass.

'You know the way up to the old trailer park. He's still in the same old caravan.' He spoke as though directing me to some picturesque spot on his estate which I had visited years earlier. There was about him then – perhaps there always had been – a sensation of time speeded up, an expectation of impermanence.

'Just make sure he's all right.' Peggy was still pale and trembling, but the will had come back before the colour in her cheeks. As I turned to go, they clung together, she full-length on the sofa, he kneeling before her with his arms round her neck, like a doomed couple in an opera.

The best hope was that Ed would not be there. Even if he was still lurking in the bushes outside the rented house, Joe was far better equipped to deal with him. As I drove through the town, past the old men sitting out on their verandas, I heard myself mumbling out loud like a child, please let him not be there, please let him not be there.

The police sirens were audible from the main road. As I turned off up the track to Lake Drive, I could see the revolving lights through the trees. The caravan was surrounded by police cars, besieged. Its windows were smashed in, and there was a policeman with an automatic weapon standing by the steps.

'Shot himself. One hell of a mess. Blasted the caravan to pieces first. Pump action shotgun, like that fella in Arizona. Wife had taken a powder with the kids. He wasn't a permanent resident.' But they seemed to know about Peggy too, for as soon as they heard my English voice, they asked me to take them to her.

Peggy did not make a good impression on the police, deliberately not, I imagine.

'He said I was a pricktease,' she said. 'Well, I told him, nobody's ever called me that before.'

'Had he any reason to say that?'

'It's always so hard for one to say, isn't it? I mean, one never knows, does one?'

'Knows what, ma'am?'

'What kind of impression one's making.'

VII

Low Dudgeon goes recruiting –
Love cut short –
Broderia revisited

The lift at the Baltic Military Club was often out of order. It was a pity to be denied a ride in the delicate open oval cage. The wire scrolls and finials of this enchanted casket scarcely reached above shoulder height. On its upward journey it passed through strange central European realms. When the lift was not working, there was a darkling scramble up the heavy-banistered stairs to reach the next light-button. The low-watt bulb glimmered so briefly that the older Estonian and Polish couples would have little hope of making it. Their tired grumblings could be heard from the stairwell below, mingling with the smell of bortsch and cabbage soup to convey a general air of hope departed. As the little cage passed the second floor, sometimes the glass doors the far side of the hall would be open and you could see the long dining-room with its windsor chairs and warming-pans. Even if the glass doors were shut, you could also see a tall cadaverous man with sad blue eyes pacing the narrow space beyond them, a former Polish cavalry officer, now the Club's secretary. Sometimes he would be out in the hallway, walking up and down the black and white lino tiles with his hands clasped behind his back. As the lift rose past him, he would turn and smile and make a half-bow to the passengers. He seemed a long way off, perhaps because the light was so dim. It was hard to say whether he was waiting for some delivery or repair man, or whether this pacing was part of a perpetual tour of inspection, the commanding officer making sure that everything was in good order. Perhaps he simply needed the exercise. The pacing, these dimmed courtesies, conveyed a sharp and painful melancholy, which it was hard not to associate with the monotony of exile. On Tuesday nights, the chairs were cleared away and a lady in a flame-coloured satin frock played Chopin and there was dancing. That too was a sad sight to the lift passengers rising at a stately pace, like indoor balloonists, to the top floor and Keith Trull's apartment.

Up here, there was not a smidgeon of melancholy. Light, cool, airy, modern, white, spotless. Trull himself was carefully grubby. Above the decaying sneakers and the creased baggy chef's trousers billowed a faded canvas smock of sorts, but not the sailing or painting sort. Caught between the clean flat and the grubby owner, guests were vulnerable. Even the most retiring characters might feel that they were conspicuous for some reason or other – too conventionally dressed, too flashy, too bonhomous, too awkward. As they stood there just inside the room, it was precisely at the moment of maximum vulnerability that Trull would come forward with his pleasant, rolling gait, adjusting his dark glasses and his smile, to put them unanswerably at their ease.

Trull's success surprised me, I confess. This may just show how original he was. At that period, his gothic tales – your creepy stories, as Peter Dudgeon had called them – looked like remaining a minority taste. Now that a row of those electric blue and raw orange dust-jackets is to be found on almost every bookcase, their oddity has long become normal. For my own part, I never found the stories at all hypnotic. They were too contrived, the scene set too mechanically for my taste. As a rule, Trull would take only a couple of pages to describe the quiet suburban household, the golf-clubs in the hall, the woman returning from shopping or the man bringing the dog in from a walk in the park to stumble upon the Threat outside the back door or lurking in the morning post or lying on the unmade bed.

The Threat did not have to be crude or palpable. It might start as merely an unease, a dim awareness that something was wrong, a first presage that the Other had silently crept into their lives and would not be dislodged until it had exacted its Price.

It was easy enough to see how Trull had finessed his reputation as a master story-teller: the short sentences and short paragraphs, the simple characters, the use of large imprecise adjectives to suggest the unspeakable without risking bathos, the skilful timing of the coming-up-for-air scene in which the victim is allowed an hour's respite from the Horror. All that demanded mere talent. Where Trull's genius lay was in his subtle insistence that he *was* a genius but of the kind which only unpretentious readers could understand. He was too great for the highbrows. Because he was not afraid to entertain, they, poor fools, were liable to mistake him for a mere entertainer, a teller of tales, failing to understand that there was nothing mere about that high old calling. The interviews he gave, rarely and reluctantly, of course, were an integral part of his art. The dark glasses warned of the impenetrable depths, but the rude cherub's mouth smiled a welcome to them. When the interviewer would gently press him – 'that scene with the baby, wasn't that a bit too . . .' Trull would, with an equally gentle complicity, reply, 'oh, did you think so? Well, I *wondered* but then you read the newspapers and people do the most awful things, don't they?' He let on that under the leather jacket he was a cosy old body. He flattered not only the taste of his readers but their imaginations.

Although I did not much care for his books, I too was flattered and won by his attentions. It was a privilege to sit in his cool white flat overlooking the secret walled garden, to watch his adeptness in dealing with people. He inspired the sort of confidence an old-fashioned priest must have given, the feeling that there was someone bustling around the parish who was at ease with his neighbours while also being on familiar terms with the forces of darkness. In some devious way his stories may have been an answer to religious hunger.

I watched him mixing interesting drinks (he was one of the first people to revive cocktails, till then thought of as a ludicrously pre-war habit). There did seem something magical about his ease and knowingness. How effortful by comparison now looked the shortish life of Walter Scrannel who had died the previous spring. Because Scrannel had seemed so great to me, I was taken aback by the brief and niggardly notices of his death. Perhaps that was why I tended to think of him at odd moments such as this, here in Trull's flat where the air sang of success. My mind was still running on my memories of Scrannel when the other guests turned to welcome someone new with a brightening look on their faces.

'Look, here comes Joe. Haven't seen him for ages.'

'He's been in the States, making his fortune.'

'My dear, I thought his face was his fortune.'

Joe came into the room, buttoning his blazer with his stubby hands, like a member of the Kennedy family, which at that moment he looked not unlike, mop-haired, tanned and freckled. How had his teeth become so white? I remembered them as English yellow. And his skin had cleared up too.

Even his entry into the room seemed staged. He might have been waiting in the bathroom until his handlers gave him the nod. He passed through the little gathering – no more than ten of us – with the friendly fluster of one who would love to stay longer if only these people round him were not moving him on. Me he greeted like the floating voter who could make or break his chances. My prickly response only encouraged him to treat me in the role of the loveable old curmudgeon he had always known.

'How long have you been away?' I asked.

'Three years and three months to the day I dropped out.'

'I think of it more as taking off than dropping out.'

'Right. Going to the States like that meant I had to grow and grow fast.'

'I've heard it's terrific – the hot-dog business.'

'No, I meant grow as a person. Still the same old Gus. And anyway it's location catering now. Fifteen trailers so far and we're moving over the State line next month. Arizona here we come.'

'Do the Americans resent you doing so well?'

'No, they like it. I'm a curiosity. They don't have the British hang-ups about success. When I started selling Joe's Limeyburgers, they really enjoyed the joke.'

'So you're going back?'

'No, I've sold out, put some of the money in a prospecting

business, just for kicks. But I want to do something with this old country. And I wanted to see Peggy again of course. She stuck it for nearly a year, you know. Trull said she was coming tonight.'

And in she came a few minutes later, the same mild amusement on her face as in that bewitching encounter in The Gryphon. She leant, gasping in mock exhaustion, against the shoulder of a cadaverous man with sad blue eyes who had come in with her. It was the club secretary.

'Oh Trull, why does your poor little lift not work? The Count had to drag me up the last two floors. You know the dear Count. We met a million years ago, or was it two million?'

'The wheel of time whirls on but some people do not change.' He made a whirling gesture, followed by a bow, both gestures drenched in melancholy.

'How the gallantry brings it all back. The Count taught me the mazurka or was it the polonaise, when we were all *much* younger. Oh hi honey, how are y'all?'

'Fine, just fine, honey,' Joe said, 'C'mon, give Big Daddy a hug now.'

'Oh Big Daddy, big hug. Hominy grits 'n' French fries coming right up.'

This twitter continued as they embraced and then embraced again. The club secretary stood, a little stiffly, at their side. I thought of cool arms smeared with tomato sauce and onions and that low voice calling teasingly through the steam from the back of the trailer. Dust, low hills, blue sky, emptiness.

'You know that's the first time I've set eyes on her since we split, oh months ago,' he said after we had left the party. 'That was all fake that greeting. She made me promise that whenever we met again we should look pleased to see each other. She could not bear to be cut, she said. We were never the same together after the rape.'

'The . . .' I had heard perfectly well.

'He had her, you knew that, surely. It shouldn't make any difference, I know, but it did.'

'I don't think I – '

'It was worse for her to start with of course. She kept on saying to me, are you sure you don't mind and stuff, and I said of course I didn't. But then after a bit it got to me too, the feeling of having been defiled, and I started getting the asthma again whenever – well you remember I told you.'

'Please, Joe.'

'Oh all right, I'm sorry. But I had to tell someone. I was bursting because I know people are saying that I got tired of her because of the age thing, and I didn't want to explain about what happened in the States because that would be horrible for her too, and as you're the only person who knows about that, well unless you've told anyone else and I'm sure you wouldn't have, I thought you could somehow explain to people.'

'Explain to which people?'

'Well, you know, Trull, for example.'

'I don't think I could explain anything to Trull. In any case, I should have thought it would be simpler to accept what people are naturally thinking.'

'No, but it's not the truth. I'm still desperate about her. I know I'll never meet anyone like her again ever. And I can't bear to think of it as being over because in a way it can't ever be over. You must be able to see that, surely. Look, can I come out to dinner with you? I don't know anyone else in London, except Peggy and she's going off with Trull and that Polish chap.'

'I'm meeting Gillian. Come along if you like.'

'Great. I'd love to see her again.'

'You didn't use to think so.'

'Well, in the States you learn to be much more open to people. You don't prejudge. They're not always negative like we are. They look for – '

'The best in people.'

'No, I thought you'd say that. They look for the positive. When they see an opening, they go for it, and they respect anyone who does the same. Have you ever read *Atlas Shrugged*?'

'No.'

'Or *Erickson of Idaho*?'

'No.'

'I'm not surprised. Nobody over here would read anything like them. Well, out West, everyone reads them – truckdrivers, housewives, company presidents. They are books about men who make things happen – a chap who drives a railroad through Indian country, or someone who gets a grain elevator built against overwhelming odds, real heroes of our time. They are the kind of books that give you the courage to go on when you're feeling like packing it in. There were some lonely times out there, especially after Peggy left, and I used to pick up these books in drug stores and airports and they gave me a kind of relief. Because the thing is, you have to image yourself as positive. You must think successful. Unless you have role models you begin to question your values, and that's fatal.'

He began to tell me the plot of *The Waters Parted*, the story of a penniless longshoreman with no formal education who designs the biggest dam in the world but is frustrated by a reactionary conspiracy.

'Upper-crust types, bankers, landowners, oh and a priest, a really creepy character. Quite often there's a bad guy who's a priest. I expect they're not very good books really but they've got something.'

He looked at me for encouragement. He was unanchored, on the loose. When we met Gillian at the restaurant later that evening, he locked her in a frantic embrace, as though claiming sanctuary. Being by himself seemed to make him panicky. He might have been a man on the run, trying to scrape acquaintance with a couple of strangers in the hope that the posse would stream past without noticing him.

Gillian was brilliant with him. When he stared at the menu with frantic unseeing eyes, she chose for him and asked him the right questions, about what he had been doing and what he found special about America, questions which nobody else would ask him. I felt like a dim and ancient husband, which I almost was, we were so settled down together since I had come back from America. In return, he asked after their shared relatives, joined in family jokes about members of the family he can scarcely have known, in view of the strained relations between his mother and her brothers.

'My mother hates America. She thinks it's too materialistic,' Joe said. 'That's why I like it. Materialism is the only religion for a man with his eyes open, that's what it said in *Rock Standish, Brain Surgeon*. Perhaps I'll give it to my mother for Christmas. She doesn't believe in Christmas, which will make it even better. She's such a bitch my mother. She doesn't like Peggy but – oh, I'm sorry, Gillian.'

'Carry on. It's not news to me.'

She laughed at the thought that there could be any family estrangement left to surprise her. Perhaps her gaiety, her courage in the face of such an indifferent world might have grated if she had not, quickly but without any kind of calculation, made it clear how little she expected from anyone. Or it may be that my own fondness for her has edited out the things about her that did grate on refined observers. It was not necessary to be choosy to find the voice, the laugh, the bright lips, the throwing back of the heavy raven hair all a little too much. By now, I loved it being too much, and the sound of her calling up the stairs and the unwithheld energy of her. And though she was noisy, she was so welcoming that she encouraged confidences. And her explosive responses – 'how rotten', '*too* awful' – were somehow more cheering than the soft and caring tone which confidantes usually cultivate.

'Well, she doesn't care for Peggy, and of course she thought the whole affair was terrible, but now it's over she blames me and won't speak to me.'

'Is it a feminist thing, about treating women badly, do you think?'

'I don't think so,' Joe said. 'I think it's more about sticking to something once you've started.'

'But being in love isn't like knitting a sweater,' she said. 'You don't have to finish it just because you've started.'

'Do you think so?' Joe gave her his grateful look. 'I never know what the Monkey thinks about things like that. She's a very uptight person.'

That no doubt was how many people would have seen her, but Mrs Follows had seemed to me unnervingly open. After all, the first evening we met she had described to me her entire philosophy of life, her discontent with married life, her detestation of conventional society. And her dislike of materialism did not sound all that different from the ethics of the books that Joe had described – the same impatience with inherited creed and the old junk of what called itself civilisation, the same longing to clear the terrain and get moving.

'I'm staying in Low Dudgeon's box room, you know.'

'All the rooms in that flat are box rooms. How affected of him to talk as if it was a stately home,' Gillian said.

'He wrote to me specially to invite me to stay when I got back. Which was decent seeing I've only met him twice.'

'Decent? That must be the first time anyone's ever called Low decent.'

'Well, I know his politics aren't everyone's cup of tea.'

'His politics are shit.'

Joe looked at her with admiration. And when he took us back to his box room at his uncle's, he threaded his arm in hers.

As we clattered up the steps to the top floor, a voice came through the half-open door on the landing – faint, querulous, somehow biblical: 'Joseph, come in and say hullo to my friends.'

Low Dudgeon sat in his wing chair by the fire in the little sitting-room, flames leaping high though it was June outside. Long fingers clasped the arms of the chair, sallow head pressed against chairback in a cardinal's death mask.

At first sight, a clubman's room, bachelor quarters of the old sort, Spy cartoons in thick wooden frames, spindly tables beside buttoned chairs, heavy maroon curtains. Yet something askew about it. The smell was stale enough but not of homely tobacco; it was devotional, oriental, also lavatorial – frankincense, myrrh? The chairs were shabby like chairs in a club, but they had a foreign look to them. And the coloured engravings on the wall were unsporting, literally: a cock with all its feathers torn off and a crowd of jeering, grinning punters looking down at it from the sides of the ring, a dog mangling some bleeding stump of an animal, a stag at bay on the edge of a pond, the water already turned raw red with its blood.

'I am too old to move. Nigello will get you all drinks. Ah, I see my near-niece bringing up the rear. I am afraid we are a rather masculine group this evening, my dear.'

A large pasty character of some twenty summers rose and began pouring us beers. He was wearing a tweed jacket and grubby cavalry twill trousers. A skinny youth with a crew cut, in a white T-shirt, as pallid as the other, was sitting upright on the edge of the matching wing chair the other side of the fireplace. His thin arms were folded across his chest.

'Gosh, a fire,' Gillian said. 'You are an unhealthy lot.'

'The draughts, my dear, the terrible Kensington draughts. We are not all as blooming as you. I am sure your young man will be glad of a fire. Nigello has been out all day, *distributing*.' He gave the word a saucy lilt, charging the activity with erotic significance. 'And poor Sprat too. Sprattie suffers terribly from asthma, don't you? Look at his pigeon chest.'

'My name's Spencer, Sprat's just what they call me.'

'I'm an asthmatic too, or used to be,' I said.

'Are you? It's the dust that gets me, that and animals. Any kind of animals, cats are the worst.' He had a soft country voice which I could not quite place. And his thin white face lit up when he smiled – one of those smiles which have a secret inward look, as though the smiler was unaware of anyone else in the room.

'This is not a doctor's surgery, Sprat. We are not interested in your symptoms. We simply like to have you around as an object of pity.'

'I don't mind being pitied, you know. Most people can't stand it, but I don't mind. Gets you a bit of attention.' When he smiled again, I did not like him quite so much.

'You may think that I have not yet attracted the flower of England's youth, but do not be misled by appearances. Nigel is a computer programmer, a public-school boy to boot, only an old Sedberghian but we can't be choosy. And Sprat is an industrial chemist. Between us we have quite a few technical possibilities at our disposal.'

'Uncle John is a qualified electrical engineer,' Joe explained to me. 'And he used to be a merchant banker too.'

'Your family pride brings tears to my old eyes,' his uncle chortled. 'Our financial expertise remains a little deficient, I am sorry to say, and I fear we cannot look for much help from the sons of David in these matters.'

'What do you mean?' Gillian said. But Low Dudgeon ignored her and turned to me.

'Now then, Gillian's young man,' he said, 'what would you guess we were discussing here tonight?'

'I've no idea,' I said.

'The application of new technology to membership recruitment. What could possibly be more innocent than that?' He trembled with glee. 'Nothing disreputable about it, is there? Not a whisper of sedition. Now then, Nigello, don't wolf down that beer so fast. We have work to do.'

'At this time of night?'

'The night is our best recruiting time, dear near-niece. In fact, we had better be off, I fear.' He rose to his feet. How neat he was – the suit, the dark tie, the polished shoes.

'Well, mind how you go.'

'I am in safe hands. The boys always drive. Sprat's a very careful driver, aren't you, Sprat?'

At the door he paused, his eyes suddenly alight with malice.

'And Gillian, my dear, how is your poor mother? Have you seen her much of late?'

'I saw her this evening,' Joe said.

'Oh *you* saw her, did you, Joseph? That must have been . . . complicated. Nigello, you look puzzled. We are, I am afraid, a complicated family. I doubt whether they taught you about such things at Sedbergh.'

'She seemed pretty well,' Joe said.

'*Pretty well.* That is good, that is excellent. To seem pretty well after all her ups and downs, that is quite an achievement. Give

her an ex-brother-in-law's love when next you see her, won't you?
I should so love to see her myself down in the West Country. No,
no, do stay. There's plenty more beer in the cupboard.'

'I wouldn't stay in this place if you paid me,' Gillian said after
he had gone.

'It's only temporary,' Joe said.

'I wouldn't stay here a minute.'

'I think, you know, he's lonely, really, Uncle John.'

'He deserves to be lonely.'

'You're a very definite person, aren't you, Gillian?'

'Am I?' she blushed.

'I could use someone like you in my business.'

'Oh I don't think I'd be any good at that sort of thing.'

He tried to persuade her that it would be her sort of thing.
She deflected the invitation in a light jokey way which irritated
him. There was to be no impiety. He could make jokes about his
ventures, but nobody else. It was an edgy fretful evening. The
room seemed airless, the airlessness of a change in the weather
coming.

'God, it's stuffy in here. I can't breathe,' Joe said.

'You are an old wheezer,' Gillian said. 'He's grown out of it.'

'Well, touch wood,' I said. 'I haven't had another go since the
one I had in Footprint when Ed gave me breathing lessons.'

'You lucky sod,' Joe said. He looked at me without affection.
Even our old bond, perhaps our only bond, had frayed. 'I'm still
a martyr. George still has to go everywhere with me.'

'George?' Gillian said.

'My asthma pillow. He's been with me for years. Actually, this is
George Two. The rubber perished on George One. Lugging him all
over the States was too much for him. He passed away in Omaha,
Nebraska.'

'Oh poor George, what a bore for you.' Sympathy flowed from
her in copious gouts. She turned towards Joe, leaning forward as
she swept her long dark hair out of her great dark eyes. I felt
stranded.

'Anyway, the flight plan is roughly like this.' He began to talk of his project, but not with the childish delight I would once have expected of him. Instead, he spoke in a jerky, almost distrait way, as though the details were being extracted from him under hypnosis. I was so mystified by this odd way of talking that I did not take in the gist of what he was saying. By contrast, Gillian sounded her normal practical self. Were the mailing lists targeted, she wanted to know? Did he know anything, but anything about jumpers and cardigans? Why on earth would any sensible woman want to buy from him and not Marks and Sparks?

Yet listening with only half an ear, I began to get the feeling that these were questions even I could have asked, and that there was something inward, incommunicable or at any rate not yet to be communicated about the scheme which she had not cottoned on to, indeed had not suspected the existence of. And as her questions redoubled into a frenzy of practicality, he seemed to divine this too, and his leprechaun smile melted his truculence.

'Oh we'll sort that out as we go along,' he said.

'Surely you ought to have it organised properly, in advance,' she said.

'Don't worry. It'll be fun. You can keep me in order.'

She shrugged off this overture.

'Where will you store the stuff?'

'Oh at home, in the stables.'

'But what about your parents? Won't they mind? I mean, who wants their home stuffed with cardigans?'

'No, it's all right. There will be room in the Big House. They've had staff trouble and a lot of the kids have gone.'

The thought of his parents' misfortune further perked him up. A kind of gaiety suffused him, an indifference to difficulty, what could only be described as a spirit of adventure.

It must have been a fortnight later that I took Gillian down to begin a summer stint working for Joe. The weather had broken, not that there was much to break. The springs of my Morris Minor yelped and splashed along the desolate track to the farmhouse. The barn was piled high with plastic packages faintly glimmering in tartan and heather patterns. In the lee of these woollen stacks,

Joe's father was crouched at a long table on trestles, slapping labels on packages which were passed to him by his wife. She passed them along the table with a violent motion and a little too quickly for him, so that he barely had time to wet the label with a brush and slap it on before the next one was jostling it. In the dusty half-light of the barn – not much improved by a hurricane lantern swinging from the rafters – his work seemed like a punishment inflicted as a result of some terrible miscarriage of justice. His little balding head nodded to and fro as he moved to slide the labelled parcel down a makeshift chute consisting of a barn door with a hurdle on each side of it. At the end of this device stood Joe tossing the parcels into the back of a Transit, utterly cheerful like one of those Dickensian urchins whose high spirits are undampened by the most foul and dismal surroundings. The scene in fact carried me back to those days when a whole family might be condemned to suffer together in the Fleet or the Marshalsea, still keeping up appearances, Joe's father still wearing his tweed suit and regimental tie, for example, but without any real hope of release, certainly with no definite end to their imprisonment in sight. The dimness of the light, though, lent Mr Follows's labours an almost poetic melancholy. The futile haste with which he tried to keep up with his wife reminded me more of Mr Manette muttering hopelessly to himself over his cobbler's tools.

The labels had a border of thistles and shamrocks with, in the middle, 'Pride of the Isles – Genuine Jerseys from the Genuine Knitwear Co.'

'Which isles do they come from?'

'The British Isles, of course,' Joe said. 'Bankrupt stock from Brod's knitwear business. You know he went belly-up. Made a cock of his cash flow and then quarrelled with Freddy Svoboda.'

His mother stopped work and, to my surprise, made signs of wanting to be introduced to Gillian. By now used to the loose-limbed nature of the Dudgeon family, I had not expected them to have met before, although Gillian's mother had once been married to Mrs Follows's brother. But I had expected the Monkey to keep up her brusque indifference to strangers, or possibly to the human race in general. I could not make out whether she greeted Gillian so warmly because she was a woman or because she was so unmistakably capable and brisk. Perhaps it was simply the prospect of a new pair of hands.

'Thank God you've come. Him can't stick on labels for toffee.'

'You do shove them at me, Monk.'

'Gillian's going to do the accounts,' Joe said.

'Well, thank heavens Himself won't be doing them. He's made a complete mess of the Big House accounts.'

'Oh Monkey,' Joe's father said, in a wistful way, not so much denying the accusation as regretting her bringing it up.

I looked across at that impassive building. On that thundery oppressive day, there were no children's faces at the window. According to Joe, there were even fewer children left there now, two or three at most. The staff trouble had blown up into something worse, but he was not sure what. There had been complaints about the manner in which the children had come to the Big House from their own strife-torn countries. Money had changed hands somewhere along the line. Nobody blamed Mrs Follows directly, her motives were obviously unimpeachable. But had she exercised the proper supervision? Had the paperwork been properly checked? The vagueness of the accusations made them all the more damning. The very name of the charity – the Big House Trust – which had sounded so friendly and secure, began to take on a sinister resonance. No doubt there were, if one knew where to look, professional jealousies at work. Mrs Follows had no qualifications, the staff were all amateurs too, and in any case was it really right to take children away from their parents in the first place? Were there not unpleasantly imperialistic overtones about the whole business? These susurrations, faint at first, began to take on a hostile coherence. And, Joe explained, his mother was no good with the press, too lordly. If he had been there, he could so easily have explained away the business of the mess on the stairs. The little Chinese girl had a tummy upset and Mrs Watkins had been late in to work.

Joe was probably right. Had he been in charge of the Big House, it would have been recognised as a fine humanitarian enterprise. All the same, as I walked round its great square bulk that cold windy summer's evening, I could not help shivering. Standing there unfenced under the bruised downland sky it was a place of secrets and of confinement. The sodden green corn grew right up to its back door and stretched away to the horizon. Yet the vista was suffocating rather than liberating. Although I had been here several times, I had still never been invited inside. Fragments of excuses had been offered on earlier visits; some new children had just arrived, new arrivals were always jumpy with too many strangers, it was best to leave them a day or two to settle down; the place was really too chaotic to be shown off at the moment, but perhaps next time . . .

But this time as we strolled into the lee of the barn, Mrs Follows came towards us out of the shadows.

'Here,' she held out two new sleeping bags, still in plastic wrappers. 'I've just had a brainwave.'

'I didn't know Joe was selling camping gear.'

'No, no,' she said, 'you're sleeping in there, in the Big House. You and Gillian.'

'Oh, I thought . . .'

'The staff's walked out and someone must keep an eye on Suna and Timmy. They're coming from Barnardo's in the morning.'

'What . . .'

'To collect them. Suna and Timmy are the last two.'

Her voice was brusque, not broken. The end of her dream seemed if anything to have made her more vibrating with energy and impatience. She brushed aside Gillian's condolences.

'Hopeless trying to start anything in a country like this. We're off to the Horn of Africa in the morning. At least the camps there won't make this ludicrous fuss about qualifications. Here are the keys. I must go and pack.' She clattered off up the stairs to the stable flat. The flounce of her fringe reproached us for holding her up.

The Big House was silent, and dark. The sound of our footsteps on the lino. The smell of old cooking in the passage. Grubby toys seen through an open door, a dusty black-board, a climbing-frame half-dismantled. Upstairs, the cooking smell gave way to the smell of old urine. In each of the draughty bedrooms, the walls were lined with two-tiered bunks, empty, stripped of bedclothes, the mattresses stained and lumpy. Between the bunks were hung a series of cheap prints of English paintings – The Hay Wain, Salisbury Cathedral, The Blue Boy. At the end of the passage, we heard the sound of a child sobbing. A tiny moon-faced girl in a dirty pink dressing-gown was sitting on the edge of the lower bunk comforting an even smaller brown boy. Night had fallen and a branch of the ash tree outside was knocking against the window pane. At the sight of us, the girl began to recite the alphabet and tried to make the boy join in, but he just stared at Gillian.

'Should I get some toys for them?' I whispered.

'No, it's all rubbish downstairs. We'll . . . have a pillow-fight instead.'

Gillian pulled all the mattresses off the bunks, tugging at them with the same angry impatience as Mrs Follows, then ran up and down the corridor collecting pillows which she then threw at me. The children stared at us for a minute or two, then, as she threw pillows more gently at them, began to return them. As we trampolined across the sea of mattresses, buffeted by the pillows sailing across the high-ceilinged room, we became light-hearted, free for a moment from the brooding impatience and discontent with which Joe's mother had saturated the place.

'Now now, what's all this then?' Joe's parody of an authority-figure, policeman or schoolmaster, was swallowed up by his irritation. The pillows we threw at him were returned perfunctorily. 'Must you really make the place a bigger pigsty than it is already?'

'Oh Joe, it's their last night.'

'Lucky little sods.'

'You are in a mood.'

'I've just heard that the Monkey's putting the whole place on the market.'

'Poor you, your home and everything, where will you go?'

'Oh I know where I'm going all right. The plans are well in hand. It's just infuriating when they never tell you what they're up to.'

'Well, do you ever tell anyone what you're up to?'

'That's quite different. I do have rights, you know. Shorewinds was bad enough, but this . . .'

'What do you mean?'

'They're putting all the money into this crackpot scheme in Africa. When you think what a mess they've made of this place. I'll sue the bitch. You just can't do that to a son, not in England. I'll sue her, and that silly old fool. I'll break them both. Look at this fucking place. Look at it.'

Timmy began to cry again.

'Don't you worry. You'll be out of this shithole soon enough. You're all right.'

'Cool it, Joe. Don't frighten them.'

'I'll frighten them if I fucking feel like it.'

Under the naked ceiling light, his hair seemed to flame. His broad sandy face shone with fury as he saw the money melting into the African wastes.

The children had become accustomed now to his shouting. He tousled Timmy's hair with his left hand while fiercely gesturing with his right. There seemed nothing contradictory about the two motions. We too watched him like people watching a natural phenomenon, a geyser or small volcano spouting. He neither moved us nor disgusted us.

After he had gone, we lay on mattresses on the floor in the room next to the children, Gilly and I. The moonlight through the uncurtained window caught a corner of Gainsborough's *Mrs Siddons*. We were too long for the child's mattresses and our bare feet picked up splinters from the floor. We whispered the awe we felt for Joe's rage at being denied his inheritance.

'Shameless, isn't he?'

'Quite shameless.'

The sour smell of the urine mingled with the sweet heavy fragrance of Gilly's scent. In the darkness, I imagined the full curve of her mouth smiling at the thought of Joe's shamelessness and I reached over to kiss her. The denial she whispered back to me was not to be questioned.

In the morning, we heard the knock of the Barnardo's people and took the children down with their battered brown cardboard suitcases which were supposed to look like leather. It felt like taking puppies to the vet to be put down. After the Barnardo's van had driven away, we gathered our own belongings and locked the front door behind us. Only then did I realise that we had not bothered to look round the Big House in daylight. And when I looked back at it from across the yard, it looked as secret and closed as though our night there had been a dream and I had never been inside it at all.

We had, for some reason now lost in the memory of those slippery days of love, developed a habit of talking in the clipped tones of forties war films. My part was to combine the concise elegance of Noel Coward with the manly reticence of Trevor Howard, hers to be pure, brave, catch-in-the-throat Celia Johnson. Going out, even for five minutes, to post a letter or buy cigarettes was to be treated as a devilish wrench of a parting.

'You won't be long, darling.'

'I'll be back soon.'

'Promise. Twenty Seniors, you won't forget.'

'I won't forget. Not ever.'

Meeting too, after being apart for half-an-hour or less, was to be played with the most intense repressed emotion.

'You're back.'

'I'm back.'

'I didn't expect you. Not so soon.'

'Are you pleased?'

'Oh. Yes. Very pleased.'

The surge of counterfeit feeling with which we charged these monosyllables began gradually, without our noticing, to become genuine. In our moments of fiercest affection, we took to talking in this way as well, and in our torpid aftermaths of pleasure too, in fact especially in these, for then the clipped exchanges were so in contrast with the lazy feeling in our limbs that they were as refreshing as a cold drink or a cigarette. It was in one such aftermath that I noted idly that the words in these dialogues were virtually interchangeable between the two partners. Their lack of masculine or feminine inflection may have come naturally to their author, but they achieved their strange vibrancy only in the mouths of heterosexuals. Was all this just a dramatic trick, a mere slick inversion of normality, a way of upsetting the audience's expectations? Or did it awaken some deeper echo? Did it stir that ancient dream, provoke some vague recollection of our pre-sexual past, of an Eden where we did not have to play at being male or female?

'Happy, darling.'

'Very happy.'

'John.'

'Yes, Diana.'

'Oh, John.'

Gillian was better at it than me. The part came more naturally to her. In some ways – her courage, her indifference to what other people thought of her, especially her indifference to being thought old-fashioned – she was a kind of throw-back.

A fortnight after she came back from Joe's, I had found her reading a letter. She put it away, quite slowly, in her handbag.

'You mean . . . there's someone else.'

'Oh dear John. Dearest.'

'You were always too good for me, Diana.'

'No, don't say it.'

'We said we'd be straight with each other.'

'I'm so utterly wretched.'

'Go to him. Please. You must.'

Having made certain calculations and looked back at old diaries, I know now that this was *the* letter. The scene we were playing was real, or at least would have been if I had not been so dense (but then the denseness was part of my part). It was a week or two more before the reality became clear even to my dim eyes, and then there were no John-and-Diana scenes, no noble repression of feeling and nobler renunciation. Instead, a snarling, white-faced dialogue lasting on and off for three days, sometimes conducted face to face, sometimes over the telephone, twice shouted through front doors, first her entry-phone, then through my letterbox, followed by two abusive notes, both by me, written on paper from a kitchen reminder pad which was all I could find at that minute, so that under the reposeful Hockneyesque chalk vignette of cabbages and carrots, the words written in the red felt-tipped pen (attached to the pad by an irritating bouncy red plastic coil) seemed all the more violent and deranged. I remember standing by the cooker, scribbling at shoulder height on the pad, which had been fixed to the wall, my arm aching, the blood drained from it but the rage and humiliation pumping away as though it would never run out. And somewhere in that effluent-choked stream ran a faint streak of satisfaction, fierce and black, at the totality of my anger with her.

But only with her. Joe was curiously immune. He was one of those special pieces on the board that could not be attacked in these circumstances, although at a different stage vulnerable to some quite low-ranking piece. It was not that I was under any illusions about who had started it. He was simply out of play, beyond or beneath blame, an object, a toy. Such indifference seems hard to credit in retrospect, but jealousy has an errancy which makes its target hard to predict. Maintenon-Smith: Stendhal analyses jealousy with the precision of a chemist in his laboratory. From my limited experience, if Stendhal had a chemistry set at all, it was one suitable for ten-year-olds only.

Then, as I was being wafted upward on an escalator at Holborn or possibly Tottenham Court Road, a peculiar fancy overcame me. What if – and no sooner had I thought of it than in the sweet disorientation of the moving staircase it seemed an iron certainty – what if she had moved on to Joe because he still had asthma and I had grown out of it? Put like that in bleak print, it sounds crazy. My state was certainly frantic, but then the imagination often gains a useful yard or two at frantic altitudes. The thing about Gillian, the undeniable thing, was and is that she is a carer.

She needs to look after her fellow creatures – ponies, hens (as will be seen later on), men. It may not be essential that the creature in question should need looking after, but it does help. Like any other talent, the nurturing gift has to be exercised, and I wasn't giving her enough roadwork. Since I had lost my asthma, I had lost my power to attract her love.

The explanation may seem eccentric, and self-deluding too. More obvious explanations are that Joe was more attractive, more dynamic, richer and generally had more of a future. But even in my chagrin, I did not despise Gillian enough to think her likely to be seduced by such qualities. In fact, I was so chagrined just because I worshipped her heroic determination to rise above material motives.

She would never desert an invalid lover. If only I had my asthma back, she would still be at my bedside. And so I began to pleasure my imagination by pretending that nothing had really happened. Gillian was still with me, still listening for the first uneven gravelly breathing, waiting to hand me the puffer, despite my false protests that I didn't care to be nannied, still reluctant to leave the room until my breathing was calm again.

Even on the train riding north through the dozy cornfields of September, I indulged the fancy that I was going to join her, instead of complaisantly going to stay with them (now that his parents' house was sold, Joe had acquired premises up there, I was told, but it was all still hush-hush). My eye was caught by a farmhouse in the dusky brick of the Midlands nestling at the edge of a rolling great wood, somewhere near Cannock Chase, and immediately I imagined spending the summer there with Gillian, bathing in the stream beyond the wood, watching the ashes feather under the breeze, and then shivering and beginning to wheeze a little as the evening dew came down and feeling her comforting arm around my neck. These blowsy daydreams are worth mentioning only because they recur long after they were irremediably shattered, proving yet again how stoutly the imagination can resist facts.

What else is asthma for but to teach you how not to let yourself be upset? But Gillian in her pink suit had swept into my life, unexpected, unasked for, a glorious social albatross. To fall in love with an albatross is embarrassing enough without adding the undignified antics of jealousy. She wrote to me. The puppyish bounce which had become so dear to me in the flesh did not translate well to the page. Narrators, especially narrators who are going to be betrayed half-way through the story, ought to fall in love with mysterious, unknowable women whose essence is eternally, tantalisingly withheld. Gillian was unknowable too, but only if you got to know her well enough. She wrote letters which were the literary equivalent of the pat on the cheek she used to give me when we met, followed by a pat on the bottom, both pats affectionate and appraising like a farmer greeting his prize pig:

How are you, Disgusting. What have you been doing apart from farting and scratching your balls? I have been reading the complete works of Proust and Kafka, and I am taking A-levels in nuclear physics and accountancy. Otherwise, there is not much happening here except for the fantastic snogging in the packing department. Next week, we are going on a works outing to Southport where we shall all get filthy drunk and lose our virtue.

Ciao. G.

Narrators who receive such letters should leave the stage as quickly as possible.

Joe's car was low, silvery and slithery as a salmon. A Merc, he said, with plenty of poke.

'Like the bus,' I said.

'What bus?'

'The bus we used to come down from Smithy's in.'

'Oh that. The car came with the firm. Much too grand, like everything else. Old Brod had such delusions. Thought he owned Courtaulds, not a clapped-out single-shed weaving mill and a dud knitwear business. He went totally ape at the end. That's what brought on the final coronary.'

'So you've . . .'

'I started by taking the stock, then the Official Receiver said why don't you take the whole shooting match off my hands, as a going concern, of course. The O.R.'s a great bloke.'

'So you . . .'

'You see before you a wicked mill-owner, complete with six-figure overdraft.'

He laughed. We drove down a long red-brick avenue. Side-streets with cobbles and gleaming front doorsteps flashed past. Through the milky, steamy haze, chimneys were to be seen. To my southern eyes, landscape still as mysterious as a coral atoll.

We swung off the main road, down a side-street. The car sighed and mumbled on the cobbles. On the street corner, four or five men in flat caps with thin, brick-red faces were standing in a huddle.

'Where are the whippets?'

'I had to let forty men go, half the workforce,' Joe said, putting on his serious face.

At the bottom of the hill, by the muddy stream, reared the great italianate castle with its battlemented tower. Half its windows were broken and stuffed with rags now. The railings round the car park were broken down and overgrown with hedge parsley and willow herb.

Inside the battered swing-doors, we turned right, into the board-room with its wooden panelling faded to an ashen hue. The old ashen-cheeked butler in his black coat stood by the table holding a tray of drinks.

'A dry sherry, Ayscough, and the same for my guest.'

'There are some chops today, sir. Would you care for chops?'

'No, thank you, we'll eat at home.'

'Very good, sir.'

'Miss Parkin has gone for the day, but she says to remind you Mr Ramsbottom wanted a word.'

'*Thank* you, Ayscough.' Joe became testy as this Lancastrian pantomime threatened to get out of hand. He had no gift for purposeless fantasy. I warmed to the thought of Brod weaving away in these alien dales, at first no doubt dedicating the whole enterprise as a work of gratitude to his adopted country and county but then coming to revel in it for its own sake.

'I thought we ought to have a drink here first.'

'I'd forgotten what an amazing place it was.'

'It's a shithole. Brod left it all in a terrible mess. We're only just starting. You'll have to come back in a year or two. But I didn't bring you here to see the mill. I thought we ought to have a talk first.'

'Ought we?'

'Don't you think we should?' He looked at me with genuine surprise. His distracted, peevish manner vanished in his astonishment, as though I had taken him out of himself by performing some remarkable circus trick.

'If you want to,' I said.

'Well,' he paused, not so much embarrassed, I think, as musing how best to put the matter to an emotionally defective person. 'Well,' he said. 'Gillian and I, we're together now, as you can see.'

'I can.'

'Yes,' then fearing from my blankness that I had failed to take in what he meant: 'For good, permanently.'

'Ah.'

'At first, we wondered whether it was an infatuation, just an infatuation, and so we decided not to say in case it was, and then the right moment for saying seemed to have passed.'

'I don't think I want to hear all this.'

'Anyway, when you said you'd like to come up here – '

'You invited me to come.'

'Of course we did. It was an open invitation, you know, to come any time. A standing invitation,' he said, as though this firmed it up further.

'Well, then, don't make it sound as if I imposed myself on you.'

'Good heavens, that's the last thing I meant. Only I just thought we ought to get everything out in the open. Don't you agree?'

He stood there cupping his glass of sherry between both hands, panting for approval. I put my glass down on the polished table and walked out. Behind me I heard the butler coming in to ask if Joe was quite sure about the chops. This gave me a twenty-yard start down the draughty passage. At the end, I could hear the whirr and clatter of the weaving sheds. From an office to the right, three or four girls came out for lunch. The dusty air was suddenly full of perfume. I blinked back the tears of humiliation and pretended to be bustling along towards the weaving sheds. Behind me, I heard Joe embroiled in personnel management. Good morning, Mrs Pickup, hullo Daphne, oh Miss Pilkington, excuse *me*, do you come here often? Now then, ladies, now then. His voice sounded homely and gravelly. I stood waiting for him to catch up, staring at the grubby beige walls, scarred and streaked by passing trolleys and buffed by the shoulders of generations of mill-hands. Then I saw Joe's plaintive expression, his hands outstretched to me, and I strode on, indignation revived, into the great low shed to bathe in its clacking roar and the soothing activity of the women in their white coats and perky paper caps. I leant on the iron guard railing, as suddenly contented as though I was watching boys fishing in a deserted canal.

'No, Mr Ramsbottom, I did not ask for Number Three to be shut down. I explained that we wanted to carry on stockbuilding with the lightweight knits until mid-September and I don't care what Pendleton thinks. Look, you know, Gillian's terribly keen to see you' – voice in my ears low and honeyed now, despite the remorseless clatter – 'I mean, you will come back to lunch, won't you. Yes, Mr Ramsbottom, will you just give me two minutes.' And then somehow another voice again for showing me the knitting machines in the next shed, friendly, but distant. I might have been a party of Japanese buyers.

It's a close, he said, as we turned into the little cul-de-sac, which ended in a turning circle girt with flowering cherries and concrete driveways. It's heated, he said, as he backed up his driveway. A heated driveway, I said. You mustn't mock, he said, it's a frost pocket, we all have them. Well, well, I murmured. It's a very convenient house, a machine for living, just like Le Corpusier. Le Corbusier. That's what I said, I don't do those things any more. I don't get words wrong any more.

Gillian opened the door as we walked up the concrete path. Is the path heated too? I asked, looking at her. No, he said. Why not? Surely it's just as dangerous if you skid as if the car does. It just isn't heated, he said, Oh Gilly, here we are.

It was not just imagination or rancour. She had changed in a way which I have since come to know well. It is often called settling down or coming to terms. She looked happy, though. Her greeting was the same brisk, awkward hug. But there was no patting of any cheek.

She was enveloped in thick wool, a purple and brown hooped jersey giving the general effect of a hung-over raccoon and a deep-pile viridian skirt. The sight of her in these soft furnishings was infinitely moving. I was nearly suffocated with self-pity.

'Not slaving down at the mill then?' I managed to say.

'No, I've, well, I've retired for a bit. Getting the house ready.' Desolation dragged me further down when we moved into the cold dining room. The meal was dim and frugal: ham salad with floury potatoes and place mats that slid about on the polished table. There was an ornate gilt mirror opposite Joe. The reflection of his face made up a glum quartet. Gilly stared down at her plate like a postulant nun fearful of upsetting her chances of admission to the order.

'It's like a bloody fridge in here,' Joe said.

'Joe really feels the cold up here. It's the damp that gets to him, I think. It's terribly bad for his breathing,' she said, bending down to turn on the electric fire. These words flung from her back view – the tautened viridian skirt, the raccoon hoops – filled me with irremediable sadness. Her concern answered my fancy as pat as the answer to a question in a quiz. By growing out of my asthma, I had lost her. I had thrown away my chances when I threw away my asthma pillow. She and Joe and George Two were now an inseparable threesome.

'Do you have any friends round here?'

'Friends?' Gillian said. I might have been asking about the possibility of tiger-shooting locally.

'We don't go out much.'

'Not really at all, at the moment anyway. But there's a nice couple the other side of the Close. They *look* nice anyway.'

'We've got to tread carefully, to start with. Because of – well, we said we'd say and we'd better get it over with – because of not being married. And so, you see, we're going to be.'

'Married? Because of the neighbours?'

'No, don't be dense. That's just what brought it up.'

'Because,' I said, light-headed now and semi-hysterical (I see I have not withdrawn from the story as quickly as I intended to), 'it's not exactly romantic to get married so you can go out to dinner with a couple the other side of the close who only *look* nice.'

'Now, you're being . . .'

'They may not be nice at all. They may be terrible, you may wish you had never got married at all. Even today, you can't get divorced on the grounds that the neighbours aren't as nice as you thought they were.'

'Please, don't be like that. All I meant was that living in a place like this, the sooner we actually get married, the better for all concerned.'

'So it is because of the neighbours.'

'Listen,' Gillian with a kind of intensity which was her way of being cross, 'we're getting married because we really, really want to. I mean we don't have to go into our reasons in front of you, it wouldn't be fair, but we have made up our minds.'

'I think,' Joe said leaning forward, 'we really have sorted this one out. It's simply a question of timing.'

On the sideboards there were two china poodles and a white plaster rabbit. The green velvety armchairs in the sitting-room had white fringed antimacassars on them, and there was a low coffee-table made out of alternating strips of blonde and chocolate-coloured wood. Under the window there was a fan-shaped metal rack with records in it. Opposite the fireplace, on top of a half-empty bookcase with sliding glass doors, an orange venetian-glass vase contained dried grasses and immortelles, arranged around a serpentine piece of driftwood. These everyday objects I mentally catalogued with a fierce and snobbish scorn on the homeward journey, trying to convince myself that I was well rid of such a humdrum couple. But the softness of her mouth as she had spoken of their reasons, the familiar static of the wool as we kissed goodbye, that faint smell of toffee which mysteriously clung to her – these could not be forgotten, still less cancelled out by a pair of china poodles. And Joe standing in shirtsleeves, tousle-headed, Kennedyesque on the doorstep of the executive home, as my taxi reversed round the turning-circle (I had insisted on not being driven by him), had finally stirred something close to loathing in me. It was hard to say why his marrying her should have made me transfer my anger from her to him. But there it was. Joe was now not to be forgiven, certainly not for years and, by a part of me, not ever.

VIII The wedding

Trull hitched up his baggy blue-check chef's trousers and hoisted himself into a lotus position on the beanbag. Even in the grey November noon, the north light of the studio shone clean and bright upon him. Stubble on his plump cheeks. He was as fresh as a new-split caterpillar. He was full of himself and full of others too. I could see he was in an imparting mood.

'You seem distracted,' he said, taking off his shades and looking at me through his mild round eyes. 'I am sorry Mrs Dudgeon is not here to entertain you.'

'Mrs – oh Peggy.'

'She has given me a taste for formality. Any moment I shall start talking about luncheon. We are keeping company, you know. Of course you didn't know. I would have been so disappointed if you had. I like my love life to surprise people. It makes it all so much more worthwhile. You seem shocked. Or perhaps you just don't believe me. Let me find the reference in my journal. I always keep a note of these things. It helps to fix them in my mind. Here we are. August 3rd was our first time together. It was one of those horrible muggy days which give the English summer such a bad name. It was a marvellous afternoon. Please don't bother to explain your position. I know *you*'re not in love with her. I am just trying to arouse your sexual envy because envy is a very, very healthy emotion and all of us here in the Trull Clinic for Nervous Diseases believe in flooding our patients with as much of it as we can, in order to flush out those awkward little repressions. We want to get you good and mad, because anger is the gateway to adequacy.'

'Is Peggy angry about Joe and Gillian?'

'Mrs Dudgeon is deeply concerned whether her daughter is as yet emotionally mature enough to manage a deep relationship with the young man whom we will refer to as J. She believes that J himself is not yet ready to make a permanent commitment and that he is in any case a shallow person who does not know how to give in a one-to-one relationship. Yes, she is furious, although all she actually says is, oh I do so hope they're all right.'

'She's going to the wedding?'

'Oh I expect she will play the part of the bride's mother in her own inimitable way.'

The last thing I wanted to do myself was to attend this maimed rite, but Joe rang me up that night, wheedling and kneading with a voice that had gone warm and relaxed like something left out in the sun too long.

'You just must. It's a question of being supportive. Gillian wouldn't feel right if you weren't there. She's so worried about Peggy and you're so good with her.'

'What do you mean, good?'

'Well, you make her, you know, more normal.'

I chewed on this dismal compliment.

Yet quite how I found myself stamping my feet on the marbleised steps of the registry office remains not a mystery but one of those small surrenders whose details the memory mercifully erases. The November damp crept along the corridor and up into my heart as I stood beside Mrs Peggy Dudgeon, whose only child was to be bestowed upon Joseph Dudgeon Follows, 4 Knowsley Close, Moreton-le-Willows, Lancashire. The address of that cheerless box of a house seemed further to estrange the whole occasion. The registrar read out the details in the hostile timbre of a clerk of the court. The said Joseph Dudgeon Follows responded to the questions put to him in the subdued manner appropriate to such proceedings. By some trick of the dusty neon striplights, the bride and groom looked small and old and doomed. At the end of it, the registrar seemed the most relieved of all, and his merry ovoid features went into social overdrive.

'And you,' he said, his face suffused with advance warnings of gallantry, 'must be the bride's sister.'

'I'm afraid not,' Peggy said. 'She's my daughter.'

'Well, I'd never have guessed it.'

'I don't see why you should expect to. We are not in the least alike.'

'You must be a very proud woman today.'

'If I must, I must.'

'So lovely,' the registrar muttered, before passing on.

'Didn't go off too badly, did it?' said Joe, warm and confidential at my elbow.

'Not too badly.'

'I shall do my best, you know. My very best, I promise.'

These fine intentions left me unmoved. I could see only the total self-giving devotion which Gillian so flagrantly had for him. She stood on the blue carpet of the hotel room waiting to receive the little clutch of wedding guests. In her full dress of some silky fabric, the colour hovering too close to being peach or salmon or both at once, she was voluptuously dedicated to marriage. The frill round the scooped neck and the tangle of net and flowers in the hair enhanced the general impression that she was being given away in the most traditional sense.

'Oh you are a goodster to come,' she said with a rib-cracking hug which took my breath away. 'You remember the Colonel.'

Her father, mountainous and red-faced as I did indeed remember, had also here a kind of distinction that had not come across on his home ground. To this away fixture, he brought with him more of the dignity of his age and class. When I had seen him walking down the street outside, I had failed to recognise him and merely classified him as a colonel type. Now that he spoke, he did not seem at all nervous or fussy. On the contrary, he was assured in much the way that so annoyed people who did not like colonels of that type.

'Well, this is quite a do, isn't it?'

'Yes it is.'

'Not at all what any of us expected.'

'No.'

'Least of all me. Could have knocked me down with a feather. With a feather,' he repeated, to drive home the metaphor.

'Yes, I expect so.'

'I must say I'm absolutely delighted, especially as it's really given me a chance to get to know Joe. Funny thing, I never really met him before, you know what those Dudgeons are like. But now – well, he's giving me all sorts of good advice, about the farm. You probably noticed the old place was getting a bit run-down. Barns and fences and so on all needed looking at. Well, Joe's put me in touch with a first-rate finance chap and we're doing the whole place up, just like that. The entire exercise should pay for itself inside three years. Manna from heaven. Absolute manna. If you've got the best security in the world, which is land, then why not make the most of it? The trouble with us old buffers is we just sit on our backsides and our backsides sit on the land, and we never exploit our assets.'

As the Colonel poured out these sentiments, a kind of frantic pleasure overwhelmed the poise which had so struck me a few minutes earlier so that he was now more recognisable as the agitated character I had originally met in Devon. As he spoke of exploiting his assets, he gave a kind of breathy chuckle. Beside us the wedding cameraman was already at work. The Colonel's watery eyes glistened under the hot lights.

'Mustn't spoil the ship for a ha'porth,' he said, throwing another chuckle at me. We were fellow entrepreneurs. He looked at his daughter with affection surcharged with gratitude. By importing Joe she had brought meaning to his life. Then his great ruddy head turned to his ex-wife.

'Peggy looks well, don't she,' he said. 'Very well indeed. All the better for not being married to me. Taken her fifteen years to recover from the shock. I say, they'll want a photograph of us together, won't they, with the bridal couple and all that. Do you think she'll mind? She's been so good so far.'

'She can't mind.'

'You don't know that one. She doesn't take kindly to company orders. Well, I'd better bite the bullet. Peggy my dear, you know they'll want us old wrecks in the snap.'

She stared at him in silence. She was wearing a grey wool coat and skirt, elegant and restful to the eye. Her stockings had a grey shimmer.

'Of course, if you really would prefer not . . .'

'Colonel, I have been to a wedding before. Our own, to name but one . . .'

'I just thought . . .'

'I should straighten your tie if I were you and don't try to look as if you're thinking.'

'Well, my dear, I can only say *you* look absolutely . . .'

'I know how I look.'

She walked across to the little group standing beside the flower arrangement and took up position behind her daughter and a little to one side. The grey wool coat and skirt were a reproachful shadow to the salmon-peach explosion of Gillian's dress.

'Oh Mum, do budge up,' the bride cried, having turned round to check on the shadow.

'Come on, Pegeen, close ranks.'

'Don't call me Pegeen,' the mother of the bride muttered as the shimmery grey stockings reluctantly edged closer to her ex-husband.

'Your parents didn't come?' I said to Joe, after the photographer was finished.

He looked at me in surprise. 'You really thought they'd be here? As it happens, they're in Somalia, up country somewhere, but even if they'd been living in the next street, I wouldn't have expected them to turn up. Listen, I wanted to consult you about something.'

'Consult?'

'Yes, let's go in here' – an empty small dining-room. We sat on little gold chairs, facing each other across a polished table in the half-darkness, a strange twilit conference. 'This probably isn't the best time to put you in the picture, but we see each other so rarely nowadays and there's nobody whose advice I'd value more, especially because you know all the players in the game, so I don't have to sketch in all the background and some of the background is, as you will appreciate, better than anybody, pretty complex. So when I say can this be in confidence, I don't really have to say it in fact, because you already are in on the confidence, so to speak.'

'Get on with it.' His face was ghostly white in the hotel gloaming. The air of a fatigued leprechaun crouching in the lee of a storm-battered hedge. Confused thoughts of pity and irritation.

'Well, just to give you the general context, we reckon the Mill has bottomed out. We're probably trading profitably at the seasonal peaks, but the balance sheet is still heavily burdened and the cash flow position is still, well, we're a bit strapped and so when Peggy – '

'Peggy?'

'You remember that money she lent me to get started over in the States?'

'Oh yes, the ten thousand.'

'Twenty thousand, in fact, because in the end we had to show our partners a stronger asset base, well, I won't go into it all. Only the point is, she wants it back.'

'Well, can't you pay her out of your American millions?'

'My assets over there are all fully committed. I'm into oil and gas,' he said, leaning forward. 'We've got a fantastic spread of drilling rights, right across the South-West. It's going to be the most amazing thing you ever saw. They're wonderful people, the Texans, you know. They really let you hang your hat in their hall, with no hard feelings at all. They are so incredibly open. If only we could get the same attitude in this country. Anyway, I just have to get in on this opportunity because I can only describe it to you in two words, un missable.' He smiled in a nostalgic sort of way at his own joke, seeming to salute in this ambiguous twilight a happier, simpler time which bred such wisecracks. 'But of course to keep your share of the action, you have to come up with your tranche right on time, and that involves a good deal of gearing.'

'Borrowing more money?'

'Yeah. So I'm pretty close to my credit limit over there too and

I really need to raise some cash over here and so I wondered if you had any thoughts which might help us to get a hold on the problem.'

'You mean, lend you the money?'

'Well, we could approach the problem from all sorts of angles. There is, of course, the straightforward loan possibility, as you suggest. That's certainly one to think about. But I'd also like to throw into the pot the thought of a share issue, on attractive terms, naturally. You could buy options on so many shares in the Mill when it comes to market, or if you preferred to be in at the retail end, we could put together a little company to take over the Genuine Knitwear Company, well, it isn't really a company at all at the moment, technically. That would certainly be another way we could approach the problem.'

'Don't keep talking about the problem. And what makes you think I want to approach it at all?'

'I'm sorry you don't want to discuss it in that way. I thought it might be more helpful to approach it in an impersonal, totally objective way, instead of treating it as a purely personal appeal. I thought you might appreciate me approaching it like that. You always say I'm so tactless.'

'Do I?'

'Twenty thousand may seem like a considerable commitment if you think of it as a straightforward loan, but if you see it as an equity investment, or a mixture of loan and equity if you insist, then it's part of an investment strategy, a medium-to-long-term strategy, which is much more solidly based.'

'You mean, you wouldn't pay it back for ages?'

'Participation would, of course, carry with it a seat on the board and all the other privileges, including further options to take up shares on terms which might be even more attractive. In the first instance, we'd be talking about rights to a possible ten per cent of the company.'

'You're mad. It's a huge sum, and I haven't got it.'

'Or conceivably fifteen per cent. The figures are pretty negotiable, providing we can seal the deal within, say, the next month.'

'I haven't got it, and if I had, I wouldn't lend it to you.'

'Look, this is my wedding day and you're my oldest friend, so I will give you my final terms straight without frigging around, because I know when people like you say they haven't got any money they say it because they're too polite to haggle. Twenty per cent of Genuine Knitwear Limited if you sign by the thirty-first.'

'But you said it wasn't a limited company.'

'It very soon can be if you come in with us.'

'I have not got the money. I haven't got *two* thousand.'

'You're destroying me, you know that? And destroying Gilly too, if that means anything to you. I don't blame you because it's the day we happen to be getting married. That's down to me because I was stupid enough to think you might think of it in terms of something to mark the occasion with. I should have realised that people like you would see that as being hopelessly sentimental. Well, all right then, let's go back to this fucking wedding then, what's left of it.'

In the reception room, the Colonel towered huge and rosy over the scattering of guests still left. By the agitated gestures he made in our direction, it seemed that he intended a speech. Peggy was stubbing out a cigarette between the chrysanthemums in the plaster urn and realised too late what was afoot.

'In welcoming you all to this marvellous do, and some of you I know have made quite a trek to get here, I'd just like to say that it's quite an occasion for us too, because as you may know, we aren't a very family-minded family. And one of the real pluses of this wonderful marriage is that it closes our ranks because it brings together all of us who have been kith or kin at one time or another in the dim distant past. So I think Peggy and I and old John back there and Monkey and Him – that's Joe's parents, alias Rhoda and Anthony Follows, who unfortunately can't be with us today although I know they'll be thinking of us in Somalia – we'd all like to say a very warm thank-you to Joe and Gillian for bringing us closer together. Now G, as we call her in the family, is quite a girl. Ever since I put her on her first pony I could see she had plenty of spirit and she knew how to kick too and so did the pony – that was Biscuit, G, remember? Well that was all a long time ago now but she's still got plenty of spirit and I knew it would take quite a young man to catch her. Fortunately, her mother knew just where to find one and I think we should all be everlastingly grateful to Peggy for introducing her to Joe who, as we all know, is a first-rate chap with a tremendous future ahead of him. He even thinks he can make my farm pay. Well, that's my definition of an optimist. I mentioned Peggy here, well, she's a wonderful girl. If every woman could be as good a friend to her husband as Peggy is to her ex-husband, well, the world would be a happier place. I know Peter would have agreed with me on that one, Peter Dudgeon, another dear absent friend, who would have given his eye-teeth to have lived to see this day.'

'Can't anyone stop him?' Peggy hissed in my ear.

'Now then, no whispering on parade, Pegeen. I'm not going to detain you any longer. I've banged on far too long as it is. I come from Devon, as some of you may know. Now Devon's a big county and it rains a lot, but it's also a very lovely part of the world, and if ever you're passing that way, don't forget to drop in on me and I'll rustle up a real Devon cream tea for you, or something a little stronger if you prefer it.'

The Colonel had lost himself in a vision of English rural life, of cucumber sandwiches on the lawn, and curry-combed ponies standing in the paddock, the cawing of rooks in disease-free elms, the sound of evensong bells in unamalgamated parishes. As he reluctantly drew to a close with a toast to the happy couple, he seemed conscious of returning to a less friendly world from which his oratory had secured him only a temporary exeat. Yet he seemed conscious too, if only dimly, of certain reverberations and did not really look surprised when Peggy said to him: 'That was the stupidest speech I have heard even you make.'

'Oh, yes, sorry, got a bit carried away. Bound to happen, I suppose. But I thought I ought to give G a bit of a send-off.'

'*Send off.*' Peggy glittered with rage, but spoke to him, if anything, even more quietly than she usually spoke, so that I caught only her first two words. Under the mouldering greenness of his tail-coat his great body was shaken by a palsied wobbling. His agitation got worse after Peggy turned away from him and walked off to the far end of the room, which was emptying fast. The little cluster of wedding guests were lapped in unease, as darkness filled the long windows and the lighting began to seem too low for the dusk. He did not watch her go but looked into the bottom of the glass from which he had lately drunk the toast to their daughter's happiness. This gloom, this agitation drew me to him, stirring in me a warmth which a more genial mien would not have. He immediately gripped my shoulder and mumbled, apparently now retreating into terminal aphasia: 'Could you possibly . . . do you know . . .' Jumping to the conclusion, I led him up the long sloping passage, soft salmon-peach-lit echoing the colour of his daughter's dress. 'Sorry, waterworks,' he mumbled, pausing in an alcove decorated with a dried-flower arrangement in another plaster urn.

The little puddle began to spread, dark and accusing on the salmon-peach carpet round the foot of the urn, derisive libation to the shrivelled immortelles. This frailty recalled another, more humiliating still, which Joe had reported to me after Gillian had been talking about her father. 'Such a hero, the Colonel was,' she had said. 'You wouldn't believe it, seeing the silly old coward now. Did something fantastically brave when he was awfully young in one of those absurd regiments on the North-West frontier – Foreskin's Horse or something – then fought all the way up from the toe of Italy to the top, carrying his sergeant on his back most of the time, and now the poor dear can't say boo to his cowman.'

Later, when she had gone, Joe told me that, according to Peggy, the Colonel had difficulties with that side of life, that's what she called it, she said it wasn't really his thing. As I stood sheltering this great green leaky mountain, trying not to think of the runnels tracing his infirmity back down to the reception room, I hoped that he would not tell me not to tell his ex-wife. But when he had finished, he only said in a matter-of-fact way, 'Always happens after a glass or two. Better go and tidy up, just at the end on the right, you say?'

Following him up the winding passage, I noticed for the first time his limp, or rather his rolling, toppling, lop-sided gait, which somehow confirmed his greatness. I felt like a cabin-boy following some old seadog who ought to have retired to his cliff-top cottage years ago but was stumping through one last engagement, racked by storm and shell.

We stood side by side at the basins in the gents. He was combing his hair. First, he wetted the comb under the tap, like a schoolboy. Then he slowly drew the comb through the iron-grey strands, tilting his whole body to one side as though to relieve some excruciating pressure applied by the comb. He froze in this attitude holding the comb six inches above his head, then, appeased by his reflection in the glass, lowered it with the care of a crane-driver manoeuvring an awkward load. His hair now lay so flat on his skull that it did nothing to relieve the great ruddy bluff of his head. As he blinked at me with his watery eyes, smiling at me for some reason, he seemed swollen and vegetable, like a Devon combe after a downpour. His light, almost reedy voice sounded quite unnatural coming out of such dropsical bulk.

In the mirror behind him, I saw the reflection of his reflection, and so on, an infinity of red-faced colonels standing before marble basins and staring into mahogany-framed mirrors.

'Ugly mug, isn't it? Better if they didn't keep mirrors in these places.' There was something coquettish about his manner which belied the no-nonsense manliness of the sentiments. He had this quality of referring to things that other men left unsaid as being too liable to provoke trouble or ambiguity. This readiness to stop and draw attention where the orthodox observer would have taken it as natural to pass on might, I suppose, once have been described as feminine, but that would give an impression which he did not give.

'You must come and see the farm,' he said. 'See all the improvements. I'd love to know what you think.' My opinion would, of course, be worthless since I knew nothing about farming, and yet the invitation was irresistible. That surprises me now. It ought to have sounded like a painful, even daunting revisiting. Yet already some of the magic of my first visit had transferred itself to the place and away from the never-to-be-recaptured Gillian. People with modest desires make such transfers quite easily. Perhaps in some mad way I was falling in love with the Colonel as a substitute for his daughter.

'I'll arrange it so you hit off Joe and Gillian,' he added in a flurry as he dried his hands, his old fear of boring his guests rearing up in his mind.

'Oh, no, no, don't worry. I'd love to come on my own any time.'

It was in the depth of winter that I came. Our boots crunched through thin ice in the cart-ruts as he showed me round. His red face glowed with pleasure as he pointed out each silvery new gate firmly anchored to its silvery new gatepost. He hailed the man on the digger which was carving long drainage trenches down the sedge-infested fields. The man was wearing ear-muffs and could not hear us. The colonel went up to his cabin, hopped up the step and shook him heartily by the hand. In the afternoon we stretched barbed wire between the split-new posts. My hands wet from the rain and slippery from the resinous wood found it hard to get a grip on the wire-stretcher.

'Too slack, too slack,' the Colonel cried, hammering the staples into the next post with some abandon.

On the way home, blue-fingered in the twilight drizzle, he pointed to the scaffolding on the cottage at the end of the lane and told me how ingeniously Joe had managed to extract a fifty per cent government grant for its repair. This enthusiasm was like that of an idealistic landowner in a Russian novel who, in his zeal to improve both his land and the life of his peasants, finds an uncovenanted happiness for himself. In Alec's case – this co-operative afternoon had led him to insist on Christian names – the happiness was twice as touching since it was also a kind of resurrection after years of hopelessness.

He led me into the long corrugated-iron shed which had replaced some of the tumbledown farm buildings I had seen before.

'They tell me it's the biggest milking parlour in this part of the county. I call it the mootel.' He proudly guided me through the draughty labyrinth of tubes and pipes and tanks, past the black and white cows in their stalls casting their reproachful yet resigned gazes at us, into the pasteurising room and the little office with its old wooden desk and square of green carpet covering only half the floor. There was a flurry of papers on the desk and a large cardboard box on the floor, stuffed with what looked like bills. 'The manager's office,' the Colonel said, 'GHQ, otherwise known as the bugger's muddle.' In his state of elation, these self-deprecatory asides sounded purely formal. 'Joe's always ticking me off for the chaos.'

'You said you'd show me your cellar.'

'Good heavens, yes, the cellar, action this day.' He jumped up from his chair, stricken with alacrity, and led me back into the house and down the passage, keys jangling in his tremulous hand. The worn carpet gave way to cracked lino, and the lino to damp, uneven stone. He unlocked the black door leading to a narrow wooden staircase, having flicked a light switch without any result. We stood in the darkness at the bottom of the steps while he fumbled to light a match. By the light of the match, I saw wooden cases of wine stacked on either side, five or six cases high.

'This,' he said in a churchy undertone, 'is the treasure house. Twelve thousand quid's worth of claret in those boxes. Will be worth forty or fifty thousand, at least, when we come to sell it. And I can drink free until the day I die.' These last words were delivered in the darkness again after the match had gone out. Far from evoking a convivial old age, this vault-echoing boast conjured up thoughts of decrepitude and mortality.

'You could put it on your tombstone,' I said.

'Put what on my tombstone?'

'He drank free until the day he died.'

'They wouldn't like that at all, couldn't get it past the parish council.' He did not care for this line of talk.

'First growths are on the left. *Cru bourgeois* on the right and across the end. We don't expect them to appreciate so much, but I'm told they are more reliable. The market is steadier. It's a serious investment, you know,' he said, as though detecting some faint snigger through the darkness. 'The chap from the shippers was quite satisfied. I'm sorry about the smell. Place hasn't been a cellar as such for ages.' And there was a smell of rotting, more animal than vegetable, quite unpleasant but coming and going, a smell of dead rats dangling in some far-off ventilation shaft.

'Later on, we may do a little bottling ourselves, just for fun.' He seemed to have forgotten that we were still in the dark. The vision of a *cave* fit for a *château*, with cellarmen in aprons drawing off immortal juices from great oak barrels had quite transported him. He seemed to breathe even more heavily than usual, like a medium going into trance. His mind was intoxicated by the slow and marvellous chemical transformations going on within those high-shouldered bottles lying in their white wooden cases stamped brown with legendary origins. Once or twice, while I was there, I thought I caught him muttering their titles to himself. 'Brane-Cantenac . . . Ducru-Beaucaillou . . . Léoville-Barton.' Words were in any case always near the surface with him, or rather the conveyor belt between brain and lips was so short that words found themselves tumbled out into the world half-dressed and often had to be hurriedly retrieved or, as with this muttered litany of clarets, were left aimlessly going round and round, unclaimed luggage on his mind's carousel.

It is hard now to recapture the swollen bloom of such times. The business world then seemed lit by a magical light, by a kind of dissolving shimmer which blurred the hard edges of experience and turned it into a limitless, formless fluidity in which anything might be possible.

Some time later, I forget how long, I saw Joe cross an airport lounge. The blood-sheen on his briefcase sent the sun scuttling back through the high windows of the check-in hall. He greeted me in that puppyish long-lost friendly way which first gladdened me, then made me feel he was doing it on stage at some award ceremony, then gladdened me again.

'Great to see you, Gus. Fantastic. We mustn't keep meeting like this. I need to see some real people for a change. Businesswise I have to mix with such a lot of shits. I'm just off to Newcastle to close out a deal.' This was the kind of worldweary sentiment which had once been foreign to him and I suspected still was but he now knew was expected of him.

'Newcastle?'

'Oh I'm strictly UK-based now. The British property market is where the growth potential is. You heard Jim Slater say keep buying till you reach the sea. Well, I like to say I'm doing the same, only I stop when I reach the ring road. And then I'm into holes too.'

'Holes?'

'Holes, toxic waste, for the disposal of. You lease them off dozy old landowners – old mineshafts, gravel pits, quarries, that sort of thing.'

'Oh I know, that's what the Prime Minister was mixed up in, wasn't it?'

'No, that was slagheaps, reclamation – a totally different ballgame and not much of an earner either, the costs are too high. Holes are the thing, holes not heaps.'

'You mean,' I said, enchanted by this vision of honeycombs dripping with gold, the idea of literally living off air, and dank polluted air at that, 'instead of making your pile – '

'What? Oh, yes. Is that my flight?'

'How's the Mill then?'

'The Mill?' He spoke with not unkindly surprise, as though being asked about an old friend who had faded out of his life. 'Oh it washes its face. We've had to trim back a bit, but it's still worth its place in the portfolio. Even there, there are one or two possibilities.'

'What sort of possibilities?'

'Extraordinary thing is,' he said, not listening, 'Do you remember our wedding and my little proposition? Funny to think I could ever have got so worked up about a sum like that – how much was it, ten, twenty, if that. Amazing the difference a few weeks, a few days even, can make.'

'So Peggy got her money back?'

'Plus I told the bank to pay her the exact interest – nine months and twenty-seven days or whatever it was. And I sent her some flowers. Gilly said it was a shit's trick sending flowers. Do you think it was a shit's trick?'

This effort to recapture his old uncertainties fell miles short of its target. Perhaps the target was not intended to be reached. To have slipped back into our old relationship would have been undignified, not befitting our present stations in life.

'How is Gillian?'

'Tremendously well. I mean, she has to rest up a lot, to try and keep the baby. She has this trouble. She'd love to see you. She's bored stiff in bed. The doctor says – ' he paused to listen to the loudspeaker call his flight. 'I'll get her to write you.' And he twinkled off across the shiny floor, his hair a chestnut mane now in the light from the high windows. As his success blossomed, he grew his hair longer, which, in those bubbling years, reassured his staider customers that they were dealing with a hero of his time, a man who would carry them along with him. Could he himself have put this into words, or was it some instinct which told him? Perhaps he simply went to a barber who knew.

The letter came with daunting promptness, inside a week, a demonstration of Joe's will in action all the more impressive since it was the kind of letter she could have written unprompted at any time.

'*Dear Goodster,*' she began, '*Long time no hear, you may be saying. Blame it on the pony, Biscuit Two, who rolls around in the mud in our mini-paddock and needs a full-time groom or two, and the ducks and the chickens. I run a small private zoo here and have no time left for humans, apart from the embarrassing little chap or chap-ess within who makes me feel so awfully queer most of the time. He/she/it has the manners of a warthog which it will no doubt turn out to be*' – but I must not quote too much, for the reader cannot be expected to share in that feeling of erotic electricity with which her letters were charged for me, precisely because they did not deal in the language of emotion nor tried to show herself in a romantic light, even with that devious casualness with which letter-writers through the ages speak of wandering for an hour or two in a park or of seeing again a film which had once been seen together with the receiver of the letter. Even flat phrases like 'it rained yesterday' can be used to build up the poignancy. Such letters left me cold, while 'fell arse over tip in the hen-run yesterday and thought I had lost the warthog' stirred the tenderest of memories. The hearty rejection of self-reverence brought to mind everything about her which had been dearest to me, her bare feet on the boards of her bedroom, the black hair flipping over her strong white shoulders, the sway of her body going away from me to the bathroom, the delirious strength of her embrace on her return, the suddenness of her desire. When I ventured, stupidly, to try to say something of this to her, though not as I have put it here, she maintained the purity of the recollection by telling me to piss off. These letters were a true reflection of the modesty and the privateness of her self, and, even when they seem facetious, particularly then, they reflect her seriousness and goodness. It would have been intolerable to have received a letter from her explaining why she had taken up with Joe, nor, I think, could she have borne to have written one, for there would have been no way of writing honestly without dramatising herself, and so she had not written until now. But this letter did as an explanation, did more than adequately, since it showed so artlessly the kind of life she was ready for and I was not, not least the sort of challenges to her capabilities which Joe could offer, well, offer would be putting it kindly, thrust upon her would be nearer the mark.

There were other sightings too at about this time. I use the language of the scientific student because I had begun to think of Joe as a phenomenon and myself as a privileged observer, the only man with a serious telescope in the right place to follow the meteor's path. It was annoying to be in this position, there was no satisfaction in it, to me nobody looked less like a meteor, but that was how the world insisted on seeing him, and my nature is an accommodating one.

A mazy spring day in the park: sweet wrappers skittering along the asphalt path, babies tumbling in and out of their buggies, stubby crocuses beginning to show in the sparse grass. Along

222

the path came two cyclists, their pace sedate, their handlebars upright. They were wearing matching tracksuits of grey slashed with maroon. What first caught my eye was the smart grey moulded plastic clipboards they had fixed to their handlebars, fixed high on a sort of music-stand, making them look like trick-cyclists who might be going to play the trombone while pedalling along. Instead, I saw the older of the two, a lean grey-haired man, lean forward to scribble something on the clipboard while the other gesticulated at him to emphasise the point he was making. It was the grey-haired one I recognised first. Even awheel, he had that self-effacing, elusive look I remembered from glimpses of him in the Brod era, just before he shut the door quietly behind him or disappeared at the end of a passage.

'Freddy,' I called, and Freddy Svoboda gave me a hunted smile. It was only then that I identified the chunkier figure as Joe. His truncated, incomplete body lost its peculiarity inside the impersonal shapelessness of the track-suit.

'Why did you say hullo to Freddy and not to me?'

'I didn't recognise you in your cycling kit.'

'We do a couple of circuits every day. It's a way of keeping fit and having a brainstorming session at the same time. You should try it some time. It's great for the lungs. I haven't had a bad go since we started.'

'What about when it rains?'

'Then we use our exercise bikes in the office gym. Freddy adores it, don't you Freddy?'

'It makes a change.' Freddy Svoboda sat on the bicycle, leaning slightly backwards in an attitude of graceful fatigue, eyes half-closed. Was he a prematurely exhausted man in his early fifties or amazingly fit and pushing seventy? How had he drifted into the role of aide to these Napoleonic charlatans? Perhaps something about his uncommitted languor attracted them, a lordly indifference which they affected to despise but really admired. Perhaps he was simply obedient and efficient. When I read in the papers of some new company Joe was forming or some takeover battle he was throwing himself into, there would sometimes be a reference to 'the vice-chairman of the company, Mr F.J. Svoboda' or 'Freddy Svoboda and the other leading members of the Follows war cabinet', but I never heard any other of Joe's associates mentioned by name and the way he treated Freddy left you in no doubt about Freddy's rating – that of a treasured manservant: 'Freddy got us the most wonderful seats for – ' I cannot now remember what the event was; it is equally hard to imagine Joe sitting through an opera as it is to think of him submitting to the disciplined longueurs of a race meeting or a tennis match.

'Freddy prefers it when it's raining, don't you Freddy? Because there are all these fantastic secretaries in leotards stretching in the most amazing attitudes. And they all go for Freddy naturally.'

'It's rather stuffy in the gym, as a matter of fact,' Freddy said.

This talk of gyms and secretaries suggested a large organisation. Was there now a Follows House with a commissionaire on the door? I made a note of the address Freddy gave me and watched them pedal off together, dodging the overhanging lilac bushes in unison. As they rose in the saddle to cope with the gentle uphill slope, I saw that their saddles too were maroon and grey.

The address was familiar. Jenny Wren Lane was a sombre twisting street of warehouses on the edge of the garment district, not far from where I had just started work in an outpost of my department which everyone had to pass through and did their best to pass out of as quickly as they could. Follows House (for such it was indeed called) turned out to be a giant warehouse almost on the corner, only a short step from civilisation but still stamped with the formidable gloom of Jenny Wren Lane. Still, the gilt lettering on the glass doors shone bright enough: THE FOLLOWS GROUP and behind it, yes, a snuffling, bottle-nosed commissionaire in uniform. Inside, the place was spacious; the desks set wide apart under the high vaulted ceilings; the naked brickwork now painted cheerful colours: primrose, pink and sky blue. Eye-taking pretty girls were wandering about sipping cups of coffee or sitting on their desks with their feet on swivel chairs laughing and chatting with young men in designer shirts and baggy trousers. The Group seemed to have a logo too, a maroon-and-grey FG intertwined with

IX
An inconvenient attack –
A peculiar arrangement –
An unfortunate accident

The mews was unfamiliar. It looked like the best way back from my meeting with the lawyers to clear up some business connected with my father's will, a document still providing modest employment although he had been dead several years now and he had left little behind him. It was an unexpectedly twisting street not far from Jenny Wren Lane, but brighter, less desolate, lined with dress shops, mostly with 'Trade Only' cards propped in their windows. Several were whitewashed, with window-sills and frames picked out in pink and sky-blue, and garnished with window-boxes. Any hint of a Mediterranean fishing village was blotted out by the great 1950s blocks towering above them.

Leaning awkwardly against one of the ground-floor window-boxes, his elbow burrowing into a cluster of French marigolds, was a familiar figure in one of those young executive's short overcoats which had the sleek-grey sheen of some aquatic mammal.

'Oh hullo,' I said. 'Are you all right?'

'God. You,' he gasped. 'Well, you at least can recognise an attack when you see one. My competitors would probably think I was having a coronary.' He fumbled in his pocket and brought out his slinky little aluminium puffer and snapped back the plastic cap. 'Cheers,' he panted, settling his leprechaun lips round the short nozzle. We stood on the mews cobbles, a glum duo, while his clutching, heaving breath slowed and lengthened.

'Wouldn't you like to sit down somewhere? You were like me, I think, sitting was always best.'

This recollection, harmless enough I thought, irritated him.

'It's quite different now,' he said. 'More stress-related. It comes at inconvenient moments. Like with Che.'

'Kay who?'

'Guevara. You must have read about him getting asthma up in the Sierra just before they were going to attack the President's Palace.'

'I didn't know you were modelling yourself on him. I thought Lord Beaverbrook was more your asthma type.'

'Of course, I don't agree with all his views, but Che is a key figure of our time. Like him, I find it's best if I keep on the move. I'm on my way to a meeting actually, at Barney B's. Some people in tubes, from the North. They want a little insurance, for a Middle East deal.'

'Who's Barney B?'

He looked at me, wheezing melodiously now, a whisper of surprise in his voice.

'BB – well, no, I suppose you wouldn't, he's a sort of secret legend in our game. He's an associate of mine now.' He paused, then took a larger breath, I thought it was only to coax his lungs into a different rhythm, and said: 'Come to think of it, why don't you come along too and sit in, you'd be a real ally and it might amuse you.'

'The only tubes I know about are the bronchial sort.'

'Oh don't worry about that, all sorts of odd bods come to meetings as observers. You'll enjoy seeing a slice of life in the real world.' He unleashed the beseeching puppyish look. The rest of my afternoon was free, but I would not have gone along with him, except that the head of our section had annoyed me only that morning by declaring that the Department needed more management know-how and this seemed a puckish way of acquiring some.

We walked back up the mews and into a small block on the corner, nondescript without being shabby. Among the names on the brown board in the tiny hall was The Genuine Knitwear Company.

In the modest office on the second floor, dim and tranquil as a country solicitor's, a neat bright little man was sitting chewing a boiled sweet. There was a glass jar of them on his desk. Apart from the jar, the desk was as clear as if he had moved in that morning. Sitting opposite him were two swarthy bespectacled men bulging out of their double-breasted blue suits with fretful expressions on their faces.

'What kept you, Joseph? Our friends are busy men. I don't think we've met, sir.'

To my horror, I heard Joe introduce me as 'from the Department'.

'From the Department? That is a comfort,' the little man said (he had a neat, perky way of talking, like someone cheering up the terminally ill).

'He's here purely as an observer, of course.'

'Of course, but it's a comfort, all the same.' The swarthy men too looked comforted. I began to feel decidedly the reverse.

'It's an important contract,' the little man went on, 'and I'm sure all parties would wish everything to go smoothly.'

'We just want to make sure we get paid,' one of the swarthy men said.

'I hadn't quite realised – ' I began.

'You don't need to worry, my dear sir. No worries at all. These are only preliminary discussions and your presence will of course not be recorded in the minutes.'

The next quarter of an hour was of unendurable agony. The little man did most of the talking; the tubes men took turns to make it clear that they were only interested in making sure they got paid. It was at least a relief that Joe's asthma attack had delayed him and most of the details had already been gone through. As we left, Joe clutched my arm. He was convulsed with delight and had begun to breathe heavily again.

'Brilliant. If you hadn't come, it would have been touch and go. They weren't quite sure whether we were big enough to handle that size of deal with all the international political angles, although with this particular cargo they couldn't afford to be too choosy. Anyway, the premiums will do wonders for our cash flow.'

'It's monstrous. You've used me.'

'Ah, come on. It won't cost you anything, nobody will ever know, well, there isn't anything to know, is there? Remember how you couldn't help me on my wedding day, well, now you have. You wouldn't believe how few people have actually got inside that office. I mean, people who've done a lot of business with him, really big deals, they've never been there in their lives. He's taken a shine to me, I suppose, because otherwise I can't see why on earth he would want to count me in on some of the things we're working on now.'

Why should Joe not be grateful? Yet it was not his way to express gratitude so openly. He needed to believe in his own magic powers to attract help. It was a sub-division of his divine invulnerability. The helper must be made to feel, in some small degree, privileged to be able to offer the leg up. The possibility that Joe might have stayed stuck at some lower level, stranded in mediocrity, was not to be thought of.

Our meeting with Barney B had been different. Joe had been rescued, that was obvious, but rescued in a makeshift way which might not last. And he was grateful for it, but also irritable as the rescued are. No doubt Barney had taken a shine to him, in the sort of way he might have been expected to take a shine, but normally Joe would not have mentioned such a thing.

'Now you watch your step, Joseph. Look after him for me, will you, sir? He needs a guardian angel, that one,' had been Barney's closing words after the tubes men had gone, and not words that Joe cared for. 'He fusses over me, you know. I suppose it's compensation for not having any children.' Part of Joe's stock in trade, for example, in endearing himself to Maintenon-Smith and later on to Brod, was to act the long-lost son who was more biddable and amiable than any real son might have been, but he did not usually risk destroying the illusion by talking about it. I began to feel that the services Barney had already rendered him must have been both embarrassing and urgently required and that, behind the slavish adulation, Joe was regretting that he had accepted them, whether or not he had had any choice.

The terms of trade seemed to have gone downhill for him, the delicacies of those earlier filial simulations here coarsened. Barney for his part seemed essentially untouched by him, amused by Joe only in the most superficial way.

Apart from the rage and embarrassment left by my own role in the meeting, I could not get the thought of Joe's dependence on Barney B. out of my head.

That is the explanation of my behaviour when Gillian rang me a few weeks later. An older, more worldly person might have acted differently and more deviously, and looked for help elsewhere, perhaps with better results.

Gillian's voice was so plain and clear that I did not recognise it. All drawl and gurgle had gone from it. She was in hospital and she had lost the baby, she said without preliminary. It had happened when she was on her own in their new flat, but the ambulance had been quite quick. It had been awful, it was one of the great awful things that could happen, she knew now, but in a way it might have been more awful if there had been someone there. She needed to get hold of Joe, he was in London too, for work, but she could not find him anywhere. She was so sorry to bother me, but she could not think of anyone else.

The sorry-to-bother-you was the most ordinary part of what she had to say. Yet they were also the most poignant of her words. Is it a miscarriage, I asked foolishly, as though making sure by using the word, while even at the time wondering why there was not a shorter one. Oh yes, I'm afraid it is, please find him if you can, she said.

Recalling these words which touched me so makes me reproach myself more sharply for what I did next. A sense of crisis should have made me cunning, but still I looked up Barney B's office in the telephone book.

'I haven't seen him since I had the pleasure of your company that afternoon.'

'Have you any idea where he might be? It really is urgent – a domestic emergency.'

'A domestic emergency.' He savoured the words, as though to

him they sounded exotic, perhaps even sacred. 'Well, I suppose, in those circumstances . . .' he paused, something so alien to his quick, perky way of talking that the pause had an almost legal solemnity. 'I suppose you could try Number 23 down the road here. Upstairs bell.'

'Do you have the telephone number?'

'No use phoning, I'm afraid. The phone's downstairs and they'll all have gone home downstairs.'

'You couldn't possibly go down yourself?'

Sharp intake of breath. 'I'm afraid I have an engagement, my dear sir, in fact, I'm late.' He paused, playing back these words to himself. 'No, I think it's better if you go.'

By the time I got there, the winding cobbled mews was dark and lit only by fake carriage lamps at niggardly intervals. Revisiting the street so soon, and at night, I felt I was walking on to a stage where the scenery was representing some period of my earlier life but crudely, lifelessly done by painters who had no real knowledge of the subject. I passed the spot, now in the shadows, where I had come upon Joe recovering from his asthma attack, and pressed on into unknown regions, round the bend in the street, where the lights gave out entirely. Number 23, a little showroom or workshop, was dead as such places are at night.

Bell, short-breathed, halting buzz. The silence of bells unanswered, then faint, distant scuffling scratching in the burrow. The tweak of an upstairs blind and a pale woman's face, a straggle of blonde hair across her brow, peered out through the smeary glass. The blind fell back and soon heavy footsteps coming downstairs promised a decisive response.

'What on earth are you doing here?' Joe said, rumpled, truculent, doing up his shirt-buttons.

'It's Gillian.'

'How the hell did she get the address?'

As I explained why and how I had come, a disagreeable pleasure overcame me, one of those warm, trickling oversweet feelings which are at the same time fierce in a tremulous sort of way. He was at my mercy, if only briefly, and the sweetest of the sweet revenge was in the predictability of his crumbling. He was instantly awash with emotion, three quarters of it self-pity no doubt, but near tears none the less, standing on the doorstep, barefoot. The shirt was one of those broad-striped shirts with a soft white collar which were just becoming a cliché.

The lights went on upstairs, and now I could see the painted sign above the upper windows which said in a sans-serif, lower-case type: onora designs.

'Shoes,' he said. 'I must put on some shoes,' and disappeared up the narrow stairs behind him without asking me in.

'What do they say? How is she?' The salmon-motor, gleaming silver even in the dark, was further down the mews. He threw his briefcase into its soft depths and pushed me in after it. The urgency of his will reasserted itself. His capacity to feel so instantly, the sureness of his misery, put him back on top. I had never envied him more.

Outside the hospital, there was a hamburger stand, a bower of light and warmth beside the grey, rainstained block of the maternity wing.

'She is all right, isn't she?' he beseeched.

'Fine, I think, fine.'

'It would be all right to have a hot dog first, before we go in, wouldn't it? I am starving, and it looks like being a long night. Or a hamburger? Would you prefer a hamburger?'

'No thank you.'

As he waited for his hamburger, he inspected the equipment with a professional's eye.

'You want to get one of these new ten-inch American deep pans, cuts costs by twenty per cent, more if you're doing good business.'

'What's it to do with you?'

'I'm in the business, my friend.'

'Well, you can fuck off out of it then.'

'My pleasure. And go easy on the ketchup, if you don't mind.'

As we walked into the hospital, this high, frantic manner changed direction.

'I always wanted to have children, you know. Always, even when I was a kid myself, to make up for my childhood, or my non-childhood. I thought Gilly would be such a brilliant mother. Don't you think so? Don't you think she'd be great, and now it's not going to happen. Thank you Sister, Ward Three, Third floor. I know she's only a staff nurse, but they all like to be called Sister. It'll be just terrible, not having kids. I mean, I know the doctor will say there's no reason why we shouldn't have lots, they always say that, but once you start having miscarriages, you go on having them.' He talked in a low confidential murmur but with force, so that the nurse escorting the old man in the dressing-gown up in the lift with us could not help catching scraps of what he was saying. 'There's something pathetic about childless couples, don't you think, absolutely pathetic. They join keep-fit clubs and go on huge long holidays with each other, but it's all pretty pointless really. I don't like pointless things. I mean, when you get down to it, that's the point of marriage, isn't it – kids.'

The lift-gates slid open with a clashing clunk.

'Would you mind vacating the lift as quickly as you can?' said a voice trying to hide its panic.

The stretcher rattled past us into the lift. Behind it one doctor in a dirty white coat was saying to another who was still struggling to get his white coat on: 'Come on, Terence. It's a quickie.'

At much the same moment we caught sight of Gillian's thick black hair and beautiful white skin almost eclipsed by the sheet over her. Lower down, the sheet was soaked in blood. Joe leaped back into the lift as the gates clunked shut and the two of them were carried back down again. I could just see him bending over her in front of the panicky porter before they all disappeared from view.

The night was crowded with thoughts of death, waking, half-waking and asleep, cemeteries awash with blood which turned out to be ketchup and then turned out to be blood again, gates clanging remorselessly shutting out all prospects of happiness, then opening again to show comfortable little scenes of ordinary life, some kind of competition at a village fête in progress, lads throwing gumboots, a cycling club breaking into single file in a narrow lane, some old women in a day-room eating their mid-day meal of plaice and chips. Although erotic visions of Gillian came and went in between these humdrum scenes, there was no sign of Joe in any of these sequences. The conscious and the semi-conscious had agreed to disbar him from night thoughts, on the grounds that they had had enough of him in real life.

Daybreak unleashed him.

'Well, I said it was going to be a long night. Five pints she had. Not bad for a beginner. Two legs and an armful, I said. Hancock, you remember?'

The revenants of returning day can be worse than the soft grey phantoms they have displaced. I waited till he said the doctors had told him she was going to be all right and then I said goodbye before the gynaecological details overwhelmed me.

But he had a nose for my fastidiousness, sniffed it out, toyed with it, left it as though bored and then came back to worry it again like a cat with a crippled bird.

'It's not the ovaries themselves, Gus,' he said. 'They turn out to have been perfectly healthy all along, after that scare about the cysts. They now think the trouble is an infection in the ducts or possibly one of the ducts and has spread to the other.'

'I don't want to hear it. I know it's awful for her, but I don't want to hear about it.'

'Gus, I need to talk about it, I need to talk to someone because Gillian doesn't like discussing her health. She really doesn't like to discuss it at all.'

But in the end, the complaint turned out to be something quite different, and worse. When the cancer was first diagnosed, I was, against my will, the first to know, not from Gillian herself, for she lay white and brave in her hospital bed and talked about friends and the news in the newspapers and the characters in the wards. Meanwhile, the distraught Joe rang me at almost all hours, not the small hours of the night which would have evoked the sympathy of extreme situations, but in the middle of the morning, as I was in the middle of a meeting.

'They think they can go in by a different route,' he would say. 'It would shorten the operation and mean a smaller scar. It's a question of equipment. We're getting Burrows-Knott over from Tommy's. He's been pioneering the technique.'

Sometimes he himself appeared to be calling from some office or boardroom – there would be background sounds of men burbling or typewriters whining. Once I thought I heard the sound of a club tickertape and clinking glasses as Joe was trying to explain the improvement in Gillian's blood count. I could not quite understand the motive behind this wish to keep me so closely in the medical picture. Was it because of the nature of Gillian's illness? Would he have been so relentless if the tumour had been somewhere else in her body? Had I been singled out for punishment or for some strange triangular communion?

'Look,' he said. 'I don't think you've quite got it. Let me show you.' He began drawing with a fine felt-tipped pen on the paper tablecloth. 'There are the fallopian tubes . . .' I remembered that square sandy fist drawing with his fine draughtsman's pen those gross cartoons of the staff at the sanatorium. Even here, with this rough medical diagram, his touch was light, his line fluent.

'What do you think of the place?' he said. 'Do you really get the feeling of a proper brasserie? I called it Shorewinds after Uncle Pete's house, Onora's designed the whole thing, including the menus. You notice everything's in lower case, because she hates capital letters.'

Through the whitewashed vault came the rumbling of a train overhead, menacing or comforting or both.

Glancing closer at the menu, I recognised in its illustrations of seaside scenes, which pursued without ever quite catching the blank hedonism of Dufy and Hockney, some familiar sights: the breakwaters and tank traps rearing out of the shingle, the lifebelt festooned with rope on the creeperclad façade of the Mariners Rest, the windblown thickets of tamarisk with the gables of Shorewinds peeping above them – precious settings for a kind of freedom I had not known (and still do not know) how to grasp. But the life had been so bleached out of them by Onora's primary-colours-only pencils, her limp hatching, her dull mind's-eye-view of what such scenes ought to look like that they were as remote as other people's holiday snaps.

'There, do you see, that's where you had that terrible asthma attack, just above where it says coquille St-Jacques. Oh damn. Billy, could you change this table-cloth?'

The white wine had stained and discoloured the dimpled paper cloth. Joe's drawing of his wife's ovaries instantly became an Old Master's fragment, an age-blotched page torn from one of Leonardo's anatomical notebooks, made poignant by its age and simplicity. Fresh table-cloth, another bottle of Shorewinds house wine, another train rattling overhead, and Joe began to talk about children, and the importance of heredity as opposed to inheritance. He must have children, but the children must have nothing from him. To me the question seemed out of date, a subject no longer worth arguing about, but to him, I could see, it went to the heart of things. If life was what you made of it, then it could not be made for you. Interfering with the instruments would give a false reading; the whole batch of results would be worthless. The competitors must start level, stripped down to their natural endowments. Then back to the ovaries again.

'In the end, you know, they had to take the whole lot out. So there's no hope at all. That's it. We've had it.'

'You could adopt, I suppose, later on, when she's better.'

'*Adopt.* You haven't been listening to what I was saying. You haven't listened at all. It has to be my child, has to be. That's the whole point. I don't settle for second-hand stuff. No, that was a joke. These rolls are stale, Billy, these rolls are stale.' His misery, greedy, attention-hungry gannet, began to eat up the restaurant as he started prowling the tables. Even the diners enjoying the far corners of these airy arches felt invaded and shrank from his attentions.

'What do you think of the sweetbreads? You were quite right to choose them. I always have them. And you had the sprigged ham. Not too salty, I hope. We used to have trouble with salty hams.' The cowed diners mewed their gratitude.

He was wearing a blue blazer, rather too bright a blue, with little dull-glowing buttons and a broad silk tie, of a rich canary hue, flared linen trousers in a gentler yellow. He tossed a salad for a couple of severe-suited women with a cheeky brio which they felt they had to respond to.

Lovely, they said, lovely, as though they had never seen a salad tossed before.

After lunch, we sauntered out into the street, a dusty meander in the lee of the great dusty brick viaduct. The smell of paint from the Cyprus Re-Spray and Valeting Centre next door. Cars parked any old how. Dull rust-proofed flanks. Wings with the headlamps removed or masked with tape waited for their glossy metallic coats. A frieze of green olive branches in grubby plastic was strung above the arch leading to the oily tenebrous depths of the workshop. Joe viewed this scene with disfavour. Bloody disgrace, he said, luckily their lease is coming up soon and they won't be able to afford to renew. He turned back to contemplate the plate-glass window of Shorewinds glinting in the westering sun. The potted plants in their haddonstone urns, the gay little green and white awning over the door, the gold lettering on the glass echoing the arch above it – all gave him visible satisfaction. Coming along, coming along, he said, turning to toss me a smile, which never quite reached its destination, because at that moment a burly shortish man in a heavy tweed suit thrust himself between us.

He had a cropped head like a bomb and looked tough as a truck. His tweed was of an anguished heather mixture. He was about five foot five inches of concentrated rage.

'So here you fucking are,' he said and swung a fist in the direction of Joe's chin, hitting him fractionally below the ear. Joe put up his hands and the man immediately lowered the bullet head and butted him in the stomach with great force, making the uppercut look more like a feint opening. But this exhausted the advantage of surprise, and Joe locked his arms round the bomb-head's chest and held him in a clinch until he himself had recovered his breath. Then he released his grip enough to give him room to knee bomb-head in the groin. That was the graceful part of the contest. Then, as in most real-life fights, it was mostly a matter of grabbing at elbows, tugging at jackets, wild swinging punches which pummelled the air or grazed the shoulder and desperate staggerings in search of balance. They careered through the parked cars before falling over a bonnet lid which was leaning against the arch waiting for a respray. The dust and the clanging and swearing suggested the clash of Roman shields against barbarian skulls. They picked themselves up and stood there panting and glaring at each other, purple in the face and chest heaving.

'I told her I'd get you, you fucking wanker.'

'I don't know what the fuck you think you're doing, you stupid little cunt.'

'You need teaching a lesson, you fancy ponce. You just keep away from her.'

They stood toe to toe, held back by invisible seconds, swapping their threadbare war-cries, more impressively gladiatorial now than when actually locked in combat. Joe went into a loud, chain-rattling preliminary wheeze. As this tightened into the familiar silent heavings of a major attack, he clutched his chest with a certain theatricality.

'Christ, he's having a heart attack,' – an impressed bystander. The crowd by now had reached a respectable size. There is no more alluring street sight than the spectacle of men in suits fighting.

'Wanker,' bomb-head muttered.

'He's sick.'

'Grown men . . . it's disgusting.'

'He's putting it on. There's nothing wrong with him. He's a wanker.' Joe's assailant was aggrieved at being cast as the heavy rather than the chevalier.

'It's . . . only . . . an . . . asthma . . . attack,' Joe gasped. 'I'll be all right . . . in a minute. You must run along now, Pod,' he jerked his head down the road, making the most of the suffering.

As the bomb-head man stood there irresolute, the afternoon sun shining on the silver bristles of his skull, a car door slammed on the other side of the road, and a blonde woman began to walk towards us with the deliberate walk of a police officer. She swept her long fair hair out of her eyes with that familiar slow gesture and greeted me with a warmth that was less familiar, before turning to the bomb-head man.

'Pod, you said you used to be a fighter. You're *rubbish*.'

'Well, he got me in among those cars.'

'I think you'd better get back to your dear little antique stall, because *I*'m not going to mind it for you and that woman says she's got to get back to Brighton.'

'I'm not staying here with these wankers, I'll tell you that. Give me the fucking keys.' He snatched them from her slender fingers and stumped across the road to a huge tail-finned car of some age. The engine awoke with an unsilenced roar, and he surged off into the teatime haze, bristle-head crouched over the wheel.

'Oh that, Pod Pease . . . a street trader. What he mostly trades on is being an East-End character. He seems to be a friend of Onora's.'

'You're not very good at being sarky, you know, dear,' Onora said. 'It doesn't suit you.'

'And you know what does suit me?'

'I haven't the faintest idea, and I can't say I really care. You've been to his poncy restaurant, then, have you?'

'Yes,' I said, 'and it – '

'Was absolutely delicious, wasn't it, and so nice to have the *patron* swanning around and asking you whether you enjoyed those soggy little pieces of toast with the fish paste on them and whether the cat's piss was quite dry enough for you and would you like a quick fuck in the manager's office?'

'Onora, please don't. I've got this attack and I'm still a bit winded.'

'Going for the sympathy vote, are we? Well, you'll have to try somewhere else. Ever thought of trying your wife for a change?'

Her pale face seemed unmoved by what she was saying, as though she had passed into regions of desolation which were impermeable to feeling. Her eyes and lips were so pale that what could have seemed a humorous cast of feature in someone else seemed in her to mean nothing at all. She might have belonged to a different species whose features we had no means of reading, leaving us quite unable to tell whether they were angry or happy or in pain. The little constellation of spots between the corner of her mouth and her chin, fainter now than when I had last seen her, seemed the most expressive, most human thing about her.

'Onora's been working like crazy on our new range of designs for the next show. We're going back into synthetics.'

'We're going back into synthetics. Aren't we lucky?'

'Look here, O, I've had quite a time.'

'Little man, you've had a busy day and now you're tired and want to go to bed. Well, you can make your own arrangements, that's all I can say.' This final phrase was spat out with a desperate sob and she turned away to hide her tears.

It was soon after this encounter outside the Cyprus Re-spray and Valeting Centre that the first signs of real trouble began for Joe. And although the trouble bore no relation to that dust-up underneath the railway arches, they became interwoven in my mind, so much so that I never since have come across the national flag of Cyprus with its crossed olive branches without thinking of the difficulties which my friend began to run into at around that time.

The fire at the Jenny Wren Hotel would not normally have attracted much attention, for this was the time of fires in tenth-rate hostels and hotels, those sad stucco barracks which kennelled problem families, non-English-speaking waiters and the senile and destitute. But a freelance photographer happened to be passing and the light of the blaze from the lower floors created strange and wonderful effects. The bony limbs sticking out from billowing nightdresses, the anguished faces and the unpinned hair of the old women being brought down the ladders – well, there was bound to be a hunt for the guilty men and the trail led quickly enough to Dudgeonvest Developments, and although the fault was electrical and Joe said he had not skimped on the wiring or indeed on any part of the conversion, the company's policies came under hostile scrutiny. Perhaps it would have been better if Joe himself had not turned up at the scene and attempted to help the firemen.

The landlords were not to blame, the inquest ruled, but the bony limbs and the billowing nightdresses could not be winkled out of the memory. There was an acrid smell in the air, a sense of things having gone wrong somewhere in the vicinity. When I walked past the place a day or two later and peered through the black and twisted beams, there was nothing at all left of the Good Office.

We were sitting out of the wind, the Colonel and I, in a trellised nook he had made round the corner of the house. The view of the valley was denied us. All we could see as we sat in our overcoats was shrubbery and the log shed and a bit of the back yard. Faces were upturned to catch the late spring sun. We treated ourselves warily like convalescents as we levered ourselves out of the wicker chairs to exchange Sunday newspapers. The Colonel was fascinated by the new business sections. The way he read out items was drenched in wonder as though he had been reading some romance of mediaeval barons. Yet anxiety could not be kept at bay for long.

'They seem awfully fussed, these chaps. Don't know why they keep going on about liquidity. Joe just says not to worry, it's a bridging problem, all the companies are fundamentally sound.' His great red face turned to me beseeching, rheumy eyes screwed up against the sun. 'You see, we've got to sell the second tranche of the first growths to meet the borrowings. I mean, that's quite separate from the farm overdraft and we're still waiting for the grant. Can't expect it all to be plain sailing, I suppose. We'll be over the hump by the summer.'

This phrase pleased him. The thought of the seasons and nature's renewal gave him confidence. Business too appeared to him a miraculous process of growth and decay and then growth again. He walked over the great concrete floors of the milking parlour awestruck that he should have played a part in the construction of this cathedral of milk. 'We're awfully lucky, you know,' he said as he reverently closed the door of the pasteurising room behind us. 'I hope you won't mind, Low Dudgeon's coming to dinner. He keeps me in touch.'

'I've got the legs of that boy,' John Dudgeon cackled, leaning over the dinner table. 'He thinks he's fast, but I've got the legs of him. The moment I saw those girls lugging electric typewriters up the stairs I knew what was up. Went straight up there myself and typed an anonymous letter to the borough planners on his own typewriter, reporting an unauthorised change of use on my top floor. Waved the letter in his face and got free use of one of his girls whenever we want her.' His lizard-face was all glee. 'A delightful girl too, a Catholic girl but not, I fear, a virgin. She has been well reamed by person or persons unknown.'

'John, now John.'

'I do so hope you got my latest mail-shot, Alec?' Dudgeon inquired.

'I did,' said the Colonel, 'and I threw the muck straight in the waste-paper basket.'

'One day, you will wish you had learnt every word of it by heart. Offers of support are flooding in by every post. I got two more wing-commanders yesterday. The times are stirring.'

That at least was not to be denied. Nobody knew what was coming next. Unease nibbled at the platitudes of public men. Hope – wild, unpractised hope – infected the propaganda of every sect and groupuscule. So vague and impalpable were the dangers that it was impossible to be sure of the answers to them. This might turn out to be anyone's day. And in the remotest country retreats, disturbed as yet by nothing more sinister than an occasional motorbike scramble, retired military men sat down at their desks and set their fountain pens to work in bright blue ink no longer seen elsewhere, underlining their rank and decorations with a quavery hand. Low Dudgeon showed me a bundle of letters; all spoke admiringly of his work and said that it was about time somebody had had the courage to stand up and be counted; several enclosed a stamped addressed envelope; one, stretching over five or six pages, signed himself 'A Member of The Silent Majority – eighty-three years of age and suffering from angina but still game for a scrap.'

'They seem a bit long in the tooth.'

'My dear Alec, these good people simply provide the sinews of war. We *recruit* elsewhere.' The snake-like crooning with which he spoke made the press gang of Nelson's day sound benign by comparison. He had the light of expectation in his glittering yellow eyes. The Colonel's offer of port was refused, the coffee pushed away undrunk. A fresh white handkerchief in the breast pocket, a manly fragrance about his person, a tie as blue as the wing-commanders' ink – he was ready for the call, if only to the television studio.

'Is your wine venture prospering, Alec?'

'Oh, ticking over,' the Colonel replied, with unvarnished panic in his voice, 'We have our ups and we have our downs, but we're managing.'

'I am delighted to hear it.' He rose from the table, glowing with malice, yet also with that touch of impatience to be seen in those who have a rendezvous with destiny, especially when destiny seems a little late in showing up.

'Oh you've heard about my poor nephew Joseph,' he said with a shot of distinctly Parthian intent. 'He's having a rather awkward time. Some of his City friends seem to be somewhat nervous about him having his office in my house, I can't think why.'

When questioned, Joe was abrupt, in puzzled truculent mode. 'It's all bloody silly politics. I wish I'd never been near the place. Barney who I thought would be solid is just about the worst. Absolutely furious that I used his name to the others.'

'The other whats?'

'Oh you know. They've got this stupid notion in their skulls about Low being prejudiced, just because they read in the papers some rubbish that that Nigel chap spouted at a meeting. I mean, you know Low. He's an odd fish but there's no real harm in him. People say these things about Ikey Mos and that sort of stuff but they don't really mean them, do they? Anyway, it couldn't have happened at a worse time. Credit's terribly tight and the bank's playing total silly buggers. But we're not here to talk business.'

'What are we here for then?' He had summoned me at half an hour's notice to his darkened restaurant. The last customers were just going out into the grey afternoon. The waiter brought china tea on a tray. As I took up my cup, I saw beneath it an Onora drawing of the old fort where she had disappeared with Joe.

'I'm sorry. I was so desperate I had to talk to someone. And I'm in meetings all evening. It's terribly difficult to talk about it at all. But I have to do something about it soon, and if I miss the chance I may regret it always.'

A curious imperviousness to his appeals settled over me and I began to play the ego game, counting the number of times he said I, then drifting off from this childish pastime into wondering whether other people had felt the same mixture of irritation and tedium when forced to listen to the great egomaniacs of history, whether underlings had nodded off or thought disrespectful thoughts when Hitler was outlining plans for the invasion of Russia, but then I woke up.

'So you see when it was a hundred per cent certain that Gillian couldn't have children, the whole Onora thing was put in a different context. But she didn't tell me about the arrangement, not all at once, to test my reactions, she said. It was the same for the others too, she explained, not that this made much difference to me, really.

'What arrangement?'

'It really is terribly difficult to say, which I expect is why I'm making such a horlicks of it. Anyway, what happened first was that O said she wanted to have a child, she didn't want to get married because she didn't believe in marriage, but she did want to have a child, and she wanted to have it now while she was still in her twenties so it would have the best possible chance to be healthy and absolutely OK. How did I feel about being the father of such a child in such a situation? Well, I said I'd have to know more about the situation first. She said that was about the first sensible thing I'd ever said to her in the – well, in all the years we'd known each other. But I'd have to wait till next time to find out the rest. The first thing was simply to find out my reaction to her having a child with me.'

'What did she mean next time?'

'Next time we met. Well, to be absolutely precise, we had a

sort of private language and we called whenever we met "a time" – you know, like in a whorehouse because she said that was what our relationship was like. It wasn't at all really, but sometimes she likes to make a joke of it and sometimes she doesn't. You know what she's like.'

'Not really, but go on.'

'So anyway then next time she says, right, here's your next part of the message – it was rather like a treasure hunt when you only get the clues one at a time. You are not going to be the only father of this child. I don't believe in the nuclear family and in jealous, possessive fatherhood. My child is going to be proud of not knowing who her father is (she's taken up using female pronouns to do for both, like they do now). So I said I didn't quite get it. And she said that's all you get till – '

'Next time.'

'Exactly. Well, by now I was beginning to get into a bit of a state what with business pressures and so on. And so I came round a couple of days before our next Wednesday five o'clock. Silly thing to do, of course, because I saw the bloody man Pod Pease leaving, but I didn't tell her I had because I thought the information might come in handy. There she was anyway, lying on her bed all – well, languorous, just as she was when we first saw her, and of course I couldn't resist, regardless of what might have gone on earlier. Afterwards, she looked amazingly pleased and said, right, now I can tell you the full terms of the arrangement.'

'Which were?' I was annoyed to find myself leaning forward, my elbow making the teacups chatter.

'There are going to be three of you, she said. I've chosen you all specially and you've all been asked whether you like the idea of giving me a child. But what I haven't told any of you until afterwards is that the condition is that (a) none of you will try in any way to have anything to do with the child after she's born and (b) none of you is to know who the other two are. The point of having three is that you can't be sure which one to be jealous of. It's a new sort of eternal triangle, she said with one of her silly giggles.'

248

'So what did you say?'

'Well, first of all I pointed out to her that as usual she's screwed things up. Because she hadn't told me afterwards, she'd told me before. And she giggled again and said, oh no she hadn't, this was afterwards. In fact, not that it mattered but I was the third. Of course, she'd have to keep on trying for a bit with all three because you could never be sure of conceiving the first time. So then I lost my temper and shook her and all that, but when I'd calmed down, she said, well? So I said that we seemed to have started, so I supposed I was already part of the arrangement, so I might as well carry on. I was in a fairly desperate state anyway, I suppose, or I'd have walked straight out of the door, but I didn't.'

'And now you wish you had?'

'No, I don't, not really. The awful truth is that I wouldn't have liked to have been left out. I wouldn't like her to have a child and me not to be part of it. You see how far gone I am.' He gave me a smile which was intended to be rueful in his old manner but which came out false and woebegone.

'I can't see why you're telling me the whole thing.'

'Well, I said to her, all right, but the only condition I don't accept is that I shouldn't know who my co-parents are. It's just too undignified the three of us being used as an anonymous sperm bank. But, Christ, what a mess.'

Soft umbrous twilight came down upon the restaurant. A waiter in off-duty check shirt and jeans slouched past us. A jingle of cutlery as another waiter began laying the tables at the far end of the room, slowly, cerebrally, like a man playing some complex game which demanded thinking several moves ahead. The man from the bakers wheeled in the evening batch of loaves on flat wooden trays. At the back of the restaurant, lights were being switched on. Kitchen clang and clatter. Air laden with the warm fresh smell of the bread. The melancholy of the darkening afternoon had begun to lift, but not from Joe.

'It really gets me down, the betrayal, you know. I expect it all sounds like a joke to you.'

'No, of course it doesn't.'

'The only thing I'd always given Onora credit for, always, was that she was absolutely straight. And now she does this. I mean, she's really betraying all three of us. Of course, she must have been having affairs with all of us at the same time already, but somehow that doesn't seem quite so bad. Speaking personally, I didn't expect to be her only lover. I'd have preferred it, sure, but I didn't expect it. But now – this.'

He stared down at his square truncated fists, sandy block-hewn misery. I began to see the beauty of this strange triangular contract. How neatly it trussed up three individual self-esteems and tied them together, before dropping them into these polluted waters.

'You see, anyone who tries to break the terms of the deal will simply be frozen out. She just won't speak to him or let him see the kid. I mean, that's if he tries to claim that he's the father. But she's got us the other way too. If one of us can't stand the continual humiliation and tries to pretend that the whole thing is a fantasy, she can point out that he signed up to the deal.'

'So you're going along with the whole thing?'

He turned and looked at me with a sudden revival of his old impish-thuggish grin.

'Of course I'm not. Not for a single minute. Did you really think I would? She's not going to get away with it. Once you start letting other people cut your deals for you, you're dead in the water.' He was delighted to have tricked me with his hangdog put-on.

'I don't see . . . how are you . . .'

'As long as the triangle stays a triangle, she's got us where she wants us. Any one of the three who moves to assert his rights or to try and slide out of the whole thing will simply be brought to heel. But suppose the triangle isn't a triangle any more, suppose the three of us get together and agree to settle on one of our number as The Father, quite arbitrarily, without blood tests or anything like that, and agree that all payments to support the child will be made through him and by him, then she would have to accept that and play ball unless she wanted to deprive the child of every penny that might be coming to it. You may think that's moral blackmail, but it's no worse than what she's doing to us.'

The lights came on across the restaurant, section by section, until they reached our corner. We blinked, conspirators discovered by accident, perhaps not even sought by the authorities, or not at that moment.

'But how . . .'

'Well, I know one of the other studs must be Pod Pease and he'll be easy enough to deal with, because I know for a fact he has a wife and two children in Walthamstow, and he might appreciate, you know, a little easing of his cash-flow problem, not to mention his trouble with the Customs and Excise. So all I have to do is find the third man and see if we can do business. And that's where you come in.'

'That is where I do not come in.'

'No, hold on, listen. All I'm asking you to do is keep your eyes and ears open, listen around town. Sooner or later, you're bound to get a whisper. The third man, think of it as a sort of quest.' And he began to hum the Harry Lime theme with a nasal buzzy hum.

'It's terrible for my asthma, all this strain,' he said. 'And I'm getting these dizzy spells too. It's absolutely vital to sort things out as quickly as possible, in the interests of the child. Onora doesn't realise what she's doing to all of us, including herself. I mean, she's the one most at risk, she's the single mother.'

'Why shouldn't she kiss you all goodbye, get an au pair, bring up the child on what she earns from her designs?'

'She's not like that. She can't really live without men. Believe me, this is the only way. We just have to find the third man and cut the deal.'

'There is no *we* about it.'

'What would you like, a Negroni or an Americano? Cuba Libre?' He wanted to move on.

'I'd like some more tea. And Gillian, your wife Gillian, how does she fit in to the master plan?'

He answered without hesitation, as briskly as if this was the question he had been hoping to tease out of me, a question which did me credit as well as assisting the progress of the meeting.

'She's a major player. We have to get this thing settled quickly without hassle, for her sake really, because then we can get into this godparent-style relationship quite naturally. After all, Onora really does need all the help she can get, so we can make it a joint sort of effort, bringing up the baby and bring Gilly in on the whole process.'

'Who's that dodging about outside?'

Outside the window, darkened now, a man's head was bobbing to and fro between the lower-case sans-serif letters of the Shorewinds sign.

'It must be Pod. I don't want another punch-up just at the moment. I really don't feel up to it.'

'But according to your plan, don't you have to make your peace with him?'

Joe groaned. He seemed harassed, heavier in the face. The lights had been on for a few minutes now, but he was still blinking, still looked trapped by their brightness. He got up and walked towards the door. The dodging man was waving now as he ran up and down outside the window, his hand flapping a series of crazy accents on top of Onora's letters. As he came out beyond the sign, also making for the door, I saw that he was older and slighter than Pod and wearing thick-rimmed spectacles.

'It isn't Pod,' I said, but Joe had already unbolted the door and let in Barney. The sight of Barney did not lessen Joe's gloom, nor did Barney look any less agitated now that he had been admitted. They came back to the table with uneasy smiles of welcome already fled.

'This is an out-of-the-way place and no mistake. A pleasure to see you again, young sir. You're looking well. I can see you're following the recipe for a long and happy life – stay out of the property business, especially at a time like this, isn't that right, Joseph?'

'Yes, yes,' said Joe. He ordered another pot of tea from another waiter coming on duty and stared after him as though suspecting some kind of treachery below stairs.

'We have painful business to tidy up, young sir. You won't mind us, will you? I know you can keep a confidence.'

252

'Perhaps you'd prefer to have a drink at the bar,' Joe said.

'I'm quite happy with tea. Don't mind me,' I said, provoked by his anxiety to be rid of me. Barney by contrast seemed eager to start on the agenda before I could be hustled away. He began to take papers out of a black briefcase which was preposterously new and gleaming beside the worn, economical aspect of everything else to do with him.

'Do you really need to do all this here? I don't care for my customers turning the restaurant into a boardroom, you know.'

'Well, it is out of hours, Joe. And some of these bills are getting on a bit. I mean, there's one here is growing whiskers on it.'

'I know, a hundred and fifty twelve per cent at three months, due June 30, two hundred at two per cent over MLR at six months, one hundred – '

'What a memory. You know, young sir, as soon as I set eyes on Joe, I knew he could make figures talk. If only we hadn't had that trouble with the tubes people, I wish we'd never got the business. No offence to you, sir, very grateful we were for the comfort of your presence, but I should never have let Joe talk me into that one. Dribbled into the desert sand, that one did. Not nice people to do business with, not nice at all. And what they're doing with those blessed tubes just doesn't bear thinking of.'

'Come on, Barney, what do you want, separate cheques, personal or what?' He took out a fistful of cheque books – blue, green, grey – and spread them out on the table. These inconspicuous little book-lets seemed strangely precious objects, like the different-coloured editions of *Pilgrim's Progress* which were all Mrs March could afford to give her daughters on Christmas Day. As he began writing out the cheques, I reflected that I had scored a peculiar cat's-paw revenge. By helping, quite unwittingly, to seal a deal that was better lost, I seemed to have sealed Joe's fate.

'Just as it says on the face of the bills, my dear Joseph – BB Investments, Barnabas Credit and Loan, and the other two to the Beulah Trust, after my dear mother. Now talking of family, I must admit I was surprised when I heard about your connections, I can't pretend I wasn't. Well, you may say, we can't choose our uncles and aunts and nor you can. But I've got my connections too and to be honest with you they don't care for the address. It's his uncle, I say, family's family, you can't blame the boy. You don't have to live with your uncle, they say, you don't have to do business under his roof. Well, what can I say to that? You tell me.'

'All right then, BB, is that all?' Square sandy fist scrawling across the cheques, even now something childish, frowning, effortful about the way he wrote – his head on one side, elbows splayed outwards. He pushed the cheques across the table with his square stubby finger pressed on them as disdainful as a croupier dealing cards. Barney read the cheques with a slow deliberateness which seemed alien to him: 'Now this is one I don't know, Excellent Food and Wine Company. Really I don't recall having any business with a company of that name.'

'It's the company that owns this place.'

'Ten-year lease on a railway arch, is it? That's an asset, I don't think, as my dear old father used to say. If it isn't too much trouble, I'd be happier with another one. What about the Broderia Mill Company? Why, I can remember the day they stood at 120 and Mr Brod entertained us, most regally, at the Dorchester Hotel, all the managers came down from Lancashire and we had a conjuror, quite brilliant he was.'

'I don't want to weaken the cash flow position at Brods just at the moment. One cheque's as good as another.'

'If you can cash it, Joseph, if you can cash it. Well then, I won't be choosy. Never pick at your food.'

Joe stared unseeing at the window, barely responded to Barney's parting politeness, showed him out and locked the door behind him, then walked quickly to the back of the restaurant. I heard him make a telephone call, then another, and another. Then the slam of the toilet door behind him.

The waiter who had come in wearing the check shirt and jeans was in his white coat now and loading up the sweet trolley. I watched him arranging the familiar selection on the trays: the peeled oranges in syrup, the trifle with the sweet rusks embedded in its creamy topping, the profiteroles in their chocolate-dripping heap, the strawberries, English now and swollen in the high season. The waiter stood back and admired the array as though he had never achieved such perfection before.

At first the sound of breaking glass from the back of the restaurant sounded like one more kitchen noise, but then there was a loud yelping sort of groan and the sound of running feet. My own feet seemed to take an eternity to reach the toilet. A waiter in a vest stood aside to let me pass, holding open the door for me. The door had a jaunty silhouette of a man in a sombrero on it.

Joe was sitting on the seat, fully clothed. Blood was pouring from his right wrist, soaking his white shirt-cuff and spilling down his trousers, dark as dark against the chalk stripe. The other wrist was bleeding too, much less badly, only a scratch it looked. The wash-basin was filled with bloodstained glass fragments.

'Lucky I'm left-handed,' he said looking up at me with a sad puckish smile. 'What a stupid accident.'

On the way to the hospital in the manager's car, Joe began to babble at him about percentages and waiters' wages and the menu – was it too predictable? – and the lease – was it really worth trying to buy the freehold, or should they look around for new premises? The manager – a tall, skinny, fair man of disagreeable aspect, an ulcerous Scandinavian look he had with close-set Scandinavian eyes – answered with a gentleness and good sense that made Joe's questions sound all the more hysterical, although the questions themselves, taken one by one, were the sort of questions one would expect him to be asking. Before we were half-way there, I began almost to feel that he was Joe's keeper, had been so in fact for ages, and that Joe's ownership of the restaurant was a fantasy that had to be indulged if he was not to become more frantic still. Then as we turned into the forecourt of the hospital and saw the sign NO CASUALTY DEPARTMENT HERE, Joe began to sob in a convulsive way, dry-eyed to start with, then with tears running down his cheeks, and as we turned out of the forecourt again to make for another hospital, he threw himself against me and clutched my knee with his good hand.

When I visited him the next day, his spirits seemed restored.

He was sitting up in bed, with mint-fresh pyjamas and gleaming white bandaged paws. And he had his ox-blood briefcase on his bedside table.

'Well now,' he said. 'That was a night to forget, wasn't it? I'm so clumsy these days. As you can see, there are one or two pressures on me at the moment. Still, things will calm down when we get to Ireland.'

'Ireland?'

'Did you not know? I must have told you.'

'No,' I said.

'We're moving to Ireland, the whole works.'

'What on earth for? You're not specially Irish, are you?'

'Well, on my mother's side, I am apparently, as it happens, but I've never been there and that's not the reason. No, it's strictly business reasons.'

'I didn't know Ireland was a tax haven.'

'Well, it isn't really, but it is kind to incoming investors who are going to make things happen. And for tax purposes, I really need to be offshore of the offshore.'

He smiled the old puckish smile, sadness gone now he had a glimpse of the open road again.

'All you have to do for me while I'm gone,' he said, 'is track down that third man.'

'I wouldn't dream of it,' I said.

'Oh come off it,' he said. 'Isn't it rather intriguing, the whole thing? I mean, wouldn't you yourself really like to know? I mean, you don't want to have to do anything dirty to find out, but you'd just like the information to float into your hands, wouldn't you? In business, you come across quite a few people like that.'

'Joe, I didn't come here to – '

'No, of course you didn't, I'm sorry. I really am,' and then he used my name in that old winning way, with the perfect pitch of a dog-whistle. 'The right hand is rather giving me gyp, but I don't have to take it out on you. You'll be our very first guest at Drizzle Hall, spelled Drishill but sounds awfully like Drizzle the way the locals say it. You'll love the house, it's sort of a fake

Gothic monastery. It's even got a reflectory' – and he grinned at me, willing pander to my pedantry.

'Whereabouts is it?'

'Near the border, in fact, awfully near the border so I picked it up for a reasonable price. Taxwise, it's the perfect place to operate a UK–Republic–Isle of Man roundabout.' His bright face invited me to go on and ask him to explain, but I had no curiosity at that moment and could not have cared less what a roundabout was.

'But what about all your things over here?'

'I don't have a penny left in this country, not a single penny. If I wasn't on the Health, I couldn't pay my bill in this place.'

'You mean you're broke?'

'I didn't say I hadn't got a penny anywhere else. After last night's little embarrassment, I sold the lot this morning – the property business, the mill, the restaurant, everything. There was a terrible queue behind me for the phone in the corridor. My crock of gold is across the water now, or very soon will be. It's a little crock of gold, but it's better than nothing.'

'What made you sell everything all at once, like that?'

'When Barney calls for his money, you sell. In his funny little way, he's the angel of death, businesswise. I suppose he must have heard about the dry holes in the States. Luckily, there seem to be people over here who haven't yet.'

'But how can you find buyers so quickly?'

'Oh there are always buyers around. In fact, you encourage them because they're the ones who tell you what the business is worth. So you can always ring them up and they'll make you an offer – half what it would be normally because they know you're in a hurry. Freddy Svob will be coming round with the outline agreements to sign later on today. So, to all intents and purposes, I'm out.'

Feeling slow and dim as an earthworm, I left him exulting in his escape, glowing in his hospital sheets, the swagger of his sling now verging on the heroic. And then I heard no more of him for several months. If he came into my thoughts at all, I assumed he must be occupied with moving into his Irish home.

X

Fisha's party –
Joe fails to turn up –
Pod Pease feels at home

I travelled up alone in the cage. Its creaks and whimpers as it began to ascend made me also feel old. Former trips in this lift seemed remote in time, as they were – it must have been five years since the wedding now. My hands resting on the cold metal of the scrolled and foliated railing gripped a dead past. As the cage reached the level of the Baltic Military Club, I was prepared to see heart-slapping changes: the whole place dark and dusty, the furniture under dust-sheets perhaps, or tables and chairs piled with their legs in the air; the club secretary, if he had not died, creeping down the end of the passage, shrunken and bent, probably in carpet slippers. But there he was standing just outside the cage, with chest flung out in the stand-at-ease position, looking brisk and five years younger than when I had first seen him. 'Good evening,' he boomed. Startled, I managed only a weak wave as I rose towards Trull's flat and the babble of carousing bookmen.

Why the party for Fisha's book was being given there was beyond me. To start with, I thought, the book did not need a party. *Up Pigotts* was a bewitching compote of old photographs, engravings, excursions into folklore, taped reportage from old farmworkers who could remember working with horses and their wives who could remember the hardships of gleaning along with snippets of local dialect and song collected by the author. It was so alluringly put together, right from the dust-jacket which featured the cover of the old Ordinance Survey maps, brown with a green border, and the royal coat of arms and the country scene with an open touring car pausing in the lee of a bosomy wood beside a high-fingered signpost. Fisha was so at ease with the past. She traced its half-effaced contours with impudent sureness and knew how to tease our grandparents without condescending to them so that all their snobberies and fears came alive. And then, to fend off the temptations of blandness, there was also a radical streak running through the text, nothing crude but a sustained undercurrent of avidity for justice, buttressed by stern facts. The idyllic sepia photograph of haymaking would be captioned with statistics of the wages and hours endured by the brown, staring women in their kerchiefs. Fisha's ferocity only added to the book's charm.

'There, you see that's what it was really like,' she said, pointing to an early-nineteenth-century engraving of two dozen murderous-looking villagers marching down the road in heavy boots with padded jackets and rough gauntlets. The caption: '*Off to the Assay. The present-day ceremony is a bowdlerised version of the original, which was a violent ice-maul and each year produced severe injuries and sometimes deaths. The Up Pigotts team was especially renowned for its toughness and regularly routed the young gentlemen from the university*.' On the page opposite, a romantic water-colour of the same period showed the gentle wooded slope where Joe's lodgings and Fisha's former home now stood. On a grassy knoll, a couple of villagers were strolling arm-in-arm.

Already you could see the book was a success. Fisha was surrounded by publishing men in spectacles and corduroy suits. She blushed as they told her which bits they had most enjoyed. She was dressed in a long print dress, mostly green with orange and brown flowers, large, floppy cabbagy flowers, William Morris rather than Laura Ashley. The dress had smocking across the front and frills at neck and cuffs like a little girl's frock, and perhaps because it did not fit her, she seemed out of proportion, Alice after drinking the growth mixture. Her arms shot out of the slightly puffed sleeves.

I wondered how mad she was now and then thought that somehow being slightly mad would not matter so much if she was famous, provided she did not panic. A hint of melodrama

in the outward manner was the mark of genius. I heard her say
'but smocks were so *practical* for haymaking,' and I felt she was
all right.

In fact, she found it hard to come down from her high. When
we talked, she provoked me into a crabbed worldliness. Her book,
I heard myself saying, was just the kind of thing to take our minds
off the crash.

'What crash? Have you had a crash? I don't drive motor cars
myself. I go everywhere in a governess cart now, so quick and
pretty, and Dido loves going to the Empire Stores because they
always give her a lump of sugar. You remember the Empire Stores?
It's still got those lovely beeswax cubes on strings as you go in.'

'No, no, I meant,' but I could not bring myself to form the
words Stock Exchange.

'We should have some pictures of you in the governess cart,'
said a happy man in a sage-green corduroy suit. 'Bailey would
love to do it, or Donovan.'

She asked who Bailey and Donovan were, and the man in the
sage-green suit was happier still.

'Everyone in the village loves the book. Old Mr Treadgold was
only cross because he wasn't in it and Mrs Watson was because
she was born there and could remember the mummers coming into
the servants' hall and singing with great bunches of buttercups in
their hats: 'We be mummers, that we be, hey down dilly, come for
you to see, dance and sing, all in a ring, hey down dee.'

The men in suits had been talking among themselves about
whether they could afford a top photographer. They missed the
first bit, but when Fisha started singing and doing an ungainly
dance, hopping from one foot to the other, their attention was fully
engaged. Perhaps Morris dancers could be hired for the signing
sessions, one of them suggested, but Fisha said Morris dancers
were suburban, and her rebuke thrilled them. What they liked was
the way she went on talking, not least (although they would not
have put it like that, even subconsciously) when they were not
listening. She's a real self-starter, that one, I heard the happiest
of the men in corduroy suits say later, enjoying the thought of

not having to exert himself to ensure that her talents were fully displayed.

Keith Trull came up. I hardly recognised him. He had discarded the chef's trousers and the shades, and was wearing a neat dark suit and gold-rimmed spectacles of the type worn by Nazi war criminals. He had the polite impersonal mien of a consultant welcoming patients to his surgery.

'It is such a success, isn't it? I'm so glad we were able to help Fisha. Peggy was keen to do it because she was such a friend of her father's. In fact, she's also badgered half the publishers in this room to publish W.R.S.'s collected papers, but none of them will touch it because they know the papers are in such a hopeless mess. But *Up Pigotts* will sell a million, I know it.'

'Not your kind of thing, though, I suppose, is it?'

Trull looked at me in feigned amazement and took off his war-criminal's glasses to rub the mist off them, gazing at me with mild myopic eyes.

'On the contrary, I'm into country matters now, didn't you know? We're moving from here to start a butterfly farm, in Suffolk.'

Something about this announcement made me suspect that he had, in fact, only just thought of the plan.

'You aren't, I don't believe it.'

'Well, it may be organic farming for a start. But butterflies are my long-term goal. I've gone through urban squalor and out the other side. You know, all we wanted was a day return to the ghetto, we never wanted to get stuck in the shit.'

'I can't keep up with you.'

'You don't have to any more. It's slow-down time. The long rallentando of the twentieth century – aren't you just crazy about that phrase? We've got to learn to watch the chrysalis weaving its cocoon and really watch, like it was our very own cocoon – oh, look here's Mary. You do know Mary, don't you, Mary Scrannel. You must. I'll leave you together to pick up the threads.'

I had scarcely ever heard her first name before (her husband had only once used it in my hearing) and now I had it indecently flung at me three times in as many seconds. The sight of Fisha's mother filled me with pleasure as well as an urgent desire to dissociate myself from this casual first-naming. She was plumper still than I remembered and sadder, the plumpness advertising the sadness. Her dress like her daughter's came from an earlier time, in Mrs Scrannel's case the 1940s and elaborate teas lingered over in the causeries of department stores long since closed.

'I knew I wouldn't like that man. Fisha told me about him, and I knew I wouldn't like him.'

'Oh that's all right, Mrs Scrannel. Nobody likes him.'

She looked at Trull's departing back view with as near a glare as her forget-me-not eyes could manage.

'I expect you're surprised to see me here. I didn't want to come, but I had to keep an eye on Fisha. It was an awful dilemma because obviously it would not be fair not to do everything possible for Fisha's book, but I couldn't trust anybody else to cope. When she gets tired, she gets so fretful. Luckily, Mr Trull told me that Mrs Dudgeon would not be here. Otherwise, I don't think I could have managed it. I mean, of course I'm grateful for her taking so much trouble about Fisha and then trying to get Walter's papers published too, but I shouldn't think many people would really want to read them now – Professor Mudge tells me that unfortunately Walter's sort of philosophy is going out of fashion. And anyway, I would just much rather she didn't.'

She gave a kind of shudder, and clasped her arms round her as though she had just come into a chilly room.

'All that deceit. I hate deceit. You knew too, I suppose' – but this said wearily, not with bitterness, or so I thought.

'Well, yes, some of the time, I can't remember exactly, but – '

'Well, you must have been awfully young, and even if you had told me, I don't know what difference it would have made. It was having to be grateful to her for arranging his holiday that I can't forgive. Well I can't forgive any of it, to be honest. I thought of killing her, quite often. When I couldn't sleep, I would think up ways of doing it, quick, unobtrusive ways, like *that*.'

I had noticed how close she seemed to be standing to me, and she scarcely needed to move. I felt a mild jabbing pain in my left side and looked down. She let me see the plastic toy flick knife before she put it away in her handbag with a chuckle, not a malign chuckle, more like a comfortable acknowledgement of some pleasant remark, a compliment about her cooking perhaps.

'I feel so much better now. You can't imagine.'

'I hope that wasn't a dress rehearsal.'

'Well, you never know. Being a widow means you can keep people guessing. It's one of the few compensations.'

She chuckled again and gripped my arm as fiercely as Fisha had gripped my arm on the night of the Assay. The forget-me-not eyes looked into mine, giving as little away as a cat's eyes. It should not, I suppose, have surprised me that some of Fisha's qualities had been inherited from her mother and not her father, but the qualities now on display were not to be expected.

Now and then, I could see that Mrs Scrannel had an ear cocked in Fisha's direction, alert for a worrying change in her daughter's voice, but from the occasional snatches I caught Fisha still seemed to be under control. As I passed by to find her mother a drink, she was talking rather loudly, but only about the Iron-Age hill fort which had been obliterated by the new housing estate. When I passed her on the return journey, she had switched subjects.

'You see, it's not just a quaint piece of academic nonsense. In the middle ages, it was incredibly violent.'

'Yes, you say in the book, don't you, that villagers were quite often injured or even killed.'

'What I didn't say in the book was that it was also a local version of saturnalia with a rather peculiar erotic rite attached, a sort of midwinter renewal ceremony.'

'Oh wasn't it rather a pity you didn't put that in? I think the readers might have enjoyed it.'

'I did not wish to sensationalise anything. I hate books which try to dredge up all the dirty bits out of the past. Is that the sort of book you want to publish?'

'No, no, not at all. I just thought that, you know, for the sake of completeness . . .'

'Because I hate squalid little men who are only interested in the smutty bits in history.'

'Of course, I entirely agree, I only – '

'If you really want to know what the rite was, I'll tell you. They chose four sturdy matrons and entrusted them with the task of finding Cock Robin, that is, finding the chap with the smallest private parts in the entire village. They could go anywhere and ask to see everything. I mean, they could come in here and ask you and you'd have to show your little red willie and then – '

'Darling, I'm awfully sorry but I think we ought to go now.'

'But Ma, I'm just telling these men about poor Cock Robin and how he gets chased across the ice stark naked.'

'Felicia dear, we did agree to catch the 8.50.'

'Ma, look how they've gone all red in the face. They said I should put in about Cock Robin in the book, but actually they are all terribly embarrassed, so I must have been right not to put it in. Oh, you are red, like one of those apples they cover with arsenic to make them look like Worcesters.'

She was wild now and out of breath, pale with sweat on her forehead, swinging her body from side to side, but not violently, more as though lulling herself.

'I don't want to go,' she said. 'The party is just beginning.'

'Mr Trull won't want us here all night.'

'You said you detested Mr Trull, so why do you care what he thinks?'

'Well, it is his flat, dear.'

'Is Joe here, do you know? I hoped Joe might be here. Do you know Joe? He knows Joe, and so does my mother, but you don't know Joe, do you?' The publishing men shook their heads and looked eager to know Joe. 'Well, Joe is a very good-looking boy. Or rather he was a very good-looking boy, but the last time I saw him he was fat and red in the face, just like you, except he's too young to be fat and red in the face. Anyway, when he wasn't fat and red in the face, I fell madly in love with him. Madly, desperately in love. But of course you can't imagine it. And of course Joe didn't love me, not a bit, as a matter of fact, he didn't know me at all, but I knew he wouldn't love me, not ever, so I knew – '

'Fisha, please.'

'So I knew I had to give myself to him. That was the only hope, that he had me and *then* he might love me. Well, he might not too, but even if he didn't, I would have memories. And you must have memories, you just must. If you haven't got memories – oh well, you just must, that's all. So I put on these silly clothes rather like the suit you're wearing, no, not you, the young lady in blue at the back there, very like that really. And I made him take me out and then I *gave* myself to him.'

'Fisha, my dear.' It was Trull, neat, controlled consultant to the human race who put his arm round her waist. 'It's been a wonderful party, and I can say that because I had nothing to do with the organising of it, and I really am sorry it has to end, but the restaurant, you know – '

I saw Mrs Scrannel looking at Trull with a dawning confidence on her face gradually overcoming her dislike. There was little or no aggression in his competence. He simply knew what was best. His cherub's lips hinted at pleasures yet to come. He was not a spoilsport. At least that was how he seemed to me, but not to Fisha.

'Fisha my dear,' she said, not trying to parody his voice, but quite flatly, reflectively. 'I didn't know we were so well acquainted. Are we old friends, I had quite forgotten, which is strange because I don't forget things, even about the time when I was ill. My memory is not photographic, but it is quite adequate.'

'We're going home now, Felicia.'

'Can't we stay and wait for Joe? I want Joe to see my party.'

'The party's over, dear. Look, they've all gone. You just sit down while I get your coat.'

Ordinary easy chairs had found their way into Trull's sitting-room now that he had taken up being ordinary, but there was still a bean bag covered in some tribal textile pushed against one of the white walls, and there it was that Fisha chose to sit, her long white arms propped on her wide-apart knees, the green dress billowing over the squashy bulges of the bean bag. Her face cupped in her hands was pale and sweaty, with a drained sort of purity about it.

That was the last time I saw her, although I believe she is still alive, living somewhere near Pigotts Hill, with her mother. She has been sighted now and then. She was seen at the winding-up meeting of one of Joe's companies, rising in a kind of white shift from amid the ruck of aggrieved creditors but not making a great deal of sense. Immediately after her first book came out, she did take part in several signing sessions in bookshops around the country, but her response to her admirers was so unpredictable that in the end her publishers decided to take her off their roster. She was too daunting for all but the most ardent admirers to approach her, and even they never felt quite the same about her books after they had met her. The sad and dislocated side of her was not so obvious in *Up Pigotts*, which had the carefree quality that first books sometimes have, but in *The By-passed Village* and *Best End of Neck*, which came later, a more recriminating tone prevailed. Her detestation of modern civilisation seemed to stretch further and further back into the nineteenth century. 'I don't mind her hating motor cars,' her publisher said, 'but she now seems to resent every invention since the wheel, and I'm not even sure she approves of that.' It was when she began to abuse the sort of people who might be her readers that he took fright. The phrase – 'the generations of cold hearts who squatted in Georgian rectories' – jarred on him particularly: 'it might be all right in a Marxist text-book, but we do have to keep one eye on the coffee-table market, and anyway it isn't even good English.'

All the time she sat there on the bean bag, pale, moon-browed, with her knees wide apart, rocking from side to side as though crooning herself to sleep, I half-hoped, half-dreaded Joe would come in. However terrible the effect of his arrival, it would at least undo the agonising state of paralysis which her talk had locked us into.

But Joe was not coming. Only someone as crazy as Fisha would have expected him to. Even if there was no warrant out for him, as far as I knew, he was already being spoken of in the past tense, to my surprise quite kindly spoken of, at any rate to start with.

Now that he could be openly described as a shyster and fly-by-night (after all, he had shied and flown), he began to be thought of fondly by some people who had previously been immune to his charms. Friends who had always found my affection for Joe incomprehensible talked as though they themselves had never not had a soft spot for him. Partly this was because they did not wish to be thought of as hard-hearted to a man on the skids, but also they convinced themselves they had always known how to appreciate a buccaneer.

The warming towards Joe cooled off again when the quantity of chaos he had left behind became clearer. The new owners of several of the companies that he had managed to sell soon came upon sizeable liabilities which Joe had failed to disclose to them but which did not mature until he was clear of the country. Then there were half-a-dozen companies which, contrary to his boasting from his hospital bed, he had failed to sell. These went into liquidation with the swiftness of the last of the bathwater. The Broderia Mill and the Excellent Food and Wine Company did not prosper under their new owners and soon joined the liquidator's list. The Colonel's wine business must have been one of the first to go under, for it was only a week or two after the party for Fisha's book that I received a letter from Gilly recording her father's distress.

Oh the poor old bugger moons about the cellar, counting the few bottles they've allowed him to keep because he said they were his and not the company's. I can hear him moaning below the floorboards like a fart in a thunderstorm. He comes up with his sad red face all covered with dust looking like a leper which he thinks he is now. I keep on telling him that all great men go bust from time to time or have to scarper like Joejoe, but he doesn't believe it, because he remembers all about bankrupts having to resign from clubs and regiments, although he resigned from all his years ago anyway. The worst was when the chap who's bought the mootel put a fence across the top of the paddock, below the ha-ha. Quite unnecessary unless he's breeding cattle which can jump six feet high, but it was barbed-wire round the soul of the poor Colonel. He feels he's living in a concentration camp, which I suppose failure is especially when you can see the evidence of it all around you.

Things aren't much better over here in the Emerald Isle either. The poor fugitive from justice is totally spastic with his bandaged paws. He gets awfully cross when I go away, even to see the Colonel. He still can't cut up his meat and he also gets awfully cross when I turn it into glorified mince. You must come and see us soon. There'll be a wailing in the sheiling if you don't. Oh and Joejoe says, would you keep an eye on Onora, he says she's pregnant and she's the sort of person who doesn't really have many friends, not friendly friends anyway.

I had no intention of running this errand. Somehow the importunity was all the worse because it came from this maimed runaway. The tenacity of his will seemed especially indecent now, but as it happened, within a week, I ran into her quite by chance, not far from where I had run into Joe when he was having his asthma attack.

She came down the street towards me, far gone now. The tent-like denim dress was only just big enough. Her long neck and skinny shoulders seemed cruelly bare under the blue denim. She had the starved look of a poor white in the depression, starved and pure – her skin had cleared up and the beauty of her long sad boat-shaped face was unimpaired. She greeted me as though we knew each other very well, and had seen one another only a day or two earlier. She wanted to know how I thought the miners' strike would turn out and whether cyclamates really caused cancer. The sight of her golden hair in the dusty summer street set me adrift.

'You do stare, don't you? Haven't you ever seen a pregnant woman before?'

'How are you feeling?'

'Oh she kicks now and then, but I quite like the company.' Her smile was so placid that I found it hard to imagine that she could have invented the arrangements with which she was torturing Joe.

'Would you like to sit down?' I asked. 'Shall we go and have a cup of tea somewhere?'

'I'm afraid I must get back. I've got some designs to get off, but it's lovely to see you.' All at once, a great odour of solitude, sad and sour, came from her. I felt her longing to be a million miles away.

But, as I turned to go, she said: 'Oh well, then, you might as well come back – and have a cup of tea.' Aware how cool she had sounded, she smiled to let me feel I had not cadged the invitation. Yet the way she tacked on the phrase made having a cup of tea at this or perhaps any hour sound an unbearably stuffy pastime. For my part, I had only made the suggestion out of politeness, but now the desire to see the little flat above the workshop became stronger. From the dust and the grubby white paint along the walls of the stairs – little more than a splintery ladder – it looked unlikely that anyone at all lived there. We might have been a couple sent by a house agent to view a vacant property. Onora herself gave no impression of arriving home. She stared briefly up the stairs, with a mild curiosity as though not expecting much. Beyond the door, to my surprise, male snuffling noises could be heard.

'You go on in there,' she said, prodding me in the back, snuffling herself in an amused way. The room was low and grubby-white like the walls, with white pillowy sofas and white melanine designer's table and easel. The only spot of colour was Pod Pease squatting on the bed in shirt sleeves, scarlet braces supporting the trousers of his heather-mixture suit.

'Oh hullo,' he said, 'she picked you up instead of the secretaire, did she then?'

'What's a secretaire?'

'Piece of furniture, too good for the likes of barrow boys like me. So I send her out to find what old Madders is charging the quality, then I know what he'll let it go to the trade for.'

'The veneer's all cracked at the sides and the flap is bowing badly, Pease. He's asking three-and-a-half, but I could see from his ledger he's had it eighteen months already, so I bet you could get it for half that, but I wouldn't touch it.'

He scratched the silver bristles on his bullet-head, but vigorously, not in a thoughtful way. He seemed uninterested in Onora's report.

'You're the one I saw with the Follows bloke, the one that scarpered to Ireland.'

'Yes.'

'Didn't get anything out of me. This one here wanted me to sell him some stuff when he was riding high, but I can tell a welsher a mile off. Anyway, he was pig ignorant, asked if I had any Sherrington furniture.'

'He can't pronounce things properly.'

'Doesn't say much for a public-school education, does it?' He sat on the bed in his braces grinning at me, not in the slightest put out by my arrival. In fact, he looked tremendously happy to be there in this studio attic bedsit or whatever it was. For him too it was a kind of refuge.

'She looks lovely when she's pregnant. I love pregnant women, don't you? That madonna look. If I was a woman, I'd be pregnant all the time.'

'Shut up, Pease, you know fuck all about it.'

'That's just it. It's the mystery that lures us on, lures us on to our doom.'

'I don't know why you think it's *your* doom.'

'Because we can't do it, that's why. There we are, kings of the universe, and we can't do the simplest most basic thing in the entire universe. You know, there are these men who have phantom pregnancies when their wives fall, swell up like balloons they do.' She threw a cushion at him, he caught it and promptly stuffed it inside his heather mixture trousers and crossed his hands over the monstrous swelling with a seraphic expression of fulfilment on his broad bullet-face.

'You're boring, Pease, you know that, terribly boring.'

'That's all the English can ever say. You're most frightfully boring.'

'I've had enough of your East End cockiness for one afternoon.'

'Well, I don't pretend to be anything I'm not. It's all original veneer.'

He rose to go, then put his arm in Onora's. They stood side by side, Pod Pease still with the cushion inside his heather mixture trousers, posing poker-faced.

'There. Tweedledum and Tweedledee.'

They had the swollen stomachs but not the disturbing menace of the Lewis Carroll illustration. In fact, there was a weird serenity about this odd couple. Their being so ill assorted was relaxing. They reminded me more of some early Flemish masterpiece: the pale pregnant bride rapt in her own destiny while the coarse-grained husband is himself also stilled for a moment by the peace of the situation and distracted from counting-house thoughts by his wife's beauty. I could see now why Pod Pease had rolled in the dust with Joe.

Pod removed the cushion, picked up his jacket which had been lying in a heap on the floor like some summery Highland tussock and put it on, straightened his tie with care, and combed his bristle with his fingers, deploying the kind of surplus violence that would have been needed to get through a tangled mane.

'Well, angels hover.' And he broke into a little trot as he was off through the door and down the stairs.

'Let's sit down for five minutes,' she said. 'We haven't really talked.' Her voice was Midlands flat, with a confident edge which made you pay attention to what she said, even when there was nothing much to it.

'You've wondered about who the father is.'

'Well.'

'Go on. You must have. You couldn't not.' A teasing smile rippled across the long, sad, boat-shaped face.

'All right then, I couldn't not.'

'You couldn't possibly guess the answer.'

'How do you know I couldn't?'

'Has Joe told you? I made him promise he wouldn't, but he can't keep a promise, or a secret, so it was silly to expect him to.'

'He's told me something.'

'Oh then he has. Because you wouldn't say Something unless he'd told you about the Arrangement.'

'Well, yes, but he didn't really explain what the point of it was.'

'Don't you see, to be free. I had to have a baby, I really had to, but I just don't see why I have to *live* with a person just so I can have a baby.'

'Yes all right, but why the threesome? Why not just go along to a hospital?'

'And have some creepy medical student's child? You don't understand. I wanted my baby to have a really nice father, only a sort of anti-father, so he had to be someone I liked, so I chose very carefully. No, I'm not going to say who I chose.'

'I wasn't asking.'

'I could see you wanting to know. Anyway, that's the secret and that makes it fun as well as a good arrangement, don't you think?'

'Odd sort of fun.'

'Don't be draggy. Anyway, you can guess who most of them are, but I'm not going to tell you whether you're right or not.'

Just then I remembered what the Flemish masterpiece I was thinking of really looked like. The husband was not bristly and bullet-shaped like Pod Pease. On the contrary, he had been, still eternally was, pale, tentative, concerned for his wife. Pod had imposed himself on a scene of great delicacy of feeling.

'I forgot the tea,' she said, and got up to reach down two Coronation mugs from their hooks above the sink in the corner. 'What I really like about this place is there's nowhere to cook. You just have to go out. My mother cooked and cooked – cakes and scones and soda bread and stews and Queen's pudding and spotted dick, and bread-and-butter pudding. I couldn't stand the smell of it. I think people who are always thinking about food are disgusting.'

Her long pale arms reached up again to bring down the packet of tea bags and the milk-bottle. 'I hate making things complicated,' she said.

'Will they all be allowed to see the baby?' I asked.

'Oh yes. I don't want her to have any hang-ups about not being allowed to meet this or that person. That's the kind of heavy family scene which we're getting away from. They'll all meet her quite naturally as friends.'

'But suppose one of them wants, well, wants to be more than a friend.'

'He won't be allowed to. We won't let him.'

'You can't stop him wanting.'

'He'll just see it's no good. Anyway, men don't really mind about babies. They pretend to sometimes but they don't really.'

What gave her this idea that she could invent her own destiny? While I was with her, I was buoyed up by her self-confidence. As long as she was blind or indifferent to the snags in her situation, perhaps they really did matter less. Perhaps the driving force of her will would enable her to bump her way over the obstacles. Yet once out in the street again, that same misery overcame me as I had felt when she had initially turned down my suggestion of a cup of tea. The possibility of something terrible happening to her loomed up again, with a bruising lurching force. This thought – that she was somehow doomed – came round in my mind for several weeks after, as unnerving in its regularity as the beam of a lighthouse.

But in fact, she had at the expected time a healthy eight-pound girl, which she announced in a defiant notice in the papers which I missed at first because it was inserted under her first name without any mention of her surname, let alone of any man – *ONORA, to onora of onora designs, a healthy eight-pound baby girl, both doing brilliantly.*

At first, it seemed better not to be the bearer of this news, then it seemed cowardly not to bear it, especially if they had already read it for themselves, although they too might have been looking under Onora's surname. And so I threw it into a long rambling letter I wrote to Gilly. To my eyes, this casual parenthesis jumped out from the page as though written in foot-high scarlet capitals. I could not tell how it had been received, since the letter I got back, almost by return, was preoccupied with other news.

Silly old Joejoe. You'd never guess what the stupid bugger's gone and done now, just as his poor little paws were on the mend, had a stroke no less. In the profession we call it a small cerebrovascular accident, but in layman's terms, Mrs Follows, it is a stroke, unusual in a chap in his early thirties but it does happen, has he been overdoing it a bit recently? Quite a bit, I said.

273

That would be it then, the doctor said, if you need any moral support, I could put you in touch with Father O'Kelly Mahon, he's a grand man in a tight spot. Was this quite the moment, I thought, but here I am cutting cucumber sandwiches for the both of them and poor Joe upstairs staring at the ceiling.

XI

A sort of haven – Gillian's hens – Father O'Kelly Mahon and the Irish Constitution, an overview

The sedgy fields under an injured sky lulled me, or would have if the taxi had not so brutally assaulted the unlevelled humps in the road. 'She hasn't got a spring left in her body,' the taxi driver said, 'where'd you say the place was, I don't come out this way much, not the sort of place you'd go for a crack.' 'Why not?' I said. 'Excellent fellows they are in their way you know but not much for conversation.' 'Who . . .' 'Oh they've a reputation for it, they have, he's as close as a Cockburnstown man, they'll say. Mind you, I don't know the truth of it, but the border throws a long shadow and, whew, you'd need to be a bloody kangaroo to navigate this stretch.' Beyond the sedgy pastures grazed by bony-rumped brindled cows, mountains rolled low and mauve across the horizon. Now and then a whitewashed bungalow crowded the edge of the road, taking refuge from the boundless desolation of the landscape. We passed a fir plantation. Some of the trees were snapped off halfway up the trunk. 'Now that was your genuine hurricane, all the way from the Gulf of Mexico and no pit-stops.' He laughed and started the windscreen wipers as the mist thickened into proper rain.

The lodge was masked by a dripping thicket of rhododendrons and he missed the turning the first time. My first sight of the crenellated gateway with its crumbling hatchment was achieved through the back window of the old Austin Cambridge taxi, as it reversed through the arch, before turning round on the grass. At the smeary gothic window of the lodge, a woman's face appeared, alarmed by the reversing taxi, and then disappeared. 'What a place, you'd be lucky to get a dog-cart through that arch,' the taxi-driver said, as we bumped on down the mazy drive past untidy heaps of felled or fallen timber.

Through the ever thickening rain, I could see a small group of people coming towards us up the drive. There were three of them, a man, a woman and a child walking side by side. They were carrying cheap brown suitcases tied up with string. The man also had a large cardboard box tied up with string. They interrupted their disconsolate trudge and stood at the side of the drive to let us pass. The woman seemed to catch sight of something in the cab and pointed her finger at it or me. As we drove past, I heard a rattle of stones hit the back of the cab. Out of the small back window I could see the child making some gesture at us. 'Now there's a grand Drishill welcome for you,' the taxi-driver said. 'They'll be from the Abbey for sure.'

The drive curled round a little low scrubby wood. Beyond, I could see grey crenellated towers like the lodge's. As we approached the long Victorian gothic façade, the rain above us and the gravel beneath our wheels both grew heavier and softer. The taxi suffocated to a halt. On the low steps in front of the white gothic-arched door a burly elderly man was leaning on a stick, muffled up to the bridge of his nose.

It was only when he had limped close up to me and he had pushed down his scarf to allow him to speak that I realised it was Joe.

'You,' he said, 'bloody good.'

I was ready for the obvious effects of the paralysis, or thought I was: the limp, the dragged-down side of the face, the halting speech. But it was the expressionless features that shook me most. All animation had fled. The interrogating brightness of his eye, the leprechaun crinkling of his cheek, all that had gone. He fumbled with the scarf and tried to stuff it in the pocket of his dirty old fishing mac, losing his temper when he could not manage it, then pausing deliberately before holding out his left hand awkwardly, palm downwards, for me to clasp.

'Bloody good,' he said again.

The white gothic-arched door opened and Gillian came out with a surge of healthy energy.

'Oh you goodster, come on in both of you, the silly fool would insist on waiting outside for you, because it takes him so long to sort himself out, so now he'll get pneumonia as well. And how was the journey? It really is the back of beyond, isn't it?'

'It was fine, except we were stoned as we came down the drive.'

'Oh that must have been the Tooleys. It's so awful. I said they simply must take the taxi back, but they just wouldn't.'

'Bloody awful,' Joe said.

'Now then, darling, no skiving. He can talk perfectly well when he tries, but they do find it easier just to bloody away. There was a French poet who said nothing except fuck it for fifteen years. I've read loads about the whole ghastly thing, so I'm quite an expert. And he's so fantastically much better than he was when I wrote to you.'

Through the long windows of the drawing-room, I could see the corner of a lake, and low mauve hills beyond. Joe stood at the window and stared at the view with his unmoving face. He turned to me and said in a still, slow, dragging voice, lower than his old voice: 'Welcome to Drizzle.'

'You see,' Gillian said. 'He can do it perfectly well. It takes time, but he can do it.'

I admired the high room with its vaulted ceiling and great fireplace. Gillian was about to reply, then checked herself and looked at Joe.

'It was,' he said and then stopped, gathering his strength for a special effort, 'it was the refectory.'

'Got it right at last,' I said.

'Bloody good,' Joe said.

'The Cockburns left all their pictures and furniture behind, so we've got an instant stately home for practically nothing.' Round the walls, portraits of men in red military coats and blue naval uniform looked down on the three of us. 'We practise on the portraits,' she said.

'How do you mean?' I said, but Joe had already started.

'Hon. George Cockburn, MP; Thomas Cockburn; Thomas Frederick Cockburn, Admiral of the Blue.' His lips slowly made the shape of a kiss at each 'b' in Cockburn and blew a soft horn on Blue.

'We do it after meals, like brushing your teeth.'

The rats had got at some of the pictures, and the paint on them was perilously thin. It was easy to see why the Cockburns had left them behind, skied there on the cream walls.

After lunch, the physio came and we left Joe to do his exercises with her. Gillian and I wandered out through the mild air down the path to the kitchen garden. The sky was lightening behind the hills, and the soft suffocating drizzle had lifted. Now the sound of raindrops falling from the bushes accompanied our squelching footsteps. The fruit bushes were heavy with raspberries and currants fattened with rain, the silvery drops slithering down the red berries. She gathered great armfuls of spinach for dinner, splashing herself with raindrops, and then thrust them into my arms to allow her to gather more.

'You must come and see the hens.'

'Do hens eat spinach?'

'Don't be a moron.'

In an angle of the high stone wall, there was a hen run. The tall henhouse nestled in the corner. It was an odd structure with a conical slated roof supported by white pillars with the gaps between the pillars boarded up with creosoted timbers. 'It used to be a summerhouse. Generations of Cockburns must have done their courting and jilting in it and now my darling hens lead their funny little lives there with that silly fat cockerel throwing his weight about, and them pretending not to notice.' The brown and cream hens ran clucking about the hen run. She had scattered their feed from a battered beige fishing bag she had slung over her shoulder. 'Look at him strutting up and down pretending to be above it all. Now who on earth does he remind you of?' She bent double to reach through the hatch and lift the eggs from the straw. The smell of chickenshit soured the soft air. She held up the eggs to me with a smile of triumph.

'You look as though you had laid them yourself.'

'Oh how I wish I had.'

'I'm sorry.'

'Forget it. How is that girl's baby?'

'Fine, I think.'

'Joe was awfully worried about her. I'm sure there's no need. She's one of those skinny bints who's tough as old boots really.' A huge sense of remoteness came over me as she said 'bints', that curious thin old-fashioned word. It was one of those reminders she handed out now and then that she was not going to be hustled out of her time and class.

'Joe wanted to go over and see the baby, to see if there was anything he could do, he said, but I think it was a bit more complicated. Anyway, he couldn't. He's not nearly well enough yet, and even when he is, he still can't, because of the financial hoo-ha which has suddenly turned awfully nasty for the poor thing. Come on, my dears, eat up your vitamins like good clucksters. That's Molly, the gingery one there, she's such a hopeless gossip, she never starts eating till the rest have nearly walloped the lot.'

There were no warrants out for him, not yet anyway, she said. The tangle he had left his affairs in was too dense to be unravelled into precise charges as quickly as that. Anyway they knew he had been ill, and so even if there had been any extraditable offences involved, no Irish court would send him over. He was safe, for what that was worth, she said, brushing aside the clumps of willow-herb which all but blocked the path to the lake. The air was heavy again now, and the midges knotted and then dispersed again, tickling the tops of my ears with the promise of worse to come. Our arms were still full of great dark green bunches of spinach, its faint bitterness seasoning the air.

'There, you can see Cockburnstown.' Squares of grey and white the far side of the dull-steel water. 'That's the peat-packing factory, they're awfully proud of it, and the place that makes chain-link fencing for the Maze prison, they're even prouder of that. It's part of the export drive. And you see that rickety tower beyond on the hillside. That's a guard post for the border, on our side. Apart from the towers, this bit of it is just a barbed wire fence anyone could hop over.'

Through the gravid air I could only just make out the spidery shape she was pointing at. From where we stood, it was little more than a blob on stilts. It seemed a flimsy thing to be protecting us, as flimsy in fact as the whole long meandering border, although for Joe it was no less than the guarantee of his liberty, for what, as Gillian had said, that was now worth.

'In the evening, we'll play Scrabble.'

'Joe too? Isn't that torturing him a bit?'

'No, he likes it, as long as we take it slowly. He really does like trying at things, for short periods anyway until it all becomes too much for his concentration. But he really is getting better all the time. After all, it's nearly a year now.'

The evening loomed full of menace. Did even Gillian know what she was doing? Might not the mutual effort of the game finish off poor Joe, the obstinate refusal of the brain circuits to release a seven-letter word beginning with 'q' unleashing a fatal arterial deluge? My apprehension increased as dusk came down with unnerving promptitude and just as promptly Joe limped into the little octagonal dining room wearing a claret-hued smoking jacket which seemed to promise melodrama. His sad, dragged-down face remained quite still as Gillian cut up his meat for him, so still that it came as a surprise when his mouth opened and the chopped morsels disappeared down his gullet. Above us, the dim portraits of departed Cockburns came into their own, the threadbare canvas and feeble draughtsmanship treated kindly by the candles on the table.

From certain twitchings of hand and mouth, it became clear, to my surprise, that Joe was in a hurry to finish dinner, or as much of a hurry as he was capable of. It was not until the three of us were seated at a green baize folding card table that he became still again. Beginning at last, not without difficulty, to understand some of the signs and gestures in his now restricted repertoire, I could detect his eagerness to demonstrate the undimmed force of his will.

'House-rules are there is a two-minute time limit,' Gillian said, 'so we don't get in a tizzy thinking we might be missing some fantastic long word and Joe's words score double. You start.' I did Abacus. She hung Stoop on my s. Joe went sideways with Pot, I went down again with Trill, Gillian across with Limb, Joe down with Baby. Panic seized me that his words were about to form some terrible significant pattern which could leave us all distraught. I found it impossible to look at the board as his good hand slowly shuffled his pieces into place for his next turn. For a moment, I could not spot where he had made his word.

'Come on slowcoach. There it is. Bob.'

'That's a proper name,' I said.

'No, it's not. Bob your hair, bob sleigh, it means lots of things.'

'So it does,' I said, and Joe's lips parted in a slow experimental way which more or less amounted to a smile.

And then in some peculiar manner, quite without conscious effort, I slowed down too and adjusted to the dragging pace of the way we were playing. Joe rarely produced a word of more than three letters and often took longer than two minutes to produce it, not to mention the equally slow fashion in which he counted his score, placing his square finger deliberately on each piece as he counted. A state of happiness in which one recognised the futility of things and felt quite at home with the futility. Recognition of futility not the same as despair – hazy recollections of Scrannel's lecture at the Pipes of Straw flitted in and out of my thoughts. Outside, the wind got up. The logs in the grate did some chuckling and hissing. In a proper story, the man in the claret-coloured smoking jacket would have begun to recall a chance meeting in a highland bothy or a Malayan trading station thirty years before. But this is not a proper story.

As it was, Joe said:

'Log. L,O,G. One and two makes three and two makes five.'

'Five, that's right, darling.'

The words I made seemed to shorten too, entirely of their own accord, as the evening went on. I was quite unaware of trying not to humiliate Joe. It seemed more that the rhythm of the game demanded three- or four-letter words and that anything longer would be as gross and galumphing as taking big steps in a minuet.

When some word of Joe's charmed her, she would stretch out her arm, glowing pale in the firelight, and pat his paralysed cheek. How strange it was to feel envious of a man in Joe's state. I began to think cold actuary's thoughts about his life expectancy. After the decent old-fashioned period of mourning, well then – might not the resuming of it be a fiercer, more golden thing than the first time round?

'Come on, Gus, your turn. I seem to be looking after two hemiplegics now.'

After the game was over, we climbed the stairs together, the three of us, arm in arm, taking the broad shallow treads one at a time with a rest on each, at the pace of a soldier's slow march.

In the morning, a commotion. We sat at breakfast, Joe and I, making our way through the cereal, scrambled egg and bacon, and toast and marmalade, as though stocking up for a day of unremitting physical exertion. Joe talked slowly about the house and the fields around it let for grazing at a rent barely enough to pay for the fencing, the timber too low-grade to be worth the carting away, the lake so choked with weed that even local fishermen would go ten miles to fish any other water. I gazed out of the narrow gothic windows – the dining room was on the ground floor of one of the corner towers and looked in three directions. These glimpses of the landscape of failure might be comforting to a visitor. They aggrieved Joe. It was a cruel blow that he had been struck down in this countryside and not in the busy fields and trim plantations of southern England. The fates had known what they were about when they plumped him here.

'Bloody awful,' he said, staring out with motionless grim face at the straggle of fallen timber beside the path to the lake where we had walked the evening before.

It was at that moment that Gillian came running into the room, rosy-cheeked, out of breath.

'Come and see, the hens, quickly, they've all gone.'

Quickly was beyond our powers. Joe took up his stick and limped out into the hall.

They had not all gone. Half-a-dozen were still huddled between the summerhouse hen-coop and the angle of the wall. Brown and cream feathers littered the floor of the hen-coop and were also to be seen on the path we had come along. A few feathers floated around us in the mild morning air, suggesting that the hens had been spirited aloft or snatched by some great bird of prey.

'It must have been more than one fox, to take so many. Oh my darling Molly's gone, and that silly fat rooster.'

'It's no fox, look at the wire.' Joe's deliberate voice made me think of the quick brown fox jumping over the lazy dog. He thumped the ground with his stick.

The chicken-netting had been cut to leave a gap at ground level about two foot square, large enough for a child to crawl through.

'It must have been Seamus. Little Seamus Tooley. The bloody little bugger.' She sat down on the ground and wept, her white aertex shirt shaking with the sobs. We tried to repair the chicken-netting. I was sent back to the house to fetch some wire and on the way caught sight of a brown and cream hen skulking in the raspberry canes and made a feeble effort to catch it, but it fled squawking deeper into the raspberries and I let it be.

When I came back to the hen-coop with the wire, Joe was still thumping the ground with his stick. He was incoherent with rage. Now and then, he got out a 'bloody awful'. Gillian was already recovered and began threading the wire in and out of the netting to keep in the remaining hens. Then I remembered the hen in the raspberry canes and set off after it. The long tendrils slashed at my jacket and slopped raindrops down my neck. Up against the netting at the far end, the hen had cornered itself and was squawking in a panic. I took off my jacket and threw it over the hen. Loose change cascaded into the leafy depths. The hen tried to squawk its way out, but I managed to scoop it up in the coat and take it back and release it into the hen-run. Joe was standing there thumping his stick, inconsolable then and more so as the day went on. He went out again to count the remaining hens, told Gillian to get on to the police (but she refused), to ring the insurance, to pursue the Tooleys' friends and relations in Cockburnstown. Nobody mentioned that if he had not sacked the Tooleys none of this would have happened, assuming that the Tooleys were indeed the rustlers. His indignation was not to be queried.

That night, our Scrabble was shortlived. The game was blighted by the absent hens.

'Where are they now? Will they eat them or sell them, do you think? I don't know which would be worse. Oh, I'm so tired. Being burgled is so exhausting.'

The next morning, we all noticed the gaps on the dining-room walls immediately.

'That was the Admiral of the Blue. And that was Henry Cockburn who died young. Now we really will have to get the police.'

'Chickens I can see. But can the pictures really be the Tooleys too? I mean, what would they do with them? I can't imagine there's a fence in Cockburnstown.'

'They'll come back. To take the other pictures.'

'Don't be stupid. They just wanted to annoy us.'

'They'll come back. I'll sit up.'

'Sit up, what do you mean?'

'With my stick.' He thumped the ground with it.

'You're not serious. What would you – oh all right.'

We left him that night, sitting up stiff as a board in his winged chair, with his hands clasped on his stout briar.

In the morning, there he was still. The curtains still drawn, the frowsty smell hanging around from the night before. There was a shawl over his knees now and his head lolled against the wing of the chair. He looked dead rather than asleep. No more pictures had gone, but the telephone rang to say that cattle with the Abbey brand on them had been seen wandering along the Dublin road a mile or two beyond Cockburnstown.

'If this goes on, the other servants will leave. They'll say the place is bewitched or something.'

'Bloody awful.'

Two mornings later, opening the front door to taste the day, I fell over something soft and fluffy on the doormat. Looking down, I saw a pile of brown-and-cream feathers. The smell was so loathsome I had to take several deep breaths of outside air before going in to report to Gillian and Joe. I felt like handing in my own notice before the servants handed in theirs.

Gillian received each fresh atrocity with granite fortitude. Englishness typed her reactions and protected her from collapse. She accepted that she was irremediably abroad and there was no point in trying to understand what was happening to them.

Joe retreated to his office. This little octagonal room in the other corner tower matched the dining-room in shape, but was otherwise on a different planet. Telex, computer, word processor, flow charts on the walls, telephones – here was Joe's bastion against Irishness, his personal offshore island, floating cool and piloted in a feckless sea of Tooleys. Safe in this room he began to speak more fluently, even now and then with a little life in his face.

'Oh I could always keep figures in my head,' he said when I complimented him on remembering a telephone number. 'Figures are my scene.' In that part of Joe's brain, no doubt, everything was as calm and ordered as a banking hall, while only the thickness of a wall away in the verbal section desperate rescue workers drenched in blood fought to contain the disaster. In this little room, a fresh confidence swept over him. Here he was his own man again (perhaps even Gillian's self-giving was in the end a little cramping).

'We must go to Dublin,' he said, 'to see the lawyers. You must drive me.'

'To Dublin? Couldn't you telephone?'

'No, we must go.'

He was stolid, immovable.

'Oh yes, he's been going quite often these last few months, once a fortnight or thereabouts. It's . . .' she paused. 'Oh, a change of scene, really. You are a goodster to take him.'

The next morning, I went into Joe's study to collect his briefcase for him. One of the narrow gothic panes had been smashed, and a wet wind was blowing through the little white octagon, scattering the heaps of soot which had been flung across his machines, great black heaps of the stuff, so that the golf-ball of his electric typewriter peeped out like some little trinket in a lucky dip.

'It's all so petty,' Joe said slowly. Lacking the capacity to express surprise, he made it sound as if soot was regularly dumped on his office equipment, soot-dumping being a tiresome custom of the country which he had not yet discovered how to avoid.

'Why soot?' I said, but on reflection soot seemed like a fitting sort of protest against domination by technology.

'There's no pattern to it. You just don't know what to expect next,' Gillian said. 'I suppose that's par for the course with the Tooleys. I know it sounds silly, well, it is silly, but I would almost be easier in my mind if they were bombing and booby-trapping. It's these horrible senseless little tricks that get on my nerves. At least in Dublin you'll get away from the Tooleys.'

We drove, Joe and I, in silence through the sedgy injured countryside. Grey, watery green, only an occasional yellow splash of gorse on the hillside. Now and then he read out, in both languages, the names of the places we were passing through, staring straight in front of him. This broken mesmeric incantation of the pure Gaelic vowels and then the hybrid English ones helped me to concentrate on the driving, since it needed no answer. When he uttered an ordinary English sentence, it did not immediately sink in.

'I still have needs, you know.'

'Oh yes. What sort of needs do you mean?'

'You know.'

'I see.'

'The doctor said people won't understand. You'll have to tell them.'

'Well, thank you for telling me.'

'Ballygrogan,' he said, as we rattled down another long grey single-streeted village.

When we came closer to the city, a kind of agitation seized him. I wasn't sure whether it was a pleasant agitation or not. He directed me silently through the long brick terraces of the north of the city. I peered at the shabby doors and pediments, the damaged fanlights, enchanted and saddened by the Georgian townscape and its decay.

'Do you mind waiting half an hour. Just round the corner here. I have a call to make.'

'I'm the chauffeur.'

In the side-street, the decay was completer still. Dirty children, as dirty as urchins in an old *Punch* cartoon, were playing in the puddles on the pavements. Glass was missing from the fanlights, the rickety sashes of the windows wedged shut with cardboard. Joe got out, reached clumsily for his stick and hobbled across the road, taking time to find his feet after the car journey. On the steps of the house, two young men were sitting, both thin as celery stalks. They got up as Joe crossed the road, and I could see that they had been seated upon shabby cushions and also that they too had walking sticks in their hands. As Joe came up the steps they raised their sticks at him, and I was seized with alarm. But they merely crossed sticks with him this way and that, as though rehearsing some mediaeval foreplay. Then the two of them pretended to bar his way before raising their sticks to make an arch over his head. I could see the smiles on their thin faces. They sat down again, adjusting the cushions under their bony bottoms, as he disappeared through the open door.

It may be that men who are incapable of experiencing passionate love are those who feel most vividly the effect of beauty: at any rate that is the strongest impression that they can receive from women. The man who has experienced the beating of the heart caused by the distant sight of the white satin hat of the woman he loves is surprised by how cold the approach of the greatest beauty in the world leaves him.

I could not think why I had plucked the Stendhal from the shelf in my bedroom to while away these chauffeur's waits. The AA Members' Handbook was more diverting. I began trying to memorise the ferries and toll-bridges of the British Isles and then moved on to the international registration letters for cars. Malaysia, Botswana and the Central African Republic were the most surprising.

The door opened and a plump, dark woman, more a girl really, showed Joe out. She was wearing slippers, a red T-shirt, and a dark skirt. He pointed across the road to the car. She looked briefly in my direction, kissed him on the cheek, then went indoors closing the door behind her. The two thin young men got up and began their stick routine again. Joe joined in perfunctorily and then walked across the road.

These brief seconds will always stay scorched on my heart, and not only because of what Joe said next: 'Those poor buggers.'

'Oh they haven't got . . . ?'

'Yes. Druggies. There's a lot in this area. The lawyer's in Merrion Square. We have to cross the river.'

He was quicker at the lawyer's office.

'After breakfast will you watch him pedal?' Gillian said the next morning.

'What?'

'You know, like in the old days, on the exercise bike. I've cleaned the soot off. I know it sounds boring, but he does like an audience.'

'But can he really – '

'He's slower now, of course, a lot slower, but he still likes to set himself a target. He's aiming to reach Crossmaglen by Christmas.'

Joe was ready for me when I put my head hesitantly round his study door, not sure which door to take out of the narrow passage leading to the turret room. Already he was seated on his bike in the old maroon and grey tracksuit, outlined against the window and the misty light of a Drishill morning. Something flat about his outline, not Egyptian now but depleted, insubstantial, ghostly.

'You must clock me,' he said. 'If I go too slow, boom.' He made an exploding gesture with his hands. I saw he had stuck a red strip over the speedometer between five and ten miles per hour.

'The IRA get me if I – ' he stabbed a finger at the low side of the dial.

Obediently I sat at his side watching the needle hovering just on the high side of the red strip as he pedalled with excruciating slowness, leaning his body from side to side to put all his weight on each pedal in turn. It seemed unlikely that a real bicycle would have stayed upright at such a pace, let alone evaded a terrorist ambush. Joe's broad face, contorted by the effort, went alternately maroon and grey like the tracksuit. After a lifetime of this purgatory the milometer clicked up another mile and Joe allowed himself a brief rest before starting up again.

'Turn round. Got to get back home again,' he said. 'Bloody awful.' The game, if game it could be called, appeared to involve a return trip through the terrorist badlands. Even here at the limit of his physical resources or perhaps especially here, Joe could not resist dragging in some kind of gamble. If he went on too far before turning around, he would in his mind's eye fall off and be doomed to lie exhausted on open moorland while hard-eyed killers pumped lead into him. If he set too easy a target, he would have failed himself. As he gasped his way back from no man's land, he began to slow down, the needle now and then strayed across the red strip and I found myself urging on the gasping figure crouched over the handlebars.

'You can make it,' I heard myself say as the door opened and Gillian brought in a priest.

'Joe, you remember Father O'Kelly Mahon. He's come about the Tooleys.'

'Don't let me interrupt your game. Exercise is a wonderful thing for the health.'

Joe collapsed into a convulsive gasping fit, threw his head back to suck in some air, and began wheezing heavily. Father O'Kelly Mahon seemed to pay scant attention to these symptoms. He was a tall skinny man in his sixties with thin mobile lips, the dry stony sort of Irishman. Over his shoulder he had slung a black airline bag. Indeed, his brisk demeanour spoke of airports and conferences and of impatience with parish chores, though his cassock had the grubby shiny wornness of the churchmouse-poor priest. He looked as if the Church had not treated him well, certainly not in his own opinion. And indeed, he opened the conversation with a certain aggrieved kind of self-confidence.

'Now this is a delicate mission I'm on, highly delicate. I have some experience of diplomatic work, did you know that, Mrs Follows? I used to be chaplain for state affairs to Archbishop McQuaid. Between you and me, I was more suited to that type of work, I'm not really a parish man, not at all. The Archbishop was sorry to lose me, especially after my work for him on the constitutional negotiations. The constitution wouldn't be the same without you, OK, he used to say. They all called me OK at that time. The passage about respect for the family, well, I had a stronger wording up my sleeve, much stronger, but I think you can still detect a little of my handiwork in clause . . .'

Joe was still coughing and wheezing and could scarcely speak, but just managed to mutter 'Tooleys'.

'You call me to order, sir, and you are right. I need a touch of the bridle now and then, you'll find that to be so, but since I left the clergy house at Mullingar, I have not been accustomed to civilised conversation and I have lost the hang of it. Now as to the Tooleys, they are not an easy family. I would be the last man to pretend that. They do not take kindly to discipline, but then they are not used to it. The Cockburns, God bless their memory, lived in the Irish style. They were Protestants for form's sake only, you might say. And they knew the Tooleys like they knew every inch of the Bog of Drishill. Now you'd be wanting something rather different out of Tom Tooley and Doreen, something more in the modern management line. But you see, Mr Follows, that's the trouble. Critical path analysis is meat and drink to you and me, but it's a closed book entirely to a dear soul like Tom Tooley.'

'He is not a dear soul,' Joe coughed out the words with discomfort, although he was wheezing more quietly now.

'Now I'm sorry to see you take that line. Tom is an in-and-out performer, I'll grant you, but he's a decent fellow underneath. The thing is not to drive him. He won't be driven. He's a man that likes to work at his own pace, if you know what I mean.'

Joe snorted.

'Well now, let me put it another way to you. To be honest with you, I wouldn't choose this particular line of argument, I don't care for it at all, but there's plenty of people in Cockburnstown who want to see the Tooleys get their job back and they said to me, now then, OK, you be sure and tell the man out straight. So let me put it like this, hypothetically if you like: the Tooleys have lived in this place one hell of a long time and they have piled up a heap of friends all over the country and as I am sure you know, this is bandit country as the phrase goes. We're not in County Kildare now.'

'Are you – '

'No, no, I know what you're going to say. And I don't want to upset you in your distressful state of health, that's the last thing I want. I'm merely placing the facts before you. Now I believe there have been certain deplorable incidents within the demesne over the last couple of days. That's all pure hooliganism. There's no authority behind it at all. But I can't promise there won't be more substantial incidents to follow. I have no direct knowledge of such things, you understand. And I would give anything to prevent them coming to pass. That is why I have taken the liberty of coming along.'

'Bloody awful,' Joe said.

'Now I'm sorry you should take my visit amiss. Mind you, I'm not surprised. You're a man of spirit and a man of spirit does not take to being advised. So I won't push my luck.'

'We're fantastically grateful for the advice, Father,' Gillian said. Joe began pedalling again with a fierce and sullen mien. The other three of us, grouped round him amid the office furniture, were as collusive as a case conference of social workers.

'Just so long as you understand the lie of the land,' Father O'Kelly Mahon said.

'It's awfully kind of you,' she said.

'Is there perhaps some other work here that Tom Tooley could have a go at?' I hazarded.

'If we put our thinking caps on, I'm sure we could come up with something.'

Joe stopped pedalling and glared.

'Bloody awful,' he said and with a great drunk-seeming swing of his arm gestured at the door.

'I think perhaps he's had enough for one day,' Gillian said.

'I gather your drift entirely,' said Father O'Kelly Mahon, hitching up his shoulder bag and making for the door.

It was the next day I was due to leave Drishill Abbey, and I was about to call in on the turret room to say goodbye to Joe when he got in first by getting Gillian to summon me to him. 'He wants a heart-to-heart,' she said, trying not to sound annoyed to be left out. I would much rather she had come along. Her presence would have prevented him burdening me with any embarrassing messages.

He sat, not on the exercise cycle, but at his desk in the corner, looking out over the grey-green fields and the black waters of the lake, or the corner of it he could see from there. His gaze was mortally glum. Not that he was short of things to be glum about: his state of health, his exile, his childless marriage, his lack of occupation, as well as the rotting timber in the woods and the weed-choked lake where the fish were dying.

'Bloody awful,' he said, but with a spurt of sprightliness which led me to guess he was referring to my going.

'I'm awfully sorry to be going. It's such a marvellous place.'

'Long way,' he said. 'Long way away.'

'That's what's marvellous about it,' I said and tried feebly to describe how much I had enjoyed my stay, which was true enough, for the remoteness of it all had been cool and sweet, despite certain freakish upsets.

He did not appear to be listening. His stony face had the dragged-down look again. The cold light through the long window had petrified his features.

'Could you do something for me?' he said, speaking now at the pace of a normal conversation. These changes from zombie to ordinary human being had become more frequent as my stay had gone on and he had become accustomed to my company, but they were still unnerving when they happened, making me feel as though his inner self had been observing me closely all the time behind the ramparts of his aphasia and had now decided to come out and switch to the human mode.

'Well, yes, of course, anything legal.' The jocularity was intended to fend off the sort of errand I dreaded, principally being asked to take a message to Onora, or worse still, having a pair of bootees or a fleecy matinée jacket for the baby thrust into my hands. But for the time being, he seemed to have given up hope of re-establishing contact in that direction. At least, he had not spoken of it at all, and even in his present state it was hard to think of him as too shy to confide his most intimate hopes.

A few moments later, I would willingly have carried a dozen matinée jackets and the most cloying message, couched if necessary entirely in baby talk, rather than execute the commission which he turned out to have in store for me. There is a temptation, quite a strong temptation, to record in these pages exactly such a sentimental scene, however perverted the sentiments, instead of the truth of what happened next.

'You saw Bridie. She's a great girl. She does everything she can – to help. But she can't manage, not the whole bit.'

'Yes. Quite,' I said vaguely, not quite knowing what I was agreeing to.

'So I have this – ' he waved an arm, retreating into word-lessness.

'This what?'

'Bloody awful,' he said, then paused. 'I'll show you,' he said after a moment or two.

He fumbled with a key on his key ring and eventually managed to unlock a drawer in the desk and brought out a flat cardboard box only a few inches long, that peculiar deep crimson cardboard used by old-fashioned chemists, the same crimson as the oval box which contained my yellow pills. I took it as a mark of friendship that he should be showing me some new device to help his breathing, and I leaned forward, seized by a keen interest which was both professional and comradely. Once again we were to be asthmatics together as in the old days, members of the great fraternity of the bronchially strangulated. My interest grew when I saw the neat little rubber bulb linked to a miniature contraption of tubes and rings.

'Wonderful how small they can make these things now,' I said.

He looked at me, his ruined features suddenly revived by his amazement.

'You know these things? I would not have expected . . .'

'Well, not this model exactly, but the general . . .' My voice too trailed into speechlessness as I looked more closely and it became clear that the device was not of respiratory application. As he lifted it out of the flat box, it became possible to read the legend, discreetly placed on the inside of the lid in the sort of decorated script used by William Morris in the Kelmscott Chaucer: 'ITHYPHAL, the Infallible Reviver, medically approved.' As I was reading this, he reached over the desk and placed a small slippery object in my hand. I looked down and saw what looked like a fragment of a balloon. He entrusted it to me with the same care that Eeyore lavished on the burst balloon he had received as a birthday present from Winnie the Pooh.

'Thing's bust. Bloody awful,' Joe said. 'Can't get a new one in Dublin, because of the priests, and I can't go to Belfast any more.' This was the longest speech he had made in the week I had been at Drishill Abbey. Never had the hopelessness of exile been made more manifest.

'I'll see what I can do,' I said and hurriedly stuffed the terrible thing into my pocket.

'John . . .' he said, and again 'John' and then words failed him.

'John who?' I said, leaning forward as though attempting to catch his last words, fearing that he had forgotten my name and was calling me John.

Surely he could not have mistaken me for John Dudgeon. Or worse still, had he, perhaps without meaning to, in his bombed-out attic of a mind, stumbled on the memory of our John-and-Diana dialogues, disloyally confided to him by Gillian and stored up as ammunition for some suitable moment?

'Bell,' he cried in a cracked voice. 'Bell.' And then was silent again.

'Bell, ring, telephone, bell, book and candle, front door bell?'

'No, no,' he muttered, 'John Bell.'

'Oh,' I said, 'John Bell and Croyden.' The name of the famous West End chemist's caused him to smile in his old irresistible leprechaun's way and I smiled too. The mere mention of this temple of pharmacy had bathed the whole project in respectability. True, he had landed me with a mission of paralysing embarrassment. Yet it was hard not to admire his dauntlessness.

'I'll tell them to be as quick as possible,' I said, 'and to send it under plain cover.'

He nodded as though I was tying up the loose ends of the most routine piece of business in the world. He then permitted us a pause, not so much for reflection as for any other subject to declare itself. After a minute or so of silence, he got up and held out his good left hand to me. His farewell was laconic, the farewell of one man of action despatching another on a mission the hazardous aspects of which it would have been demeaning to allude to. There was a marmoreal quality to our goodbyes. And before I had closed the gothic-arched door behind me, he had turned to contemplate the long damp view over the neglected parkland.

The finality of the whole business sent me stumbling down the long dim passage from the turret room. My legs felt weak and out of control. As I reeled out in the hall, it was not surprising that I cannoned into Gillian. In such a tottery state, I was bound to bump into something. But it was a surprise when she let out a loud squawk, the most perfect imitation of a hen's squawk that could be imagined. When I recovered my balance, it became clear that no imagining was required. She was in fact carrying a hen, a startled, indignant bundle of brown and cream feathers.

'Oh you have upset Perdita. She's not used to musical bumps or even unmusical ones.'

'Perdita?'

'Lost and found again. She's the one you rescued from the raspberries. When the new lot arrive, they're all going to be called after Shakespeare heroines. There's a real non-stop talker who doesn't know it yet, but she's doomed to be Portia.'

The hen gave a guarded, suspicious sort of cluck. Gillian bent her dark head and nuzzled the brown-and-cream feathers of the hen's neck.

'Oh you fluffski, what shall we do without that silly man who keeps bumping into us?'

'Only once.'

'We can see he's an incurable bumper, can't we, Perdy? Bump, bump, bump, he goes.' Even the gentle imitation bumps upset the hen again and set her clucking.

It came to me that I was sadder now to leave her than I had been when she had gone off with Joe. The hen nestling in her bosom against the hooped jersey (from the little boutique in Church Street where I had waited outside for her) was a lucky bird. Downy, squawky, clawed and beaked and wattled, bright-eyed and bird-brained, creamy-feathered, and smelling, quite faintly, of chickenshit, it seemed as good an emblem of love in its various aspects as could be hoped for. Beside Perdita or the thing itself, how thin and dull were the usual analyses of love. Maintenon-Smith: you will find that Stendhal is a fearless deep-sea diver into the submerged life of the emotions. From where I stood, he seemed to go about as deep as a schoolboy with a ping-pong ball and a rubber breathing tube. Would Stendhal have had a clue how I felt standing in the damp hall while Perdita clucked on and the rain drummed on the glass roof of the little cupola? The jersey had orange-and-blackcurrant hoops and I had not liked it from the first, because it made her look like a rugger forward. This criticism had not gone down well at the time but she had since adopted it and would say, 'there's nothing like a rugger bugger to keep you snug.'

'This is goodbye then.'

'Don't say goodbye. Don't ever say goodbye.'

he can see that it is essentially a religious parable about the loss of innocence. The book after that is going to be a whodunnit set on a Viking longboat in the eighth century. I had originally thought of incorporating it in the present book with the Thai rent-boy as the detective, but then I realised that by the time we got back to the eighth century he would just be a Hideous Thing and quite incapable of working out how long it would have taken Harold Snagtooth to climb the main mast and kill the look-out during a Force Ten gale. Literary endeavour is a solitary and gruelling pursuit,' he said with a doleful sigh, removing his war-criminal's spectacles. 'You go and wander round the glasshouses. I've got some office chores to finish.'

Peggy put on what I suppose was a baseball cap, but it was such a silky grey thing that it looked Parisian. 'The glare through the glass,' she said, 'my old eyes need shading.'

On the sliding door of the first glasshouse, Trull had written 'Tropical Butterflies hate draughts. SIDLE through this door.' Peggy slipped through and held out her slender hand to beckon me through the exiguous gap, even now turning the gesture into some larger kind of invitation.

'The sun's gone in. They'll mostly be roosting,' she said. In the tangle of leaves and trunks, it was hard to see more than the occasional huge butterfly, flitting silent and drowsy above us. The heat was suffocating, damp, rising from the shiny waters of an ornamental pond. Other visitors peered frustrated through the foliage, looking for the flash of iridescent wings. We jumped as a loudspeaker opened up somewhere above us with sounds of cawing, cooing and the occasional shrill yelp: 'it is dawn in the tropical rainforest,' a metallic voice-over twanged through the din, 'and like other creatures of this fantastically rich habitat, the butterflies are beginning to stir from their perches.'

Trull's voice was honey-laden with menace. 'There are 37,000 species of butterfly in the forest. Hundreds of those species are now at risk from *this*.' A terrifying crash disturbed the animal orchestra. 'Every week another area of forest the size of Gloucestershire is cleared by the loggers and ranchers to provide hamburgers and rare hardwoods for us here in the Western world.' The visitors instinctively huddled together, startled by this unexpected assault upon their life-style. 'So remember next time you go to McDonald's or buy a mahogany coffee table, you could be destroying for ever the habitat of these unique and lovely creatures.'

The visitors began to move on, nettled by being got at thus after having paid good money. But at the far end of the glass house they found their way barred by an austere figure in green operating-theatre kit with war-criminal's glasses. Trull stood with cherub smile on his lips and ear cocked in ecstasy to his own commentary which clearly was going to be heard to the end.

As he moved on to describe the life cycle of the butterfly, far from dying away, the note of menace if anything became more alarming still as Trull explained the fragility of the butterfly's existence. Even that joyous frolicking dance of courtship which so enchanted the tender-hearted lover of nature was a perilous pastime.

'You will see here and there butterflies whose wings are ragged or torn-looking. Most of this damage is inflicted by other butterflies during their often violent collisions before copulation. Although butterflies' eyes are such large and complex structures, their sight is feeble. They can see the general outline of objects, but they cannot clearly distinguish members of other species from their own kind. When laying her eggs, the female butterfly often seems to be guided by the sense of smell rather than by sight.'

And not only butterflies, I said to myself, as the sweat trickled down between my shoulder-blades.

'Now, after you have looked your fill upon these magnificent creatures, you may wish to stroll through to your native heath. In the temperate house you will find most of Britain's best-loved butterflies enjoying their natural surroundings. You will also be able to purchase a selection of the caterpillars and chrysalises which we have bred here especially for you, so that you can turn your own back garden into a haven for butterflies. Remember, do not touch the butterflies. These insects will die if brushed aside by careless hands.'

302

In sombre mood, we filed through into the next glasshouse past a grinning Trull. Something about the portly little man in sandals ahead of me was familiar. As the tour went on, he was being increasingly irritated by the slow progress of his wife who was on two sticks. She was rather more broken down than he was and found it hard to manoeuvre along the narrow paths between the dense tangle of jasmine and passion flower.

In the temperate house, Trull's commentary became more lyrical, softening the customers up for the climactic moment of sale. He told us of the plants the butterflies preferred for nectar and for laying their eggs on and the other plants their caterpillars fed on: mignonette and hedge mustard, cuckoo flower, buckthorn and milk parsley for the swallowtail, wild strawberry for the Grizzled Skipper, restharrow, ground-ivy and thistle and false brome as well as the indispensable nettles and, of course, buddleia, the butterfly bush.

I was musing on this pastoral catalogue with its sweet echoes of Shakespearean lullabies and Victorian watercolours when the portly man in front of me turned round and spluttered: 'Calls himself a conservationist, con man more like.'

'What do you mean?'

'Releasing into the wild insects bred in captivity is sheer murder. Half of them will die and the other half will corrupt the native breeding stock.'

'But if they're native butterflies?'

'Natives my eye. Half of these so-called British butterflies are complete immigrants. Haven't bred in this country in recorded memory.'

'Is there some trouble?' Trull hovered.

'You ought not to do it, you know.'

'Do what?'

'It's a scandal.'

He had the look of someone who is not used to getting angry in a public place. His wife plucked at him with flustered little hands.

'They must know what they're doing, Derek.' Her soft pink funny face with its surprising dark eyes looked round at the rest of us, appealing to us to stop the trouble somehow.

'Meriel, isn't it?' I said.

She looked at me with eyes unstirred by recognition.

'You wouldn't remember . . . the old days . . . the Mariners?'

'The what?' A stranger at my elbow said.

'Oh the dear dear Mariners,' she said, still not recognising me. 'Derek, this is a friend from the Mariners days.'

'I'm not deaf, you know. I'm sorry, but I can't quite – '

'I was there the day Peter Dudgeon collapsed.'

'Oh *that* day, what a day that was.' He spoke with sudden zest as though we had witnessed some great sporting triumph together.

'All dead, now, of course,' he added, on a more elegiac note. 'As dead as the butterflies they sell from this bloody place.' He waved at the glass case with his rolled-up *Daily Telegraph*.

'If you don't like it, you can get the hell out of here.' Trull, nettled to be out of things, reasserted himself.

'Delighted, the sooner the better. Just thought I ought to show the flag. I'm local rep for LABE, the League Against Butterfly Exploitation, it's only a small outfit so far, but we're gaining members at a rate of knots.'

'Get out.'

The decrepit couple trotted out, he exhilarated at having made a stand, she waving me a tremulous goodbye. The last I saw of Derek he was thrusting his *Telegraph* back into his shopping bag with the brio of an officer returning his sword to its scabbard.

'Keeps them happy, I suppose, stupid little people,' Trull said.

'He'll probably put a spell on you with his *Daily Telegraph*. You remember, he used to be a wizard with Peter Dudgeon and the rest of them.'

'Of course I remembered. Instantly. I wasn't going to give him the satisfaction of letting him know it. Right then, I'll leave you to look round,' and he hurried into an office at the far end of the glasshouse. For the first time in years, I remembered that he walked with a little swaying sort of strut.

'What peculiar friends my ex-husband had. Let's go back in the bungalow. Trull will be hours,' Peggy said, and took my arm. That faint – what was it, hesitation, breathlessness – before the word 'bungalow' sounded the same old quaver, mocking yet enhancing. 'We've got so much news to catch up on. Are you happy?'

But that was only a polite introduction.

'Joe's getting better, isn't he? Everyone says so. Slowly of course, but better. I don't think I could bear to see him. You know what I'm like with ill people. Anyway, my dear daughter has made it very plain, awfully plain really, that she doesn't want me to come over. She really is stalwart, Gillian, isn't she? You admire her so much, don't you?'

I conceded this soft imputation with the same embarrassment as if I had been cajoled into admitting an interest in Shire horses.

'Perhaps I should go over, just once. Do you think? He must get lonely. Such a pity he can't see that baby.'

'The baby?'

'Oh I know all about that. Trull and Onora are always talking about it. If you ask me, I think the whole thing is a little bit overdone. Having children is difficult enough without adding *complications*, don't you think?'

We sat on a low sofa in the little sitting-room. Through the open window, I could smell the wallflowers and hear the distant chatter of the visitors. The same deep repose I remembered from our tea together in the Gryphon Hotel had me in its clutches. Indeed, I was sipping her tea again – smoky china tea but strong, not exquisite – when a sudden groan from the other side of the wall startled me into choking. It was a long squeezed-out groan, an expression of terminal despair, and soon followed by another, louder, then a quieter moan, of resignation. Then the cycle was repeated: long groan, loud groan, dying moan.

'What on earth is that?'

'Oh that's poor Rickshaw. He tries to sleep through the afternoon, but he always gets the dose wrong.'

At the sound of our talking, the groans stopped, and there was a knocking against the wall, intended perhaps as a protest at our talking in the next room but so deliberate and spaced-out that it came out like the knocking at the beginning of a French play.

'We can't have that,' Peggy said. 'He's either got to go to sleep properly or come and join the grown-ups.'

She got up and went into the passage. Doors opening. Low mumbles. She came back, severe as a school matron.

'He's coming along,' she said.

The figure in blue pyjamas was as pale as I remembered, but thinner still and frailer-looking now. That bleached look seemed quite drained of life. He lowered himself into a wicker chair, gripping the arms of the chair.

'Tea,' he said. 'Oh good.'

'Bad Rickshaw. You made the most frightful noise.'

'Did I? Oh did I? I am sorry.' He seemed to be searching his mind for the details of events that had happened years ago. 'I know you,' he said, looking at me.

'Of course you know him.'

'Do you like butterflies?' he enquired.

'Yes I do.'

'I saw dozens of Purple Emperors once. In Greece. Dozens. Very common there.'

'Are they?'

'Not so common here. Rare in fact, very rare.'

'Yes.'

'Rickshaw, don't be boring.'

'I couldn't sleep. I can't get those pills right.'

'It says quite clearly on the packet.'

'I know but I can't remember whether I took one or two before.'

'Why don't you write it down then?'

'Write? Oh, I can't write, not at all, not yet. When I'm better, I'm going to write.'

'Well, I should hurry up and get better then.'

'Yes. Yes, I will.' He looked up at her with sad grateful eyes. 'I thought I would be better when I came back from the hospital. But it's so difficult. Oh you are kind.' Through the mists of his melancholy, here could be traced the ruins of his old charm, overgrown now.

'Do drink your tea, Rickshaw, I can't think why you find it so hard to remember to eat and drink. When I'm ill, I eat like a horse.'

'Do you?' He smiled and drank his tea.

Peggy's chiding seemed to do the trick. She handled him with a deftness which seemed born of quite long experience, and that was surprising in view of her acknowledged impatience with ill people. Rickshaw must have his tedious moments, repeating himself, harping on his condition as melancholy-mad people do, not to speak of the taut silences that were also to be expected, the stuttering placating nothings, and the alarming ferocities blowing up out of the nothings. It seemed unlike her to have gone through all of this.

Trull bustled in, unpopping the top buttons of his green uniform with the irritable haste of one who has performed half-a-dozen appendectomies on the trot.

'Jesus, the bloody public. I sometimes wonder whether it's worth letting them in. That Derek man we used to meet with Peter D, he knows as much about butterflies as a face flannel. When one's only trying to do one's bit for conservation.'

'Trull dear, Rickshaw's had a ghastly afternoon too. Couldn't get a wink of sleep and then we woke him with our chat.'

'Poor old Rickers. Well, I've got some news that will prop your pecker up, Rickshaw. I've just been talking to Onora on the office phone. She's coming down on the 7.23 with you-know-who. Baby Bubbins, isn't that nice, Rickshaw? You love Baby Bubbins, don't you?'

He glared at Shay, his war-criminal's glasses glinting with jocular menace. Trull clearly expected this news to have an instant effect, and so it did.

Shay bent forward in the wicker chair, and pressed his fists to his mouth. His head trembled in a peculiar convulsive fashion. His mouth seemed to be nibbling at his hands. There was a childish concentration about him, like a child who has been told that if he imitates a nibbling rabbit very hard he will get a present.

'No, no. I can't.'

'Oh come on, Rickshaw. Just stay up and say hullo. It'll mean a lot to Onora, and Bubbins is really taking to you, I can see she is.'

'No, no.'

'You did say to me once how you liked babies. You told us that lovely story about that Afghan tribe and the baby rolled up in the carpet. They were Afghans, or Pathans, except that's the same thing, isn't it, and you call them Pat-hans, don't you?' Peggy was crouching beside the sobbing figure and stroking his back, massaging the pale blue pyjamas with a gentle circular motion.

'No, I can't. Can't.'

'Rickshaw, some day you're going to have to take responsibility for your actions, you know. You can't just leave it all to other people to clear up after you.' Trull was firm, magisterial.

'Not my actions.' The voice little more than a faint whimper now.

'My dear Rickshaw, I'm afraid they were. In fact, I can't think of any actions which could be more unmistakably yours.'

'May not be me.' These phrases came out like the speech-scraps of a dying man in a mystery story, although in this case the mystery was melting fast.

'No, but you're the only one she can lean on, aren't you, Rickshaw? Because that East End antiquaire has got a wife and kids, hasn't he? And Joe, well, poor old Joe is unavoidably detained elsewhere. So you're the only one.'

'But you said . . . you said . . .'

'What did I say, Rickshaw?'

'You said it would be a kindness.'

'So it was. A great kindness. She needed you, Rickshaw, and she still needs you, needs you very badly, I'd say. Wouldn't you, Peggy?'

'Yes she does, but Trull . . .'

'No but-Trulls, please. Rickshaw, this girl is all alone with her Bubbins. Now you may say she's not a girl at all, but a fully grown woman with her own business and all that, and a woman who's had a lot of men in her time, so she ought to know her way around

308

by now. But the point is she doesn't. She is really just a babe in arms *with* a babe in arms. And she needs someone to help her, and she's quite willing to let you help her because, well, because she thinks you're not a threat to her independence. You see she's still got all these ideas, but she's got enough sense to know she needs someone to lean on. She doesn't want a full-blown husband, who does these days? But she does want a little help.'

'I can't help anyone. Not now.'

'I don't mean now, of course I didn't mean now, but when you're better.'

'Better?'

'You are going to get better, don't pretend you don't know that. Everyone gets depression these days and everyone recovers from it. So when you're better, all you have to do is simply take the little top base above her and say hullo to her and Bubbins whenever you're here but come and go entirely as you please.'

'You said . . .'

'I said what?'

'There would be no complications.'

'Well, there aren't any complications. You need some sort of base now your mother's gone, and Onora needs a little company. I can't see what could conceivably be simpler.'

'You told me I wouldn't have to live with her.'

'Well, I don't call that living with her. I call that friendship. Don't you want to see Bubbins?'

'I can't. I can't.'

He got up, head bent, hands still clenched in the nibbling position. He walked out of the room with a scurrying walk, gone without a word, at any rate without a word that any of us could hear, for he was mumbling like a priest at his breviary. Indeed, he was somewhat holy in his madness, carrying with him into that state his native intensity and purity.

'Will he really get better?'

'Oh yes, they all do now, like I said. The crack-up started when his mother died. Said he felt rudderless, wished he had a family but he couldn't cope with the responsibility. Well, you must admit it looked like a heaven-sent opportunity for him to *be* part of a family with the minimum of responsibility. He could enjoy a kind of floating parenthood. Onora was thrilled. She'd always worshipped him from afar, she said. Well, she didn't waste much time before she got down to worshipping him at close quarters. It all was like a dream, Rickshaw said. Onora was convinced from the start that he was the one. Of course, as soon as the baby was born, there was no doubt. Are you sure you can't stay and see for yourself? Bubbins really is rather enchanting even to an old Herod like me.'

'I'm afraid I do have to get back.'

'And then it all became a bit much. It turns out, you see, that Pod Pease is absolutely terrified of his wife and as soon as she got wind of the affair, she attached the old ball and chain with a vengeance. She goes with him everywhere now, the pub, the antique markets, the loo probably. So there was no chance of him getting near Bubbins. And then Joe was ruled absolutely out of court. And suddenly Rickshaw realised that he was the one in every sense, not just a once-a-month zoo-and-McDonald's father but the real thing. And he just couldn't face it, poor lamb.' Trull's rude cherub lips had come back, fleshed up and filled with blood by the excitement. He had taken off the war-criminal's glasses and his round eyes were sleepy. He was drowsy-gorged, a mosquito the morning after.

Peggy lay on the sofa, her slender bare legs dangling over the end, her hand over the eyes in a migraine-mime.

On my way out, I wandered through the butterfly house. A youth in a T-shirt and jeans was just locking up. Some of the butterflies had already gone to roost, their folded wings black against the green and silvery-green buddleia leaves. But several fritillaries were still fluttering about the airy spaces between the bushes. One attached itself to a Red Admiral and the two of them swooped up and down in a giddy dance of I could not tell what – conversation, courtship, provocation, war?

It would have been heartless and thoughtless to pass on to Joe any of the news of Rickshaw. And it turned out that, unless I had done so in the next couple of weeks, it would also have been impossible.

'Ah, is that you? Thank heavens I've caught you. It's Alec here, well, the Colonel, Gillian's father. Have you heard the news?'

'What news?'

'They've been kidnapped. Joe and Gillian. By the Fenians.'

'I don't believe it.'

'Nor did I. But there's a note, you know. They left a note, stuck on Joe's exercise bike. The police didn't find it till the morning after. Low Dudgeon thinks it's all a put-up job. Typical of his nasty mind.'

'Why isn't there anything about it in the papers?'

'There's a news black-out, according to the chap from the Fraud Squad who rang me up. They always have a news black-out, you see, to keep the kidnappers in the dark.'

'Why from the Fraud Squad?'

'Yes, that is odd, isn't it? They seem to be handling the thing this end. He asked me all sorts of questions, rather personal some of them were, but I thought it was best to give one hundred per cent co-operation. You never know what may turn out to be relevant. They are asking for two million, you know. Totally absurd. I couldn't raise twenty thousand since I had my smash-up, not two thousand probably. Low Dudgeon's got a bob or two, but I wouldn't like to – '

I tried to stem the flow and was swamped by his flood-panic. The best that could be done was to promise to find out what was going on and get off the line. It was a relief to talk to the neat dark man from the Fraud Squad, although he was as puzzled as the rest of us. His name was Jervoise. He spelled it out for me.

'There's nothing wrong with the note, mind you, it's just what their ransom notes are always like, uses the right code-name and so on, but then everybody knows the code name nowadays. It's just that it doesn't seem like them to lift an undischarged bankrupt who is also liable to face certain charges if he ever returned to this country. I don't say he would definitely, but he might have to. And then there's the fact that the note was typed on Mr Follows's own typewriter. Sounds a leisurely sort of kidnapper to me. Normally, you see, they have the note or message prepared in advance and delivered separately. So you see – '

'You think they might have faked it.'

'You said it, sir, not me. But we are taking it one stage at a time at the moment.'

'There was this family they quarrelled with, the Tooleys.'

'Oh yes, we've spoken to them. He's doing very well now, as a roofing contractor in Galway City. Seems as mystified as the rest of us.'

I could not utter words like preposterous and inconceivable. For, reluctant though I was to agree with John Dudgeon, it was possible to see how Joe might have conceived one final adventure along these lines. This would in fact be the ultimate first: the cripple despaired of by the doctors (a little exaggeration was pardonable in such matters) who staged his own disappearance and fooled the police of three nations. True, so far he did not appear to have fooled the police of one nation, but no doubt the plot would have other twists to it which would make the story more plausible. I could see Joe roughing out the scenario, as he would have called it, perhaps on the same bicycle clipboard to which he had finally attached the ransom note. As this fancy scampered further out of control through my disordered mind, I noticed the Fraud Squad man looking at me and reading my thoughts as plainly as if they were written on a motorway sign. It was too late to explain that I suffered from a peculiar moral defect, namely, the inability to suppose my friends incapable of any crime, however foul or insane. A mumbled protest that it all seemed very unlikely was the best that could be mustered.

'Unlikely? Indeed, it does, sir. But then you take the alternative hypothesis, that Army Command in Donegal gives the local Provo snatch squad the go-ahead to seize an undischarged bankrupt without any of the usual financial or security checks. Not very likely either, is it?'

'Aren't you giving them rather too much credit?'

'There, if I may say so, sir, I think you are falling victim to the

Pat-and-Mike syndrome. Today's IRA is a highly sophisticated outfit, not like the cowboys we used to have to deal with.'

'But oughtn't we to say that Joe's a bankrupt wanted by the British police, just in case they don't know.'

'Well, sir, if that is the scenario, are we going to be the first to tell them, because we might be signing your friends' death warrant, might not we? After all, what use would they be to them then?'

'So what do you suggest we do then?'

'We just sit and wait, sir, let them make the first move.'

After leaving the airless little office, I began to think of all the things I might have told Jervoise if he had not started talking about syndromes and scenarios: for example, that Joe really had got away with quite a lot of money, although he might not wish, in normal circumstances, to have that fact known; for another example, that I could not in a million years see Gillian consenting to take part in such a monstrous deception.

And then I thought again that it might be best to wait and see if the kidnappers, if they existed, were aware of Joe's real cash position. Later still, on the tube home, I was overwhelmed by another thought, that Gillian might, precisely because of her nobility, go along with this cheap and shabby trick. Rather than watch Joe pedal hopelessly towards a blank horizon, she might, just might, against all her instincts and principles, indulge him in one final break-out.

It was, after all, a comfortable fantasy, if fantasy it was, much less grim than the thought of the two of them cowering in some damp farm outbuilding, listening to the rain on the corrugated-iron roof or the conversation, by turns brutish and tedious, of their captors. In the days and then weeks that followed, we heard nothing. And the thought of their illicit exile began to take hold: a villa on the outskirts of some South American capital, Bogota perhaps, bought with money laundered through Switzerland and Panama, not that they would care much about the colour of the money out there; stables thatched with pampas grass; Gillian breaking rough half-breed colts in the paddock, while awaiting admission to the local bridge club; Joe keeping fit out on the shady veranda, the whirring of the exercise bike broken by the chirping song of the cicadas, doing a few local property deals to keep his hand in, mixing with some of the rough diamonds he always liked, possibly even a German or two with a remarkably blank past, then, as time went on, first Joe then Gillian taking to the tequila, she obediently following him over the brink into alcoholism, but still the pulsating heat, the shrill cries of the parakeets, the distant peaks violet in the sunset, pearly grey at dawn . . .

It was precisely in those days of waiting and surmising that I began to notice something unexpected beginning to happen. I was driven one night by some newish acquaintance to a restaurant they said they had been lucky to get a table at. 'Its proper name is Carousals, but we call it eating underneath the arches,' the wife said with a winsome toss of her maple-syrup mane. The same waiters were still there, including the one who had showed me so slowly to where Joe was crouching with his bleeding wrists, the same manager with the Nordic moustache, even, it seemed, the same sweet trolley with the peeled oranges bobbing in their syrup as the trolley rattled over the quarry tiles. But now the place was crowded, tables pressed against the wall, the raw brickwork scraped the bare arms of women who looked much like my hostess.

'I used to come here before,' I said, 'it was often empty then.'

'How gloomy. But you can't have, it was right In the moment it opened.'

Quite soon afterwards, I heard two women complaining that the silk her husband had brought her back from Hong Kong seemed really rather shoddy compared with her Brod shirt. The miraculous revival of the Brod silk mills was apparently one of the few recent success stories in British textiles.

'They got the place dirt cheap,' my informant said. 'Sold off half the land for housing, turned the old weaving shed into an industrial heritage museum, and then intensively marketed the designs they inherited from that chap, you remember, the one who went belly up and scarpered, to Ireland, I think.'

There was also a small haulage firm I remember Joe owning, which he had come by unintentionally, as part of a property deal (what he wanted was the company's yard and the derelict acres behind it). Slumbering in one of those fading little mining village-towns in the Forest of Dean, it was a charming spot for a small housing estate, but offered slim chance of haulage contracts against the big firms in Bristol and Cardiff. Then its prospects were transformed by the great strikes in the South Wales coal field and steel mills when the railways shut down for months, and strike-breaking lorries plied up and down the motorways, covered in brown dust, with wire mesh across their windscreens to protect them from missiles. The lorries of Joe's old firm were on the road twenty-four hours a day with the drivers working in shifts and lucky to get back to the Forest of Dean at night. And after the strike, the firm's record of reliability earned it a fistful of long-term contracts. Then there were the property deals that Barney finally brought off, just north of the garment jungle. For a time, until his retirement to Winchmore Hill to look after his ailing but still formidable mother, he was said to be one of the country's top half-dozen property men. If Joe had kept his share of those deals, he would at least have been in the top dozen.

A little later on, the man who had bought the hamburger franchises and the American property interests and oil and gas rights from the receiver sold them on again for a sum which at first I assumed to be a misprint. And even today, I occasionally notice some firm with a faintly familiar name changing hands for a million or so and some fragment of Joe's conversation floats back to me: 'when these options mature, they'll have no choice but to . . .' 'Reversions are fantastically cheap just now . . .'

But then there are no prizes given for prematurity. Timing is everything. Buy at the bottom of the slump, better still buy in wartime, and you can't go wrong, my informant said, the next best thing is to buy only from receivers in bankruptcy. The posthumous splendour of Joe's empire – huge, glittering, towering out of the depths – was as unreal as some Victorian steel engraving of Babylon in its heyday. The graves of failed entrepreneurs are unmarked. Even successful ones have to import their own marble and hire their own historians. The Tomb of

the Unknown Tycoon will never be paid for by popular sub-
scription.

But then that had probably been Joe's mission, not to be
appeased in his lifetime but to stir things up, stir people up
too. He had been the human equivalent of the mast cells which
inflamed our bronchial tubes, discharging their malign granules
at pitiless intervals. He had been wished upon us to make trouble
for our own good – at least if you believed that trouble was what
we were here for, and in their different ways Onora, Peggy, Fisha
and Gillian all did believe that. Perhaps that was what asthmatics
were for – to act out the unappeasability of things. It was nice
to think that we had our uses and that our wheezing was not
in vain.

As the evidence piled up that Joe's enterprises had contained
some vital spark which needed only a following wind to fan it into
flame, I noticed that I was thinking of the man himself as deader
and deader. There seemed no point in him outliving failure on
such a scale.

By the time the call from Jervoise came, its news was genuinely
startling to me.

'They've found them, sir. They're all right. Tired and washed
out like a couple of drowned rats, but all right. They were tied
up in an empty council house on an estate just outside Dundalk.
Quite unharmed, physically anyway. The Gardai got the tip-
off last night. They wanted me to express their thanks to you,
sir.'

'To me?'

'Your scheme worked a treat.'

'My scheme?'

'You won't have seen the big articles we had inserted in the
Irish press. About how we were going to press charges against
this bankrupt fugitive financier and how that was going to put
a strain on the Anglo-Irish relationship because extradition in
this particular type of case had never been applied for before.
All legal codswallop, mind you, but the Irish were most co-
operative. The villains dropped them like hot potatoes within

forty-eight hours. After all, not merely were they now holding a couple of penniless individuals, by letting them go they could set the scene for a nice little Anglo-Irish punch-up, couldn't they?'

'Thank heavens. Why do you think they dared let them go, though? After all, you thought they might simply bump them off, didn't you, for fear of being identified?'

'Well, sir, that was one possibility we had to take into account. But then, you see, they were masked throughout the proceedings, weren't they, so there was no danger of Mr and Mrs Follows recognising them later. Standard procedure now on all snatch operations, is masking.'

'Is it really?'

'We had to explore the possibility of a put-up job, collusion or an outright fake. But it does bear all the marks of a regulation-style Provo mission.'

'That must be a comfort.'

'We're most grateful to you for confirming our own view. Between you and me, sir, I'd have preferred to put the story out a good deal earlier.'

'Would you?'

'Anyway, all's well that ends well. A truism, I know, sir, but truisms are often very true, aren't they? When you think, we could have been responsible for two deaths, you and I.'

The Colonel said Joe and Gillian did not want visitors yet, but he himself did.

'It's like living in a prison camp down here with all this barbed wire. Expect that fellow will have searchlights up soon. He seems to farm all night as well as all day. I sold him the paddock a fortnight ago. The house is really too big for me now with Gillian over the water, so I expect that will have to go too. Sorry about the brown ale, the last of the good claret has just gone at Christie's. The plonk I usually get at Sainsbury's isn't half bad, but the car's in dock at the moment, so I'm restricted to the village shop. Still, mustn't moan, it's glorious news, isn't it, really glorious. There's nothing like freedom. Here's G's letter,

I told her you were coming, and she says her memory's gone for all addresses except home.'

Goodster,

It's absolute bollocks what the shrinks say about a bond forming between the grown-napper and his victims. We hated them from first to last. They were rude and smelly and THICK. *Joe tried to have one of those super-sophisticated chats about ideology and nationalism and all that, and they hadn't a clue. Nor has he, poor old hemiplegic, but compared to them he's Einstein. And it's bollocks too about grown-nappers being fantastically idealistic and chivalrous. When I explained about the curse looming, they said the foulest things you can imagine. They were evil, not silly playing-at-evil, like Low Dudgeon, but stupid-evil, the real thing. And when they discovered, or thought they discovered Joe had no money, they were angry like small children, only children with huge big meaty fists and thick sticks which they threatend Joe with. So when you hear we are quite unharmed, remember that quite unharmed, being translated, means scared stiff, cold as ice, with sores all over our bottoms, and diarrhoea like Niagara. Whoever invented people needs His Head examining. He should have stuck to hens who are all well and send their love and so do I.*

PS. The funny thing is, being a hostage did wonders for Joe's asthma. He didn't wheeze once all the time we were in durance vile. He's back to square one now, though, the poor old grampus.

'Pity about the asthma coming back,' the Colonel said, 'You'd have thought the shock might have done the trick permanently.'

'Stress reaction,' I explained. 'I wonder whether they would have let them out anyway, in the end. Perhaps there was no need to brand Joe as a bankrupt and fugitive from justice.'

'Well, he is a bankrupt,' the Colonel said.

'Yes, but not a real bankrupt, not in Ireland anyway. Now they'll think he's a crook and, worse still, a failed crook, one without any money.'

'The great thing is, they're free. We can't know whether any other way would have worked. Low Dudgeon still thinks it was all a put-up job. Extraordinary thing is, Low's demobbed his stage army and rejoined the Conservative Party. Paid me his sub last week.'

On Sunday, the Colonel read the lesson: St Paul plaintive,

thunderous, overbearing, sore with everyone, especially his faint-hearted followers. On and on went the catalogue of boasted suffering: in labours more abundant, in stripes above measure, in prisons more frequent, in deaths oft; thrice was I beaten with rods, once was I stoned, thrice I suffered shipwreck, in perils of waters, in perils from my own countrymen, in perils in the city.

But the Colonel was so elated by Gillian's rescue that he read the whole passage in a voice suffused with chuckling happiness, as though it were a well-loved bit of the *Pickwick Papers*. His mood seemed to tickle the tiny congregation in the tiny grey church. They all burst out of the service in a rattling good humour, competing for the pleasure of congratulating the Colonel. Perhaps it was his last moment of true happiness. His health began to go downhill soon afterwards. His money trouble went from worse to worse. Gillian was less and less able to leave Joe and come over from Ireland. The Colonel communicated his growing melancholy in the usual torrential way he flooded his surroundings with his feelings of the moment. Yet I found his company soothing and would often go down to Devon and hear stray wisps of news of them all. He was in fact my only source, for Drishill seemed to be cut off by more than the Irish Sea. There were no more letters from Gillian. Perhaps her ordeal was now too dour and grinding. Trull and Peggy I never saw, nor Onora until that sports day which brought my asthma back.

The doctor was quick to calm me with a name for it. What you probably have now, he said, is intrinsic asthma, the sort that mostly comes out in middle age. Unlike the extrinsic asthma of youth, it has nothing to do with dust or feathers or even stress. The episodes tend to be straightforward physiological reactions to upper respiratory infections, bronchitis, that sort of thing, nothing psychological at all, but his hands made a calming motion which suggested otherwise. I could not help thinking that second-time-around asthmatics might be responding to a different set of allergens which scientists have not yet managed to isolate, of a sort which would raise bumps only on the soul's anatomy: boredom, for instance, or sexual failure, or fear of death or self-hatred. No, self-hatred is not quite the right word, more a kind of uncomfortableness with self, like being strapped into an aircraft seat next to a restless loudmouth. Had Joe too been told that he was an intrinsic now, or was he still clinging proudly to his theory that his tubes were unusually narrow? Perhaps in the interests of science we ought to resume our crippled games of blow-football, and discover whether he could still beat me as in the old extrinsic days.

In this damp westerly air, it is towards evening that an attack comes on. At half-past-six or seven o'clock, I find myself sitting in the old leather armchair unearthed from the shed at the back of the local antique shop, with the puffer at my elbow. It is pleasant at such times to numb the bronchial tubes with some television documentary, preferably the ones about travel or nature which tend to be on about then. I had switched on without looking at the listings and was cheered to come across the familiar scene of a man in a bush jacket walking up a stony hill, turning now and then to camera as he explained where he was heading in an only slightly out-of-breath voice: 'We are going to meet one of the most elusive men of our time . . . one of the last great travellers . . . a man who has found freedom in the high and empty places of the earth.'

And there was Rickshaw, bleached and thin but wiry-looking again, no longer frail, squatting under the scant shade of a wizened tree, talking to an old tribesman with a scrubby beard. Strolling now with the bush-jacket man along a stony track with distant views of mountains: 'Yes, I do travel quite light. One needs so little. A pair of boots, a pair of eyes . . .' Then he told a tale of a wandering rogue from those parts, a timeless tale of effrontery and disguise and come-uppance. And the old spell came across through the flickering black-and-white television in the damp cottage, and I no longer needed my puffer. But the interviewer was not to be denied his last word. As Rickshaw strolled off in the lengthening shadows of evening towards some rough mountain caravanserai, no doubt expecting The End to come up across his wiry back view, the camera cut to the man in the bush jacket: 'What is it that drives on this solitary man with a host of friends, this scholar who prefers the simple folk, this marvellous talker who goes for days without seeing another human being? What strange inner compulsion is it that leads this much loved man to walk alone?'

I did not feel like answering these questions. After all, was Rickshaw's solitude so very different from all our solitudes, except that it photographed better? It was then that it occurred to me to call Drishill Abbey. They would not yet have settled down to Scrabble. They might welcome a voice from the past. The Colonel had passed on the phone number to me – it had been changed 'because of the Fenians' – I had kept it by me as a kind of ambiguous thing which might come in handy one day, but I was not sure for what. Now, all of a sudden, it seemed cold and unnatural not to use it.

The number rang. In my mind's ear, I heard it ringing long and shrill down the chill passages of the Abbey. Then the click of an answering machine (they must have started dinner already) and the slow dragging voice I had come to know since the stroke: 'This is Follows On plc. There is nobody available to handle your call right now, but . . .' I heard him out to the beep and then gently replaced the receiver.

A Selected List of Fiction Available from Mandarin

While every effort is made to keep prices low, it is sometimes necessary to increase prices at short notice. Mandarin Paperbacks reserves the right to show new retail prices on covers which may differ from those previously advertised in the text or elsewhere.

The prices shown below were correct at the time of going to press.

☐ 0 7493 0780 3	**The Hanging Tree**	Allan Massie	£5.99
☐ 0 7493 1224 6	**How I Met My Wife**	Nicholas Coleridge	£5.99
☐ 0 7493 1064 2	**Of Love and Asthma**	Ferdinand Mount	£5.99
☐ 0 7493 1368 4	**Persistent Rumours**	Lee Langley	£4.99
☐ 0 7493 1068 5	**Goodness**	Tim Parks	£4.99
☐ 0 7493 1492 3	**Making the Angels Weep**	Helen Flint	£5.99
☐ 0 7493 1364 1	**High on the Hog**	Fraser Harrison	£4.99
☐ 0 7493 1394 3	**What's Eating Gilbert Grape**	Peter Hedges	£5.99
☐ 0 7493 1216 5	**The Fringe Orphan**	Rachel Morris	£4.99
☐ 0 7493 1510 5	**Evenings at Mongini's**	Russell Lucas	£5.99
☐ 0 7493 1509 1	**Fair Sex**	Sarah Foot	£5.99

All these books are available at your bookshop or newsagent, or can be ordered direct from the publisher. Just tick the titles you want and fill in the form below.

Mandarin Paperbacks, Cash Sales Department, PO Box 11, Falmouth, Cornwall TR10 9EN.

Please send cheque or postal order, no currency, for purchase price quoted and allow the following for postage and packing:

UK including BFPO   £1.00 for the first book, 50p for the second and 30p for each additional book ordered to a maximum charge of £3.00.

Overseas including Eire   £2 for the first book, £1.00 for the second and 50p for each additional book thereafter.

NAME (Block letters) ....

ADDRESS ....

....

☐ I enclose my remittance for ....

☐ I wish to pay by Access/Visa Card Number

Expiry Date

George Gordon, cousin to Byron, heir to a desolate Scottish estate, superficially enjoys a brilliant career: he dines at Malmaison with Napoleon and Josephine, excavates the Acropolis, shares a night in a hayloft with Metternich, inherits the Earldom of Aberdeen, marries two beautiful women, becomes Foreign Secretary twice and then ultimately Prime Minister.

Yet Lord Aberdeen remains an awkward, tragic figure, increasingly at odds with his times, shattered by repeated bereavements, loathed, abused and eventually driven out of office by his fellow countrymen for his doomed efforts to prevent the Crimean War.

'A triumph' Allan Massie
The Scotsman

'Mount is a fresh and brilliant historical writer; he brings a haunted and scorned statesman sympathetically to life and makes the past breathe again'
Sunday Times

'Anyone for wit? Anyone for elegance? Anyone for style? The novella is back'
The Times

'*Umbrella* has a powerful, melancholy and peculiarly English charm ... a most affecting story'
Sunday Telegraph

Cover design: Button Design Co.

ISBN 0-7493-9543-5

9 780749 395438

MINERVA
FICTION
UK £5.99